Girls, Guys, and a Tangle of Ties

Galynne Matichuk

ISBN: 978-1-7341117-0-5

To my most amazing children, N!ck and GrAce,

I hope that I have modelled for you, through my life and this book, the power of connection, perseverance, and fervent prayer

CONTENTS

ACKNOWLEDGMENTS

I'm able to write about ties because I have been blessed with so many amazing connections.

To the camps where I've worked, Birch Bay Ranch, Circle Square Ranch, Teen Time Ranch, and Teen Reach Adventure Camp, I have such wonderful memories of crazy fun and miraculous moments. Of people and pranks, lakes and lessons, long days and sleepless nights, and the hand of God everywhere. To the staff and campers I've worked with and known, if you think that you recognize yourself within these pages, you might be right. A special shout out to Mike, who first told the stories of *Hardships* and *Molly the Moth.* I did my best, but no one tells those stories like you. How can I even begin to sum up all the ways that these camps have blessed my life? I guess I'd have to write a book.

To my Bible study friends, what a joy to walk with you and watch as you build your lives and dreams. Thank you for encouraging me with mine. Special thanks to Tiffanie and Wynnie - your comments had a huge impact on me and the plot. Thank you, Maggie, for listening to the Lord. I needed your timely nudge. Angie, everyone should have a friend like you. Don't blush, it's true. Hugs to all of you!

To Kathy Ide, my editor, who took a wild field of words and after much weeding, brought forth order and harmony. It is a painful process to be pruned, and yet look at the growth that has come.

To my parents, Tom and Grace, who first showed me a relationship of healthy ties. Thank you for your wisdom and encouragement. I couldn't have written this book without you. That's partly because you forced me to go to camp when I didn't want to go, and thus began the adventure. Thank you for knowing what I needed and holding firm. Your fingerprints are on each page.

To my sister, Leanne, who has hung on through my best moments and my worst. Thank you for your unwavering loyalty and support. You've read every version of this book, and there were many. Thank you for your wise counsel.

To my husband, Chris, you've always been a courageous risk-taker. Thank you for helping me turn my timid steps into a leap of faith. And forgive me for judging your hat. I didn't know the story. You were the first Darren, and you formed the first Men in Hats.

To my children, N!ck and GrAce, thank you for you listening and offering insights far beyond your years. Nothing escaped your keen ears. You've watched me fulfill a dream of mine. I can't wait to watch you fulfill your own.

And to the Lord, remember when I made a New Year's Resolution to write a book? And thought I would finish in one year? How naive I was. And how faithful You have been. During the eighteen years it has taken to complete that resolution, I have soared in confidence, wallowed in despair, thrown up my hands and walked away, run back and started again, laughed out loud, cried buckets of tears, and danced with joy. Every page of this book is soaked in prayer. Through it all, You have carried me. I can only hope that I have represented You well - your grace, mercy, sense of humor, and above all, your fathomless love.

1 CHANGE OF PLANS

The early-morning sun streamed through the kitchen windows above the sink but couldn't drive the chill from the room. A shiver ran through Kelly's body, and a strand of long brown hair fell across her eyes. She brushed it away and focused her attention on her father as he placed a set of pale-green luggage in the center of the room. She'd been expecting a moment like this for the last few weeks. And now it was here.

Kelly perched on the edge of the wooden chair, her back stiff and straight as she stared at the bags. The suitcases seemed to crouch together, as if preparing to attack and drag her away.

"Why is my luggage out of storage?" Kelly turned to her mother, seated across the table. "I thought we had a deal. If I improved, you wouldn't send me to the hospital program." She braced herself for a fight.

"Improved?" Her father snorted as he took a seat beside his wife. "Gaining half a pound is hardly progress."

It could have been. At least if it were true. But she hadn't even improved that much. However, now was not the time to confess that she'd manipulated the results.

"We're not sending you to the teen recovery center." Her mom concentrated on pouring a small amount of milk into a steaming mug of coffee. With slow and deliberate movements, she picked up a spoon and stirred. "Your father and I met with your counselor last week. She's heard great things about a church camp that's not too far from here."

So she wasn't being rushed off to the eating-disorder intervention program. Kelly relaxed, but only slightly. Camp was still a form of punishment. Most likely for what happened last weekend.

Kelly's mom gave her a tentative smile. She slid a plate with a banana and a blueberry muffin toward Kelly, who ignored it.

"I'm too old for camp." She was also too old to have her mother feed her. Especially since she'd stopped eating breakfast months ago, along with every other meal she could skip.

Kelly's mother leaned back, a frown creasing her brow. "The counselor recommended that you work there as a volunteer for the summer."

Two whole months? No way. Being stuck at some religious camp would ruin all her plans.

Her mom raised the cup to her lips and took a sip. "You can't spend your vacation sitting around with nothing to do."

No fear of that. Kelly had already planned an intense summer program of daily hikes, bike rides, and speed walks. Of course, all that exercise would be worse, in her mom's eyes, than doing nothing. Particularly if she lost more weight.

But Kelly knew the plan to send her off to camp wasn't just about keeping her busy. It was also about keeping her away from her friends—and her boyfriend, in particular. Or ex-boyfriend, thanks to the disaster last Saturday night.

"I'm not qualified." Kelly took a deep, steadying breath. She wasn't about to surrender without a fight. "I don't know anything about church camps. I've never even been to one."

Kelly's father dismissed the argument with a wave of his hand. "Experience isn't necessary. The director told us they offer a two-day training program that will cover everything you'll need to know."

Kelly shook her head as she imagined a cabin full of hyper campers. "What if the kids don't like me and beg for a new counselor?"

Her mother gave a faint laugh. "Don't be so melodramatic. All the neighborhood children adore you. You're the first person who gets called whenever someone needs a babysitter."

That was true. And Kelly did enjoy hanging out with all her little buddies. But she couldn't let her mother's compliment sway her. Kelly turned a wary eye to the suitcases. The bright rays of sunshine glinted off the partially open zippers, making the silver rows of metal gleam like razor-sharp teeth.

"You'll be a sophomore next year," her father cut in. "Time to think about college applications. Volunteer experience looks great on a resume."

That was her dad, always practical and thinking of the future. But Kelly was thinking ahead too. And this was about more than the summer. Her social future was at stake if she couldn't patch things up with Aaron. The icy fingers of panic seized her, and she found it hard to breathe. She couldn't imagine her world without him.

Kelly scrambled for a different tactic. "But I won't know anyone at camp."

Her father raised an eyebrow. "Considering how much time you spend on the phone, I'd say you don't have a problem making friends. And this will give you the chance to make some new ones."

But that was the point. She already had plenty of friends, although lately they'd been blowing away like dry leaves in a windstorm. Which wasn't too surprising. Just the natural consequence of being dumped by the most popular guy at school. Even if she could use some new friends, she didn't want to meet them at some stupid camp. Especially since anyone working there was likely to be a boring spiritual nut.

Kelly looked straight into her father's eyes. "Are you punishing me for what happened with Aaron?"

Her father's hand came down hard on the table. "Aaron is a different matter, and we've already dealt with him."

Yes, they had. By forbidding all contact with him. Of course, Kelly had no intention of obeying, which they'd probably already guessed. It's not like they could stop her, unless they sent her away. Which was exactly what they were doing.

"I know I broke a bunch of rules, but it's not what you think."

"Really? You stole my brand-new car, snuck off to a party, and your drunk boyfriend almost drove you home. Did I get anything wrong?" Her father leaned forward.

Yes. No. Kelly studied the floor. Telling the truth now would only make things worse. At least for Aaron. And she wasn't a snitch.

"Don't I get any credit for calling home?" Kelly spat out the words.

Her mom took a sharp breath. "Thank God you did, or someone might have been hurt. Even killed."

Kelly shuddered as she remembered the expression on her parents' faces when they arrived at the party and found her dad's Corvette Sting Ray parked in the driveway with a seriously hammered Aaron behind the wheel, keys in hand, and her in the passenger seat. The hurt in her mother's eyes. Like she didn't recognize her own daughter. And her father's barely-controlled fury as he pulled Aaron out of the car.

"Don't even try to tell me it's not what I think." Her father's voice cracked. "I know what I saw."

Maybe, but he'd missed a few things. Like the fact that she was already crying when they drove up, and not just after she'd been caught. And she'd been trying to grab the keys away from Aaron, not pass them to him.

In a last-ditch effort, Kelly launched her final weapon. Brutal honesty. "You think some lame religious camp is going to fix me. I'm not broken, and I don't need help."

An awkward silence descended on the kitchen. Kelly's mother lifted the cup to her lips, but her hands shook and brown liquid dripped over the side. She lowered the mug and glanced at Kelly's father.

Watching them through narrowed eyes, Kelly felt a stab of remorse for causing her parents so much grief over the last year.

They thought they were being discreet, but she'd overheard the whispered conversations. And their desperate prayers.

Kelly's mother turned toward her, mouth set in a firm line. "The hospital called last night to tell us that a spot opened up in the treatment center for eating disorders."

"But you just said you wouldn't make me go." The words tumbled out of Kelly's mouth. She didn't belong there. Just because some doctor said she was anorexic didn't make it true. Sure, she'd lost some weight over the last year. Okay, a lot of weight. But all the popular girls were skinny, and that's what guys like Aaron found attractive. She knew exactly what she was doing.

"We aren't sending you...at least not yet." Kelly's mother cleared her throat. "I told the hospital we'd already signed you up for summer camp. But I can call back and tell them we changed our minds."

There was no way out. She was being sent away, and her only choices were a religious camp or a treatment center. Kelly shot her mother a scathing look. "I'll take camp."

Her mom nodded. "Training starts on Friday. That's just two days from now. Why don't you go upstairs and start thinking about what you'd like to pack."

Kelly could have sworn she heard a snarl coming from the suitcases. And the sound of metal jaws snapping shut on her summer.

2 A THIEF, A TORNADO, AND FOUR UGLY HATS

Kelly stepped out the front door of her home and into the chilly morning air. Every other house on the street remained dark as the neighborhood slumbered. The only movement came from her father, loading her suitcases into the back of the family car. Kelly avoided his concerned glances in her direction and checked her phone...again. She'd sent a flurry of texts to her friends about leaving for camp, but only a handful had replied. And those few responses consisted of lame comments about having fun and vague plans to catch up with her later.

A cool breeze lifted the wisps of hair that had escaped from her ponytail. Close to a week had passed since that disastrous night with Aaron. More than enough time for him to tell everyone he'd dumped her. And why. Even though she'd expected to be shunned by the popular crowd, it still hurt.

"Kelly! Wait!"

Kelly watched a pair of familiar figures hurrying down the sidewalk, and a relieved smile stretched across her face. At least two of her friends hadn't forgotten her, although she didn't consider herself close to either girl, at least not anymore. Annalisa was too busy chasing guys. She changed boyfriends the way some girls changed nail polish. Kelly used to consider Lucy one of her better friends. But Lucy got a new boyfriend and started hanging out with a rougher crowd, partying hard every weekend. Rumors had it she was experimenting with drugs. And Kelly knew what others didn't. They weren't just rumors. Lucy missed a lot of school and ended up failing the last semester.

Kelly looked at the two girls, somewhat disappointed they'd been the only ones to show up to say good-bye. But considering the cool response to her text messages, Kelly wasn't in a position to be picky.

"We thought we'd missed you." Annalisa paused to catch her breath. "I've been worried about you after that breakup with Aaron."

Not likely. The only thing Annalisa liked more than guys was gossip. She was hunting for juicy details. But at least she might have information about Aaron.

Kelly's eyes followed her father as he stepped back into the house. The moment the door closed, she grabbed Annalisa by the arm. "Have you talked to him? How mad is he?

"You don't want to know what he's saying about you."

Kelly winced. Annalisa was right. She didn't want to know. He'd said enough in the furious texts he'd sent on Friday night. She'd heard him insult his previous girlfriends, but never thought he'd trash talk that way about her. She'd been wrong.

"He said you got him into a ton of trouble." Annalisa shrugged. "His parents are furious. They might even pull him off the school basketball team. And it's all your fault."

Kelly frowned. Annalisa didn't have to look so pleased as she delivered the news, although she shouldn't be surprised. Annalisa wasn't the only girl eager to cozy up to Aaron now that he was available.

"I hope you have a great time at camp." Lucy tugged on the long t-shirt she was wearing. "At least it's better than summer school."

Kelly couldn't argue with that. She'd have the chance to be outside, and maybe even get a golden tan. Her poor friend would be stuck in a stuffy classroom all day with a pile of homework to occupy her evenings. But it was Lucy's only chance to earn the missing credits and finish her freshman year.

Annalisa popped her gum loudly, a habit that had always annoyed Kelly. "You sure blew it. Do you know how many girls would do anything to be with Aaron?"

Kelly kicked a loose stone on the ground. Yeah, she did. And so did he. She glanced back at the house. "I have to find a way to talk to him. But my parents are monitoring my calls and texts."

Annalisa pulled a phone out of her back pocket and handed it to Kelly.

With fingers trembling, Kelly dialed Aaron's number. He answered on the second ring. Kelly took a half-step to the left and turned slightly. Not that it would do any good. Annalisa and Lucy were standing inches away and couldn't help but overhear every word. And Annalisa had leaned closer, to make sure she wouldn't miss a thing. Annoyed but without any better options, Kelly kept her voice low as she begged Aaron not to hang up. She swallowed back tears and begged his forgiveness for calling her parents. It was a mistake. She'd been stupid. And she pleaded for a second chance.

Kelly's whole body trembled as she waited for Aaron's response. When he finally spoke, she cringed at the anger in his voice. Aaron said he'd think about it. But a week was a long time, and he was doing his best to forget her. And then he hung up.

Not an outright rejection. But it wasn't much better.

The front screen door squeaked as it swung wide, and Kelly's father returned carrying her sleeping bag and pillow. Kelly shoved the phone back into Annalisa's hands.

"Let me guess. He's still mad."

There was no need for Annalisa to speculate. She'd heard every word.

And there was no use denying it.

Annalisa popped her gum again. "No guy is going to date you now."

Kelly gave a miserable nod. She knew it was true.

"Well, have fun at camp. Catch you later." Annalisa took off down the driveway, no doubt eager to find Aaron. And offer any consolation he might need.

"He's not worth it." The words tumbled out of Lucy's mouth. "Don't let him drag you down." Without waiting for a response, she hurried to catch up with Annalisa.

An odd statement. And unexpected. Lucy's life had become a complete mess. Seemed out of place of her to give advice about being dragged down.

Kelly's father tapped her on the shoulder. "You need to leave your phone at home."

She pulled out her lifeline and clutched it close to her chest. "Why? I told you I wouldn't use it to contact him." Which was true. She'd used Annalisa's phone instead.

Her father held out his hand. "It's camp policy. No electronics."

Kelly sighed. Not surprising that a religious camp would have stupid rules to isolate everyone from the outside. She shoved the phone at her dad.

Kelly's mother got into the car, and motioned for her to get in. After suffering through a tight farewell embrace from her dad, Kelly climbed into the front passenger seat and slammed the door. With arms crossed and jaw clenched, she determined to remain silent for the forty-five minutes it would take to reach the camp.

While her mother kept up a constant stream of chatter as she drove, Kelly tuned her out and focused on the scenery. Far too quickly, the familiar homes and streets of her neighborhood disappeared. Tight-packed communities gave way to farms with faded wooden barns and rusty tractors. Kelly felt a sharp pain and realized she'd been chomping on a fingernail, a nervous habit she'd broken years ago. She clasped her hands in her lap to keep them still.

The rising sun cast a golden glow over the fields. The morning dawned fresh, bright, and hopeful. But not for her.

For the past two days, she'd worked on her parents from every angle. They'd refused to change their minds about camp, but at least she'd managed to negotiate a compromise. Rather than commit to the entire summer, she only had to stay for staff training and the first week of camp. Ten days in all. After that, she could choose to come home if she wanted. Which, of course, she would. But then she'd have to face Aaron...and try to convince him to take her back.

Kelly tasted blood and caught herself gnawing on her nails again. She jerked her hand away. She stared out the window and watched mile after mile speed past, taking her away from the trouble back home. She might have been thankful to escape her problems with Aaron, except that she was heading straight toward the dreaded unknown.

As the car turned off the highway and onto a bumpy dirt road, her mother's voice broke into her thoughts. "There it is: Timberlake Camp."

Kelly took a few steadying breaths and gazed up at the large arch that spanned the entrance, towering over them. Weather-worn lettering had been cut deep in a thick beam of reddish wood. It loomed above them, rustic, solid, and imposing.

As the car rolled onto the property, Kelly's mother gestured toward a set of buildings to the left. "I read an article about the camp's horseback riding and vaulting programs. Apparently, they're some of the best in the country."

Unwilling to break her silence, Kelly turned her attention to the bright red barns with black-shingled roofs, the gleaming silver metal of several small corrals, and the large oval riding arena surrounded by spectator stands. Pretty impressive...for a church camp. Not that it mattered, as she wouldn't be spending much time near the barns. Her only contact with horses had been on a kindergarten field trip to a petting zoo. And that had been limited to a few quick pats. She'd been intimidated by the thick bodies and dangerous hooves. And when one pony nibbled on the tassels of her coat, she'd run from the corral, shrieking that the beast was trying to eat her. She'd spent the rest of the morning playing with the bunnies.

A woman strode out of the arena, leading a sleek brown horse. Wearing dusty boots, worn jeans, a faded shirt, and a cowboy hat that looked like it had been stepped on a time or two, she was the perfect image of a ranch hand.

Kelly's mom stopped the car and rolled down the window. "Excuse me!"

The woman turned in the direction of the car. "Can I help you?"

"I'm Sherry Martin and this is my daughter, Kelly. She's here for the volunteer staff training."

The woman's face lit up with a smile so warm Kelly almost made the mistake of smiling back. She tied the horse to a hitching post, then approached the car. "Welcome to Timberlake Camp. We're glad to have you. I'm MaryAnn, the director's wife. We've spoken on the phone several times."

Kelly glared at her mother. It wasn't hard to guess the topic of all those conversations. No doubt her mom had related all the details from her doctor's reports. And probably signed this woman up to act as therapist, counselor, and prison guard.

MaryAnn didn't seem to notice the tension in the car. "I'd take you to the lodge myself if I wasn't running late this morning. But it's not difficult to find your way around." She gestured ahead. "If you keep driving down this road, you'll pass the camper cabins and staff rooms. Boys are on the left and girls are on the right."

Of course a religious camp would keep the genders apart.

MaryAnn leaned into the car and spoke to Kelly. "We have five female camper cabins but we're only using the first two during staff training. You can drop off your suitcase in whichever one has space. After you've settled in, follow the road till you get to the lodge. Staff training starts in half an hour. I believe most of the other volunteers have already arrived."

Kelly forced a polite smile. All the other good little staff members were probably eager to begin the week. Kelly couldn't wait for it to end.

Kelly's mother thanked MaryAnn, then edged the car forward. The gravel lane that stretched before them was bordered by thick trees on both sides. Kelly glimpsed narrow paths running through the trees, most likely shortcuts to the various activity areas. The place felt relaxing and peaceful. For a brief moment, Kelly felt a twinge of regret that she wouldn't be staying long enough to enjoy it. But she pushed the feeling aside and focused straight ahead.

Kelly's mother parked beside a row of cabins connected by a common roofed veranda. Kelly grabbed her suitcases from the trunk, hauled them up a couple of creaky steps onto the porch of the first cabin, and entered. It was a large, plain room with five bunk beds. The threadbare rug had long since lost its original color, but it blended well with the dull brown walls. Along the back stood ten wooden lockers and a few makeshift shelves.

Each bunk already had a sleeping bag spread on top of the mattress. Suitcases lay open all over, with clothes and personal items strewn about the room. It looked as if there'd been a massive slumber party among friends. And no space for anyone else to join in.

Kelly tightened her grip on her suitcases as she stared at the disorder. The room seemed to shout at her. "You're alone. Unwanted by your friends at home. And unnecessary here." The message felt like a slap in the face.

Kelly's mother stumbled up the steps, arms clutching the sleeping bag and pillow. She poked her head into the room. "This one looks full. Let's check out the next one."

The second cabin was equally plain, with an identical arrangement of bunk beds, wooden lockers, and makeshift shelves. Only half of the bunks had been claimed.

Kelly's mother dropped her sleeping bag onto an open bed. "I'll be back in a minute." With a furtive glance at Kelly, she left the room.

Kelly spread out her sleeping bag and pillow. She opened her suitcases and pulled out a few bathroom items, which she shoved into an empty locker. It would be a waste of time to unpack more. No use getting comfortable if she wasn't staying beyond the mandatory week.

After stowing her luggage under the bunk, Kelly wandered around the simple room. Names and dates had been carved into many of the bunks. She traced her fingers over the etched letters, trying to imagine the faces of the girls who'd stayed there. In the back corner, one camper had chiseled the words *Best week ever* across the frame. Kelly's lips stretched in a grim smile. The best part of this week would be when it was over and she could go home.

The door creaked and Kelly's mother reentered, carrying a canvas bag. "I packed a few of your favorite snacks." She held the sack out to Kelly. "You've made progress these last few weeks. Your doctor and I don't want you to slip back."

"I don't need that." Kelly crossed her arms. A childish gesture. But she wasn't taking the food.

With a heavy sigh, Mom set the bag beside the pillow on Kelly's bunk. "I'll leave it here. In case you change your mind."

No chance of that happening. But it was pointless to argue. She'd throw it out later.

Kelly's mother glanced at her watch. "You'd better get going. Staff training is about to begin."

As Kelly followed her mother out of the cabin, guilty thoughts swirled in her head. Her mom was wrong. There hadn't been any progress. She'd just come up with new ways to manipulate the exams.

The family doctor had been monitoring Kelly's weight for the last few months, charting her gains and losses. On the first four visits, they'd watched her weight plummet. But at each of the last two appointments, to the delight of the doctor and her parents, Kelly had gained a half pound. It wasn't much, as her father had pointed out. But to her mom, it marked the first small steps toward recovery. Little did they know that Kelly altered the results. The first time by hiding coins in her socks. The last time by drinking a full glass of water just before she stepped on the scale.

Mom stopped near the edge of the veranda. Lost in thought, Kelly nearly crashed into her. They both giggled, like old times when they used to have fun together. Then Kelly caught herself and turned away.

"The bathrooms and showers must be in here." Kelly's mom gestured to a door on the left.

They stepped inside a long, narrow hall. A large bathroom opened up on their right. Kelly counted ten sinks with mirrors, eight showers, and eight bathroom stalls.

"It looks roomy." Kelly's mother returned to the hall.

Not with five cabins full of girls.

Kelly checked her reflection as she left the bathroom. Anxious brown eyes stared back at her, still puffy and slightly red from days of crying. Earlier that morning, she'd swept her long brown hair into a sleek, high ponytail. Thinner than it used to be, though she hadn't mentioned to anyone that her hair had been falling out in small clumps. But the style was fast and easy, and it showed off her cheekbones. Not that it mattered. Aaron wasn't here, and there wasn't going to be anybody else to impress.

Kelly tucked a stray strand behind her ear and caught up to her mother. They continued down the hall, passing open doors that revealed small rooms with single beds and a few wooden shelves. Probably for staff members who weren't assigned to a cabin. Kelly felt a flicker of hope. Maybe they wouldn't need her as a counselor after all. If they gave her some other job, she might be lucky enough to have a room to herself.

When they reached the end of the hall, Kelly and her mother stepped outside. The morning sun had vanished and drops of rain fell softly but steadily. Kelly's mom opened the car door, but paused before sliding in. "I could drive you down to the lodge."

"No need. I'm sure it's not far." She certainly didn't want to be seen walking in with her mother, like a scared child on the first day in a new school. Even if that was how she felt.

Her mom stepped away from the vehicle and caught her in a fierce hug. "Please give this a chance. You'll have a good time here. I know you will."

Kelly pushed down the aching desire to return her mother's tight embrace. "We made a deal. One week." No point in giving false hope.

"Ten days. And you can always stay longer if you change your mind." With a final squeeze, her mom released her. "I'll be praying for you."

What good would that do, talking to a God that didn't exist? And if He did exist, He sure didn't care about her.

Kelly waited for her mother to drive out of sight before making her way toward the large building farther down the road. A wood plank stretched across the top, announcing "Timberlake Lodge."

The building looked like it had been modeled after an old-fashioned hotel. Weathered boards created a rustic aura. The walls were decorated with horseshoes, cowbells, wagon wheels, and spurs. Kelly rolled her eyes at the overdone western theme.

As she stepped onto the porch and reached for the silver door handle, she hesitated. Her mind flashed back to another door with silver handles. On a two-story building with sheer white walls, and long halls filled with the sharp smell of disinfectant. She could have been entering the hospital instead, confined within the program wing and unable to leave. Suddenly, the lodge didn't look so bad.

The moment she stepped inside, Kelly was swept into a rush of noise and activity. In a large space to her right, about thirty teenagers hung out in groups of three or four. A few girls sat cross-legged on a set of risers, chatting as they braided one another's hair. Several mixed groups of guys and girls stretched out in front of a variety of board games. In the middle of the room, four boys carefully balanced playing cards on a tower that was as high as their shoulders. Off in a corner, another guy played an upright piano, rather badly, while a group tried to sing whatever tune he was pounding out.

An urge to turn and chase her mother's car down the road swept over Kelly. She felt out of place here. Like an outsider. Or an interloper. These volunteers clearly knew each other. They'd probably been coming to camp together for years. Kelly missed her friends, and wished that at least one would have chosen to sign up with her. They were probably off doing something fun together. Without her.

The piano player brought his song to a crashing end and immediately launched into a new one. He wore a wide-brimmed fishing hat with an unattractive mix of blue, green and brown. Three other guys in the group sported the same ridiculous headgear. Kelly hoped they weren't part of some hideous staff uniform. She might be stuck at a lousy religious camp, but she still had her pride. There was no way she'd put that ugly thing on her head.

A burst of cheers drew Kelly's attention to the largest group, where half a dozen girls gathered around a tall guy who looked as if he'd just stepped off the pages of a teen heartthrob magazine. Broad shoulders. Styled blond hair. Lightly tanned skin, chiseled jawline, and intensely-blue eyes. Kelly couldn't stop staring. He was even better looking than Aaron. And she hadn't thought that was possible.

The hottie raised his hands above his head, then swung them down as he bent into a low crouch. Suddenly, he exploded off the ground, his arms swinging back over his head, knees tucked into his chest. At the end of his flip, he stretched out his legs and landed on his feet. The girls squealed and cheered like a pack of hyenas.

As the handsome gymnast straightened and nodded to his adoring fans, his eyes met Kelly's. He grinned and winked at her.

Kelly's cheeks warmed, and she looked away. No need for him to think he had a new member in his high-pitched group of admirers. She might have considered signing up, except her name was already at the top of the list for Aaron's fan club. Unless he'd crossed her off.

Still, she hadn't expected to find anyone so smoking hot at a Christian camp. The boys in the church youth group back home were nice enough, but most were a little geeky.

She couldn't help but wonder what it would be like to go out with a religious guy. Would he push her to do things she didn't want? Like sneak her dad's car keys? Then blame her for everything that went wrong, like Aaron had? Probably. Lucy made lots of comments about her boyfriend getting his way all the time. Seemed fair to say that males were all alike.

A small movement distracted Kelly. One of the hat-wearing guys slipped away from the singing group and crept up behind the girls seated on the risers. A slender teen with long, flaming red hair held the finished braid of the girl in front of her. With the other hand, she picked up a golden barrette. But before she could secure the braid, the hat-wearing stalker snatched the hair clip from her fingers and dashed off across the room. Screeching in rage, the girl leaped to her feet and gave chase.

As the barrette thief snaked his way around the room, the girl roared behind him, blasting through the tall tower of playing cards like a whirling tornado and sending them flying into the air behind her. She charged through board games, scattering pieces everywhere. Teens leaped to the side to get out of her path.

The bandit headed straight toward Kelly, one hand holding his hat to his head and the other brandishing the golden hair clip high in the air. As he raced past, he waved the barrette right in front of Kelly, practically daring her to take it. So she did, snatching the clip from his fingers.

The thief flailed wildly in an attempt to regain the treasure, but his momentum carried him out of reach. The red-haired girl raced up, and Kelly tossed the clip to her.

The girl's look of surprise was quickly replaced by a pleased grin. "Thanks."

Kelly smiled back. "No problem."

Turning to the hat-wearing bandit, Kelly held up empty hands, then burst out laughing at the look of shock on his face.

A sudden piercing blast made her jump. She spun around to find MaryAnn in the doorway, holding a whistle to her lips.

"Everyone head to the gym."

The moment of shared fun was shattered. The redhead returned to the group of girls she'd been with earlier, and the thief joined his hat-wearing pals. The other volunteers surged past Kelly and down the hall. MaryAnn tucked the whistle into her pocket and motioned for Kelly to follow her.

There was nowhere to go except straight ahead.

3 STIRRING UP TROUBLE

Kelly sensed trouble the moment she followed MaryAnn into the gymnasium. At first glance, it looked like a typical school gym. Basketball hoops stood on opposite ends of the room. A variety of sports equipment lay stacked in bins against the far wall. Thick black lines crisscrossed the floor, marking court boundaries. But it was the items arranged in the four corners of the room that caught her attention. And aroused suspicion.

Each station held a different set of toys that seemed more appropriate in a daycare center. Kelly spotted gymnastic mats, hula hoops, soccer balls, bags of marshmallows and a wading pool filled with water and ice cubes. It had to be some kind of bizarre obstacle course. She hoped participation was optional.

MaryAnn directed the teens to line up against the back wall. Then she flashed a warm smile. "I'd like to welcome all of you to Timberlake Camp. For those of you who don't know me, my name is MaryAnn. I'm married to Bill, the camp director. He'll join us later."

Kelly scanned the faces of the other teens. Judging from their comfortable and confident expressions, she guessed that she was one of the few new volunteers.

"Our first set of campers will arrive in two days. That means we have a lot of information to cover in a short time. If you haven't been to camp before, the next forty-eight hours may seem intense. But don't worry, we'll get you through it."

Kelly raised an eyebrow. MaryAnn made it sound like camp work was difficult. How hard could it be to babysit kids all day?

"Now, what's the main reason that campers come to camp?"

Kelly fought the temptation to shout, *Because their parents force them.* Probably not the answer MaryAnn wanted to hear.

The other volunteers called out more appropriate guesses.

"To ride horses?"

"Hang out with friends?"

"Learn new things?"

"Get away from home?"

"Have fun?"

"All of the above, but especially the last one." MaryAnn gestured to the stations. "And the key to having fun is to get involved–no matter how unusual, scary, or crazy the activity may seem."

Kelly stiffened as her gaze strayed to the small pool with the floating ice cubes. She could handle unusual and scary. Even crazy. But she had no intention of looking like a fool. That was a sure way to get pegged as an outcast. The breakup with Aaron had already marked her as a reject at home. No need to continue the downward trend at camp.

"I'd like you to form teams of four. Once you're in a group, introduce yourselves. I'll explain the activity in a few moments."

Kelly couldn't help but glance toward the smoking-hot blond guy, even though there was little hope she'd find a place in his group. Sure enough, he was already surrounded by at least eight girls.

"Want to join us?"

Kelly whirled around and looked into the bright green eyes of the redheaded tornado. Behind her stood the clip thief and the lousy piano player, both still wearing the geeky hats.

Kelly considered the trio for a moment. They formed an odd group. But at least someone had invited her to join them. Their offer was much better than standing in a corner, waiting for MaryAnn to force someone to let her in.

"That'd be great." She gave a small wave. "I'm Kelly."

The thief tipped his hat, revealing unruly brown hair. "My name's Darren."

Kelly studied him as he jammed the hat back on his head. Not particularly cute. But his golden-brown eyes were friendly, and his roguish smile added an offbeat charm.

Darren gestured to the piano player. "This is Mike."

Mike's long, skinny form towered over her. He probably ate whatever he wanted and never gained a pound. Some people had all the luck. Although Mike's good fortune had run out when it reached his abnormally large ears, which stuck out from under his hat, giving him a comical look.

Darren poked the tornado in the arm. "That's Sheila. She's really picky about her hair."

Without warning, Darren put Sheila in a headlock and messed up her long locks. She screeched and fought back, finally freeing herself. "Touch my hair again and I'll cut your worthless hat into little pieces."

"Worthless?" Darren raised an eyebrow. "We paid good money for these hats. Fifty cents each."

Kelly stifled a laugh. She couldn't decide if Sheila and Darren liked or hated each other. Maybe a little of both.

Mike stepped between the combatants and extended his arms like a referee. "Enough bickering, you lovebirds."

Sheila snorted, then turned to Kelly. "Don't believe a word he says." She finger-combed the tangles in her hair. "I haven't seen you here before. Is this your first time at Timberlake?"

"This is my first time at any camp."

Sheila's face lit up. "You're in for a great summer."

Yes, once the week was over and she could go home. But Kelly felt a prick of doubt. Home to what? Repairing things with Aaron? Which meant more apologizing. More groveling. And more covering up for his lies by taking all the blame.

Several shrill tweets interrupted her musings.

MaryAnn lowered the whistle as the volunteers fell silent. "Today everyone will be competing in an obstacle relay race."

The teens erupted in a mixture of cheers and groans. Kelly felt the grim satisfaction of knowing she'd called the activity correctly. Except for the part about it being optional.

MaryAnn moved to the far corner of the room and stood by the wading pool. "All teams will start here. Using only your feet, you must flip out two stones from the bottom of the pool. I'd suggest removing your shoes and socks, but the choice is yours."

A guaranteed soaking with icy water? It seemed a little juvenile, and it sure wasn't Kelly's idea of fun. But she could handle it.

MaryAnn trotted to the next corner. "At the second station, you'll find a hula hoop with a marshmallow tied to it. While holding the hoop, you have to eat the marshmallow without using your hands."

Not happening. Kelly's lips hadn't touched sugar in close to a year, and she wasn't about to start now. She'd be skipping that station. As soon as she thought of a way to avoid it.

MaryAnn moved on. "Next, you'll summersault ten times across a mat."

Another problem. Even two or three somersaults made Kelly nauseated. After ten, she'd spew the glass of water she'd had for breakfast that morning all over the gymnastic mats. That would make a strong impression, just not a good one.

MaryAnn moved to the last corner. She held up a brown belt with a knee-high nylon stocking tied to the middle, weighted down by a small ball in the toe. "At the final station, you'll attach a belt around your waist, with the stocking hanging down behind you like a tail."

The teens burst into laughter. Kelly did not. She failed to see how the odd contraption dangling from MaryAnn's waist had anything to do with staff training. Unless to prepare them for playing ridiculous games with the campers.

"The runner will swing the sock and ball between his or her legs and hit another ball on the floor, knocking it past the pylons at the far end of the mat."

Surely this activity was designed to make the volunteers look stupid. And Kelly didn't do stupid. Especially not in front of a hot guy with amazing blue eyes.

"Then you'll run back to the start and tag the next person in your group. The first team with all their members back in line wins." MaryAnn pulled several strips of green paper from her back pocket and waved them in the air. "Each member of the winning team will receive a coupon for five dollars at the camp store."

The teens cheered as if MaryAnn had offered bars of gold. Kelly shook her head. Nothing at the camp store could motivate her to eat sugar or throw up in public.

Kelly turned to inform her team they'd just lost a player. She found them already in a huddle, whispering strategies. "I'm out," she announced.

"You have to participate." Darren yanked her into the circle. "We can't be disqualified in the first competition of the summer. We may not win with Sheila in the mix, but we have to try."

The comment earned him a sharp jab in the ribs from Sheila.

Rubbing his side, Darren moved to the left of Mike, out of strike range. "Sheila can start. I'll go second and make up any time she's lost. Kelly, you watch what we do and race third. Mike will be our anchor man."

Before Kelly could protest, MaryAnn blew a long, shrill blast. "Line up behind the yellow line. First runner to the front."

Mike grabbed Kelly by the shoulders and dragged her into place behind Darren, taking his position at the back. And blocking her escape.

MaryAnn counted down, with the teens joining her. "Three! Two! One! Go!"

The gym erupted in a roar of noise as the first racers took off. Sheila tore off her shoes and socks and jumped into the pool. Her feet kicked water everywhere as she tried to lift a stone from the bottom. She managed to remove her first rock, then a second one. As Sheila leaped over the side, she narrowly missed being wiped out by a girl who slipped and fell. The fallen teen hopped up, completely soaked. Kelly winced at the sight of blood dripping from her elbow. With the barest glance at her wound, the racer continued to search for stones.

Apparently everyone was playing this kiddie obstacle course to win. And blood appeared to be no excuse for quitting.

"Move it, Sheila!" Darren and Mike jumped up and down as if that would help her run faster.

The other teens screamed encouragements and insults at their team members. Kelly's heart beat faster as she got caught up in the excitement. She shouted Sheila's name, even though her new friend probably couldn't hear it over all the raucous cheering.

At the next station, Sheila snuck up behind a fellow racer and positioned the marshmallow between the edge of her hula hoop and his back. With the sweet treat stabilized, it was easy to grab with her teeth. She was the first to leave the second station and rush to the mats.

Darren and Mike leaped high, punching the air in frenzied joy. Kelly bounced on the balls of her feet. Darren wasn't the only one who liked to win.

Sheila started her summersaults before she even reached the mat. After rolling the required ten times, she staggered as if crossing the deck of a ship during a violent storm. But she managed to navigate a crooked path to the last station, attach a belt, and knock the ball across the line without much difficulty.

The moment Sheila touched Darren, he took off running. He didn't bother to take off his sneakers, just plowed into the pool, spraying water over the other racers. Ignoring their screams of protest, he launched two stones out of the pool and jumped out. When he got to the marshmallow, he managed to swing the entire white blob into his mouth on the first try, increasing the team's lead.

Kelly took her place at the starting line, straightened her shoulders, and shook out her arms. She had no idea how she'd deal with the problem stations. But her team was in first place, and she wasn't going to let them down.

Darren flew through the last two obstacles and sprinted back to tag Kelly. With a burst of nervous energy, she raced to the wading pool, pulled off her socks and shoes, and launched into the icy water. Ignoring the biting cold, she dug her toes under a rock and flung it out. The second rock proved more difficult. Her feet grew numb as she tried to flip one stone after another out of the pool. Precious seconds ticked by as she squandered her team's advantage. Finally, she trapped a small rock under the sole of her foot and slid it up the side and over the edge.

Spurred on by the cheers of her teammates, Kelly ran to pick up the hula hoop. Imitating Darren, she swung most of the marshmallow into her mouth. But rather than swallow it, she pretended to choke. Stumbling to a nearby garbage can, she spit out the gooey mess. Sugar avoided. Mission accomplished. But she'd wasted even more time.

Gritting her teeth, Kelly raced to the mats and rolled five times before a wave of nausea washed over her. On the sixth roll, she careened off to the side, crashing into a hard body. When she looked up, she found herself staring in the angry blue eyes of the blond hunk, her limbs entangled with his. She opened her mouth to apologize, but a second wave of nausea swept over her. She snapped her mouth shut. The only thing worse than throwing up on the gym floor would be upchucking on him. He pushed her foot out of his face and disappeared, tumbling down the mats.

Kelly had lost count of her somersaults. But she no longer cared.

She stumbled to the last station, where the hottie and a tall, dark-haired girl were tied for the lead. Her fingers trembled as she attached the belt to her waist. On her first attempt to swing the hanging sock through her legs, she completely missed the ball on the floor. This was harder than it looked.

The dark-haired girl's stocking swung back and to the side, knocking against Kelly's hand. In a reflex move, she grabbed it. And saw her chance to get back in front.

Kelly pitched the girl's stocking toward the blond hunk's sock. They connected in midair and wrapped around each other, becoming hopelessly entangled. With a cry of outrage, the girl clawed at the snarled socks. Kelly caught a glimpse of the hunk's surprised face before she slipped around him, knocking her own ball past the pylons and reclaiming the lead.

Awash in a mixture of panic and pride, Kelly raced back to her team and tagged Mike, who took off running.

Darren was doubled over, laughing so hard his hat had fallen off. "Brilliant move," he sputtered when he'd recovered enough to speak.

A beaming Sheila gave Kelly a congratulatory high five. "Impressive run. We're going to win for sure."

Kelly felt her cheeks flush. She'd done well, but at a price. She'd tripped up the cute guy twice, crashing into him on the mats and tangling his sock with an opponent's. His team was sure to lose, and it was her fault. Aaron would never have forgiven such sabotage. He not only liked to win. He *had* to win. She could only hope this blond hunk didn't feel the same. The last thing she needed was to get on the wrong side of the cool crowd on her first day at camp.

Mike raced through the activities like a crazy man. After guiding the ball past the pylons at the last station, he tore toward the finish line and slid in as if scoring a home run. Then he leaped up and pulled his team members into a crushing group hug. Caught up in the center of the screaming, jumping, and whirling vortex of her teammates, Kelly could hardly breathe for laughing.

After several minutes, Darren broke out of the circle and put Sheila in another head lock, messing up her hair again. When she got loose, she chased him all over the gym, shouting death threats to his hat.

A sharp cry of "unfair" caught Kelly's attention. She spun around to find the tall, dark-haired girl at MaryAnn's side, gesturing in Kelly's direction.

Mike rushed toward MaryAnn and the protesting girl. "There was nothing in the rules about tying up other competitors," he shouted, waving his arms. Darren hurried to join him, with a furious Sheila in pursuit.

All eyes focused on Kelly, including the intense gaze of the hot blond. Though surrounded by giggling girls, he stared at Kelly with a curious expression. Was he disgusted at her clumsiness on the mats? Angry at her interference? Or did he admire her bold and clever move with the nylons? She couldn't be sure, but she thought the corners of his mouth tilted upward in a grin. A faint smile flitted across Kelly's face, and she tucked the pesky strand of hair behind her ear again.

It looked like she'd been forgiven. Perhaps there was hope for the week after all.

4 THE STRANGE ASSIGNMENT

Kelly stood in the gym beside her team members, glowing with pride as they were declared the winners. When MaryAnn handed her the five-dollar coupon, Kelly stuffed it into her back pocket. She enjoyed the thrill of victory, but the prize was useless. She wasn't about to buy any junk food at the camp store. The only other items were probably cheap trinkets or religious stuff. For a moment, Kelly considered offering the prize to someone else. Then realized she'd have to explain why she didn't want to use the coupon herself.

MaryAnn gave another blast on the whistle.

Kelly winced. At this rate, they'd all be deaf before the campers arrived.

"Time for our first campfire. It's raining, so we'll stay indoors today. You have a fifteen-minute break before we start the session in the front area."

The volunteers surged toward the door leading out of the gym and flowed into the dining hall. Kelly stuck close to her team.

"So Mike," Darren said in a loud announcer-style voice, "to what do you attribute our success today?"

"I think we owe it to our hats. They went on *a head* while everyone else followed."

Mike and Darren howled over their joke, while the other teens groaned. Kelly stifled a giggle. She liked puns. Not that she was any good at coming up with them herself. But her dad was a master at finding a double-meaning jest for any occasion. Although he hadn't been cracking a lot of jokes lately. That was probably her fault.

Darren and Mike waved their coupons and tipped their hats to every volunteer in gloating celebration. "If they aren't careful," Kelly murmured, "someone will make them eat those ugly hats."

"What did you say?"

Kelly hadn't meant for Sheila to hear her comment. "I just think those hats are a little...weird," she stammered.

"Obnoxious would be a better word." Sheila raised an eyebrow. "Want to stir things up?"

"What's your plan?" Better not to commit to anything until she heard the details.

Motioning for Kelly to follow, Sheila stepped out of the wave of volunteers. "I need a Coke."

Kelly looked around for a soda machine but didn't see one.

Sheila walked to the back side of the kitchen's serving counter and reached behind a stack of plates on a low shelf. When she straightened, she was holding a silver-and-red Coke can. Not something that Kelly would ever drink, even if it had been diet.

"I stashed it here before the relay." Sheila pulled off the tab and took a long swig. "You want one? I have lots more in my room."

"No, thanks. Soda makes me burp." Which was true. Kelly didn't bother mentioning the real problem, which was the 140 calories per can.

"I drink about three of these a day--one at each meal."

So that's what fueled the tornado. Sugar, carbonation, and a heavy dose of caffeine.

Sheila took another swig from the can. "I've got to steal Darren's hat to pay him back for always messing up my hair. Want to help me?"

As Kelly studied Sheila's eager grin, she felt the warmth of acceptance. A far cry from the cold shoulder she was getting back home. Ten days at camp was a long time. She could use a friend to add a bit of excitement. Kelly grinned. "Count me in."

"Great! If we can convince Marcie to join us, we'll be set."

"Who's Marcie?"

"My best friend from last summer. We got into all sorts of trouble together."

Another girl as bent on mischief as Sheila? That would be like having a pair of tornados collide. And she'd be caught in the middle. Kelly frowned. She didn't know how they punished troublemakers at camp, and she didn't want to find out.

The two girls caught up with the last of the group as they entered the open area at the front of the lodge. A semicircle of risers, stacked three high, was a quarter filled with the teenagers.

"Marcie!" Sheila shrieked. "You made it!" After hopping over a few volunteers, she gave an enthusiastic hug to a plain-looking girl in the second row.

"Sorry I was late, but my violin lesson ran overtime."

Kelly stared at the girl's matching plaid T-shirt and shorts, knee-high socks, brown loafers, and short, straight hair with an uneven fringe of bangs. Solemn eyes peered back through thick dark-rimmed glasses. It all added up to one thing. Sheila's friend was a nerd.

"I bet you're in the Robotics Club at school." The words left Kelly's mouth before she realized she'd spoken.

"Yes, I'm the only girl." Marcie's face glowed with pride. "We came in second place at the state competition. Were you there?"

Kelly felt a measure of relief that Marcie hadn't been offended by her blundering comment. "I didn't go this year." Or any other year. Robotics wasn't her thing. Even if it had been, she wouldn't have joined. Aaron and his friends mocked all the academic clubs. Sports was their idol.

Sheila plopped herself down beside her friend. "Marcie's going to be famous one day."

"Famous for what?"

"I'm not sure yet." Marcie pursed her lips in contemplation. "But it's my life's ambition to be notable for some outstanding academic achievement or worthy contribution to society."

Kelly fought to keep a smile off her face. And her mother thought *she* was melodramatic. "How did you two meet?" Kelly had a hard time imagining how a tornado and the future pillar of progress had become such good friends.

Shelia gave Marcie an affectionate punch in the arm, causing her to wince. "We were part of a leaders-in-training program at Timberlake last summer. We had sessions all morning. In the afternoon, Marcie and I were assigned to indoor maintenance work."

Marcie rubbed her arm. "The only good thing about that job was getting to know you."

"There's nothing like washing toilets together to cement a friendship for life." Sheila flashed a sly grin. "But we had plenty of fun too."

Kelly could see nothing amusing about cleaning bathrooms. She turned to Marcie and raised an eyebrow.

Marcie gave a deep sigh. "During the leadership camp, we painted the dock in neon colors, duct-taped the doors to the boys' cabins shut so they had to crawl out the windows, and spray-painted the pigs and goats."

Kelly laughed at Sheila's idea of fun. Clearly, the redheaded tornado wasn't happy unless she was involved in some type of mayhem.

Listening to the stories reminded Kelly so much of Lucy. When some crazy stunt happened at school, Lucy was always the first suspect. She'd been the one to slip the sign "Honk if you like ice cream" on the back of the unsuspecting principal's car. Kelly heard that the poor man was a nervous wreck by the time he got home. On April Fools' Day, she gave a candied onion-on-a-stick to Aaron in the cafeteria. He took a huge bite, and immediately started gagging in front of everyone. Aaron wasn't used to being the butt of a joke, and wouldn't talk to the prankster for weeks. Lucy would have loved camp, and it wouldn't have been hard to convince her to sign up. But that was before the partying and new boyfriend changed everything.

Sheila lifted her shoulders in a modest shrug. "But all that was just a warm-up. Since we weren't on staff, we had to convince our mentors to go along with us. And they took the credit for our ideas."

"*Your* ideas." Marcie gave Sheila a disapproving frown.

"But this year, we can do a lot more. And we won't have to share the glory."

"Or the punishment." Marcie crossed her arms. "I'm not interested. I have my future reputation to protect."

"But you don't want to be known as some dry academic. Think of how this will be recorded in the history books." Sheila raised an arm with a dramatic flourish. "'The brilliant Nobel Peace prize winner, Marcie Johnson, is also known for her mischievous genius. In her first notable escapade, Ms. Johnson was part of a trio who pulled off the biggest prank in the history of Timberlake Camp.'"

Marcie gave a slow nod. "That would add a light, personal touch to my list of scholarly accomplishments."

Kelly couldn't hold back a snicker, which she quickly converted into a cough. How could someone be so smart, yet so gullible?

Sheila wrapped her arms around Kelly's and Marcie's shoulders and pulled them close. Her eyes glowed with anticipation. "We'll be famous. Campers for summers to come will speak our names with reverence."

Kelly shook her head at Sheila's over-the-top drivel. But she couldn't deny the appeal of being included in a daring band of rogues.

The high-pitched blast of a whistle caused Kelly to jump. Again. MaryAnn stood behind a podium in front of the risers. Kelly considered asking Sheila to adjust her plan. That annoying whistle should be the target of their theft instead of Darren's hat.

Despite several more tweets, most volunteers continued talking. As MaryAnn raised the whistle to her lips again, a tall, rugged man strode up beside her. An immediate hush fell over the group. With his worn cowboy boots and hat, jeans, and flannel shirt--all in black--he looked like a tough sheriff from a western movie. The only thing missing was a shiny silver star.

MaryAnn sighed. "At least my husband can get your attention." She smiled at the man beside her. "In case you haven't met him, I'd like to introduce Bill, the director of Timberlake Camp." She stepped aside. "They're all yours."

Bill scanned the room in an unhurried manner, making eye contact with each person. Kelly squirmed. It might be wise to stay on the right side of the law while she was at camp, which could prove difficult with a prank-happy friend like Sheila.

Bill strode to the fireplace and picked up a stack of white paper. He gave them to a girl on the end of the front row. "Take one and pass the rest on. MaryAnn will hand out pencils."

For several moments, the only noise in the room was the shuffling of papers. And the annoying sound of popping gum.

Bill held up a blank sheet. "I want you to draw your idea of romantic love. Use words, symbols, or anything else to represent your thoughts. Signatures are optional. If you'd like to add color, you'll find markers in a box at the front."

"You're kidding, right? That's so lame."

Kelly whipped around, looking for the brave but stupid person who had questioned the assignment. She spotted her at once, standing off to the side with one hand on her hip. Miss Attitude looked like she belonged at a photo shoot, not camp orientation. Blonde hair cascaded down her back in artfully arranged curls. Designer jeans and a pink-sequined tank top showed off a perfect figure. Her pouty lips and coy expression could have graced the cover of any teen magazine. And she was blowing huge bubbles with bright pink gum.

"No, Cindy, I'm not kidding." Bill glanced at his watch. "And you're late. Spit out your gum and join the group." He turned to the rest of the teens. "I'll collect the pictures in ten minutes."

Amid the flurry of papers rustling and pencils scratching, Cindy strolled to the garbage can, spit out her pink wad, and headed for the back of the group. Kelly thought she detected a faint blush on her cheeks.

Sheila leaned over. "Don't let his gruff manner fool you. Bill's great."

"Until you break any of the rules," Marcie corrected.

"We would have gotten away with painting the dock if you hadn't blabbed everything the moment we sat down in his office."

Marcie gave a loud huff. "How was I supposed to know he only wanted to tell us to move to a different room? I didn't want to get kicked out of camp."

A sudden thrill shot through Kelly. Could volunteers be sent home for causing trouble and breaking rules? She hadn't considered that option. Kelly closed her eyes and pictured her mother picking her up and driving off the ranch property. But even as she envisioned heading down the imaginary road to freedom, imposing stark-white walls loomed before her.

Kelly's eyes flew open. If she got expelled from camp, her mother wouldn't drive her home. She'd step on the gas and head straight to the hospital...and the lockdown eating-disorder program. It would be far better to stick it out here for ten days.

Sheila waved her hand dismissively in the air. "Bill wouldn't send us home. Probably just make us clean the barn or something. Besides, we were demonstrating enthusiasm and camp spirit."

Marcie scoffed. "Oh, we showed plenty of spirit scrubbing the paint off that old wooden dock for the next two days. And I had the blisters to prove it."

Bill took a few steps in their direction, eyes narrowed. Both girls bent their heads and began to draw.

Kelly stared at her blank sheet. How was she supposed to draw "romantic love"? She excelled in Drama, but floundered in Art. Kelly chewed on her pencil tip as the minutes ticked by. Completely stuck for inspiration, she snuck a peek at Marcie's paper. Neat, concise rows of crisp handwriting flowed down the page. Kelly counted fourteen lines. Most likely a Shakespearean sonnet. She tapped a frantic rhythm on her blank page. Writing scholarly poetry might work for a brainiac like Marcie, but there was no way she could pull that off.

Kelly turned to her left, desperate for an idea. Sheila's hand zipped back and forth across her sheet, filling it with bold images. A knight with sword and shield battled a fire-breathing dragon as a redheaded princess watched from the dragon's lair. Of course Sheila would portray romance as an exciting adventure. Even if the dragon looked more like a sick cow. Kelly was happy to know she wasn't the only Art flunky.

"Five minutes left."

Bill's words set Kelly's heart into a flurry. She couldn't turn in a blank sheet of paper.

A vision suddenly popped into her head. Kelly's pencil flew as she sketched the outline of a guy. She added descriptive labels with arrows pointing to the appropriate body parts. Blue eyes. Cute smile. Blond hair. Broad shoulders. Tanned muscles. Cool clothes. Along the border, she scrawled other traits. Funny. Athletic. Smart. Popular. With a giggle, she added a cat and a car, along with the comments "Cat optional" and "Cool car recommended but not required."

After decorating the rest of the paper with hearts, she studied the picture. It wasn't a great work of art, that was for sure. But it was creative. As she studied it, she realized that very few aspects matched Aaron. However, she had managed to create a reasonable resemblance to the gorgeous blond sitting somewhere behind her. Grateful that signatures were optional, Kelly left her work anonymous.

"Time's up. Turn them in." Bill and MaryAnn navigated through the tiers, collecting the sheets. Once they'd gathered them all, Bill returned to the podium and shuffled through the pictures. "Let's see what we have here..."

Kelly sucked in her breath. He'd given no warning that he'd be displaying the pictures, although she had to admit a certain curiosity to see what the others had drawn. As long as her own work remained unidentified.

Bill held up a sheet. "Ah, yes, the standard red hearts and long-stemmed roses. I have a feeling we'll see quite a few papers with those traditional symbols of love."

Polite applause for the boring picture.

Bill displayed another sheet. "Fancy boxes filled with expensive chocolate. The food of love."

Kelly grimaced. More like the food of fat. She'd convinced herself long ago that she didn't like the taste of chocolate.

Bill shuffled through his stack and held up Sheila's page. "Nicely done. Love often inspires acts of chivalry and great exploits."

"That's mine," Sheila shouted. Which was unnecessary since she'd signed her name in big letters at the bottom of the page and clearly cast herself as the lovely redheaded damsel in distress.

"Here's a picture showing a couple locked in what appears to be either a passionate embrace or some type of wrestling move."

Giggles floated through the rows.

"We have several pictures of couples kissing."

The campers hooted and hollered as Bill waved the sheets.

"It appears no one is brave enough to claim these."

No surprise there. Who wanted to confess, to the director at a Christian camp, that they defined love as two people groping each other?

When Bill looked at the next paper, he burst out laughing. "I'm glad Darren signed this one, but I don't think that was necessary."

As Bill displayed the image, the male volunteers broke out in spontaneous hoots and hollers, the girls in groans. Darren had drawn a fancy red sports car and written "Love is a two-door hardtop Enzo Ferrari with a 6.0-liter, 660-horsepower V-12 engine." Perched atop the roof was a hat that looked exactly like Darren's. The words "Men in Hats in Cars" was scrawled on the side door.

Bill raised an eyebrow. "Men in Hats? Is that what you and your comrades are calling yourselves this summer?"

Darren stood and tipped his hat to the crowd. Mike and the two other guys sporting matching headgear rose to their feet and grunted in unison. Bill waved them down.

Sheila dug an elbow into Kelly's ribs. "They don't know it yet, but the Men in Hats are about to lose a member. And we're about to gain a hat."

Kelly nodded, although she really didn't want the ugly thing. Or the trouble that was bound to come with it.

Bill moved on to the next picture. "It's not hard to tell who drew this one, either." He held up a drawing of a tree with a heart carved into the trunk. Kelly squinted to read the names inside the heart. *Cindy and Joel.*

As the volunteers let out a smacking of kissing noises, Kelly glanced behind her. Her heart lurched when she saw the picture-perfect model snuggling close to the blond heartthrob, a smug expression on her face. Kelly could almost hear her purring with pleasure at all the attention.

Kelly twisted around. Of course the camp hunk had a girlfriend. A strikingly beautiful, confident, very thin girlfriend. She knew the rules. Popular guys only picked the most attractive girls. And Kelly wasn't in that category. She'd been beyond lucky to catch Aaron. Now she was in danger of losing him. If that happened, she'd never get a chance with anyone so elite again.

"Joel's boiling," Marcie said in awe, gazing at the cozy couple.

Kelly wrinkled her nose. "What does that mean?"

Marcie exhaled, as if it took great effort to explain the obvious. "It means he's hotter than hot."

Sheila scowled at the pair in the back row before turning away. "Marcie's trying to come up with some new phrase that she hopes will catch on and become known around the world."

Well, she'd have to keep trying, because *boiling* wasn't going to make it out of camp, much less go global.

Kelly glanced back again, and immediately wished she hadn't. Joel's arm lay casually across Cindy's shoulders, and he toyed with the long strands of her shiny hair, wrapping them around his fingers. A reminder of the way Aaron used to cuddle with her. And probably never would again.

"Guess Cindy's back in favor," Marcie said. "Wonder how long that will last."

Kelly opened her mouth to ask Marcie what she meant, then shut it quickly when she saw the sheet of paper Bill was holding up. Her picture–of Joel!

Bill tapped the page. "Now, this is an honest portrait. A scientific diagram analyzing attraction. And the artist got it right. Most of us focus on external things like physical appearance and material possessions."

Kelly wished she could ask for her sheet back. She wanted to make a few changes...like ripping it into tiny pieces before throwing it in the garbage. Because guys like that were jerks. All of them.

Bill continued to flip through the drawings. Most repeated earlier themes. A few artists, however, were bolder in their designs. One page had a huge dollar symbol in the middle. Another showed a broken heart with tears. The final picture had the word *sex* written in big letters across the page. Kelly expected Bill to be shocked or upset. This was a Christian camp, after all. But he added the picture to the rest of the stack without any reaction at all.

Kelly's gaze wandered over the volunteers. Was there a girl in the group facing pressure from her boyfriend? Or had the word been written by one of the guys, because that's how he defined love? Which confirmed what she'd already suspected. Teens were pretty much the same everywhere, even at a Christian camp.

Bill tapped on the stack of sheets. "You've done a good job. Every one of these pictures contains images that are commonly associated with love. Well, except for the Ferrari."

Darren snorted.

"Any idea why I asked you to draw pictures of romantic love?"

A girl from the middle row waved a hand. "You're looking for an instructor for the craft cabin and you want to see who's artistic?"

Bill chuckled. "Good guess, but wrong."

"You're warning us that we're not allowed to kiss at camp?" suggested a guy in the back.

"No. But since you brought it up, I'll remind everyone that we don't encourage romantic relationships among the staff, at least not during camp. If you're already seeing someone, don't attract any attention to yourselves when the kids are around." He stared pointedly at Joel and Cindy until they slid apart. But only by a few inches.

Bill strode to the fireplace. "At the end of the summer last year, we surveyed the campers. Along with some other questions, we asked, 'What topic would you most want us to discuss at campfires?' Far and away, the number-one choice was boyfriends and girlfriends. The second and third choices centered around fighting with parents and problems with friends. Almost every camper wanted us to talk about some type of relationship. But romantic love was the clear winner."

If Bill had given the survey to Kelly's crowd at school, he would have gotten the same results. She couldn't think of anything that mattered more to her friends. Or to her.

Mike waved a long, skinny arm in the air. "I still don't get why we had to draw pictures. Unless you wanted to make fun of people who can't draw."

Bill shuffled through the stack of papers and pulled out a simple and poorly drawn sketch of a boy handing a flower to a girl. "Yours?"

"I have the right to remain silent." But Mike's bright red face answered for him.

Bill walked to the far wall and tacked up Mike's drawing. Right in the center.

"Did you have to do that?" Mike groaned.

There was an awful lot of wall around Mike's sketch. Kelly hoped Bill didn't plan to display all the pictures, although that might give her a chance to grab hers and shred it later.

Bill returned to the podium. "This was a test to see how much you know about love. You drew a lot of great pictures, but there's more to romance than chocolate, roses, and kisses. And sex. No one passed, because every sheet of paper is missing one crucial item."

Kelly frowned. She thought her picture had been quite thorough, except for the blunder of choosing a playboy for a model.

Bill surveyed the room. "Any guesses as to what was left out?" When no one raised a hand, he took a blank sheet of paper to the podium and began to sketch. "I guess I'll have to draw a true picture of romantic love myself."

In less than a minute, Bill held up his page. He'd drawn a bunch of ropes, stretched across the page. Kelly squinted at the image. Was she missing something?

After a moment of silence, comments started flying.

"That's it?"

"What do the Boy Scouts have to do with love?"

"Hey, I thought this was a Christian camp! That looks a little kinky."

Bill appeared shocked that everyone had missed this obvious item. "No picture of love is complete without ropes."

Marcie raised her hand, straight and high. Bill nodded to her.

"Aren't we supposed to teach the campers about Jesus so they can be saved?"

Kelly rolled her eyes. Time for all the Christian stuff. She'd been dreading this moment.

"Yes," Bill said, "our first priority is to teach the campers how to have a personal relationship with Jesus." Bill walked to the wall and pinned his picture beside Mike's. "We're going to start by talking about romantic love. Then we'll finish with the greatest love of all."

Kelly had heard people talk about God's love a thousand times. She'd gone to church since as far back as she could remember. It was going to be a long week if she heard "God is love" and "God loves you" all the time. Maybe there was a way to sit near the back and skip out on a few of the campfires so she wouldn't have to listen to all that meaningless nonsense.

Marcie pushed her glasses farther up her nose. "I still don't see how talking about ropes is supposed to teach campers about God."

Kelly didn't get it either. But unlike Marcie, she didn't see the point in complaining.

Bill's gaze roamed across the teens. "In order to explain how it all works, I'm going to need two volunteers to help me demonstrate a couple in love."

If he picked Cindy and Joel, Kelly just might throw up.

5 CARDBOARD AND ROPES

Kelly squeezed her eyes shut, unwilling to watch Bill choose Joel and Cindy as his nauseatingly perfect example of a couple in love.

"Behold our volunteers."

Bill's announcement launched a wave of laughter from the group. Not the reaction she expected. Kelly's eyes snapped open.

Bill stood in front of the podium with a life-sized cardboard cutout of a boy and girl propped up on either side of him. Someone had taken a great deal of care with their hand-sketched faces and trendy painted outfits.

These were the chosen "volunteers"? Kelly let out a relieved chuckle at the strange couple.

Bill swept his arms toward the duo. "These two characters are going to help us teach the campers about love."

"Hey, Darren. Is that guy wearing a cardboard belt?" Mike called out in a loud voice.

Darren peered closely. "I don't think so. That would be a *waist* of paper."

The volunteers let out a mixture of chuckles and groans. Even Bill cracked a grin before sending a warning glance toward the comedians. Mike and Darren seemed able to pull out a pun for any situation. And probably would. All summer long.

"How about introducing us?" a teen called out.

Bill put his arms around the stiff couple. "I want to avoid using the names of any campers or staff members. With the huge number of people coming through this summer, that will be next to impossible. So I'm just calling them Guy and Girl."

Whistles and shouts of "How ya doin', Guy?" and "Looking good, Girl!" resounded around the room. The enthusiastic reaction surprised Kelly. She doubted the campers would be this thrilled about large, flat cardboard dolls with unoriginal names.

Bill moved the figures about a foot apart. "Once upon a time, Guy saw Girl and Girl saw Guy. Guy asked Girl if she wanted to go to a movie. She said yes before he finished the question, and they went on their first date."

"It's not that easy!" Mike's protest was supported by murmurs of agreement from the males in the group.

Kelly agreed. Aaron hadn't just walked up to her one day and asked her out. It never would have happened if they hadn't taken the same drama class. Acting wasn't Aaron's strong suit. He'd been hoping for easy credits. That's why he chose to partner with her on the first project. He just saw her as the best route to a top grade.

She'd fallen immediately for Aaron's charm and confident attitude, and spent many late nights working alone on the script for their two-person play. Two weeks and three acts later, Aaron had an A+ and Kelly had an invitation to sit with the popular crowd at lunch. But any possibility of a romance seemed hopeless.

The breakthrough came when one of her new in-crowd friends told her that Aaron thought she was funny and cute, but too fat for him to date. She immediately went on a starvation diet. Four months later, she'd dropped close to thirty pounds, and Aaron asked her out on Valentine's Day.

Mike was right. Getting asked out wasn't easy.

Bill sent Mike a pointed look. "Back to our love story. Guy and Girl watch a movie, then go out for ice cream. This date creates a connection between them."

Bill motioned to the back of the room. MaryAnn came forward, holding a handful of long, thin green ropes. Reaching into the bundle, Bill selected a rope. He tied one end of it to Girl's hand and the other end to Guy's hand. "We'll illustrate that connection with this tie."

Bill stepped back and gazed at the cardboard couple. "Now, this first date doesn't form a strong connection. Girl and Guy don't discuss politics, religion, their goals for the future, or how many children they would like to have someday. They're not in love. In fact, they aren't even sure if they like each other at this point. Girl is actually disgusted with Guy when he burps the alphabet."

The males in the group roared. Kelly rolled her eyes. She could never understand why boys found revolting bodily noises so entertaining.

"Guy is unimpressed when Girl talks all evening about her past boyfriends." Bill raised a hand in the air and continued in a falsetto voice. "And then there was Larry, but he didn't like my cats. After that I dated Jim, but he didn't like shopping. And then..."

The girls hissed and booed in support of Girl. Kelly had to side with Guy on this one. It drove Kelly crazy when her popular friends talked on and on about their past boyfriends. But if she was being honest, that was just jealousy. Since Aaron had been her first real boyfriend, she couldn't join in.

Bill rapped on the podium to restore order. "Let's say Guy and Girl overlook their first-date blunders and continue to see each other. He takes her to a monster truck rally, where she gets a splitting headache from the exhaust fumes." Bill fastened another green rope between the two cardboard cutouts. "She takes him horseback riding and he falls off twice. Guy says rude things about his horse, which Girl pretends not to hear." Bill attached another green rope. "Every time they do something together, a tie is added and their connection becomes thicker."

Bill's lecture was amusing but nothing brilliant. Kelly's thoughts drifted. If she weren't here, she'd be in the hospital. When she toured the facility with her parents before school ended, they'd received a schedule that showed every day crammed from dawn to bedtime with individual counseling, group therapy, cognitive behavior modification, and classes on nutrition and health. No cardboard and ropes in that program. Just weight scales and medications. Or intravenous lines and feeding tubes, if things didn't go well. Kelly shifted and stretched her legs. The childish paper cutouts weren't exciting, but they were better than the alternative.

"After a year of dating, Guy and Girl get married." Bill paused until the smooching noises stopped. "Fast forward seventy years. Guy and Girl have spent a lifetime together. Both have gray hair and wrinkled skin. Imagine them sitting on a park bench, holding hands."

That'd put a few creases in the cardboard.

Bill motioned for MaryAnn to join him. "True love never stops adding ties." Working quickly, they secured the entire supply of ropes between Guy's and Girl's hands. When they'd finished, the ties were so thick it looked as if the couple was holding a tree trunk between them.

Bill stepped back from his creation. "This is our new picture of love."

Kelly tilted her head as she considered the scene. This wasn't the kind of breathtaking, overpowering type of love that could be turned into a blockbuster movie. But the connection was obvious and strong. Just like her relationship with Aaron...until it completely fell apart. And now she had to wonder. How solid had their connection really been? Especially when a week's absence might make him forget her.

Mike gave a loud, exaggerated cough. "Do you understand this, Darren?"

"A frayed knot."

Kelly chuckled. *Afraid not.*

"Should we grab a few ropes and skip out?"

"Nah. I'm tied up here for the rest of the summer."

Once again, the volunteers reacted with a mixture of groans and cheers.

Bill raised an eyebrow. "Do either of you have anything worthy to contribute?"

Darren leaned forward. "Yeah. Like Mike said, it's not that easy in the real world."

"You're right." Bill nodded to MaryAnn. She loosened a handful of ties and snaked them through the other ropes, even winding a few around Guy and Girl. Within minutes, she'd created a tangled mess.

"Now, that looks like my love life." Mike grinned.

"At least you've got a love life." Darren gave him a fist bump.

Sarcastic troublemakers or stand-up comedians? Kelly couldn't decide which role the hat-wearing friends played best. Maybe it was a combination of both, with a heaping measure of class clowns.

Bill stepped in front of the cardboard characters and lifted the knotted ropes. "Not all romantic ties are good. Some tangle and others strangle. They don't always lead to happy endings. During the next week, Guy and Girl are going to show the campers, and all of you, how to keep love straight in the complicated world of dating."

Kelly sat up a little straighter. What if Bill actually had some advice that could make her relationship with Aaron right again? Maybe the campfires would be useful after all.

Marcie's hand shot up. "I still don't see where God fits in."

If Mike and Darren played the clowns, Marcie had the role of class brain. And she seemed determined to be the one annoying student who wouldn't give up until she was satisfied with the answer.

"God is involved right from the beginning. Romance was His idea." Bill started detangling the ties. "God created Adam and Eve, put them together in the garden of Eden, and said it was good."

"They were naked, and God said that was good too!"

Kelly laughed more at Mike's audacity than at his joke. He didn't quit either.

Bill turned to Mike. "This isn't the garden of Eden. Clothing is mandatory here."

A lopsided grin stretched across the face of the self-appointed camp jester. But Mike was smart enough to stay quiet...this time.

Bill finished unfastening the ties, then carried Guy and Girl off to the side and leaned them against the wall. He returned to stand in front of the volunteers. "Even though God created and blessed romance, it isn't the most important relationship we can have. The most life-changing connection the campers can have is with Jesus. And that relationship will influence all others."

Silence fell in the room.

Kelly stared at the ropes dangling from Bill's hands. This tie thing kind of made sense. Well, not the God part. But the stuff about romance. Her fingers drummed a staccato rhythm against her leg.

Her relationship with Aaron was a mess. If she still even had one. Maybe she'd be able to figure out a way to straighten it out. But what if she couldn't? She imagined herself walking past Aaron, alone and rejected. She could almost see the smirk on his face. Unless...there was someone else. She could get another guy. A really hot guy. Someone like Joel. If she could walk by with him at her side, that would show Aaron that he was wrong. He'd think twice about dumping her. Maybe even want her back. And all those false friends wouldn't act so smug if she showed up with Joel's arm around her. Besides, with Joel at her side, she might not even want to hook up with Aaron again. Unfortunately, this scenario was never going to happen. Joel was connected to Cindy by those stupid ties of love, and she could never compete with Cindy's cool perfection anyway. Yet there had been that look at the end of the obstacle race. It was probably nothing. But what if it wasn't? She could still see his eyebrows arched with curiosity. The mouth tilted in an amused grin. And that settled it. As long as there was a thread of hope, she was hanging on.

6 LET THE COUNTDOWN BEGIN

Kelly's thoughts were so focused on the absurd hope of connecting with Joel, she barely heard Bill's lunch announcement. But his words struck the other volunteers like a flash of lightning. Chaos erupted as close to thirty teenagers stampeded into the dining hall as if they hadn't eaten in a week. Which was close to true in Kelly's case. And she intended to keep it that way.

Kelly pulled in her arms and legs to avoid being trampled.

"I'll grab us a spot," Sheila yelled over her shoulder as she leaped into the mob.

Marcie remained seated beside Kelly, eyebrows knitted together as she looked out the lodge window at the rain, now pouring relentlessly.

Kelly rubbed the goosebumps on her arms. "Kinda chilly in here without all the people crammed together."

"The world is a cold place."

Kelly stole a sideways glance at Marcie. She was staring into space, as if looking at something far away.

Kelly hoped Marcie didn't expect a reply to her odd comment. She didn't have one.

Marcie stood. "I think the cabin windows are open. I'd better go shut them. I don't want my violin to get wet."

Kelly coughed. "You brought a violin to camp?"

"Daily practice is the key to advancement."

Kelly couldn't argue with that. But it also cut into having a social life. Which probably wasn't a huge concern for the uber-ambitious Marcie.

Kelly latched onto the easy excuse to skip out on the meal. "I was just going to run back to the cabin and grab a sweater. I can check on the windows for you." It was true. She'd been shivering all morning. Then again, she usually felt cold, even when the weather was warm. Her counselor had blathered on about how her metabolism had slowed because she didn't have enough body fat. But she'd rather be cold than fat.

"Thanks." A look of relief passed over Marcie's face. "I'm in the first cabin."

Kelly slipped out into the gray afternoon, and jogged up the road. When she entered Marcie's cabin, she spotted a dark, oblong case on one of the bunks, along with a neat pile of thick textbooks. Marcie's bed, no doubt about it.

A composition notebook lay open next to the violin case, and the bold printing and underlined scrawls caught Kelly's attention. She glanced at a few lines. *Sloppy finger work. A five-year-old could play better. Pitiful performance. The festival is next week. Second place is no better than last place. Practice harder!* A quick flip through the book revealed page after page filled with the same type of comments. No wonder Marcie thought the world was a cold place. She had a heartless tyrant for a violin teacher, one who used humiliation and threats as motivation. Kelly wondered why Marcie put up with such abuse, and why her parents paid for it.

A cool breeze blew through the windows, and Kelly wrestled the rusty panes closed. Then she headed for her own cabin. Once inside, she sank down on her bunk and flopped back on her pillow, eyes closed. The quiet stillness of the room felt oppressive. She had little chance of catching Joel, and a solid chance of catching heat for taking part in Sheila's prank. The week ahead stretched before her like a long, dreary road. It would take forever to reach the end.

Forever. The word stirred a forgotten memory. She was five years old, her hair up in pigtails, crying at the kitchen table because her father had left on a trip. The first he'd ever taken. She asked her mother how long he would be gone. When her mother said it would be five days, Kelly sobbed even harder, declaring that was *forever.*

With a compassionate smile, her mother pulled out a white sheet of paper and a purple crayon. Kelly dried her eyes on a sleeve, then watched her mother draw large boxes across the page. One for each day her father was gone. In the last box, she drew a huge happy face. She secured the chart with magnets in the middle of the fridge, then passed the crayon to Kelly. Every evening Kelly crossed off one of the boxes, watching the day of her father's return draw nearer. And she skipped to bed with a smile on her face.

The memory gave Kelly an idea. She strode to her locker and flung open the door. After rummaging through her few belongings, she pulled out a pad of paper and a pencil. She returned to her bunk and drew a large rectangle on the top sheet. She divided it into ten segments, labeling each with a different day. Two days for staff training, Friday and Saturday. Eight days with the campers, from Sunday to Sunday. She considered the chart with a grim smile. No matter what happened during the day, she'd be guaranteed one happy moment each evening when she marked off a new box.

Kelly shoved the makeshift calendar under her pillow. No one else needed to know how much she didn't want to be here.

Her stomach rumbled, protesting its emptiness. Kelly glanced at the canvas bag her mother had left on her bunk. It was easy to guess the contents. Mom knew all her weaknesses. She'd probably packed a peanut-butter-and-honey sandwich. Glazed donut. Banana-nut muffin. All loaded with calories. The temptation had to be removed immediately.

She picked up the sack with her thumb and forefinger, as if the canvas were poisonous, and walked out of the cabin to the girls' bathroom. With a feeling of rebellious delight, she dumped the whole thing into a garbage can.

Kelly returned to the cabin and rifled through her suitcase, looking for a light sweater. She had just slipped one over her head when the door swung open. Cindy burst into the room, carrying a long-stemmed red rose, a small heart-shaped tin, and a card. Not hard to guess where they came from. Another girl followed close on Cindy's heels. They checked their laughter at the sight of Kelly.

Kelly took a deep breath. It wouldn't hurt to be friendly. Maybe she'd read the Cindy wrong. She sent a warm smile. "Hi. I'm Kelly."

Cindy looked her up and down with icy blue eyes. "Hello." One word, spoken in a frosty tone.

Nope, she'd read Joel's girlfriend right. A stuck-up princess.

Cindy gave a careless shrug, then walked to her bunk at the back of the cabin. The other girl hesitated, then followed the blonde's lead.

Kelly left the cabin, wrapping her sweater tight around her body in an attempt to stay dry.

There was no reason for Cindy to be so nasty. But she probably didn't see other girls as friends, only threats. The popular group at school was full of aggressive girls who were always on the defense, chasing everyone else away from their guys. It would serve the snotty blonde right if someone snatched Joel away from her and wiped the smug confidence off her face.

As Kelly returned to the lodge, she congratulated herself on her timing. The group had just started to migrate from the dining hall back to the risers in front of the fireplace. Ignoring the tantalizing smells wafting from the kitchen, she slid in beside Sheila, who was munching on a massive chocolate-chip cookie.

"I saved a place for you at lunch. But it's too late now. They've already put the sandwiches away."

Exactly what she'd hoped for.

Marcie nibbled on an equally large cookie. "You could have *knit* a sweater in the time it took you to grab one."

Kelly reached into her ever-present bag of excuses and pulled one out. "I had a headache so I laid down for a bit." A small lie. But the truth was too complicated. And personal.

"I think the desserts are still out." Sheila waved her half-eaten cookie in Kelly's direction.

Kelly's mouth watered from the savory aroma drifting toward her. "I'll pass."

"They're awesome. The camp cook is as cranky as a cornered crab, but she's an amazing baker. She owns a bunch of restaurants, and they've won all kinds of awards."

From champion restaurant owner to summer-camp cook? That seemed a long way to fall for a top-ranking chef, if she really was all that good. Kelly didn't plan to find out.

MaryAnn rapped on the podium. Kelly hoped that meant she'd lost her whistle.

"Time for the fun stuff." The director's wife passed out a stack of thick booklets.

Kelly took one and flipped through page after page of small type. It didn't look fun. More like school. Third-period History, to be exact.

"We're going to read through the entire package together." MaryAnn ignored the groans and complaints.

The booklet covered every aspect of camp life: curfew times, safety issues, the daily schedule, rules for the dining hall, procedures for each activity station, and a map showing out-of-bound areas. After an hour, Kelly was drowning in details and no longer needed to lie about having a headache.

When they turned to the last page in the booklet, the volunteers cheered and several stood and stretched. MaryAnn waved them down.

"I've invited Tony, a former counselor, to share an inspirational story about his personal experiences working with campers."

Kelly rubbed her throbbing temples, hoping he wouldn't take too long.

A grizzly bear of a man lumbered forward. Everything about him was massive. Big shoulders. Big hands. Big nose. Even his unruly hair was bushy and in need of a comb. Or industrial-strength scissors. Kelly would have been frightened to have him as a counselor. Maybe he kept his campers in line by threatening to eat them.

Marcie shivered. "They say he's done time in a juvenile detention center."

Sheila tossed her head. "No one's been able to prove that."

"That's because records are sealed once a minor turns eighteen, as long as three years have passed without any new offenses. The only exceptions are serious felonies."

"And you know this how?" Kelly asked.

Marcie shrugged. "I sat in on a preliminary law course last year."

Of course she did. Between violin lessons and the Robotics Club. And whatever else she did in her quest to become famous.

Sheila lowered her voice. "Tony's the chief supplier behind most of the camp pranks."

Perhaps that kept him in touch with his criminal past.

Tony growled and pounded on the podium. "You're going to be outnumbered. There will be eight kids in each cabin and only two counselors. You'll have to take your campers canoeing on windy days or horseback riding in the rain and mud. Campers will start food fights, refuse to change their clothes, and keep you up all night. If you have a bed-wetter, your cabin will smell like pee."

Kelly's nose wrinkled. If Tony wanted to get their attention, he'd done a good job.

"You may spend all summer working in a stuffy craft cabin, covered in paint and glue. Or find yourself washing a mountain of dishes in a hot and humid kitchen. Worst of all, you may end up on the cleaning crew, scrubbing dirty bathrooms and unplugging toilets."

Groans of disgust filled the room. Tony's eye's glinted, and Kelly suspected he was enjoying the reaction.

"Camp is hard work. Your job may not feel significant to you. But whether you're teaching horseback-riding lessons, mowing the grass, or leading cabin devotions in the morning, you can do mighty things for God this summer and make a difference in the lives of these campers."

Kelly didn't care about making a difference. She just wanted to survive the ten days and go home. Preferably without dealing with any plugged toilets.

MaryAnn stepped forward, her eyebrows furrowed into a frown. "Thank you, Tony."

She sounded anything but thankful. She'd asked for inspirational, and Tony hadn't delivered.

"We'll take a short snack break."

Since she couldn't retreat to the safety of the cabin again, Kelly followed Marcie and Sheila to a table. She smelled the brownies before she saw them.

"I've been waiting all year for one of these!" Sheila picked up a plate of the thick brown squares, grabbed two, and passed the plate to Marcie. "If only I had a Coke. But I forgot it in the room."

Marcie chose a gooey brownie and took a big bite. Closing her eyes, she sighed. "They're even better than I remember. They're *gruper*!" Another square disappeared before she handed the plate to Kelly.

Kelly passed the sweet treats to the volunteer sitting across from her. "Gruper?"

Marcie took another mouthful before decoding her word. "Great plus super. Gruper. I think that could really catch on."

Think again.

"You're not even trying one?" Sheila stared at Kelly as if she'd just turned down a stack of hundred-dollar bills.

"I don't like chocolate," Kelly lied.

Sheila reached for another brownie. "I never met a piece of chocolate I didn't love."

Of course not. Chocolate was full of sugar, which appeared to be one of Sheila's main food groups.

"Doesn't anything tempt you?" Marcie's glasses might be thick, but her eyes missed nothing.

Kelly was ready with another tried-and-true excuse. "I've got a nervous stomach. It acts up in new situations."

Marcie gave an understanding nod. "I have the same problem when I get stressed or overwhelmed."

Then she should have left her college-level summer reading program at home. Along with the violin.

After the break, Bill gathered the volunteers back into the fireplace area. "It's time to reveal this week's job assignments. For those who have signed on for more than one week, you'll rotate through several of these areas throughout the summer. I've asked the activity leaders and other staff members to describe their stations before I call out the names of their assistants."

Kelly's foot tapped a nervous beat on the floor. She pressed down hard to keep it still. This job assignment would be a major factor in determining the pleasure or pain of her camp experience. She wasn't sure what she wanted to do. Other than be partnered with Joel, of course. But whatever her job, she hoped it wouldn't require holding a toilet plunger while sporting a clamp on her nose and a wearing a hazmat suit.

A girl wearing a tie-dyed shirt stepped to the front and introduced herself as Amy, the craft leader. The only thing brighter than her multi-colored shirt was the toothy smile stretching across her face. "The campers will be weaving friendship bracelets, painting rocks, and using a pottery wheel to create a clay vase." Amy waved her arms in animated motions while describing the week's projects. "We'll have a great time."

Not Kelly. If she got stuck as an assistant in the craft shack, she'd have a lousy time. Guaranteed. Art projects weren't her thing. Neither was sitting around all day undoing knots or cleaning up paint spills. She needed to be active, burning calories.

Kelly felt relieved when Bill called the names of two other girls.

But archery didn't sound much better. As the instructor explained the joy of turning young campers into experienced marksmen, Kelly stifled a yawn. Too much watching and correcting. She was glad to receive a pass on that activity as well.

The two male volunteers who had been chosen cheered and high-fived each other. Kelly hoped she'd be that happy when her name was called.

Stan, the canoe instructor, described the various skills that would be taught on the lake. Kelly leaned forward. Finally, an activity with potential. She could get an excellent upper-body workout and a golden summer tan. But with zero experience on anything that floated, she wasn't likely to be chosen. Sure enough, Bill called two different names.

Tony lumbered to the front.

"I'm the maintenance director. I take care of anything messy, dirty, or broken. My tool shed is out of bounds. Check with me if you have a job that needs to be done. Ask with a chocolate bar in your hand, and the work will get done faster."

Bill coughed. "I didn't hear that."

"A plugged toilet costs double."

Tony appeared to be adding to his rap sheet of alleged criminal activity by operating a black-market system that dealt in chocolate. Which made the five-dollar coupon in her back pocket more valuable than Kelly had thought. It might come in handy if she needed to buy her way out of an unpleasant job.

"Bob will be working with me this week."

Kelly felt another wave of relief. It couldn't be any fun working with Tony on maintenance. She heard a loud groan from behind her. Bob must have had the same thought.

A tall, regal lady with graying hair pulled into a tight bun took Tony's place behind the podium. She looked like she hadn't smiled in years. And might have forgotten how.

"My name is Katherine. I'm the head cook. I run a no-nonsense kitchen. My staff starts early and stays late. You'll work through meals and won't be able to hang out with your friends or with the kids."

Kelly's foot tapped again, matching the frantic beating of her heart. She hadn't thought anything could be worse than working on maintenance. Except kitchen duty. She didn't mind long hours or isolation from the staff and campers. And she had no quarrel with mountains of dirty dishes. But she couldn't take the temptation of being surrounded by food all day long.

"Lady Katherine," Sheila whispered, "runs the kitchen like it's her personal kingdom."

Marcie nodded. "If you ever get caught stealing a leftover dessert from the fridge, death would be preferable to her punishments."

"I heard a staff member had to scrub pots until her hands bled. That was just for sneaking an apple."

"Her second-in-command, Sandy, is constantly cracking jokes. She's the only thing that makes kitchen duty bearable."

Kelly didn't care. This Sandy could keep them laughing from morning to night. They'd still have to clamp her in handcuffs and chain her in place to keep her locked up in the kitchen for a week.

"Working with me this week will be Sheila, Marcie, Charlie and Kelly."

Kelly could almost feel the cold steel manacles closing on her wrists.

"I always get the lousy jobs!" Sheila didn't bother to keep her voice low.

Lady Katherine sent her a withering look.

Marcie took a deep breath and let it out slowly. "At least we're all together. If I have to spend a week peeling potatoes, I'm glad it will be with friends."

"But I'll never get a chance to see..." Sheila's voice trailed off.

Kelly's heart beat frantically in her chest. This couldn't be happening. She had to find an escape route from kitchen duty. She'd been planning to go for an early run the next morning. Jog down the road past the edge of the property, turn around after about twenty minutes and head back. It was a simple but effective route for a workout. But that's not what she needed now.

Time for a new plan. She wouldn't turn after twenty minutes. She'd just keep running. All the way home.

7 PARTNERS IN CRIME

A week of kitchen duty? A sharp pain shot through Kelly's chest. She couldn't do it. The very thought made her nauseous. She felt hot and sweaty, and found it hard to breathe.

A sideways glance revealed that the news had hit Sheila hard as well. The shoulders of the redheaded tornado sagged. She looked like she'd been poked with a pin and all the air had escaped. Which was exactly how Kelly felt.

Bill's voice rang out as he continued with volunteer assignments. "Darren, Mike, Zach, Alan, and Ben will be group leaders for the boys. Cindy, Nancy, Audrey, Jill and Hannah will work with the girls."

Sheila's nostrils flared as she snapped to attention. "That's so unfair." Her words came out in a quiet hiss. "Group leaders get to hang out with the campers at all the activities. It's one of the best jobs at camp. And Cindy and her friends got it."

Kelly looked over at the flawless blonde. A broad smirk stretched across her face. Kelly wished she could wipe it off. With a soapy dish rag from the kitchen.

A flash of black and white drew Kelly's attention back to the center of the room. A wiry woman wearing a zebra-print cowboy hat strode to the front. Once she reached the podium, she swept the hat off, revealing a long mane of jet-black hair.

"I'm Bernice and I'm in charge of the Equestrian Program here at–" A burst of cheering interrupted her speech.

"They say Bernice could ride before she could walk." Marcie spoke with obvious admiration. "She's a true horsewoman, and she's got the medals and trophies to prove it."

Of course Marcie would be a fan. She seemed to idolize success in any form, even if it required a four-legged creature.

Bernice called out the volunteers for horse staff, and every name brought a growl of rage from Sheila.

"And finally," Bill announced, "Joel will be our new vaulting instructor, with Matt as his assistant."

A deafening cheer rose from the female counselors. But Sheila's complaint, loud and bitter, sliced through the din. "Cindy will see him every day, while I'm trapped in the kitchen."

So Sheila was sweet on either Joel or Matt. Kelly gave her a nudge in the ribs. "See who every day?"

Sheila shook her head and launched into a tirade about the cruelty of life and camp directors.

Bill returned to the podium, the sheet listing the names of volunteers and their assignments dangling loosely in his hand. An idea struck Kelly like a thunderbolt. Bill had created the list. And that meant he could change it.

Perhaps she wouldn't have to run away from camp after all.

Bill cleared his throat and the teens hushed. "It's been a long, full day. In just a few moments, I'll dismiss you for supper. Afterward, the evening is yours. I expect everyone in their cabins, with lights out, by ten o'clock."

"I'm too old for a curfew," Darren protested.

A chorus of voices gave support to Darren's complaint.

Bill considered the grinning volunteer for a moment. "Darren, you may stay out as long as you like. But your hat needs to be in the cabin by ten o'clock."

Darren wore a puzzled frown for a moment, then he grimaced. "You win...even if you don't play fair. But I'm not going in until nine fifty-nine."

Kelly wondered if she'd missed something. Or if Darren had. All he had to do was throw the hat in the cabin, and he was free to stay out as long as he liked. She couldn't understand why he'd surrendered so easily.

"Dinner is served." Bill waved his hand in the direction of the dining hall, and the volunteers stood, stretched, and headed toward the rows of tables.

Kelly turned to Sheila and Marcie. "Can you save me a seat? There's something I need to check."

Sheila nodded, but Kelly wasn't sure her friend had heard. She seemed focused on Bill, her eyes shooting flaming-hot arrows at him. Which he didn't seem to notice.

Kelly stepped into the shadows in the hall, watching to see which way Bill would go. To her great relief, he exited the lodge. Alone. Kelly waited a few moments, then raced after him. "Mr. Bill, I need to talk to you."

He turned, and Kelly stared into eyes such a deep brown they almost seemed black.

"You can drop the mister. Bill is fine." His eyebrows furrowed slightly. "Is there a problem, Kelly?"

He knew her name. That didn't seem like a good sign. But she pressed ahead with her plea. "I can't work in the kitchen."

He examined her closely, his features impossible to read.

"Please." Kelly swallowed hard. "I'll do anything but that." She was trembling from head to toe. He had to see it. But she couldn't stop.

Bill pulled the folded list from his back pocket. His eyes swept across the page. Minutes passed, each one slow and painful. Kelly bit her lip so hard she tasted blood.

Finally, Bill looked up. Kelly thought she detected a slight softening at the corners of his eyes. And the barest hint of a smile. "I'll make a switch."

A flood of relief flowed through Kelly's body. For a moment, she couldn't speak. Then she managed to squeeze out, "Thank you."

"Head back inside. I'll make the announcement after supper."

As Kelly entered the lodge, she realized she'd forgotten to ask what her new job would be. But it didn't matter. Anything was better than the kitchen.

When Kelly reached the dining hall, most of the volunteers had already passed through the serving line and settled at tables. She grabbed a plate, but moved past the platters with huge portions of steaming lasagna and the trays of thick garlic bread. At the end of the counter, she found a large metal bowl full of salad. After taking a small amount, she spread it out to cover her dish. When she glanced up, she noticed a lady in an apron standing near the swinging kitchen doors and watching her. Too boldly for Kelly's comfort.

Kelly tensed. At home, her mother monitored every bite she took, constantly trying to force her to eat more. Every forkful had been a battle. Kelly hadn't expected close surveillance at camp. But at least she had lots of practice at evasive maneuvers.

Kelly picked up a bottle of salad dressing and pretended to read the label. Out of the corner of her eye, she saw Lady Katherine push through a door and motion to the other woman. With the snoop's attention diverted, Kelly put down the bottle and escaped.

After a quick search of the room, Kelly spotted her friends sharing a table with Mike, Darren, and the two other members of the Men in Hats. Mike pointed at each of his comrades and introduced them as Charlie and Zach. Apparently no one had told them it was bad manners to wear a hat at the table.

Kelly took a spot at the end of the bench and listened to the light banter. Dishes of strawberry pie sat at each table setting. Kelly pushed her slice toward the middle.

"If you don't want your dessert, I'll take it."

Second lesson in manners for Mike. Don't talk with your mouth full.

Kelly shrugged. "It's all yours."

Mike dragged the plate to his side of the table, then stabbed his fork through the crust multiple times.

"There's no need to kill it," Sheila snapped. "The strawberries are already dead." Her bad mood seemed to be growing. And she was gripping a can of Coke so tightly that her knuckles had turned white. Kelly hoped to be far away and safe from the inevitable blast when Sheila discovered that Kelly had wiggled out of kitchen duty.

Grinning, Mike pulled his fork out of the mutilated wedge. "No one else will take it now." He elbowed Darren. "What's the best thing to put in a pie?"

"Your teeth."

Every male wearing a hat laughed. The girls groaned.

Darren gave an exaggerated sigh. "It's too bad my math teacher isn't here."

"Why?"

"His favorite dessert is pi."

Laughter again. And more groans.

A loud rapping at the front of the room drew their attention. Bill stood in front of the counter, banging a large metal serving spoon on the side. Primitive, but effective. And better than a whistle. But only slightly.

He pulled out the volunteer list. Kelly tensed. She'd never been a fan of fireworks. Especially when they were about to go off right beside her. She took a bite of her salad, chewing as if it required all her concentration.

"I'm making a few last-minute changes to the assignments for this week. Hannah and Melinda will exchange roles as group leader and craft assistant."

Kelly heard cheers. The girls must have been happy with the switch. She took another bite of salad and focused on her plate, glad she wasn't the only change on the list.

"Tony is short-handed on maintenance, so Kelly will be joining Bob on that assignment."

So that was her new job. Working with the allegedly corrupt grizzly bear. Not her first choice. Not a great choice. But still better than the kitchen.

Kelly risked a glance at Sheila. She saw the shriek before she heard it.

"What?" Sheila spun to face Kelly. "Did you talk to Bill?"

Kelly gave a slight nod.

"And he let you off kitchen duty?"

Kelly inclined her head again.

Sheila flew out of her seat and stormed toward Bill. A tornado in full fury. Kelly felt a moment of pity for the man.

"You're so lucky." Marcie sighed.

Kelly was glad to have a change of assignment. But she wouldn't go so far as to say cleaning bathrooms and fixing broken items was good fortune.

"You get to work with Bob. He goes to an elite private school, and they win most of the academic and athletic awards in the area. We only get Charlie in the kitchen, and he's no fun. He barely talks."

Kelly didn't care about her partner's accomplishments. But if he was cute, the week might be salvaged. She nudged Marcie. "Where is he?"

"He's at the end of our table, in the blue shirt."

Kelly checked out Bob's broad shoulders and muscular arms. Her friends at school would have been tripping over each other to get his attention. But he might want to rethink the expensive name-brand shirt and the thick gold chain around his neck. Probably not the best apparel for maintenance. And neither was that fancy snapback cap covering a head of dark hair. Seriously, what was the obsession with guys and hats at camp? At least Bob's taste in headgear was better than the ugly fishing caps, and he didn't have three friends forming a matching hat club with him.

"Not hungry, Kelly?"

Startled, she looked up and found MaryAnn standing beside her. Or more accurately, spying on her. Kelly avoided her gaze. "We don't eat a big evening meal at my house."

Mike snorted. "You should come to my place. My mom complains that she triples every recipe and it's still not enough." Then he shoved half a slice of garlic bread in his mouth.

The others chuckled, but Kelly didn't join in. She didn't joke about food. Ever.

MaryAnn pointed at the two pieces of pie in front of Mike. "You know the rules. One dessert per person."

"Kelly gave me hers." Mouth stuffed full of food, Mike's answer was close to unintelligible.

Sensing MaryAnn's piercing gaze, Kelly nodded. "I don't like pie." The lie slipped from her lips, so smooth and easy.

Thankfully, MaryAnn moved on without further comment. She tapped Darren on the shoulder. "Eating with your hat on?"

He grinned. "Yep. We can't take them off."

The moment for the first lesson in manners had arrived. Kelly expected MaryAnn to tell Darren to remove the hat, and his three friends to do the same. But the director's wife just raised her eyebrows and headed toward the next table. Odd. And disappointing.

Darren jumped to his feet. "We are the Men in Hats!" He placed his hands on his hips, stuck out his chest, and lifted his chin. The classic pose of a super-hero. The only thing missing was a flowing cape, which Darren remedied by tucking a paper napkin into the back of his collar. Mike, Charlie, and Zach leaped up and imitated his stance, with similar white napkins trailing behind them.

"You children have serious problems," Sheila muttered as she slid back onto the bench.

The scowl on her face answered all of Kelly's questions. Somehow, Bill had withstood the storm, and Sheila was still stuck in the kitchen.

"I quit playing dress-up years ago." Marcie pointed at the limp paper capes.

So Marcie knew how to play after all. Kelly was beginning to wonder.

"Hats for all and all for—" Mike swung his arm wide in a grand gesture, but his hand collided with the pitcher of water on the table. The contents splashed over Marcie, soaking her.

For a moment, everyone at the table froze in shocked silence. Then the teens burst out laughing.

Marcie's face turned a splotchy red as her lower lip trembled. Kelly stifled a giggle. If Sheila had been drenched, she might have laughed at her dripping self. Or attacked Mike and exacted revenge. But Marcie's whole life seemed focused on achieving international acclaim, while avoiding public embarrassment.

"I'm sorry." Mike scrambled to grab napkins from around the table, passing them to Marcie as quickly as he could.

"Don't bother," sneered a voice from the end of the table. "She looks better that way."

Caught up with the chaos of the spill, the others didn't seem to hear the comment. But Kelly whirled around, eyes narrowed, searching for the creep who'd insulted her friend. She found herself staring into the smirking face of her new partner.

"She couldn't look any worse." Bob added the last comment under his breath, just loud enough for the guys seated around him to hear. Kelly looked into Marcie's wounded eyes. Clearly she'd caught the cut as well. Kelly remembered Marcie's words from the morning. No wonder she found the world a cold place. And cruel too, at least for girls who wore plaid shorts, knee-high socks, and thick glasses.

Bob's friends snickered, and Kelly watched her work partner sweep the fancy snapback cap from his head and bow several times.

A rush of white-hot anger rose within Kelly. She wasn't going to stand by and watch Marcie get picked on. Something had to be done. Preferably something messy.

"I'll get more napkins." Kelly leaned far across the table, reaching for the metallic canister of napkins on the other half of the table. Her fingers grasped it and she pretended to slip forward. As she fell, her hand knocked into a full glass of punch. The force of the collision sent the bright red liquid spraying all over Bob.

Rose-colored rivers streamed down Bob's face. He sputtered and staggered to his feet. "Watch it, you klutz! You just ruined my shirt!"

It was a shame. He was so good-looking. But such a jerk.

"I'm sorry." Her eyes sent a different message.

Bob gave her a dirty look before brushing past, heading in the direction of the bathroom. Kelly returned to her seat, passed the handful of napkins across the table, and silently congratulated herself on an excellent performance. Mike grabbed the extra napkins and mopped up the table while Sheila toweled off Marcie.

A light kick caught Kelly's shin under the table. She looked into Darren's laughing brown eyes.

"He deserved that."

So he'd been watching her. Kelly opened her eyes wide and feigned innocence. "I don't know what you mean. It was an accident."

"Of course it was. Nicely done."

Kelly examined Darren's teasing grin, but found no trace of mockery. Just amusement, and perhaps a hint of admiration.

"I'm going back to the cabin to change." Marcie kept her eyes lowered. "Then I'm going to work on my Spanish lessons. I'm trying to get ahead for next year."

Sheila leaped to her feet. "I think I'll join you. I have my own assignment. Do you have some paper I can borrow?"

The request came as a surprise to Kelly. Sheila didn't seem like the type to focus on studies at camp. Or any other time.

Marcie tucked a strand of wet hair behind her ear and nodded.

"Bill said I couldn't talk to him any more about a job switch. But he didn't say I couldn't write." Sheila's eyes glowed, a sure sign she was up to no good. "Three pages ought to do it."

A three page note from Sheila would certainly be enough to annoy Bill. And possibly earn her a second week scrubbing greasy pots and pans. Repeated attempts to change the schedule probably wouldn't sit well with him. Which made Kelly wonder. Why had it taken so little effort to convince him to make the switch in her case?

Marcie and Sheila left the lodge together. But as they walked past Cindy's table, the flawless blonde pointed at the drenched Marcie, rolled her eyes and made a comment that drew giggles from the girls sitting around her.

Kelly felt anger flare up within her again. Cindy's actions weren't much of a surprise. She was no different from the girls in the popular crowd back home. Spiteful and superficial. Too bad the pitcher of juice was at the far end of Cindy's table, or Kelly might have been tempted to trip again in a repeat performance.

Teens from the surrounding tables began to disperse. Kelly scraped the remaining half of her salad into a garbage can, then stacked her plate with the others.

A few hours remained before curfew. Kelly felt drained and would have been happy to walk straight to the cabin and collapse on her bunk. But she'd missed her morning jog and needed to make up for it.

She slipped out of the lodge and discovered a well-worn path. She spent the next hour running back and forth on the hard-packed lane, swinging her arms for maximum effect.

As the sun faded and the path grew dark, Kelly headed for the cabins. She retrieved her sack of toiletries and entered the washroom. It was a hum of activity, with everyone vying for sinks at the same time. Kelly grimaced. When close to fifty campers were added, this would be complete chaos.

When she'd finished washing up, Kelly returned to the cabin and sank onto her bunk. Her fingers twitched, missing her phone. It felt strange not to be able to call or text her friends back home. She hadn't caught the names of any of the other girls in her cabin, except for Cindy. A few girls sent her a tentative smile. Several introduced themselves and they chatted briefly about the upcoming week. But the ice princess and her small group ignored her again. Kelly didn't mind. She didn't feel like talking much anyway.

Kelly grabbed the wind-up travel clock from her locker. It was a stone-age piece of junk, and she missed the simplicity of her phone. Twisting the dials on the back the way her father had shown her, she set the alarm for six in the morning. That should be early enough to get in a run and shower before breakfast.

Not wanting the extra-early alarm to wake her cabinmates, she shoved the clock under the far corner of her pillow. As she did, her hand brushed against the calendar. She pulled it out and, with thick, dark strokes, crossed off Friday. One day gone. Nine long days left.

After shoving the clock beside the chart under her pillow, Kelly crawled into her sleeping bag. She squeezed her eyes shut to block out the sight of Cindy walking among the bunks with the heart-shaped red tin.

"Chocolate-covered cherries from Joel. He knows they're my favorite."

She didn't have to announce it so loudly. Kelly hoped the sweets made Cindy fat. Or break out in zits. Or both.

"He wrote me a note too."

Kelly peeked through slits in her eyes and watched Cindy make a great show of tacking the card to the wall just above her pillow.

Lights out couldn't come fast enough. But as Kelly buried herself deeper in her sleeping bag, her foot nudged something furry. With a shriek, she shot out and stumbled to the center of the room. "There's something in my bed!"

A few girls screamed. Everyone backed away.

Kelly stared at the motionless bulge. She picked up a shoe and threw it at the lump. Nothing happened. Edging closer, she poked at it with her other shoe. Still no reaction.

All eyes watched as Kelly slowly unzipped her bag and flung back the top. A black, white, and tan stuffed beagle stared up at her. One of her most precious possessions.

Laughter came from the other girls, part mockery and part relief. But Kelly ignored them and picked up her beloved dog. As she ran her fingers through its well-worn fur, she discovered a note taped to its stomach.

Dear Kelly,
Your beagle didn't want to be left behind. We're thinking of you constantly, and praying for you always.
Love,
Mom and Dad

Kelly stroked the long, soft ears. The dog had been a surprise gift from her father when he returned from the five-day trip. The one that took forever. Ever since that day, she'd never slept without it. She'd been so angry while packing that she overlooked it. Her mother must have noticed, smuggled it along, and hidden it after Kelly went to the lodge. An image of the bag of snacks at the bottom of the garbage can sprang to mind, bringing with it a sudden flush of guilt.

Kelly had great parents, and she knew it. It wasn't fair what she'd put them through. The rapid weight loss was bad enough, but then she'd changed her crowd of friends and stopped going to church. Her grades had suffered, and so had her attitude.

Worst of all, they'd been devastated when they'd found out she'd stolen the car and snuck off to a party. She'd told the truth when they asked what she was planning to do that night. Go to a movie with Aaron. But when he arrived, she made the mistake of showing him the hot new sports car her dad had just bought. And telling him that her parents had left for the evening. His eyes lit up at the news, and suddenly he changed his mind about walking to the movie. Said he'd rather take the car for a spin.

Kelly sat on the edge of her bunk and stared out the cabin window into the darkness, her hands stroking the soft fur of her beloved beagle. She'd argued with Aaron. Tried to change his mind.

But Aaron told her that if she really trusted him, she'd prove it. And if she wouldn't, he'd find someone who would.

So she'd taken the car keys from the rack, and passed them to him. To keep him happy. She hadn't anticipated more than a quick ride around the block. But Aaron had other plans. He knew about a party. He promised they'd just put in a short appearance, show off the car, and then head home before her parents got back. But once they got there, Aaron didn't want to leave so quickly. And then he started drinking

Kelly's hands clutched her stuffed dog. When Aaron staggered to the car, finally ready to leave, she'd panicked. And called her parents.

He'd been behind the wheel when her mom and dad pulled up. She'd been embarrassed and humiliated. And thankful.

Aaron, of course, had been furious. And it only got worse when her father yanked him out of the car and, in front of everyone at the party, threatened to call the police and have him arrested. She'd begged her dad to listen, and sworn that everything had been her idea. But Aaron didn't care that she covered for him. The damage had been done.

Maybe camp was a good thing after all. It would give her time to sort out what she was going to do if Aaron actually gave her a second chance.

Kelly snuggled back into the sleeping bag, holding her beagle close. It might be childish for a teenager to sleep with a stuffed animal, and she wondered if the campers would tease her. But she didn't really care. She needed something familiar and comforting right now. Besides, she wasn't sure she could break the habit of cuddling with it every night, and wasn't even going to try.

Someone turned out the lights, and the voices of the chatting girls hummed in the background as Kelly waited for sleep to overtake her. But her mind wouldn't stop reliving the twists and turns of her roller-coaster day. She'd caught the eye of a stunning blond hunk, been dragged into an insane plot to steal a hat, was assigned to kitchen duty then switched to maintenance in a last-minute trade. If that wasn't enough, her work partner was a complete jerk.

And that was only the first day.

8 A WALLET AND A PLAN

The muffled sound of an alarm jolted Kelly out of her uneasy slumber. Fumbling under her pillow, she turned it off before the noise woke the other girls. She lay still in the darkness of the cabin, listening to the steady breathing coming from the other bunks. No one had been disturbed. Taking a deep breath, Kelly relaxed. She wouldn't have to explain or make excuses for getting up so early. At least not yet.

Though tempted to close her eyes and drift back to sleep, Kelly forced herself to slip out of the warm comfort of her covers and into the cool room. Reaching under her bunk, she located the shirt and shorts that she'd tucked away the night before. Once she was dressed, she tugged on her shoes, eased open the cabin door, and stepped outside.

The rising sun cast a golden light over the camp. Kelly stood in the soft glow, enjoying the brief moment of peace. This was the only time of the day without struggle or pressure.

Then her stomach rumbled, shattering the moment. And just that quickly she was thrust back into the never-ending battle to lose weight. How else could she compete with girls like Cindy? She'd never be the prettiest. Or the smartest or funniest. But she could be the thinnest. It had been a badge of honor among the popular crowd, and she was the envy of many girls.

Kelly slipped past the dark cabins and headed toward the camp entrance. Jogging down the main road and back again didn't offer much for scenery, just empty fields. But it didn't matter. Nine more days and she'd be free to choose from multiple routes in her familiar neighborhood.

As she passed under the massive wooden archway, Kelly pushed herself to pick up the pace. She focused on the rhythmic crunching of gravel under her shoes. One foot in front of the other. Ignore the fatigue and the protesting muscles. Imagine inches melting away.

Kelly's breath came in shallow gasps as she reached the bend in the road. Her lungs burned, and she savored the pain of a successfully brutal pace.

Kelly paused to tie a loose shoelace. As she straightened, a movement from farther down the road caught her eye. Squinting, she saw a person in the distance, walking toward camp. The figure was too far away to be a threat, and her initial fear gave way to annoyance. She'd planned to keep her morning workout a secret.

Spinning around, Kelly pounded back down the way she'd come, considering the options for another route. The short, twisty trail she'd found the night before wasn't long or smooth enough. And she was certain to run into more people if she stayed within the camp boundaries. This road was still her best choice.

As Kelly jogged back onto camp property, she slowed her steps and wiped a hand across her sweaty brow. Frustrated at losing the privacy of her route, she grabbed a handful of rocks and flung them at the side of a storage shed. The pebbles made a staccato sound, like a series of pellet shots.

A shrill neigh startled Kelly, and a voice shouted, "Whoa!"

A bolt of panic shot through her. She'd forgotten the vaulting arena on the other side of the building. As she raced around the corner, she saw Joel, standing on the back of a massive brown-and-white horse, which was tossing its head and snorting. Joel's outstretched arms spun in circles as he tried to maintain his balance.

The horse took a leap forward and jerked to a stop. The blond hunk flew over its head. He pulled his arms and legs into a tight tuck position just before hitting the ground. Dust flew everywhere as he rolled several times. Finally, he lay sprawled out on the ground, perfectly still.

Kelly rushed to the railing. Had he broken his back? Or been killed?

A tall, lanky teen dropped the long lead rope and ran to Joel's side. "Are you okay?"

Joel slowly raised himself to a standing position, stretched out his limbs, and nodded. Kelly nearly collapsed with relief.

"I wonder what spooked Samson like that." Joel bent over to brush the dirt off his pant legs. As he straightened, his eyes met hers. There was nowhere to hide. And no point in trying to deny her guilt.

"I did." Kelly took a deep, shaky breath. "I threw some rocks at the shed."

The other teen whirled around and glared at her. "That was a stupid thing to do."

Kelly winced, and looked away. "I'm sorry. I didn't know anyone was here." She risked a glance at Joel's handsome face and was shocked to find an amused grin.

"No harm done. Besides, I needed to practice my safety roll."

"It looked really good." And she sounded like an idiot. Complimenting him on how well he'd crashed to the ground. All because of her carelessness.

The gravel crunched behind Kelly, and she twisted around to find Cindy striding toward her, looking bright, fresh, and perfect in a pink workout suit. The exact opposite of Kelly's sweaty, grimy appearance.

"What's going on?" Cindy's eyes narrowed at Kelly. "Why are you here?"

Heat rose to Kelly's face, but she assumed an innocent smile. "I was...helping Joel with some moves."

It was the truth. Or close to it.

Joel gave a light chuckle. The sound sent a warm thrill through Kelly's body.

"I can take over from here." Cindy's cool dismissal felt like a slap. "I'm ready to work on that doubles routine." She leaned coyly against the fence.

"Not a good idea." The volunteer picked up the lead line and turned the massive horse toward the exit. "Samson's still a bit spooked. You'd better call it a morning."

Kelly let out a silent cheer. She'd thwarted Cindy's cozy session with Joel. Accidentally, of course. And it had been costly, because she'd made a fool of herself in front of Joel. Again.

"Matt's right." Joel gave Cindy an apologetic shrug. "I need to help him put the equipment back and give Samson a rub. I'll catch you at breakfast." Joel waved at both girls before trotting toward the gate.

Cindy turned to Kelly, her eyes accusing. Unable to keep a grin off her face, Kelly turned and jogged down the road toward the cabins.

She gave a small sigh of relief when she found the room empty and her cabin mates already gone. Kelly grabbed her toiletries and some clean clothes, then dashed to the bathroom and took a quick shower. After changing into cut-off shorts and a loose T-shirt and pulling her wet hair into a ponytail, she considered her appearance in the mirror. She couldn't come close to the model-perfection of Cindy. No use even trying. But even perfect had to grow boring after a while. Maybe Joel should consider a change, to a girl with less perfection but a lot more humor and dramatic flair. Someone like her. Then she laughed out loud because the idea was ridiculous. And she knew it.

Kelly hurried to the lodge. As she entered the noisy dining hall, she noticed a banner tacked up on the far wall, with the words "What's your picture of love?" across the top. In the center was Bill's drawing of ropes, framed with the same green ties he'd used to connect the hands of the cardboard Girl and Guy. It was surrounded by all the volunteers' pictures. The display looked like a classroom wall, decorated with students' work. But Kelly liked it. It added a warm, personal feel to the lodge.

As Kelly approached the serving counter, delicious smells wafted from the eggs and waffles. But she passed by the hot-meal choices and moved on to the cold-food counter. She took a small bowl and dumped just enough bran cereal to cover the bottom. Skipping the sugar, she added a light splash of milk over the flakes.

Kelly had just set the milk container back on the counter when she had a prickly feeling. Looking up, she spotted the nosy, apron-wearing staff lady from the night before, leaning against the wall and spying on her. Probably recruited by MaryAnn to report how much Kelly ate. The kitchen worker gave her a warm smile, but Kelly turned away. It wasn't wise to get friendly with the enemy.

Kelly spotted Marcie and Sheila sitting at a back table. Sheila's tangled hair suggested an early-morning spat with Darren. Kelly bit her lip to hide a grin as she slid onto the bench beside her friends.

Sheila stabbed at a stack of pancakes adrift in a sea of maple syrup. A shiny can of Coke sat beside her plate. If the snoopy kitchen worker wanted to pick on someone, she could start with Sheila. Her plate might have more food than Kelly's, but the sugar-laden meal was hardly a healthy start to the day.

Raising her spoon, Kelly gestured toward Sheila's hair. "Need a brush?"

"Yes," Sheila snarled, "so I can hit Darren."

"Nothing good ever comes from retaliation." Marcie sipped a steaming amber liquid that smelled like herbal tea. "Nonviolence is the best response."

Sheila took a long swig of Coke. "Extreme force has always worked for me."

Kelly didn't doubt it.

Three sharp clangs startled Kelly, and her head snapped around to find MaryAnn at the front of the room, banging on the counter with a silver serving spoon. Still no whistle. Thank goodness.

MaryAnn tapped her watch. "We have a full day ahead, starting with a session on how to lead cabin devotions."

That shouldn't be too hard. Kelly had spent years being indoctrinated in Sunday school. She knew all the classic stories. And if she ever got stumped, the right answer was Jesus. It worked every time.

Marcie wore a look of disappointment.

"What's wrong?" Kelly asked.

"Kitchen workers don't get to be a part of devotions, because we're not staying in the cabins. We're stuck in the staff rooms."

Kelly couldn't understand why she was complaining. Marcie and Sheila got a private room to themselves and wouldn't have to babysit a bunch of campers. Lucky them.

Sheila continued to attack her breakfast. Kelly nudged her arm. "Did you give your note to Bill?"

"All five pages, filled with compelling and irrefutable arguments for my release from the kitchen." Sheila sneered. "He thanked me for the kindling and said he'll use it to start the next campfire."

Kelly feigned a look of shock, as if astonished that Sheila's plan had failed.

MaryAnn banged the counter again. "Room assignments will be passed out after lunch. There will be two counselors with each group of campers. Most of you will be working as assistant counselors and will be matched with a lead counselor. Those not assigned to a cabin will be staying in the private staff rooms."

Kelly had barely gotten settled and she might be changing cabins. At least she didn't have much to move. And she wouldn't be with Cindy any more. That was a relief.

"The rest of the afternoon will be spent moving into assigned rooms and prepping cabins for the campers who arrive tomorrow. After supper, we'll regroup for a practice campfire with Bill. Then it will be time for lights out."

And Kelly could cross off another day.

"Please clear your table and meet me on the risers at the front of the lodge. And whoever tied my whistle to the top of the flagpole had better be careful. If I find out who did it, there will be pain."

The faces of the volunteers shone with innocence, but Kelly caught Darren giving Mike a slight nudge under the table. And once MaryAnn had turned away, the hat-wearing duo exchanged knowing grins. Darren caught her gaze and put a finger to his lips. But he didn't have to worry about being ratted out. She was far more likely to thank them for sparing her and the other volunteers from early hearing loss.

All across the dining hall, the teens rose to clear the tables. Kelly looked down at the mushy brown cereal flakes. Grimacing, she pushed the bowl away.

Sheila raised her eyebrows. "You don't eat much. No wonder you're so thin."

Kelly stiffened. Personal observations made her uncomfortable, especially about her weight.

"I don't like soggy cereal." No need to mention she'd let it get mushy on purpose.

But Sheila didn't appear to be listening. She stared toward the front of the dining hall. Kelly followed her gaze. Several teens milled about, chatting in pairs or small groups. Four hats dodged in and out as Darren and his friends attempted to tag each other. Sheila seemed to be obsessed with that hat. Or with Darren.

But it was the two blond heads that caught Kelly's attention. Joel and Cindy. Walking side by side. With Joel's arm resting lightly on Cindy's shoulders, and her arm wrapped possessively around his waist. The picture-perfect blonde had good reason to hang on tight, as several other girls crowded round, vying for Joel's attention. He didn't seem to mind at all, which Kelly took as a good sign. Suddenly her fantasy of walking past Aaron with Joel on her arm didn't seem so crazy. If Joel was checking out his options, why not her? The more she played with the idea, the more she liked it.

Maybe it wouldn't be so bad to make certain she was in his line of sight. Hopefully without injuring him or embarrassing herself again.

Kelly dumped the soggy cereal into a slop bucket at the front of the lodge, then fell in with Marcie and Sheila as they headed to the risers. The top half had already been claimed by the guys and a few couples. Joel and Cindy were in the mix, snuggling in a cozy tangle of arms and legs. Kelly ended up on the front row, crammed between Sheila and Marcie.

MaryAnn frowned as she observed the couples. "You're sitting too close. I want to see space between each of you."

Kelly could have cheered. The sulking expression on Cindy's face increased her satisfaction.

MaryAnn waited until the couples separated. "And don't forget there's to be no public displays of affection during camp. If you can't remember, an evening spent with a shovel in the barn will help jog your memory."

Even better. Joel might not be as interested if Cindy was drenched in eau de manure.

MaryAnn cleared her throat and the volunteers settled into silence. "Along with your assigned day jobs, most of you will also be assistant counselors. We have cabin devotions every morning after breakfast."

Devotions in the morning and campfires at night? That was a lot of God talk. Not that Kelly planned to join in. She'd been faking her faith in her church at home for the last year, at least when she'd been forced to attend, and none of her friends had caught on. It shouldn't be too hard to keep up the act for one week at camp.

"This summer, we'll follow a booklet that Bill put together."

A homemade textbook? Kelly groaned along with the other teens. That sounded like school. And work. So much for MaryAnn's speech about camp being fun.

"If you heard about Jesus for the first time as a camper, please raise your hand."

At least a dozen arms shot into the air. Close to a quarter of the volunteers, including Marcie and all the Men in Hats. Kelly felt mild surprise. She'd assumed most of these kids had grown up with some basic knowledge of religion. Apparently not.

MaryAnn surveyed the raised hands. "That's my story as well. Now it is our privilege, responsibility, and joy to introduce the campers to Jesus, just as a counselor once introduced Him to us."

That might be a problem for Kelly, since she and God weren't exactly on speaking terms. She'd leave the introductions for the head counselor.

MaryAnn motioned for hands to be lowered. "I'd like an example of a fun way to begin the morning devotion time."

A grin stretched across Darren's face. "My counselor started each session with a massive pillow fight. It was awesome. Well, until someone stuck a boot in his pillow and flung it at another kid's face."

"That's nothing," Bob scoffed. He adjusted his snazzy snapback cap, as if to put the Men in Hats' cheap headgear to shame. "My eye was black and blue for a week after I got smacked by a pillowcase with a book in it. And it was the counselor who clobbered me." His mouth twisted in a smirk. "But I paid him back the next night. Worse than he got me. The counselor never saw the frozen water balloon coming. I heard his headache lasted three days."

Kelly already knew Bob was a chump. Now she could add vengeful to his list of fine qualities.

"Hey, Darren. Did you hear about the counselor who hit some campers with a corduroy pillow?"

Kelly recognized Mike's voice. She didn't need to hear the rest of the joke to know it was going to be painful.

"Did it hurt the kids?"

"Not really, but it made headlines."

Amidst the laughter, the other guys rushed to add their own recollections of epic pillow wars. Most of the battles seemed to end with blood. Kelly hoped the girls' cabins would be more civilized.

MaryAnn made a slashing movement, and the volunteers quieted. "It's not a bad idea to let the campers do something active right before you want them to sit and focus. A pillow fight is one way to release energy and build unity with your group. However, safety is the priority. Guys, you'll have to inspect pillowcases."

Marcie shook her head. "Sometimes I wish this was an all-girl camp."

Sheila gasped. "I couldn't survive at a camp without guys. They're like a basic need."

Kelly agreed. Food, shelter, clothing, and a boyfriend. And not necessarily in that order.

"There are multiple ways you can encourage your cabin to bond as a group." A faraway look crossed MaryAnn's face. "When I was a counselor, I used to bring an unusual color of nail polish. On the first night, I would paint each girl's nails."

Darren raised his hand, wearing an exaggerated expression of innocence. "Nail polish won't go over very well in the boys' cabins. Even if it is an unusual color."

The comment drew raucous laughter.

"Of course not," MaryAnn replied dryly. "You'll need to choose gender-appropriate bonding activities for your campers."

Mike wiped his brow in mock relief. "You really nailed that one, Darren."

MaryAnn reached for the whistle that was no longer around her neck, frowned, then spoke loud enough to be heard above the moans and chuckles. "Your cabin will be a mix of personalities. Some campers will be shy and others outgoing. There's often a bully in the group. Sometimes two. There will be immature and rebellious kids. You'll have campers who want to be here, and others who fought the whole way."

Kelly grimaced. MaryAnn could include at least one volunteer in the latter group. Kelly was sure that she'd resisted as hard as any of the reluctant campers.

"You'll have kids with various emotional and physical disorders. Some campers will be on medication, which will be kept and administered by our nurse. Many of these children have been abused, while others have led perfect, spoiled lives."

A shiver ran down Kelly's back. So many messed-up kids. Even the kids who looked great on the outside might be hiding something painful on the inside. She should know.

"Since you'll need to live together for one week, it's wise to find a way to bring the group together as early on as possible. Nail polish is optional."

Kelly hadn't considered that she might play an important part in a young girl's life. She felt ashamed. Up until that moment, she'd only been thinking of herself and her problems. As she imagined the faces of the campers who would be assigned to her, she felt an unexpectedly strong desire to make a difference in their lives. If only for a week.

MaryAnn walked to a stack of cardboard boxes beside the fireplace. She flipped open the top lid and pulled out a blue three-ring notebook, half the size of a regular binder. "If you're wearing a hat, grab one of these boxes and pass out the binders."

The notebooks came in a variety of colors, and the simple task became complicated as volunteers argued and fussed, each trying to nab their preferred shade. Kelly chose a pale-yellow binder. There were no markings on the cover except for the words *My Wallet* stenciled in black. A strange title.

"Every camper will receive one of these workbooks." MaryAnn tapped lightly on the cover.

Marcie's hand shot up in the air. "Why does it say *My Wallet* on the front?"

Mike shouted from the back row, "Maybe Bill got them cheap because someone printed the wrong words."

MaryAnn shook her head. "There's no mistake. It took Bill a couple of weeks to stencil those headings on all the binders. His fingers got so cramped he couldn't straighten them for days."

"You mean Bill added this...on purpose?" Marcie's brow furrowed.

"Yes."

"But there are a lot of easier ways to put a label on a binder."

"This was the most inexpensive method. Besides, Bill prayed over each one as he wrote the words."

"That still makes no sense."

And everything had to be rational and logical for Marcie, the overachiever. Although Kelly agreed with her on this point. Bill seemed to have wasted a lot of time and ink.

"Trust me. I promise you will understand the meaning by the end of the week." MaryAnn flipped open the binder in her hand.

Kelly and the other volunteers followed her lead. The first page contained an enlarged photograph of the lodge wall, with the "What's Your Picture of Love?" banner, Bill's sketch of ropes, and the volunteer drawings of love surrounding it. Kelly peered closely and found Sheila's dragon and princess, Marcie's sonnet, Darren's sports car, and her picture of the perfect guy. Cindy's tree with the heart was featured in the bottom-left corner. If Kelly had a pencil, she would have scribbled Cindy's initials off the tree and added her own.

Kelly turned to the next page, which showed a drawing of the cardboard Guy and Girl, connected by ties. She skimmed the bullet points written below.

Love is sharing.
As two individuals share, they create ties that bind them together.
Not all ties are good.
True love never stops adding ties.

All the main ideas from Bill's first campfire message. Kelly had to admit it was an interesting start, but she wasn't sure how Bill could keep the tie theme running for eight days. Or hold the campers' interest for that long.

MaryAnn didn't seem to share Kelly's doubts. She spoke with pride as she described the plan. "Each morning, campers will be given a set of pages reviewing what Bill shared the night before at campfire. A second set will introduce a new concept that the cabin will discuss during the devotion time."

At that rate, the binder really would be as thick as a textbook when the week ended. Kelly tilted her head to the side as she considered the notes. This wasn't the dry fill-in-the-blank format she'd expected, and the campers would go home with a souvenir of the week. The wallet name was odd, but she had to admit the binder was a clever idea.

"We've been sitting long enough. Let's head to the dining hall for a snack break. Please take your binder with you."

Kelly's back ached, and it was a relief to stand and stretch.

Sheila grabbed her arm and pulled her back down. "I thought of the perfect plan to make Darren pay for messing up my hair."

The three girls hung back and allowed the other teens to clear off the risers. The moment the area was empty, Sheila spun toward her friends. "First, we bribe one of the campers in his cabin to steal his hat for us. Then we sink the ugly thing in the middle of the lake!"

Marcie was shaking her head before Sheila even finished. "If Bill finds out, we'll have bathroom duty for the rest of the summer."

Sheila brushed aside Marcie's concerns with a wave of her hand. "You worry too much."

"You don't worry enough," Marcie shot back.

Sheila took a deep breath. "Maybe we could attach some sort of a floating device to it so we'd be able to retrieve it. After we force Darren to beg, of course."

Marcie and Kelly exchanged doubtful glances.

"What if someone else finds the hat?" Kelly frowned. "Or what if the line breaks and the hat sinks to the bottom?"

Sheila paused, drumming her fingers on her leg. Suddenly, her eyes lit up. "We could submerge it in the bulrushes by the shore.

No one will see the floater in the reeds. The lake isn't very deep there. So even if the hat sank, we'd be able to find it and pull it out."

Marcie shook her head again, more adamantly. "The lake water would ruin the hat. We can't wreck another staff member's property, even if it is unattractive and cheap."

"We could put it in a plastic bag to keep it dry."

"Scientifically speaking, it could work," Marcie admitted.

"I know it will."

Sensing defeat, Kelly gave one final attempt to steer Sheila from her path of revenge. "Is this really worth it?"

"Absolutely!" Sheila's eyes flashed. The tornado was gaining strength, preparing to touch down and rip the hat from Darren's head.

"This will go down in Timberlake Camp history as one of the best pranks ever! Our names will be spoken with reverence for years to come."

Kelly and Marcie stared at Sheila as if she'd lost her mind. Suddenly, they all burst out laughing. If they pulled this off, it would indeed be an awesome prank. If they didn't, they'd know every toilet in camp personally.

9 STAMP, TRAMPLE, AND JUMP

A sweet aroma wafted toward Kelly as she sat on the risers, listening to Sheila talk about giving swimming lessons to Darren's hat.

Sheila stopped mid-sentence and sniffed. She peered into the dining hall, where the other volunteers had already gathered at the tables. "I smell something heavenly. We'd better hurry or we'll miss out. We can talk about Operation Sink the Hat later."

More like Operation Bad Idea. Kelly would have preferred to skip both the discussion and the snack.

As she rose, the room began to spin. She froze in place and closed her eyes, swaying slightly. Had she pushed too hard during the morning jog? Skipped too many meals? The unpleasant sensation passed, and Kelly chose to disregard it. Like she always did.

She hurried to follow her friends to a back table. A plate of cupcakes sat in front of her. Light spongy muffins covered in a lemon-cream icing...so hard to resist. She glanced around the room, and spotted Cindy at a side table, pressed close to Joel. Smiling, chatting, and gazing into his mesmerizing blue eyes. But not eating. Kelly grabbed a pitcher and poured herself a tall glass of water. If Cindy could withstand the temptation, so could she.

"I'll be right back." Sheila disappeared and returned a few minutes later with a can of Coke. Her private stash, wherever she'd hidden it, seemed to be endless.

Marcie took the last few bites of her cupcake, wiped her hands on a napkin, and reached into her back pocket. She pulled out a pack of gum and held it toward Kelly. "Would you like a piece?

Studies show that chewing gum after a sugary treat prevents cavities. It also increases blood flow to the brain and helps with concentration."

"No, thanks." Research had also shown that chewing gum suppressed the appetite. But as far as Kelly was concerned, it wasn't worth the extra fifteen calories. She took another sip of water.

MaryAnn banged against the counter and called the group to order. Kelly grimaced. Surely there had to be a better way to gain everyone's attention without causing whiplash. Perhaps the whistle hadn't been so bad after all.

"Here are the cabin assignments for counselors and room numbers for staff not staying with campers."

Kelly listened closely as MaryAnn rattled through the list. She didn't care which cabin she stayed in. They were all the same. Ugly. But she hoped to get assigned to a good lead counselor. Someone who wouldn't work her too hard or watch her too closely.

"Sheila and Marcie will share staff room number eight."

Kelly watched her friends exchange high-fives. The best she could offer was a half-smile.

Marcie must have noticed Kelly's expression. "It's not like we'll be staying up late and having parties. We both have to get up early for kitchen duty, and this way we won't disturb anyone else."

It made sense. Kelly wished she could stay with them, but that would mean sticking with her kitchen duty assignment. And there was no way she was willing to do that.

"Jill and Kelly will be in cabin number one."

Kelly turned to her friends. "Which one is Jill?"

Marcie scanned the room. "I don't see her here. Some of the experienced counselors don't arrive until right before camp."

"What's she like?"

"Jill's great." Marcie gave a reassuring smile. "She was my counselor two years ago. She runs an organized cabin. Efficient. Clean. No nonsense."

Which sounded like no fun.

"She's not that bad," added Sheila. "She's never officially part of any camp mischief, but she isn't a snitch. And she covered for us last year when the boys accused of us of stealing all their toilet paper. Which we did."

So there might be some fun after all. At least Jill wasn't a tattletale.

"The rest of the afternoon is yours to prepare for the campers' arrival tomorrow." MaryAnn waved off the volunteers.

Moving wouldn't take too long. It was only one cabin over. And after she was done transferring her stuff, she'd be free to go on a walk, or perhaps a second jog.

Sheila tipped her head toward the kitchen. "We'd help you move but we have to meet with Lady Katherine for our indoctrination. Heaven forbid we put a pot in the wrong place."

Marcie nodded. "We won't be able to move our stuff until later. A lot later."

Bemoaning their situation, Sheila and Marcie left for the kitchen. Kelly grabbed her devotion binder and headed off to pack up.

The cabin resembled traffic during rush hour as the other girls scrambled to gather the gear they'd strewn about the room. There was a buzz of excitement as they chatted about their assignments for the week. A few girls said they hoped Kelly would have fun on Maintenance. There wasn't much else to say.

It didn't take long for Kelly to shove everything she'd recently put in the locker back into her suitcase. With her sleeping bag and pillow stuffed under one arm and the other dragging her luggage, Kelly struggled toward the door. At that moment, Cindy and a friend entered the room.

"Oh, Cindy, could you hold–?"

The blonde brushed past and let the door slam behind her. Right in Kelly's face.

"Thanks...for nothing," Kelly muttered. But she wasn't surprised. She hadn't expected to be best buds. Not after Kelly messed up the morning vaulting practice and committed the more serious crime of flirting with Joel. And Cindy didn't know it yet, but that was only the beginning.

After several tries at the handle, Kelly managed to get through the door without dropping anything. She trudged to the next cabin, hauling her belongings behind her. Once inside, she stood in the middle of the room, considering which bunk to take. A tall girl with a blonde bob stumbled through the door, dragging two massive suitcases and a rolled-up sleeping bag.

"Hi, I'm Jill, the head counselor. And you must be Kelly, my assistant." She dropped her luggage in the middle of the room and flashed Kelly a friendly smile. "I'll take the bunk closest to the door. You can take the one across from me."

Kelly stiffened. Was that a suggestion or an order?

"That way we can monitor if any girls try to sneak out in the middle of the night."

Kelly had no interest in playing policeman.

"Unpack first and then we'll chat. I'll be right back."

This time the order was unmistakable. Kelly stuffed down her annoyance. It wasn't worth starting off on the wrong foot.

As she waited for Jill to return, Kelly rolled her sleeping bag across the designated bunk and placed her beagle on top of the pillow. She stepped back and smiled to herself, pleased with the personal touch.

The cabin door swung open again and Jill backed in, dragging a waist-high wooden bookcase.

"I didn't know we were supposed to bring furniture." Kelly raced to grab the other end, then strained with Jill as they pushed it against the wall closest to the lead counselor's bunk.

"I'm territorial. I have to make the cabin feel like it's my home." Jill wiped the sweat from her brow and ran her fingers through her short hair. "Besides, I'm working as a counselor all summer and Bill said I can keep this cabin."

Two whole months? Kelly couldn't fathom why anyone would want to stay that long. And she didn't intend to waste any time trying to figure it out.

Jill opened the first suitcase and pulled out a thick southwestern blanket, several colorful pillows, and a large green circular rug. She stretched the blanket over her sleeping bag, tossed the pillows on top, and spread the rug in the center of the room.

Kelly knew she was staring, but she couldn't help it. Jill had brought more than a few knickknacks. She'd relocated half her bedroom.

After pushing the first suitcase out of the way, Jill unzipped the second. At least twenty books, ranging from children's picture books to paperback novels, formed a top layer. Jill gathered an armload and passed them to Kelly. "Put these on the top two shelves."

A spark of anger flared up in Kelly. Enough already. She was an assistant, not a personal servant. She whirled around, ready to tell Jill to take care of her own stuff.

"Feel free to use anything on the shelves."

Jill's generous offer and warm smile doused Kelly's annoyance.

Jill shoved a zoo of stuffed animals into her arms, followed by multiple hairbrushes and accessories, several bottles of nail polish, and enough paper, crayons, paint brushes, glitter and glue to start an art class. "Put these anywhere they fit."

Kelly's anger flared again. She grit her teeth as she crammed everything into the shelving unit and tried to stay positive. At least she wasn't the only one with a stuffed animal. When Jill handed her three framed family pictures, she held up her hands in protest. "There's no place to put those."

Jill glanced at the overflowing unit. "I'll hang them on the wall later."

After moving her suitcases into a corner, Jill relaxed on the rug and motioned for Kelly to join her.

Kelly dropped onto the soft weave. "Didn't you bring any clothes?"

Jill burst out laughing. "The rest of my things are still in my car. I'll unpack them later."

More stuff? Kelly felt a sting of envy as she considered the lead counselor's corner. Jill had created an impressive oasis of color and comfort in an otherwise dingy cabin. She glanced at her precious beagle, perched on the pillow. It looked lonely.

"I started coming to Timberlake when I was eight years old, and I've never missed a summer." Jill stretched out on her stomach, a contented smile on her face. "This is my third year working on staff. How about you?"

"I've never been to camp before. This is all new to me."

"Don't worry. Last summer, they were short of counselors and I managed a cabin all by myself. I don't need an assistant."

Had she heard correctly? Jill sounded like a bossy older sister telling her pesky little sibling to stay out of her room and her business.

"You can sit back and watch how I do things. If I need your help, I'll let you know."

Kelly hadn't wanted to come to camp in the first place. But she'd been inspired by MaryAnn's description of the campers, and now she actually wanted to make a difference. Even a small one. Which would be difficult if she was shoved in a corner and told to stay quiet.

Jill launched into a number of stories involving frustrating campers, pranks gone wrong, crazy skits, illegal cabin raids, and counselor romances. As Kelly listened to Jill's humorous depiction of camp life, her anger faded. She would have liked Jill as a friend instead of a dictatorial leader. At least camp was only for a week.

With a happy sigh, Jill stood and stretched. "My best friend, Amy, is the craft instructor this summer, and she's got to make a few last-minute adjustments at the shack. She asked if I'd help her out. I'll be back later to finish moving."

"There isn't room for another bookcase." It was part jest, part truth.

"I don't have anything quite that big. But you can have one of my bean bag chairs, if you'd like."

Kelly's chuckle turned into a strangled choke when she realized Jill was serious.

Once Jill left, Kelly used the time alone to do push-ups, sit-ups and core-strengthening exercises. If she did enough, she might allow herself an extra scoop of something at supper. Just to satisfy the nosy kitchen worker.

An hour later, Jill burst through the door, dragging two bright-yellow beanbag chairs.

Kelly glanced about the room. It looked as if a rainbow had tripped and spilled most of its color. And the campers were going to love it. "Is that everything?"

"I just have to bring in my clothes." Jill dragged a puffy bag to either side of the bookcase. "But it's suppertime right now. So close the far window and we'll head to the lodge."

Another order. But at least it sounded like a partial invitation.

Kelly and Jill walked to the lodge together, but parted ways once inside. Kelly joined Marcie and Sheila at their table. She managed to dodge the snoopy kitchen worker and eat nothing more than a few forkfuls of plain tossed salad.

Kelly relaxed, feeling as if she was finally getting into the rhythm of camp. She didn't even jump when Bill banged the metal spoon on the counter.

"Meet me in front of the lodge in five minutes for our final staff campfire."

Bill's direction was followed by a mad scramble to clean tables and head to the risers.

Once the volunteers had gathered on the steps, Bill rapped on the podium. "Let's review. The most important thing we'll do at camp this week is to teach the campers about..."

A surge of voices shouted out, "God!"

"And we're going to teach about God's love by drawing a picture of romance using..."

This time, the answers were mixed. Some volunteers shouted, "Ropes!" and others yelled, "Ties!"

Bill laughed. "Both answers are correct. Last review item. Not all dating ties are good. Some ties..."

The group hesitated.

"Trip?"

"Knot?"

"Choke?"

Bill shook his head. "The answer rhymes with strangle."

Most of the group roared, "Tangle!" But some of the suggestions caused Kelly to shake her head. Apparently not all of the staff knew how to rhyme.

"Excellent responses. Well, most of them. Let's bring out our new friends."

MaryAnn and Tony strode forward from the back of the room, carrying the cardboard figures of Guy and Girl.

"When we last saw our couple, they were a mess of tangled ties. But they have agreed to overlook each other's blunders." Bill attached several ties between the hands of Guy and Girl. "Guy promised not to burp the alphabet, and Girl vowed not to talk about her former boyfriends. They've gone on several dates. The sun is shining, birds are singing, and our pair thinks they're in love."

The teens cheered with great enthusiasm, as if this were the greatest thing to happen all day. Maybe even all week. Kelly wondered if there was a camp code she didn't know about. Like *Always act excited. Even if you're cheering for two lovesick pieces of paper.*

"Take a close look at our happy couple. They're standing with space between them. Each person is balanced on his or her own two feet. Neither one is gripping the ties too tightly or holding them too loosely. And they both have room to move."

Someone in the back row yelled out, "They're just cardboard figures."

Good point.

"Watch what you're saying!" Mike jumped to his feet, his face a picture of exaggerated outrage. "Girl is sensitive. She can't help that she's made of paper."

Darren rose beside Mike. "I agree. It's tear-able to treat her like an object."

The hat-wearing duo had started their comedy routine early.

Bill raised an eyebrow at the boys. "You know, Bernice could use some extra help tomorrow morning mucking out the stalls in the barn."

Without hesitation, Darren and Mike dropped back to their seats. They were bold and brash, but not stupid.

Bill gestured to Guy and Girl. "I present to you the impressive picture of a solid, healthy relationship. This is the standard, the ideal, the goal. It isn't complete yet, but even so, it's quite stunning."

The volunteers broke into applause.

Stunning? Kelly stared at the cardboard couple. They were flat, geeky, and tied together with ropes. If they were impressive in some way, she didn't see it.

Bill held up his hands and the group quieted down. "Now, some of you may be wondering if you missed something. Perhaps this picture of love looks too simple. Even dull and boring. What's so great about this relationship? Where's the dazzle, the chocolate, the Ferrari?"

Exactly what Kelly was thinking–minus the chocolate.

"Where are the flowers, the presents, and the kissing?"

Several girls cheered. "Now you're talking!"

Kelly nodded in agreement. She remembered those sweet early days with Aaron. Hours on the phone, texting constantly whenever they were apart, the adorable teddy bear he'd given her on their one-month anniversary. And their first kiss. He'd caught her off guard in the school hallway. Just leaned over and kissed her lips, right in front of everyone. She'd never felt so special.

Bill walked over to the paper pair and stood behind them, his arms resting lightly on their shoulders. "This relationship may not seem thrilling at first glance, but it has two important things: balance and respect. These terms may not seem romantic or sexy. But after we've looked at some less desirable relationships, I believe you'll view these concepts with new appreciation. For now, we'll start a list of New Romantic and Sexy Words and write *balance* and *respect* at the top."

Tony appeared from the back of the room, carrying an easel with several sheets of paper clipped to the top. He pulled out a thick black marker and scrawled the words across the page. His handwriting was barely legible.

As she stared at the terms, Kelly could almost hear Aaron's mocking laughter. Short skirts, tight jeans, and low-cut tops. That's what would have made his list of sexy words. And most other guys she knew.

Bill moved out from behind Guy and Girl and stood in front of the volunteers. "Before we go any further, we need to stamp on, trample, and jump all over a few myths. Like love at first sight. Sorry, but it doesn't exist."

Kelly frowned. Of course it was real. She'd flipped for Aaron the moment he'd walked into that drama class, so confident and smooth. And all it took was for Joel to look her way to set her heart beating faster as well.

"Now, it's possible to feel a powerful attraction at first sight. But that's not love." Bill pointed to the ties connecting the cardboard duo. "There is no way to have ties at first sight. And that makes it impossible to have love at first sight. It takes time to share and create a connection. That gives us our next word on the list."

Tony scribbled *time* below the other words. At least, it looked like he did. Kelly found it hard to read anything he wrote.

Aaron would have scoffed at this word too. He didn't believe in time, except his own. He said they'd only take the car for a quick ride. And then he drove to the party. And decided to hang out and throw down a few drinks. If her parents hadn't showed up...She didn't want to think about what would have happened.

Kelly fidgeted with the cuff of her sleeve. She wasn't being fair to Aaron. How could she blame him when she'd shown him the new car? And then she made the mistake of telling him her parents were out and wouldn't be back for hours. If she hadn't put so many temptations in front of him, that disastrous evening never would have happened.

Bill rapped on his podium. "Since we are stamping on, trampling, and jumping all over common love myths, I'll trash another. Some people think that if you meet the right one and if the relationship is meant to be, everything will fall into place. Like a perfect love story. If you think that's true, you've been watching too many movies."

But it wasn't just the chick flicks, which Kelly had to admit she consumed on a regular basis. That concept was in every romance novel, popular song, teen magazine, and music video she'd ever come across. They couldn't all be wrong. And things had been so easy with Aaron, at least in the beginning.

"Love is hard work. Establishing ties requires *effort* and *perseverance*." Bill stressed the two words. "Let's add those terms to our list."

Finally some words on the sexy list that wouldn't make Aaron complain. She'd put a lot of effort into her relationship with him, and he appreciated it. Funny notes slipped into his locker, quirky gifts every Monday morning, helping with his Saturday chores. Not to mention losing over thirty pounds and working hard to drop a few more. Aaron had been attentive to her as well, at least at first. Then the small presents and thoughtful gestures stopped, and the persistent demands began.

Tony jotted down the new terms, and Kelly squinted at them. Perhaps it was a good thing that Tony's handwriting was almost impossible to read. He'd misspelled the last word.

"We need to move past the belief that true love is a never-ending carnival ride filled with constant thrills and excitement. A relationship may begin with sweaty palms, loss of sleep, and angelic music. But don't be fooled by thinking that's all there is to a great romance."

Kelly shook her head. Bill was all alone on that point. Completely out of touch. Everyone she knew longed for a thrilling romance. And it could happen. The first few months with Aaron had been nothing less than fantastic. Although, as good as it had been, she hadn't experienced a happy ending. But she hadn't given up on that yet. Even though it was likely to fail. And if she was being honest, she had more confidence in her backup plan, or at least her backup guy, Joel.

"True love grows as we add ties, one by one, building a strong, unshakable bond with another person. That is the true picture of a strong, healthy romantic relationship, and the campers need to see it clearly." He paused. "So do some of you."

Kelly shifted uncomfortably. These talks were for the campers. She wasn't interested in making it too personal. Nothing Bill had said thus far would help her get Aaron back. All he'd done thus far was stir up a lot of memories, some she'd rather forget. Especially the ones that made Aaron look bad.

Bill took a few steps over to the fireplace and picked up a thick black book. Kelly recognized it at once. A Bible. She had one just like it at home. Only hers was gathering dust under her bed. But at least it was in better condition than the pitiful book in Bill's hands. Tattered pages, frayed edges, and a front cover that was barely hanging on gave the book a neglected appearance. Kelly wondered why he didn't get a new one.

Bill flipped to a passage marked with a gold paperclip. "God places the highest priority on love. He instructs in Proverbs 4:23, 'Above all else, guard your heart, for it is the wellspring of life.'"

Bill closed the book and pulled a green rope from his back pocket. He held it across the outstretched palm of his hand. "The heart is where life-changing decisions are made. If we want to be successful in life and in love, we must learn to guard our hearts by being careful with our ties."

Kelly considered the thin cord. Bill thought it would change the lives of the campers, and staff members as well. Not likely. Especially not for her. She shoved the image of the tie out of her head.

Bill gave final evening instructions and dismissed the staff. As Kelly headed back to the cabins with Marcie and Sheila, she hoped to ask questions about the sort of jobs she could expect on maintenance duty. But she never got the chance. Sheila kept up an animated dialogue with herself, alternating between bitter complaints about kitchen work and wild plans to steal Daren's hat. She paused only to take a swig of Coke. Any hope to hang out was lost when her friends yawned and said they were going straight to bed since Lady Katherine expected them at their stations before the sun rose.

Once Kelly was back in her new cabin and ready for bed, she pulled out a pen and paper and sat cross-legged on her bunk. She couldn't call or text her friends back home, but she could at least write a few letters. Ask Lucy about summer school.

Jill gave an obvious yawn. "Lights out in two minutes."

Kelly checked her watch. "But we still have half an hour before curfew."

Jill shook her head. "We need all the sleep we can get before camp starts."

As far as Kelly was concerned, it had already begun. And Jill was practicing the role of drill sergeant by treating her like a little kid.

"Do I have time to finish what I'm writing, or will that ruin the whole week?"

Jill laughed. "Go ahead, but just for a minute."

Obviously not all drill sergeants understood sarcasm.

There would be no time for letters tonight. Kelly pulled out her calendar and marked off the second square. Two days of training camp were finished. Eight days of camp were about to begin. She stared at the long line of unmarked boxes. Still so far to go.

She'd barely tucked away the paper and set the alarm before Jill flicked off the lights. As Kelly lay in her bunk with her beagle in her arms, she listened to the head counselor's deep, even breathing, and focused on her plans for the rest of the week. Avoid orders from Jill. Survive the prank with Sheila and Marcie. Help the campers in her cabin have a great experience. And most important of all, attract the attention of Joel.

One week wasn't a long time, and the odds weren't in her favor. But she'd gotten the guy of her dreams once before. It might just happen again.

10 AT WAR WITH A LAWNMOWER

Kelly dashed to the lodge, her hair still dripping from the morning shower. A huge smile stretched across her face. The day was off to a great start. She'd had a solid run with no glimpse of the annoying mystery person, followed by a long, hot shower. And she'd returned to an empty cabin, which meant no orders from Jill.

As Kelly entered the building, she noticed the list of "New Romantic and Sexy Words" tacked up on the wall beside the pictures of love. She chuckled. Someone else must have had a hard time deciphering Tony's scribbles because the list had been rewritten in much neater handwriting.

Kelly passed through the serving line, skipped the scrambled eggs and toast, and placed one small pancake on her plate. Looking up, she discovered the eagle-eyes of the nosy kitchen worker. Spying again. The silent watching made Kelly nervous, not knowing when the confrontation would come. It would be better to take the offensive and attack first.

"Is there something you want to say to me?"

"Yes." The kitchen worker took an eager step forward. "My name is Sandy, and I've been looking forward to meeting you."

The warm and gentle response caught Kelly off guard. And made her feel stupid. Kelly turned her back without answering and walked stiffly over to Sheila and Marcie's table.

She felt ashamed of her own rudeness. But this Sandy was trouble. She just knew it.

"Kitchen duty stinks." Sheila took a swig from her can of Coke and banged it back down on the table. "Nobody should have to get up so early. It's wrong." She slathered a piece of toast in a thick layer of jam.

With all the sugar and caffeine that girl consumed, she shouldn't have any problem bouncing out of bed. And all over the kitchen.

Marcie moaned. "This morning we only had to prep for the staff. It's going to be worse when the campers come. We'll have hundreds of dishes!"

"You're lucky." Sheila pointed a fork at the lonesome pancake on Kelly's plate. "You don't care about food. It's only the second day of camp and I'm already eating way too much. If I don't get some self-control, I'm going to be fat by the end of the week!"

Kelly looked away. If only they knew the truth. From the moment she woke up in the morning until she lay her head on the pillow at the end of the day, she obsessed about food. When she'd first started the diet, she just wanted to lose enough weight to be attractive, even sexy. It soon turned into constant denial and continual craving. Kelly didn't feel lucky at all. She felt cursed.

Sheila gave a quick nod in the direction of the kitchen. "Lady Katherine's looking our way. And she's wearing her angry face."

"We'd better hurry or she'll make us wash the dishes by hand."

Marcie crammed half a piece of toast in her mouth and nearly tripped as she rushed after Sheila. Lady Katherine had to be truly terrifying to provoke such absolute fear. Kelly hoped her boss wouldn't inspire the same cowering dread. Although the first glimpse of Tony, when she'd mistaken him for a grizzly bear as he shared negative camp stories during training, hadn't been reassuring.

Kelly had only taken two bites of her pancake before MaryAnn stood in front of the serving counter, beating a staccato rhythm against the metal side.

"Campers are scheduled to arrive in the next hour. Lead counselors will go to their cabins and get ready to help the newcomers settle in. All others will head to their assigned jobs."

Kelly couldn't hold back a groan. She lingered in the dining hall as long as she dared before heading to the maintenance shed.

With shoulders squared, she stepped inside. No sign of Tony. There was only Bob, leaning against a work table as he skimmed a lined sheet of paper. When he saw her, he hastily folded the note and tucked it into his back pocket. "Tony isn't here, but he left instructions. I'm supposed to check the chlorine levels in the pool, and you have to mow the lawn behind the lodge."

The first assignment. And it stunk. "I've never cut grass in my life." Kelly frowned. "I don't even know how to start a lawn mower."

"Well, there's a first time for everything." Bob shrugged as he grabbed a container of test tubes from the table. "The mower's behind the shed."

Kelly smelled a rat—wearing fancy high-top sneakers that he probably didn't want to stain with grass clippings. Bob tried to move past her, but she held out her hand.

"I want to see the note."

Bob hesitated before passing it to her. There was no doubt it was from Tony. Reading it was like decoding hieroglyphics. But the information she discovered made it worth the effort.

"This says that Tony gave you the job of mowing the lawn, and I'm assigned to test the pool water."

Bob smirked as he shook his head. "Too bad. I got the equipment first." With a satisfied chuckle, he trotted off in the direction of the pool.

What a jerk.

Kelly walked behind the shed and stared at the ancient lawn mower. It wasn't even the kind that could be ridden. She'd have to push the massive beast.

Bracing her arms, Kelly shoved with all her might. The rusty wheels screeched, then turned with great reluctance.

Kelly was drenched in sweat long before she reached the picnic area. And then she almost turned around and pointed the clunky machine back to the shed.

The space to be mowed was huge. The grass looked more like a field of tall wheat. Which might have been an exaggeration. But not by much. And according to the note, each of the eight wooden picnic tables had to be moved first. Just her luck, there was no one around to help. The day that had started off so well had taken a sharp U-turn into disaster.

Kelly approached the nearest wooden table, chanting under her breath. Alternating between "Bob is a blockhead" and "I'm burning extra calories," she grasped the sides firmly and tried to push. It didn't budge. Pulling wasn't any better. Kicking the wooden frame only bruised her foot.

Kelly paused to wipe the sweat off her forehead. She didn't care what Tony wrote in his note. She was mowing *around* the tables.

Returning to the ugly machine, she grasped the cord firmly and yanked back. The motor roared to life and Kelly struggled to steer it along the outer edge of the lawn. After a couple of passes, she looked back to inspect her work. The lines could have been straighter. But considering it was her first time, the job wasn't too bad.

When half of the area had been mowed, the machine began to sputter. Kelly slowed her pace. It didn't help. The mower coughed, shuddered, and died. Kelly pulled on the cord until her arm ached, but it refused to start again.

Feeling lightheaded, she collapsed beside the machine. She felt like crying. Or letting loose some nasty words. She was about to do both when a bulky shadow loomed over her, blocking the sun.

"Where's Bob?"

Kelly's head snapped up and she saw Tony towering above her. "He's testing the pool water."

A frown creased Tony's face. He was probably unhappy with her cutting job. Well, too bad, because it was the best she could do.

"You're not finished." Tony's frown turned into a scowl. "Why did you stop?"

"The lawn mower died, and I can't get it to start again." He didn't have to look so angry. It wasn't her fault she knew nothing about outdoor equipment.

Shaking his head and muttering something about pampered girls, Tony removed the bulging bag. "The motor stops automatically when the bag is too full." He carried it to a garbage bin by the back wall of the lodge, dumped it, and returned to reattach the bag. "Is there a reason you're mowing the lawn and Bob is testing the pool water?"

"Bob got the equipment first." She didn't even try to keep the bitter edge out of her voice.

Tony rubbed his chin. "I think I'll have a little chat with Bob." He pulled the picnic tables over to the half that Kelly had recently mowed. With ease. "Finish the job. But don't move the tables back. I'll send Bob to do that. And he can bring the mower back as well." After a curt nod, her boss lumbered off.

Kelly bit her lip, trying not to laugh. She almost enjoyed cutting the remainder of the grass. When she finished, she left the mower in the farthest corner and headed down the road to the shed. Halfway there, she passed Bob, his cap pulled low over his eyes.

"I'm sorry I made you mow the lawn." He spoke stiffly, teeth gritted. "It would be my pleasure to move the picnic tables for you and return the lawnmower."

Clearly a speech Tony had insisted he give her. "That's so thoughtful of you. Thank you." She poured as much sarcasm into the words as possible.

Bob barreled past and Kelly continued on her way.

When she reached the maintenance shack, she found Tony hammering two boards together. He paused, looking up from his work. "Did you see Bob?"

She nodded, unable to hold back a delighted grin.

The corners of Tony's mouth turned up slightly. "Take the rest of the day off. I'll meet you and Bob here tomorrow after breakfast."

So the grizzly bear had a soft side. He'd given Bob a just punishment and her a free afternoon. Maybe maintenance wouldn't be so bad after all.

Kelly returned to the cabin and found it full of campers chatting, giggling, and throwing stuffed animals around. Jill motioned to her from the back of the room. Kelly picked her way around the open suitcases, ducking to avoid a flying monkey.

Jill stood on a side ladder, helping a camper spread a blanket on an upper bunk. On the bunk below, another girl sat alone, her face buried in a paperback novel. Kelly peeked at the cover. The picture showed a powerfully built man passionately embracing a half-dressed beauty as she ripped the shirt off his muscular body. At the very least, it deserved a PG-13 rating.

The camper gave Kelly a shy glance, pushed thick glasses farther up her freckled nose, and returned her attention to the book.

"What happened to you?" Jill had to shout to be heard. "You look like you just ran a marathon."

"I had a fight with a lawn mower," Kelly bellowed.

"Not that old thing." Jill laughed. "I tangled with it years ago, and it was ancient back then. It should be put out to pasture."

Or shot and buried.

"I'm going to take the girls on a tour of the camp before lunch. Want to come?"

Kelly shook her head. "I need a shower."

Jill clapped her hands and waited until she had the campers' attention. "This is Kelly. She's my assistant counselor."

Kelly gave an awkward wave. Most of the girls smiled or called out a greeting. A few looked away. Perhaps they could smell her.

Jill pointed to the door. "We're going on a tour of the camp. Everybody outside."

A mixture of cheers and groans rose from the girls as they dropped the stuffed animals on their bunks and moved toward the door.

"I'm not going." A dark-haired camper stood in the middle of the room, feet apart, arms folded, wearing a pouty expression.

Kelly felt the hair on the back of her neck stand up. A direct challenge. The other girls hesitated, and all eyes turned to Jill.

"Your name is Joyce, right?"

The girl inclined her head slightly.

"Have you been to Timberlake Camp before?"

"Last year, and I hated it."

Kelly grimaced. Only a few hours into camp and Jill had run right into a brick wall. With shoulder-length hair, a stocky build, and a lot of attitude.

"We're all going on the tour, Joyce." Jill's tone was firm. "Since you're familiar with camp, you can choose where we go first." Jill walked to the front of the room, opened the door, and swept out an arm.

Kelly's eyes flicked back to Joyce. For several moments, the camper stood straight and unyielding. Then her arms relaxed, and she shrugged. "The only thing worth seeing is the horses."

"Then off we go. Lead the way, Joyce."

With a toss of her head, Joyce strode through the door and the other girls rushed to follow.

One point to the lead counselor for a brilliant move.

Jill peered back into the cabin. "You too, Amber."

With a heavy sigh, the bookworm rose and trudged after the campers, still clutching her risqué novel. Before she closed the door, Jill winked at Kelly.

Alone in the cabin, Kelly sank onto her bunk. Maybe it wouldn't be so bad to let Jill take the lead. At least with the tough campers.

She stretched out, too tired to make the trip to the showers. Half an hour later, the girls returned but didn't stay long before heading out the door to lunch.

Kelly forced herself to rise and grab her towel. "Sorry, Jill. I haven't taken my shower yet. I'll come as soon as I can." Or not at all.

A few minutes later, she stood in the relaxing spray of steaming hot water. It felt wonderful on her aching back. And made a great excuse for skipping the midday meal.

Kelly finally forced herself to leave the soothing flow and return to the cabin. She'd just finished drying her hair when the girls dashed back and began rifling through their suitcases. Jill entered behind them, a huge grin on her face.

"Our cabin just challenged Amy's cabin to a game of volleyball. Losers scrape the other team's plates after supper." Jill pulled a neon-yellow T-shirt from her locker. "We're going to wear the brightest clothes we have and distract the other players."

Within minutes, the campers had changed into flashy shirts and shorts. Between the vivid colors and mismatch of shades, Kelly thought the plan to blind their opponents had a good chance of success.

"Volleyball is a lame sport. I don't want to play." Joyce took her same position in the middle of the cabin. Arms folded. Attitude on full display.

Kelly sighed inwardly. It was going to be a long week.

Jill didn't even flinch. "You can sit on the sidelines and keep score if you like. But I think you'd have more fun playing."

Joyce considered the options.

"And we need a setter. It's probably the most important position. You up for it?"

Joyce gave a reluctant nod. Kelly awarded another point to Jill.

Jill waved at Kelly. "Have fun on maintenance." Jill was out the door before Kelly could tell her about the temporary release from duty. Which worked out fine because she had plans to be at the opposite end of camp. With Joel.

As Kelly trotted down the road toward the stables, it seemed that half the females in camp had the same idea. When Kelly reached the vaulting ring, it was impossible to find an open space around the corral railings. And Cindy certainly wasn't going to give up her primo position perched on a top bar.

Kelly stood behind a few short campers, watching over their shoulders. There was no way Joel would notice her in the blur of young, adoring faces. She barely listened as Joel explained what he'd be teaching in the vaulting classes that week. She was completely focused on watching him as he demonstrated a few basic moves. Mounting. Kneeling. Dismounting. Standing. Nothing fancy. Except that he was doing it all on the back of a moving horse while looking like a Greek hero.

Kelly spotted an opportunity to get close to Joel when he invited the watching campers into the ring to pet the massive horse. She moved quickly. But not quickly enough. Cindy was at his side in an instant, guarding Joel like a pit bull wearing pink lipstick. And growling at anyone who got too close.

There was no way Kelly wanted to stand next to Cindy and compete with such calculated perfection. So she lingered at the edge of the arena. She thought Joel looked her way once or twice, but couldn't be sure. Finally she gave up and took a long walk around camp. She might not be able to connect with Joel, but at least she could burn calories.

Kelly walked until supper, then turned her steps to the lodge. She found her cabin mates sitting at their assigned table, boasting about their victory on the volleyball court. Jill sat beside Joyce. A wise move. Kelly chose the opposite end of the table and parked herself next to the quiet camper, who was still hiding behind an open book. Time to stop thinking about herself and start making a difference.

"Your name's Amber, right?"

The girl nodded but didn't close her novel.

"I'm Kelly. Do you like to read?"

"Yes."

"That must be a good book."

"Yes."

If Joyce was like a brick wall, Amber was a locked door. With a "no entry" sign nailed to the front.

"Is it a love story?"

"Yes."

"Is that your favorite type of book to read?"

"Yes." Amber met Kelly's eyes for the first time. "I'm going to be a romance author when I grow up."

Excellent. An answer with more than one word. Kelly pressed ahead. "Why do you want to write love stories?"

"They're not like real life. The hero and heroine stay together forever. And there aren't any divorces." A bitter note echoed behind those words.

Unsure what to say, Kelly changed the subject. "How was the tour of the camp?"

"Okay."

"Did you see the horses?"

"Yes."

They'd regressed back to monosyllabic answers. So much for progress.

"Have you been to camp before?"

"No."

"This is my first time too. My mom signed me up." Kelly didn't think it wise to share how hard she'd fought the decision.

"So did mine." Amber lowered her book a few inches. "I didn't want to come."

A grin stretched across Kelly's face. Perhaps she'd just found a key. "Let's make the best of our first week at camp...together." She held out her hand.

Amber's brown eyes peered at Kelly from behind thick glasses. She gave a hesitant smile, closed the book, and placed it carefully on the table. Then she reached out to shake Kelly's hand. The book remained closed through the rest of supper.

After the evening meal, Bill gathered the campers for their first campfire. Amber sat on the bench and read during all the songs and skits. She didn't look up until Bill announced that the theme for the week's messages was love. Then she put down her book.

The news sparked a mixed reaction from the rest of the campers. The guys groaned and the females cheered. Which wouldn't have been hard to predict.

In a replay of the earlier staff sessions, Bill introduced Guy and Girl and defined love as sharing that builds a connection of ties. Kelly surveyed the crowd. Despite the earlier complaints from the guys, most of the campers listened attentively.

The campfire ran long, and as soon as Bill finished, Jill hurried the girls to the cabin. "Everyone sit around the carpet and nobody move until I tell you."

This must be the big bonding moment. Kelly doubted she'd be able to provide much assistance since Jill hadn't bothered to tell her what they'd be doing.

Once the girls settled in place, Jill pulled armfuls of art supplies from her shelves and dumped them in the center of the rug, creating a mountain of glitter and glue bottles, spools of bright ribbon, packs of colored pencils, and a variety of stickers. The girls squirmed in their places, pointing and squealing with delight.

"We're each going to design a name tag to hang on our bunks." Jill passed a stack of white cardboard around the circle. "First write your name on the card. Then decorate it any way you like."

Kelly grinned. Not a bad idea, and she liked it better than MaryAnn's suggestion of exotically colored nail polish. Or the bruising pillow fights most likely raging in the boys' cabins.

Fingers inched toward the supplies.

"I hate crafts. They're stupid."

Kelly grit her teeth at Joyce's permanent bad attitude and stubborn reluctance to participate in any activity.

The outstretched arms of the other girls hesitated and drew back. Joyce could be a bitter grinch if she wanted, but she didn't have the right to poison everyone around her.

"I can't draw," one camper whined.

"Do we have to do it?" another chimed in.

In less than ten seconds, Joyce had managed to douse the enthusiasm of every girl in the cabin. Kelly wondered if the idea might flop.

Instead of responding to the negative comments, Jill put her finger to her lips and motioned for silence. Then she grabbed a black marker and drew on a white card, shielding her work with her left arm. The campers craned their necks, trying to get a glimpse of the paper.

Less than a minute later, Jill held up her sheet, displaying a sketch of a girl and a dog that would have made Picasso proud. The girls stifled their giggles.

"Is that you?" asked the camper who'd said she couldn't draw.

"Yes, Emma. And that's my dog, Muffin."

"Your dog has three ears?" Joyce scoffed.

"No. One of those is his nose."

The girls shrieked with laughter. Jill capped her marker and tossed it to Joyce. "I'd like to see how many ears your dog has."

Joyce pulled the cap off the pen. "I have a cat. Named Fluffy." She leaned over her page. "And she doesn't look like a mutant pig."

"Mutant pig?" Jill furrowed her brows in mock anger. "I'll have you know I got a B+ in Art last year...mostly because my teacher graded on effort."

The girls laughed again as they reached for the supplies. Jill had gotten around the brick wall once more. And she was racking up the good-counselor points.

As Kelly listened to the chatter, she recognized the brilliance of Jill's idea. Working on the tags gave the campers a common focus and helped break down any awkwardness. Before long, the girls were passing around materials, commenting on and admiring each other's creativity.

Kelly sat back and watched, glancing from tags to faces and attempting to memorize names. Joyce revealed an inner artist, confidently sketching an adorable fat and furry feline. Everyone laughed, including Jill, as she proudly compared her anatomically correct cat to Jill's challenged mutt.

Head tilted to one side, and biting her lip in concentration, Amber worked with painstaking care on a princess in a castle. Terri and Tanya, twins who were hard to tell apart because they wore matching shirts and pulled their long blonde hair back in a ponytail, covered every available inch of their sheets with stickers. Fiona filled her tag with big, bubble letters, colored with alternating pink and purple stripes, and asked for a second tag. Nadia struggled to fill her first one. Emma and Michelle, who'd been the most reluctant of the group at the start, chatted happily as they braided ribbon to make hanging tassels.

"I'm setting a timer for five minutes." Jill tapped Kelly on the shoulder. "While the girls are finishing, you can cut a length of string for each sign."

Yes, boss. Kelly grabbed a blank tag and scrawled her name. Then she turned to Joyce. "Could you draw a beagle for me? Like the one on my bed?"

"Sure."

Joyce took the tag and propped up Kelly's stuffed dog on her bunk. As she set to work, she wore a proud smile. The first one Kelly had seen on her face.

Kelly moved about the room, passing out string and complimenting the various designs. When each girl had finished and hung her tag on a bunk, the plain cabin looked as if it had received a bright, personal stamp. Another point for Jill. She was turning out to be a clever lead counselor.

The timer rang and Jill held it high. "I'm resetting it for ten minutes. You need to get washed up and back in your bunks before it rings."

"Or what?" Joyce demanded.

"Or you'll scrape the leftover food from everyone's plates into the slop bucket after breakfast tomorrow."

With squeals of "yuck" and "gross," the girls raced off to the bathroom. Kelly helped Jill clean up before taking her turn at the sinks.

The girls managed to finish and jump into their bunks within the allotted time. As Jill stood by the light switch, counting down the final thirty seconds, Kelly whipped out the calendar. With a sigh of satisfaction, she crossed off Sunday. Three days gone. Only seven left.

Kelly shoved the calendar under her pillow just as the timer rang. Jill flicked off the lights, plunging the cabin into darkness. Immediately, flashlights beamed across the ceiling and around the room. Kelly shut her eyes tight when one shone right in her face.

"No flashlights unless you're going to the bathroom," Jill called.

The lights turned off, and the whispering began. Something whizzed past Kelly and landed on the floor with a jingle. Probably a stuffed animal with a bell on the collar.

"Oops!" a voice called, and someone fumbled in the dark to retrieve the item.

"Once lights are out," Jill warned, "no one gets out of their bed. Unless they're going to the bathroom."

"I have to use the bathroom." Joyce giggled.

Not likely.

Joyce turned her flashlight on and beamed it around the bunks. "Anyone what to come with me?"

Several thuds indicated that a number of girls had left their bunks.

"Only two at a time." Jill sounded perturbed. "And make it fast."

Joyce left with Emma, slamming the door behind them. They returned just as noisily.

Jill spent the next hour and a half calling out names, pleading, threatening, and begging for quiet. Kelly groaned and pressed her stuffed beagle against the side of her head to block the noise. But it didn't help. She'd never get any sleep if this kept up.

Kelly deducted the first point from Jill's score. Too bad. She'd been doing so well.

"Did you see that blond counselor guy?" a voice whispered.

"The tall, skinny one with the weird hat?"

"No, the one riding that huge horse."

"That's Joel."

"He's 24 karat gold."

"He's bubblegum delicious."

Kelly rolled her eyes. Instead of counting sheep, she decided to tally the number of times the campers said Joel's name or described him with some cheesy term. She drifted off around number fifty-nine.

11 SANDY'S SUPER-SPECIAL SUNDAES

Kelly slid her bowl of breakfast cereal onto the table and sank down on the bench beside Amber, who'd gone back to hiding behind a book. All around Kelly, the dining hall resounded with chatter and laughter. So much noisier now that it was packed with campers.

She snuck a glance at the cover on Amber's novel. Different characters, but still half-naked. Different pose, but still steamy and indecent. A red-tasseled bookmark marked her place a quarter of the way into the book.

Amber put her paperback down and poked Kelly in the arm. "Where were you this morning? I woke up early and you were already gone."

"I went for a jog. But I could hardly keep my eyes open. I nearly ran off the road twice." Kelly stifled a yawn. "It was impossible to fall asleep with all the noise in the cabin last night. Instead of counting sheep, I tried to count how many times I heard Joel's name. I lost track around fifty-nine."

"That's all? Then you fell asleep early, because they must have said his name at least a hundred times." Amber rolled her eyes, then dove into her bacon and eggs.

The tantalizing smells drifted up to Kelly's nose. She turned her head and took a spoonful of plain flakes.

"Joyce and Emma bragged that they didn't fall asleep until after two AM."

Kelly let out a snort. Hardly worth boasting about.

"And Joyce said she's going to get everyone to stay up even later tonight."

Why couldn't Joyce use her natural leadership abilities for good? Kelly propped her head on her arms and groaned. She'd be a zombie by the second day if the girls kept this up.

"Joel is hot," Amber continued. "But I heard he's got a really pretty girlfriend and they're totally in love. Is that true?"

The clanging of a kitchen utensil on the serving counter grabbed everyone's attention. Grateful for the interruption, Kelly didn't bother to answer.

"One of these summers, we're going to get a bell," Bill muttered. Then he addressed the campers. "Welcome to your first full day at Timberlake Camp. After breakfast, campers will return to their cabins for devotions. Following that, cabin groups will rotate through two activities before lunch and three after lunch. The store is open in the afternoon between the fourth and fifth activity. Each day will end with supper, games or free time, and a campfire. Schedules are posted outside the lodge and at the barn."

Kelly listened with envy. She had one activity. Maintenance. All day. Every day.

Some boys from a back table stood and began to walk away, but Bill motioned for them to return to their places. "Last summer, we had a problem with messy rooms. So this year, we're going to hold a contest for the cleanest cabin. A secret judge will inspect the rooms at a random time each day. Points will be awarded. Pleasant-smelling cabins will receive a bonus point, which means the boys will have to shower at least once this week."

The boys shouted their protests, as if stinking was macho.

Bill banged the spoon again to regain silence. "At the end of the week, the cabin with the highest score will win Sandy's Super-Special Sundaes."

The announcement earned a few cheers but not much more. Kelly wasn't surprised by the halfhearted response. A plain scoop of ice cream with a drizzle of brown sticky sauce seemed too boring to provide a week's worth of motivation.

A sudden crash caused Kelly, and everyone around her, to jump. It sounded like pot lids clanging together, and it came from deep within the kitchen. All heads turned as the kitchen door swung wide and a solemn-faced Sandy marched to the front of the counter. She surveyed the campers, raised her right arm in the air, and snapped her fingers three times.

The kitchen doors opened again and Sheila stepped out, wearing a black-and-white apron. The towel draped over her arm and the thin mustache drawn on her upper lip gave her the air of a proper French waiter. In her hands she carried a large glass bowl, filled to overflowing with scoops of vanilla, chocolate, and strawberry ice cream. With a curt bow, Sheila presented the bowl to Sandy and marched back into the kitchen.

The sight of the massive dish energized the campers. All traces of apathy were lost in a roar of approval.

Kelly licked her lips and tried to remember the last time she'd allowed herself to taste ice cream. Strawberry had been her favorite.

Sandy snapped her fingers twice. This time, Marcie and Charlie stepped through the swinging door, also dressed in black-and-white aprons, with matching tea towels and penciled mustaches. Each held a tray covered with a white tea towel, and they took up positions on either side of Sandy. They could have fit right in as waiters at some classy French café. Except for Charlie's ugly hat, sitting slightly askew on his head.

Marcie kept her head lowered and eyes focused on the floor, probably trying to hide her bright red cheeks. Kelly smothered a chuckle. It wasn't hard to guess the reason for Marcie's discomfort. Playing dress-up, especially with a faux mustache doodled on her face, might get her blacklisted from some future association of the intellectual elite.

Sandy snapped her fingers once more. Marcie and Charlie whipped the towels from their trays, revealing an assortment of Ziploc bags.

After setting his towel and tray on the counter, Charlie held up one of the bags. "Gummy bears," he announced. He opened the bag and dumped a generous portion into the bowl of ice cream.

Cheers mingled with boos erupted from the campers.

Marcie drew a bag from her tray. "Marshmallows." She poured the miniature white puffs into the bowl.

Another mixed reaction from the campers.

"Chocolate chips!"

Thunderous applause showed unanimous approval. Kelly gazed at the bag with warm memories. She used to sneak into her mother's baking supplies and eat the small chocolate chunks by the handful. A lifetime ago.

"Oreo cookies!"

The campers banged on the table. It was almost impossible to hear Charlie and Marcie over the noise.

"Gumdrops!"

"M&Ms!"

The campers spiraled into a sugar frenzy. They were on their feet, reaching, begging, and pleading for a taste.

"Share with me!"

"Just one bite!"

"I'll give you anything you want!"

Sandy held up her hand. When the crowd finally fell silent, Charlie reached into a pocket on his apron and pulled out a spoon. Bowing low, he presented the shiny utensil to Sandy.

Sandy lifted the spoon high and, with painstakingly slow movements, dug into the multi-colored mountain of candy and ice cream. She scooped out a heaping spoonful and crammed it into her mouth. A blissful smile spread across her face.

"Each member of the winning cabin will get one of Sandy's Super-Special Sundaes." Bill grabbed a spoon from behind the counter and took a huge scoop for himself. It was several minutes before he could speak again. "The bowl shown in this display is not the actual size. Yours will be smaller."

Kelly's jealous sigh was lost in the shrill pleas of the campers. Sandy turned back toward the kitchen with the dessert held high, ignoring the campers' hands stretched out in supplication. The closest kids tried to mob her, but Marcie and Charlie held their empty trays like shields and fended them off.

Bill set a huge chart on the counter. He traced his finger down the categories. "Floors clean of garbage and clothes. Wastebasket not overflowing. Shoes stacked by the wall and coats hung on hooks. Neat bunks. Lights off when no one is in the room. Door closed at all times."

Kelly thought of her cabin, already a hopeless mess, which suited her fine. She didn't want to win that dangerous bowl of calorie-laden corruption.

Bill lowered the board. "This chart will be updated each morning. Good luck to everyone."

"If I ate all that ice cream, I'd have a Jelly Belly."

Kelly spotted Mike's ridiculous hat towering above the camper heads at a back table.

"You could jog on a Rocky Road for exercise." Darren jumped to his feet, his horrid hat firmly fixed on his head. For now.

"But that would leave me seeing Dots. Don't be such a Dum Dum."

The two comedians both leaped onto the benches at their separate camper tables, shouting their candy name puns to each other across the dining hall.

"Maybe you could eat more Juicy Fruit. But watch out for the Gummy Worms."

"Thanks for the warning, Darren. You're a Lifesaver."

There was no way of knowing how long they would have continued if Bill hadn't stepped in with a joke of his own. "That's enough, Mike & Ike."

The campers broke out into wild applause for Mike and Darren, and Kelly joined in. She'd never met anyone as good at pulling out puns as her father. But even he would have applauded the comic duo. And probably joined right in.

Jill banged the salt and pepper shakers on the table and motioned for the girls to lean in. "Do you want those sundaes?"

Every head nodded.

"Then let's do it! We'll work on a plan before morning devotions."

Kelly forced a smile. Even if they won, there was no way she was going to eat a single bite. Then again, judging from the frenzied reaction of the other campers, it wouldn't be too hard to give hers away. Or sell it for a massive profit.

The girls cleared their table and returned to the cabin.

Once inside, Jill pointed toward the plush carpet in the middle of the room. "Get a pillow and find a place."

The girls raced to their bunks, grabbed pillows, and flopped on the floor. Amber slid in beside Kelly, her romance book at her side. At least it was closed.

"Here's our strategy for winning the clean cabin contest." Jill plucked a notepad and pencil from her shelf and tossed them to Kelly. "Take notes."

Another order. But at least she was getting used to them.

"Everyone will choose one area to monitor."

"I'll turn off the lights when we leave," Joyce shouted.

Which had to be the easiest job.

Jill nodded. "That means you'll also have the important task of doing a final walkabout before you exit."

Joyce puffed up with the added responsibility, apparently missing the fact that it meant extra work. Another good-counselor point for Jill.

Kelly scribbled down Joyce's name and assignment, scrambling to keep up as the other campers called out their requests.

"As long as each of us takes care of our task, the cabin will stay spotless at all times. There's no way we can lose."

Giddy with excitement, the girls began choosing toppings for their sundaes.

Jill carried a large box into the circle, pulled out the devotion binders, and passed one to each camper. While the girls traded, each trying to snag their preferred color, Jill reached to the bottom of the box and pulled out a bundle of pens. After taking one, she passed the others around the circle. "Please write your name on the front cover."

Kelly grabbed her binder from under her bed and returned to Amber's side. Jill passed out three sheets of paper. "This morning we'll talk about the features of a solid, healthy romantic relationship."

The devotion covered the same material that Bill had presented to the staff during the last training campfire. As Jill talked through the points, Kelly admired the amount of work that had gone into preparing the lessons. The first page showed a large picture of Guy and Girl. Arrows and handwritten labels emphasized that the pair stood on their own feet, with room to move, not hanging on to each other too tightly.

Kelly turned her attention to the girls. They appeared interested. But when Jill described the Guy-Girl relationship as a stunning picture of love, the campers looked skeptical and unconvinced. Just as she'd been. Kelly caught a few of them sneaking glances at the smoldering couple on the cover of Amber's book. Poor Guy and Girl didn't stand a chance against the raw passion radiating from the barely-clad duo.

Jill moved on to the second page and read the first line. "There's no such thing as 'love at first sight.'"

"Of course there is," Joyce scoffed. "It happens all the time."

"Instant attraction happens all the time," Jill corrected. "But shared ties take time to form."

Joyce rolled her eyes and let out a snort.

Kelly hadn't expected the campers to absorb every statement without question. But Joyce's negative attitude robbed the other girls of a chance to decide for themselves.

"There are no perfect Prince Charmings. Or flawless romances."

Kelly felt Amber stiffen.

"And the adrenaline rush of first love doesn't last forever."

Emma's brow wrinkled. "Why not? Romance should be easy if you're really meant to be together."

Jill shook her head. "Love is hard work for any couple, although most of us don't picture romantic relationships that way. That's why the last page contains a list of 'New Romantic and Sexy Words.'"

As Jill read through the list, Kelly sensed resistance from the campers. She couldn't fault them. She still had a hard time seeing terms like *balance*, *respect*, and *time* as sexy. Those words certainly wouldn't be found in the title of any of Amber's books. Or anywhere inside the covers.

Jill tapped on the simple drawing of Guy and Girl. "This is a whole new picture of love."

Joyce pointed at Amber's book. "I like that picture better."

Though she felt like a traitor, Kelly silently agreed. If she had to pick, she'd much rather insert herself and Joel onto the cover of the romance novel than the one in the devotion binder. Although she'd wear more clothes.

Jill closed her binder. "I understand that's how you feel now. But your opinion might change by the end of the week. This picture of Guy and Girl may become the most impressive relationship you've ever seen."

That would take a miracle. For the campers as well as her.

Amber traced her finger over the words on the cover. "Why is it called 'My Wallet'?"

Jill shrugged. "Bill chose the title, but he hasn't explained his reasons."

"That's dumb."

Trust Joyce to fire another shot of negativity.

"No, that's Bill." Jill laughed. "He likes to do things that seem to make no sense. Then, when we're sure he's completely off track, he spins it around and pulls out something brilliant."

Joyce tossed her head. "Not going to happen this time."

Kelly thought she might be right.

"We have fifteen minutes before we have to be at archery. Let's do a practice cleaning run while Kelly collects the binders."

Kelly nodded. Of course. She lived for such glorious tasks.

To Kelly's surprise, all the girls threw themselves into their jobs. Even Joyce. Within minutes, the cabin was spotless. Not a sock or shoe out of place.

As the girls left for their first activity, still discussing the best way to build a sundae, Kelly felt sucked into a whirlwind of dread and panic. She didn't want to get anywhere near that ice cream prize, no matter how much smaller the actual sundae bowl might be. But thanks to Jill's plan and the girls' enthusiasm, it looked like they had a good chance of winning.

As Kelly left the cabin, mutinous feelings swirled around her. Along with a cool blast of selfishness. It would be easy to leave the lights on. Or accidentally knock a coat off the rack. Just enough to lose a point or two. Maybe not today, and only if the need arose.

An image of eight disappointed faces sprang to her mind. Nine if she counted Jill. But she replaced the guilty vision with a mental picture of herself unable to stop eating the sundae. Stuffing her face with heaping spoonfuls. While Joel looked on in horror, and Cindy stood by his side, laughing.

She was not going to let that happen. No matter what she had to do.

12 A RODEO WITH A TWIST

"We have to paint the whole thing?" Kelly set her heavy can on the ground and stared in disbelief at the fence. Like a long wooden snake, it curved down the length of the camp's main road, running from the barn area, past the cabins, and down to the lodge.

"Every inch of every post." Tony held out two pairs of coveralls. Thick denim, oversized, and spattered with various shades of paint. "You can slip these on over your clothes."

Bob took a pair and held them up. "There's no way I'm wearing these." He tossed them back.

Tony gestured to Bob's paint can. "This stain is hard to get out."

Bob shrugged. "I'll take my chances."

Kelly took the overalls. Bob could ruin his name brand shirt if he wanted, but she had a limited clothing budget. She slipped on the outfit and immediately began to squirm. It was exactly what she'd expected. Hot, scratchy, and hideous.

When Tony handed her an oversized cap, she jammed it on her head. At least it obscured most of her features, and hopefully her identity.

As Tony lumbered off toward the lodge, Kelly was certain she heard him snicker.

She used the handle of her paintbrush to pry the tight lid off her can, breaking the skin on a knuckle in the process. Not the best start. With a heavy sigh, she plunged a brush inside and applied a dark chestnut color to the nearest rail.

"How long are you staying here this summer?"

Kelly nearly dropped her brush. She hadn't expected a friendly conversation with Bob, but it would help pass the time. "One week. How about you?"

"Three weeks. Just long enough to get my community service hours for school and then I'm outta here."

So they actually had something in common. Sounded like he was as eager to leave as she was.

Bob slopped stain on a post, dripping all over the grass. "Where do you go to school?"

"Skyridge High."

"Could be worse. I go to Pinecrest."

A snotty private school for rich brats. That explained a lot.

"You've got a decent basketball team. We have to break a sweat to beat you. But your school is short on hot girls and heavy on nerds."

Kelly gritted her teeth. So much for a pleasant morning.

Bob moved on to the next post. "Do you play any sports?"

"Volleyball."

"Good choice, for a girl. You don't look fast enough for a game like basketball. I prefer football. But any sport with cheerleaders works for me. Gotta love those short, tight uniforms!"

Superficial, chauvinist creep. Kelly had no interest in being shredded by Bob's sharp tongue, or hearing his shallow opinions. Better to end the conversation quickly.

Kelly turned and squinted at him. "Your tail's showing."

Bob stared at her with a blank expression. Then, he twisted around to check out his back side. Kelly hid her giggles in the sleeve of her overalls.

"What are you talking about?"

Kelly pushed the tip of her nose up, like a snout.

"Are you calling me a pig?"

"Took you long enough."

While Bob sputtered, Kelly picked up her can of paint and moved farther down the fence. Turning her back to him, she focused on the post in front of her.

Bob mumbled something under his breath, but she refused to acknowledge him. Based on the angry swish of his brush as he splattered the fence, he wasn't used to getting the cold shoulder. Or being compared to a farm animal. And he obviously didn't like it. Which was great for her. They worked in silence, with Kelly maintaining a distance of several posts, for the rest of the morning.

Just when she thought her arm was going to drop off, a group of about thirty noisy campers passed by on the road, making their way from the barn to the lodge. Kelly checked her watch. Almost lunchtime.

Without any warning, Bob appeared beside her and smeared a long brown streak down the sleeve of her overalls and over the back of her hand. "That's for calling me a pig." A second slash smeared the dark stain down the fingers of her other hand. "And that's for knocking juice on me during staff training."

Kelly gasped and stared at her skin. "How am I supposed to get this off?"

"Why would you?" Bob smirked. "Think of it as a gift of mud from my pigpen."

She preferred to think of it as a declaration of war. And she accepted, with a dripping brown jab to his cheek. Paintbrushes transformed into swords. Bob's attacks landed mainly on her overalls, while Kelly coated his clothes and arms. She almost felt guilty for ruining his fancy threads. But when Bob knocked off her cap and smeared a thick line down her nose, she no longer cared.

Focused on the battle, she didn't hear the thunder of hooves until they were almost upon her.

Kelly leaped back as six members of the horse staff skidded to a halt. She cringed at the sight of Joel among them. She'd hoped to run into him, but not when she was wearing baggy overalls and sporting a brown stripe down the middle of her face.

"You missed a spot," teased Caroline, the girl in the lead.

"More like they missed the whole fence." Matt laughed.

"What's the matter?" Bob glowered at the riders. "Too lazy to walk to lunch?"

Caroline snorted. "At least we know that paint belongs on wood, not people."

Bob raised his brush menacingly and the horse staff spurred their mounts into action, racing off toward the lodge.

Kelly whirled to face Bob. He needed to pay for her humiliation in front of Joel. She lifted her brush high but froze when she realized that Joel hadn't ridden off with the rest.

"Looks like she got the best of you, Bob!" With a wave, Joel spun his horse and sped off after the others.

A thrill coursed through Kelly's body. Joel had noticed her! And paid her a compliment. But she couldn't get too happy, because he hadn't used her name. Which made her wonder if he even knew it.

She turned back to Bob and was surprised to find him carefully applying stain on the nearest board.

"You can drop the act," Tony's voice rang out.

That explained Bob's sudden concentration and feigned innocence.

Tony strode toward them, scowling. "The fence looks good. Too bad I can't say the same about either of you."

Kelly braced for a verbal flogging but noticed a twitch in the corners of Tony's mouth. As if he was trying to hold back a smile.

"Go get cleaned up."

Kelly closed the lid on her paint can, balanced her brush on top of it, and pulled off the overalls. The stain on her skin was not going to come off anytime soon. She'd look like a fool for the rest of the week.

As she headed toward the cabins, Bob fell in step beside her. Which meant he was close enough to trip or shove into the nearest tree.

"Hey, hold up."

Kelly and Bob stopped at the sound of Tony's voice. He'd picked up one of the paint cans and brushes and joined them, leaving the other can and brush in the grass beside the fence.

"There are two bottles of cooking oil in the maintenance shed. Top shelf. That should get the stain off your skin. If that doesn't work, try the nail polish remover. It's in the same cupboard."

Kelly flashed him a grateful grin. He'd saved her week, and she wouldn't have to hurt Bob after all.

"This isn't over," Bob murmured.

"I heard that," Tony said. "And it is over. You'll be working at opposite ends of the camp this afternoon."

Welcome news.

"You know, Bob, you might want to consider a rematch. Kelly won this round." Tony chuckled.

Kelly smiled at the decisive victory she'd scored.

But her celebration was short-lived. Even with both cooking oil and nail polish, she found it hard to remove the stain. She ended up scrubbing off several layers of skin. By the time she emerged from the shower, she'd transformed from a striped skunk to a red-nosed counselor. Kelly borrowed some lotion from one of Jill's shelves, hoping her irritated skin would return to a normal color soon.

Kelly's mood improved slightly when she glanced at the clock. While she'd been in the shower, lunch had come and gone. Camp had its advantages. She'd never been able to skip so many meals at home.

When Kelly reported to the maintenance shed for the afternoon's assignment, Tony eyed her from head to toe. "The bathroom had better be as clean as you are, or that will be your first job."

"It's spotless."

Tony tossed her a pair of gardening gloves. "Bob will continue staining the fence and you can weed around the craft shack. Throw whatever you pull into a pile and I'll pick it up later."

"Thanks." Pulling weeds had to be easier than painting the never-ending fence.

Kelly found a sign marking the way to the craft shack and followed the narrow path. Her good mood faded as she approached the building, which was almost hidden among a jungle of thistles. With a moan, she crouched by the nearest patch and prepared for a long afternoon. With no chance of seeing Joel.

Three hours later, Tony came by. He inspected the pile of weeds and the cleared area around half of the shack. "Good work. And you managed to stay clean this time."

Kelly shifted her position and grimaced, her legs numb from squatting for so long. "Did you deliberately plant a crop of thistles here?"

"Of course. Weeding builds character."

"Haven't you ever heard of herbicide?"

"Not good for the environment."

"Maintenance isn't good for me." She tried to stand, but a wave of dizziness slammed into her and she nearly fell over. Probably the effects of stooping for hours. Or the paint fumes from the morning. Her rumbling stomach suggested a different reason.

"You're done for the day," Tony said.

Yes, she was. In more ways than one. Kelly limped back to the cabin, collapsed on her bunk, and didn't move until the campers burst in to change out of their riding gear. Once everyone was ready, she pulled herself to her feet and walked with them to the lodge for dinner.

As she moved through the food line, Kelly skipped the main course and filled her plate with salad greens.

At the table, she ate in silence, listening to the excited chatter of the girls.

"I didn't see you at lunch," Amber said.

"I spent the whole time in the shower, scrubbing off brown stain."

Emma leaned closer. “I heard there was a massive war between two counselors. Was that you?”

Kelly nodded.

“They said you plastered the guy!” Admiration shone in Joyce’s eyes. “And dumped a whole bucket of paint on his head.”

Kelly grinned at Joyce’s suggestion. “I wish I had.”

“From what I’ve heard about Bob, he deserved every drop.” Jill winked.

“Well, he started the battle, but I finished strong.”

The girls applauded. Jill rapped on the table. “Bill’s called for an early campfire tonight. It’ll be cool this evening, so swing by the cabin to get a sweater before heading to the fire pit.”

Kelly stuffed the last bite of salad in her mouth and washed it down with a large gulp of water. She still felt famished.

After clearing the dishes off the table, the girls made their way to the cabin. Kelly and Amber followed at a slower pace. The other campers were already leaving by the time they made their way inside.

Amber yanked a pullover out of her suitcase. “I love bonfires. They’re so romantic. I hope it’s a huge, crackling blaze.”

“As long as Guy and Girl don’t get too close to it.” Kelly laughed as she searched through her locker for something warm to wear. Now would be the perfect time to mess up the cabin. She pulled out a few sweaters for inspection, and casually dropped them on the ground. Then she slipped into a long-sleeved turquoise sweater and stepped toward the door.

Amber gasped as she pointed to the pile on the floor. “We can’t leave a mess. We’d lose points.”

Kelly grit her teeth as she shoved the clothes into her locker. “Thanks for the reminder.”

After a quick check to make sure the cabin was in perfect order, the girls exited together and made their way to the fire pit by the lake.

When they reached the benches, Amber moaned. "Where's the fire?"

Kelly stared in disappointment at the pit, empty except for a mound of gray ashes. With not a log or stick in sight.

Bill stood in front of the cold pit, arms folded and his face expressionless. He remained silent until all the campers had settled onto the wooden seats.

"Okay, everyone get up. We're moving."

But they'd just gotten there. Kelly didn't see a need to go anywhere else. It was a beautiful summer evening without a rain cloud in sight.

But Bill wasn't asking for opinions. He picked up a large bag, slung it over his shoulder, and strode past the benches. A confused murmur rose from the crowd.

"What are you waiting for?" Bill motioned for the campers to follow.

Chaos erupted as the entire group scrambled to leave the campfire area at the same time. Kelly frowned. What was Bill up to?

To Kelly's surprise, Bill didn't stop at the lodge. As he walked past, he belted out a familiar hiking song. Most of the campers joined in. At least the ones who weren't grumbling. When he came to the end of the tune, he started another.

Amber nudged Kelly. "Where do you think we're going?"

She shrugged. "Your guess is as good as mine. I just hope there'll be a bonfire when we get there."

The girls from the cabin pestered Jill with questions.

"What's happening?"

"Where is he taking us?"

"Why didn't we stay at the fire pit?"

"How far are we going to walk?"

"Where are the paper people?"

Jill held up her hands in surrender. "I don't know. This is Bill. Think of it as an adventure."

The procession headed toward the front entrance of the camp. For a moment, Kelly thought Bill might lead them right off the property. But he swung to the right, guided the group to the riding arena, and pointed into the stands.

"Stay with your cabin and find a place to sit. The show will begin in a moment."

A show in a horse arena? Kelly scratched her head. What happened to the campfire theme of love and tied-up cardboard characters? She wondered if Bill had already run out of ideas.

It took a few minutes for the group to find seats in the stands, as the male campers jostled for the top rows while the girls settled below. Bill sat in the front, staring intently at the empty arena. An uneasy hush fell over the group.

The silence was broken by a creak at the far end of the arena. All eyes watched MaryAnn climb over the railing and open a small gate. A brown-and-white calf leaped out of his narrow pen and trotted forward. MaryAnn moved to the large corral gates and swung them wide.

Seconds later, a massive black horse and a rider with a zebra-print cowboy hat came pounding through. The campers cheered and shouted out Bernice's name. Kelly remembered Marcie talking about the trophies that the head horse instructor had won and realized she was watching a pro in action.

The calf bolted and ran, with the horse thundering on its heels. Bernice threw a lasso and it settled around the calf's neck. The poor critter was yanked off his feet and slammed into the dirt with a thud. Before the calf could move, Bernice jumped off her horse, grabbed the calf's legs, and tied them tightly together. The little guy struggled but wasn't going anywhere.

Bernice's horse backed up, keeping a taut rope and dragging the creature by his neck. A surge of applause rose from the campers, drowning out the scattered feminine boos.

It was the first time Kelly had watched a live rodeo event. She admired Bernice's expert riding and roping. But it seemed harsh for the calf.

Bernice swept off her hat and bowed to the crowd. Then she released the calf and remounted her horse. The calf leaped to its feet and shook itself off. Kicking up its heels, it trotted along at an eager pace as Bernice guided it back to the pen, secured the barrier, and rode out.

Kelly craned her neck to peer at Bill in the front row. He remained seated, eyes focused straight ahead. The arena stood empty for several minutes. An awkward silence blanketed the stands, and Kelly shifted in her seat. She could only imagine what would come next.

Another creak came from the far end of the arena. The small pen swung open again. But instead of a four-legged critter bursting forth, MaryAnn walked out. And she was carrying Girl. MaryAnn marched to the center of the arena, propped up the cardboard cutout, then left.

Darren leaped to his feet. "Hey, Girl! You'd better get out of there. It's not safe!"

He'd barely finished his warning when the massive black horse burst through the large corral gate. But this time the rider was the cardboard figure of Guy. The campers let out a mixture of gasps and snickers. A figure, dressed entirely in black, crouched low on the saddle behind the paper character.

The horse raced toward Girl, and the team of Guy/Masked Rider tossed a lasso around her neck, knocking her into the dust. The duo jumped off and looped the rope several times around the body of their target. Then the masked rider stood Girl to her feet, propped Guy beside her, and secured the end of the rope around his hand. The rider jammed his hat onto Guy's head, jumped back on the horse, and raced out.

Bizarre. And that was one of the kinder terms that came to mind.

Bill hopped over the rails and walked toward the cardboard characters, tossing his sack at their paper feet. "Can anyone tell me the name of the first event we watched?" His voice rang through the arena loudspeakers.

A chorus of voices shouted, "Calf roping!"

Darren stood. "I told Girl to get out of there, Bill. Maybe you *herd* me."

A few rows back, Mike leaped to his feet. "You need to *beef* up security around here."

Darren waved his hands. "Or else this camp will experience *udder* chaos."

Cheers rose from the campers. Kelly applauded. It was some of their best material yet.

Bill sent the comedians a warning glance. "*Moooove* back to your places before I *cream* you."

Mike and Darren tipped their ever-present hats to Bill and sat down.

"We just saw an award-winning demonstration of calf roping. Does anyone know the name of the second event we watched?"

"Girl roping?" Mike shouted.

The campers burst out laughing.

Bill shook his head. "It's called Date Roping. Of course, in real life it's usually more subtle than what Girl just experienced. Most of the time, actual horses aren't involved."

Kelly gave a low snort. She couldn't see how Bill could relate the strange scene to dating. With or without the horse.

Bill reached for the bag at his feet. "Some of your boyfriends or girlfriends may not want the ties to go between you. They want to wrap ties around you, which gives them the power to control and manipulate the relationship."

Kelly cast a furtive glance over the stands. The campers looked so young. She wondered how many of them had already been shackled by dating ties.

A twinge of guilt pricked her conscience. Her parents hadn't wanted her in a serious dating relationship until she was at least seventeen. She'd resented their restriction and argued that it was unreasonable to wait that long. Especially when she had a chance to hook up with someone as amazing as Aaron.

Kelly shifted in her seat. Maybe her parents hadn't been completely wrong. Things with Aaron had been more difficult than she'd expected. And had blown up in her face.

"It's not always easy to recognize when a boyfriend or girlfriend is tying you down. Not all ropes look dangerous." Bill reached into his sack and pulled out several long strips of green ribbon. "Some girlfriends or boyfriends will try to control you with gifts. Now, there's nothing wrong with a present, unless something is expected in return. A true gift is given freely, with no strings attached."

Kelly thought about the cute stuffed bear sitting on her dresser at home. A Valentine's Day gift from Aaron. And the silver heart necklace and matching bracelet he'd bought for her birthday. Such sweet gifts and he hadn't expected anything back. Well, at least not right away. Whenever Aaron pushed her to do something she wasn't comfortable with, like sneaking out at night, cheating on homework, or taking the car, he said he'd put out for her, and it was time for her to start paying him back. But all the guys talked that way. At least that's what Lucy once told her.

A sense of shame filled Kelly. Just a few days at camp, and it was as if she'd forgotten her school chum.

Bill looped the shiny ribbons around Girl's neck and tucked the ends into Guy's hands.

"I'd like to be tied up with streamers and bows," Emma whispered.

Jill shook her head. "Not if they turn out to be a noose."

Kelly's thoughts drifted to the calf, lying hog-tied on his side in the dust. She suspected the little guy would agree with Jill.

Bill reached into the bag again, pulled out a poster, and held it high. Several large circles had been drawn on it, each with a picture in the middle. A shirt. A plate of food. A musical note. The silhouettes of people. A thick, dark line ran through the center of each one.

Bill leaned the poster against Girl's legs. "Watch out for a boyfriend or girlfriend who tries to limit your choices. Telling you what to wear, what music to listen to, who you can talk to, where you can go. Such possessiveness may seem flattering at first, as if the other person really cares about every detail in your life. Not so. They only care about getting their way."

Kelly frowned. Aaron stepped on her favorite country CD just because he hated that type of music. But he wasn't anywhere near as bad as Lucy's boyfriend, Logan. That guy had an opinion about everything, and expected Lucy to comply with them all.

Bill pointed to the last circle on his sign. "Be especially wary if your boyfriend or girlfriend wants to isolate you from your friends and family. That leaves you vulnerable to his or her control."

Everything Bill said seemed to put Aaron in a negative light. But Aaron had his reasons for refusing to hang out with her "religious friends". He knew they didn't approve of him. And that's why he stayed away from her parents as well. Aaron hadn't forced Kelly to grow distant from them. Even though that's pretty much what happened.

Bill peered inside the sack and fished out a box of tissues. "Expressions of strong emotions can be a lasso that holds you in a bad place. Don't be fooled by tears. Even the words 'I love you' can trap you into feeling that you are committed to the relationship."

That seemed more of a girl trick. Annalisa used to brag that she could make a guy do anything just by turning on the tears. Guys didn't use feelings to get what they wanted.

Then again, Aaron did get sulky when things didn't go his way. She always had to apologize to smooth things over. But it wasn't like he was deliberately manipulating her or anything. Or at least she'd never viewed it that way.

The next item out of the bag was a set of boxing gloves. A heavy silence fell on the campers as Bill attached them to Guy's hands. "Some girlfriends and boyfriends use anger, intimidation, and force to get their way."

Finally something that couldn't be pinned on Aaron. He might be strong-willed and demanding at times, but he'd never hit her.

Bill plunged his hand deep into the bag and came up empty. Turning the sack upside down, he shook it hard. Three bandages fell out. He stuck them on Girl's arms and legs. "The attacks may be physical, leaving marks on your body. Or the attacks may be verbal, leaving bruises on your heart and soul. No matter the form, abuse should never be ignored, excused, or tolerated."

A shudder ran through Kelly as she thought about the day Annalisa had pointed out four small bruises on Lucy's arm and asked what happened. Lucy said she'd run into a door. But the finger-shaped markings told Kelly she was lying.

Bill tossed the empty sack off to the side. "Before we finish, I need to stamp on, trample, and jump all over a few myths about abuse. Some people hold onto the foolish hope that the abuse will just go away. But it won't. It will only get worse. Other people blame themselves for the abuse. It's never your fault when someone else makes a poor choice."

When Annalisa refused to believe Lucy's answer that day, Lucy had finally confessed that Logan sometimes became aggressive when he'd been drinking. Or when she did something stupid. Staying with a guy like that seemed pretty stupid to Kelly.

"Some believe that if the abuser is truly sorry, it won't happen again. But it will. And you can't save them. They need to seek professional help."

Bill's words seemed so serious. Logan was just a high school student who'd messed up. But then Kelly wondered what would happen if he didn't get help. Would Logan hit the next girlfriend...and the one after that? And one day would he strike his wife and children?

Bill tugged on the rope around Girl's neck, then gestured to the poster, boxing gloves, and bandages. "Does this look romantic to you?"

The campers booed and held thumbs down. Kelly agreed.

"Tony?" Bill scanned the stands. "It's time for the list of New Romantic and Sexy Words."

"On the way." Tony emerged from the audience and hopped into the arena. No easel, no sheet of words.

Bill held up his hand. "Where's the list?"

Tony gave a piercing whistle.

The gate at the far end of the arena creaked open, and the black horse thundered through, carrying Bernice and the easel. She pulled her horse to a skidding stop with only a few feet to spare, showering the two men in dirt. Reaching down, Bernice handed the easel to Tony, then she wheeled around and raced out. The campers stood and applauded.

"You couldn't carry the easel yourself?" Bill muttered, brushing himself off.

"You said you wanted a show," Tony shrugged. As if Bill should be grateful for his creative effort.

Bill snorted. Then he looked at the easel. "Is the word *ouch* on the list of New Romantic and Sexy Words?"

Tony searched the chart. "No, that term doesn't seem to be there."

"Just as I suspected. And we won't find words like *help, too tight*, and *can't breathe*."

Or *bullied* and *bruised*, like Lucy. Or *forced to steal her parent's car*...but Aaron just got carried away because he loved doing crazy stuff with her. Liked to show her off in style. At least that's what he said. In a way, she should be flattered. He was overwhelmed by his strong feelings. He couldn't help himself. But who was she kidding?

Bill tapped the easel. "Let's add a few new words" As he spoke, he unfastened the ribbons from around Girl's neck. "Two people in love will trust and respect each other. And they'll allow each other to make their own choices. Those are qualities we can add to the list."

Tony scrawled *trust* and *choice* on the paper. And somewhere a kindergarten teacher cried, lamenting her failure to teach a bear cub of a boy proper penmanship.

Kelly stared at the barely legible words. If she sat down with her friends at school and asked them to describe their relationships, would any of them have chosen those words? Probably not. She wouldn't have chosen them either.

Bill pulled the boxing gloves off Guy and attached the ties between the hands of the cardboard couple.

"Early detection is crucial. When you're first interested in someone, he or she will look, smell, and sound great. But if a rope starts twirling above your head, don't ignore it. Walk away. Or better yet, run."

Kelly pictured the calf again, lying helpless on the ground. Had Aaron pulled her through the dirt by a rope around her neck? She'd never thought of it that way. Until now.

"Campfire's over. Head back to the cabins."

Kelly hardly noticed as campers pushed and jostled to exit the stands. She knew someone else who'd been lassoed, tied up, and dragged around. As soon as she got home, she'd tell Lucy about Bill's message at the campfire. She'd talk about the calf. And how joyful it looked once it was set free.

13 THE TRAGIC TALE OF HARDSHIPS

Kelly let Amber drag her into the jostling mass of campers leaving the stands. She hated to admit it, but the hike to the arena for the campfire message had been worth it.

Still, she couldn't stifle a yawn. Hopefully, a full day of camp had exhausted the girls and they'd fall asleep early. Or at least before midnight.

Just before Kelly turned up a side path leading to the cabins, she felt a tap on her shoulder.

"We've got to talk."

Kelly turned to face Sheila. She motioned for Amber to go on ahead.

"Staff room number eight. Come right away."

So much for a peaceful night. "Can't we just talk now instead?"

Sheila gave her head a fierce shake, and disappeared into the crowd.

Kelly considered asking Jill if she could be a few minutes late for curfew, but that meant risking a negative response. Or a direct order. Better not to tell Jill and hope that whatever Sheila had to say wouldn't take long.

As Kelly headed for the staff rooms, she heard Jill shout a fifteen-minute warning to the campers lingering on the walkway. She didn't have much time.

When Kelly reached room number eight, she gave a light rap. The door swung open and an arm reached out and pulled her in.

"What took you so long?" Sheila glanced into the hallway before closing the door.

Kelly stepped around Shelia and was momentarily stunned by the metallic glare of silver and red. She blinked several times. A tower of Coke cans covered the back wall, stacked one on top of the other. There had to be at least a hundred of them. This was extreme. Even for Sheila.

Kelly pointed to the wall of liquid sugar. "Do you think you have enough to last the summer?"

The question dripped with sarcasm, but Sheila glanced at the hoard with a concerned expression. "Just barely. If I ration three a day, I've got enough for two months. That leaves me with a few extra for emergencies or to share with friends."

"Not that she's ever offered me a can." Marcie sniffed as she perched on the edge of a wooden chair, wearing a pair of blue-and-green-striped pajamas.

Sheila tossed her head. "You won't drink it if it's warm."

"Only sugar addicts drink room-temperature soda." Marcie's chin rose a few inches. "I refuse to become enslaved to a beverage loaded with caffeine."

On Marcie's side of the room, a violin case sat on top of a short bookcase. The shelves sagged under the weight of several thick textbooks. *Advanced Algebra. Conversational Spanish. An Introduction to the Law. The Basics of Medical Care. How to Become Rich and Famous. Ten Easy Steps to Success.* And that was only the top row. But the book lying on the bed said it all. *Transform Yourself from Nobody to Somebody.* Marcie's obsessions may not be as shiny as Sheila's soda cans, but they were just as obvious.

A voice in the hall shouted a ten-minute warning till lights out.

Kelly glanced at her watch. "I have to get back to my cabin."

"This won't take long."

It had already taken too long. Kelly ached for the soft comfort of her sleeping bag.

Sheila paced in the narrow room. "Stan, the head counselor in Darren's cabin, discovered that some of his campers have a stupid plan to go the whole week without washing. Stan is forcing everyone to take a shower tomorrow night."

"Guys are so *boyzarre*. Get it? Boy and bizarre combined together." Marcie giggled at her creation. "It took me days to come up with that one."

A clear waste of time.

Sheila didn't bother to comment on Marcie's vocabulary lesson. "We've bribed a kid in one of the other cabins to borrow Darren's hat while he's in the shower."

"Borrow the hat?" Kelly raised her eyebrows. "Don't you mean steal it?"

"We plan to return it." Sheila flicked her wrist, dismissing the argument. "Eventually."

"Oh, that's different." Kelly wrinkled her nose. "I'm sure Darren won't mind at all."

Sheila continued as though she hadn't heard. "Once we get the hat, we'll sink it in the reeds. Are you in or out?"

Kelly glanced from Marcie's reluctant but loyal face to Sheila's eager expression. It wasn't a hard choice. No way was she missing out on the action. "Count me in."

"Great!" Sheila grinned. "We need a few items from the maintenance shed. You'll have to get them from Tony."

Not what Kelly wanted to hear. Her friends were asking her to raid the den of a grizzly bear. A grumpy one. "Are we *borrowing* or *stealing* these supplies?"

"Borrowing with permission," Marcie said. "We don't want to get on Tony's bad side."

True. Especially since Kelly had to work with him for the rest of the week.

"We don't need much. Just some type of strong cord, a small colorful marker that will float, a large clamp, and something heavy we can use as an anchor." Sheila rattled off the list of items.

Kelly chewed on her lip. Tony was going to want an explanation, and it would have to be a good one. "What do I tell him when he asks why I need those things?"

Before Sheila could answer, footsteps sounded in the hall and MaryAnn's voice called, "Lights out!"

Sheila leaped to the wall and flipped off the switch. The girls held their breath in the dark until the sound of MaryAnn's footsteps faded. Cautiously, Sheila opened the door. "All clear," she whispered. "You'd better go."

Kelly slipped out and sprinted down the hall. But as she passed the bathroom, a dark figure stepped out. Unable to stop, Kelly collided with the mystery person, knocking a towel off her head and revealing a long mane of wet blonde hair and a pair of unfriendly eyes.

"Watch where you're going!" Cindy wrapped her hair back in the towel.

"Sorry. Didn't see you," Kelly murmured.

A door creaked open behind her, and Kelly cringed as Sheila stepped into the hall. "Hey, Kelly," she called in a loud whisper. "Don't let anyone catch you with the supplies or we'll be in big trou–"

Sheila's voice stopped abruptly. She must have realized that Kelly wasn't alone. Took her long enough.

Cindy tilted her head, eyes narrowed.

A sinking feeling settled in Kelly's stomach as she dashed past Cindy. The chance encounter probably meant nothing. But she wished she hadn't been spotted leaving Sheila and Marcie's room. And especially not by Cindy.

When Kelly reached her cabin, the lights were already out. Jill cleared her throat as Kelly stumbled to her bunk, but said nothing. Relieved, Kelly climbed into her sleeping bag and reached under her pillow to pull out the calendar. It was difficult to see in the dim moonlight. She crossed off a square and hoped it was Monday.

Kelly tucked the paper back under her pillow and lay back, grasping her beagle in her arms. She'd worry about the prank supplies tomorrow. At the moment, the only thing on her mind was a good night's sleep. Until the giggling began. And the whispering. And items flying from bunk to bunk. No matter how much Jill pleaded, threatened, and begged for quiet, the campers refused to settle down.

Kelly pretended to be asleep, but after half an hour of constant chattering with no signs of letting up, her frustration boiled over. Something had to be done before she lost it and tore to shreds the next stuffed animal that flew her way.

An idea crept into her mind, a trick her father used when she was younger and couldn't fall asleep. Propping herself up on her elbows, she took a deep breath. "There once was a very poor boy who lived across the ocean in a small foreign country."

"A story!" several voices cheered.

"I'm too old for bedtime stories. Unless it's about ghosts."

That could only be Joyce.

Kelly sat up and pulled her sleeping bag around her shoulders. "It's not scary, but it does have an unusual ending."

And if all went well, no one would be awake to hear it.

The girls quieted down, and Kelly described the happy existence of Sam, an extremely poor boy who lived in a one-room shack with his family. She hadn't gotten far before the campers interrupted, bombarding her with questions.

"He only has one pair of clothes? Including underwear? That's gross."

"What does he wear when he washes his clothes?"

"How do his shoes stay on without shoelaces?"

"What's his sister's name?"

"No questions allowed," Kelly stated in a firm tone. That would defeat the point, which was to keep them quiet so they'd drift off to sleep.

Kelly waited for silence, then told of Sam's dream to travel to the far-off land of America.

Two girls began to whisper but were hushed by the girls in nearby bunks. The majority of campers wanted to listen, and they were keeping the others in line. Exactly what Kelly hoped would happen.

As she described Sam's struggle to earn enough money to purchase a ticket on one of the huge passenger ships, Kelly lowered her voice. In soothing tones, she listed Sam's jobs. Picking and selling pails of berries. Weeding gardens. Running errands. Performing odd jobs. She stretched each description with as many details as possible.

Stifling a yawn, Kelly paused to see if any of the girls had dropped off yet.

"Why did you stop?" Joyce seemed to have forgotten her dislike of bedtime stories.

Kelly leaned back against the hard frame of her bunk. Her eyes threatened to close, but she pinched herself to stay awake and picked up the tale again. Each time Sam earned enough money to buy a ticket, disaster struck the family. The cow got sick and died. His father needed an operation. A fire burned their home to the ground. With each tragedy, Sam sacrificed his earnings to rescue his family and was forced to begin saving again.

Pausing to listen, Kelly heard deep, even breathing throughout the cabin. Possibly even soft snoring. But two or three voices quietly begged her to continue.

She described Sam losing hope and wandering down to the docks, where a captain asked him why he was so unhappy. Sam recounted his entire life story to the captain. In detail. It was a cruel tactic, but necessary. If this didn't put the girls out, nothing would.

Kelly told of how the captain offered passage to America if Sam would work for him. Sam's job would be to entertain the passengers each day by climbing up the mast onto a narrow ledge, then jumping into a small bucket of water on the deck below. After each leap, the ledge would be raised. But the bucket would remain the same size.

Kelly stopped. Only one voice protested. She felt like cheering. The chance for slumber was in sight.

Kelly returned to Sam's successful show, where he landed every jump in the bucket. Finally, it was the last night before the ship would reach America. Despite the fierce storm that raged, every passenger aboard the ship came to watch Sam's last jump. The ledge was so high it took Sam twenty minutes to climb to the top. Just before he leaped, the ship hit a wave and rocked to the side. Sam slipped off the platform, tumbled through the air, and hit the deck.

A gasp told her one girl was still listening. So she delivered the final line. "But don't worry. By that time, Sam was used to *hard ships*." A small chuckle escaped her lips.

The room buzzed with the heavy breathing of the girls.

"That's it?" the lone camper questioned.

It sounded like Terri. Or Tanya. It was hard to tell the twins apart.

"Yep."

"Hard ships? Like hardships? You mean I stayed awake for that?"

Kelly lay back, pulled her beagle close, and snuggled deep in her sleeping bag. "I said it was an unusual ending. Now, go to sleep."

She pulled the alarm clock from under her pillow and pressed the button to turn on the light. Her heart swelled with pride. The night before, Jill had failed to calm the girls. And she'd been doing just as poorly tonight. But Kelly had marched them all off to dreamland, and she'd done it before midnight. Not bad for an *assistant* counselor during her *first* week of camp.

Kelly's eyes had barely closed when Jill whispered her name.

"Yes?"

"Thank you."

A smile stretched across Kelly's face. "No problem."

"Do you have any other stories?"

"As a matter of fact, I do."

"Could you tell one tomorrow night? Please."

A polite request, not an order. Kelly's triumph was complete. "It would be my pleasure."

The one camper still awake groaned.

14 MONSTERS ARE REAL

Questions about the late-night story started flying even before Kelly set her bowl of cereal on the dining hall table.

"What happened to Sam?"

"Did he survive the fall?"

"Did he ever get to America?"

A broad grin stretched across Kelly's face. If the campers were still talking about the story the next morning, her plan had worked. Even better than she'd hoped.

"At least let me sit down." Kelly took a seat beside Amber and pushed the ever-present romance novel out of the way with her elbow. She was pleased to see the cover was the same one as before, and the bookmark hadn't moved much beyond its previous position. Amber might be carrying the book everywhere, like a security blanket. But at least she wasn't reading it.

From her spot at the far end of the table, Jill flashed Kelly an amused grin. "When the girls woke up and discovered your empty bunk, they wanted to chase after you to get the rest of the story. But then Terri said she'd heard it all, so they surrounded her instead."

So that's who'd managed to remain awake until the end. Kelly glanced toward the ponytail-wearing twins, looking for some small detail that might help her tell them apart.

"They wouldn't let me out of my bunk until I told the ending," Terri complained.

"But the story can't stop there." Emma leaned forward. "Did Sam ever make it to America?"

"It's obvious that he died." Joyce snorted. Blunt as always.

Kelly couldn't resist teasing. "Don't forget, he was used to *hardships.*"

"That ending is so lame." Joyce rolled her eyes.

"I warned everyone before I started that it was an unusual finish." Kelly chose not to remind Joyce that she'd been one of the loudest to complain when Kelly had paused.

"Can you tell it again tonight?" Amber asked.

The other girls jumped in with enthusiastic pleading.

Kelly grinned, pleased that her story would elicit such a response. "How about a new one? Like the tragic tale of Molly the Moth?"

"Only if it has a better ending," Joyce snipped. Most likely to keep up appearances, because the dark-haired brick wall looked just as eager as the rest of the girls.

Kelly shook her head. "The punch line is worse. But that won't matter because none of you will be awake to hear it."

The campers embraced the challenge, vowing to stay alert to the last word. Kelly hoped it wouldn't take too long to drop them off. She'd have to be certain they were all sleeping before she'd be free to join Sheila and Marcie for the avenging heist of Darren's hat. That is, if she managed to get the supplies from Tony today.

Finished with breakfast, the girls started clearing the table. Kelly walked to the front of the hall to dump her untouched soggy cereal in the slop bucket. When she returned, Amber poked her in the arm. "Why is everyone standing around that table?"

Kelly craned her neck to see where Amber was looking. Several tables over, Darren stood in the midst of a crowd of campers, holding a fork and spoon high in the air. With the showmanship of a magician, he wedged the prongs of the fork around the smooth tip of the spoon. Then he stuck a toothpick through the center of the prongs. Moving with slow precision, Darren placed the end of the toothpick on the edge of a glass of water. When he removed his hands, the silver contraption balanced perfectly on the thin wooden stick. Darren's feat earned him a burst of applause from his own campers as well as those at the surrounding tables.

Kelly joined in the applause, even though this wasn't the first time she'd seen the utensil-balancing trick. Her science teacher had done the same gravity-defying demonstration during an introductory lesson on physics.

Amber tilted her head. "Darren is really cute."

So Amber had a camp crush on a counselor. How sweet.

Kelly glanced back at Darren, who'd swept his hat off his head and was bowing to the cheering crowd. He was no Joel. Even Bob was better looking. But Darren did have a few attractive features. Like his warm brown eyes. Almost golden. And his crooked, roguish smile. It was easy to see why Amber would be attracted to him.

Kelly's thoughts were interrupted by a frantic pounding on the table. Jill pointed at the front counter. "Bill's got the first day's scores for the Clean Cabin Contest!"

The campers fell silent. Bill stood at the front of the room next to the huge chart, currently draped in a sheet.

He whipped off the cover, and there was silence for a moment. Then the campers erupted into cheers of joy. Or shouts of protest. Complaints over docked points filled the air.

"We got a perfect score!" Jill screamed. The girls in the cabin celebrated with high fives.

Kelly skimmed the list. "We're in a three-way tie for first place."

Stan jumped to his feet. "Hey, Jill and Amy. Enjoy first place for now. But don't cry when you see us eating the sundaes."

"Your stinky boys will never win," Amy shouted back.

"The inspector will be killed by the stench first," Jill hollered.

So much for friendly competition. And Kelly was willing to bet she was the only person in the room hoping to lose.

Bill waved his hand to dismiss the tables, and the campers headed back to their cabins for morning devotions. Once inside, the girls settled on the carpet and Jill passed out the binders and set of sheets for the next section.

The first page featured a hairy, drooling creature with two heads. Girl and Guy stood off to the side, staring at it with fearful expressions. Kelly frowned at the ominous scene. When it came to spiritual instruction, she was used to happy Sunday school lessons with pictures of Jesus holding a sweet lamb or riding on a gentle donkey. Bill must have grown up in a different kind of church.

Jill pointed to the caption below the drawing and read aloud. "Most people believe monsters exist only in movies or nightmares." She gave a nervous giggle. "You'll probably laugh at me for this, but...I used to have the worst dreams about...rabbits."

Several girls snickered, but Kelly didn't join them. As a child, she'd suffered from frequent nightmares. Maybe not from fuzzy, long-eared critters, but other fearsome beasts that stalked her in the night.

"The dreams were always the same. I'd be in a field with all these cute bunnies, and then they'd grow fangs and attack me." Jill shuddered. "I'd run but could never get away. My mom often found me tangled in the covers, thrashing around on the floor."

Kelly understood. She'd often wake up after a night terror with a pounding heart and soaked in sweat. Though she never fell out of bed.

"I used to dream about evil circus clowns with big red noses," Emma said. "I was so scared of them that whenever a friend had a birthday party, my mom always called ahead to check out the entertainment."

Joyce leaned forward. "When I was six years old, I watched a movie about mutant monkeys and had nightmares every night for two months. My mom had to leave the light on in the hallway so I could fall asleep."

Jill gave an encouraging nod. "The good part about nightmares is that when we wake up, the killer bunnies, scary clowns, and mutant monkeys are gone."

And carnivorous dinosaurs, who were the tormentors in Kelly's dreams, and the reason her father had started telling bedtime stories to help her fall asleep.

Jill tapped the picture in the binder. "But the Two-Headed Monster is a different beast. It's real, and it's dangerous."

"Yeah, right," Joyce scoffed.

Kelly glanced at Jill's face, expecting to find a teasing smile. But Jill's mouth was set in a straight, serious line.

"Not only do two-headed monsters exist, but there is a real possibility that you could become one. Unfortunately for our cardboard couple, they're about to transform into just such a beast. Flip through the next three pages at your own pace."

Kelly considered the first picture. Guy and Girl stood in a relaxed position, connected by a familiar set of green ties. On the following page, the ropes stretched to snake around their bodies. Each successive picture showed the ties wrapping more tightly around the couple, drawing them closer together. By the final picture, the couple was bound so tightly that individual movement was impossible. The expressions on their faces showed pain and misery. Guy and Girl really did look like a two-headed monster. Whoever sketched the pictures had artistic talent. And a great imagination.

Jill waited for the rustling of pages to settle. "This mutation happened when Guy and Girl became obsessed with each other and spent all their time together. Everything and everyone else got squeezed out."

"What's so bad about wanting to be with your boyfriend all the time?" Joyce asked.

"Isn't that the best part of dating?" Emma chimed in.

"It's too much," Jill replied.

Joyce crossed her arms, signaling the return of the brick wall. "That doesn't make any sense."

Kelly didn't show any outward signs of agreement, but she was on Joyce's side. She couldn't imagine ever having too much time with

Aaron or Joel. Although she hadn't been enjoying her time with Aaron as much over the last few weeks. To be honest, it was a relief to have a break from the pressure he kept putting on her to follow his lead. Which meant breaking more rules.

Jill tapped on the picture again. "Look closely. Our couple is so tightly wrapped up they're strangling each other."

The sketch did look more painful than romantic. But surely that wasn't the only option. There should be another picture. One that showed a super close but happy couple. She and Aaron had been inseparable, and she'd been happy. Most of the time. Sure, some friends and church activities had been squeezed out of her life. But she wasn't miserable. Well, not until Aaron dumped her, passed that information on the popular crowd, and she found herself alone without any friends she could turn to for support. Which pretty much proved Jill's point.

Jill flipped to the next page. "In the next section, there's a list of 'too much' mistakes. Let's go around the circle and everyone can read one line." Jill nodded to Nadia on her left.

"Two-headed monster couples spend *too much time together.*"

"The relationship becomes *too serious too fast.*"

"There's *too much touching.*"

"The couple spends *too much time alone.*"

"There's *too much romance* and not enough reality."

"If one person decides to leave, he or she will have to tear away."

Kelly knew how messy that could get. Lucy had been having guy trouble long before she'd started dating Logan. She'd been crazy about a guy from the school's volleyball team. For three months, the two of them were inseparable. Then he said he needed space. Lucy refused to let go. She tried to hang on through constant phone calls, hundreds of text messages, long notes shoved into his locker, talking to his friends, and stalking his every move. He'd managed to tear away from her, but it wasn't easy. And Lucy's heart had been ripped apart in the process. She'd started dating Logan soon after. And even though she'd told Kelly she didn't want to do drugs, she'd given in. Maybe that was why. She hadn't wanted to lose him as well.

Jill flipped to the next page. "Fortunately, there is an easier way to separate. The antidote for *too much* is a healthy dose of *less.* The goal for our couple is *balance.*"

The next few pictures showed Guy and Girl drinking from a vial marked with a huge letter B, then separating back into two people who had ties between them rather than wrapped around them.

Kelly had to admit the sketch with balance looked more inviting than the two-headed monster.

Jill passed out pencils. "Turn to the list of 'New Romantic and Sexy Words.' The word *balance* is already there, so let's put a star beside it."

Kelly drew her star and glanced over the words. If she showed the list to her friends at school, most of them would probably laugh. She wondered if Lucy would react differently.

"Certain couples are more likely to morph into two-headed monsters than others," Jill said. "This last section shows us some early-warning signs."

Kelly stared at the final picture. A scrawny creature sat at a table, holding a fork in one hand and a knife in the other. But the plate in front of the creature was empty, and its face reflected desperation.

"How many of us look like this on the inside?"

Kelly shivered. Bill had drawn a perfect reflection of how she felt in the hidden places of her heart.

"Individuals who are most likely to turn into two-headed monsters are starving. But not for food. They're craving love, acceptance, value, and connection."

Kelly squeezed her eyes shut. She didn't want to talk about hunger, physical or emotional. But she couldn't block out Jill's words.

"When these ravenous people find a romantic connection, they hold on tight, hoping the other person will fill their empty places and satisfy their need for self-worth."

Kelly took a deep breath and opened her eyes. Why was she letting the devotion get to her? She wasn't famished for anything besides food. And that was by choice.

Jill closed her binder. "No other person can meet your deepest needs. Only God can. When He fills your empty spaces, you won't be desperately dependent on a boyfriend or any other person or thing. When God occupies the proper place in your life, then the guy you love can occupy his proper place. And you won't strangle him with your needs."

That wasn't true, at least not for her. For most of Kelly's childhood, she'd tried to serve God. Tried to be the perfect Christian. And she'd been happy. But when she really needed Him, He hadn't been there.

Kelly stared out the window, teeth clenched. She'd never forget the first day of sixth grade. That's when she discovered the popular girls had changed the rules over the summer and decided that cool kids didn't carry backpacks decorated with animals or drink chocolate milk at lunch. And no one had bothered to inform her.

At first, Kelly ignored the taunts. Her cat-adorned backpack had been a special gift from her grandma. And she didn't want to drink anything else for lunch. But the teasing got worse. Kelly prayed every morning and night that God would make the girls stop. Or move away. But nothing changed. After three weeks of constant mockery, she asked her mom for a new backpack. One with the image of a popular boyband. And she switched from chocolate milk to orange juice. Which she hated. The teasing had ended. No thanks to God.

Kelly's shoulders sagged. Those prayers had been her first real attempt to trust Him. The disappointment chipped away at her faith. She continued to pray. But it seemed as if God did the opposite of whatever she asked. She prayed to get the best teacher for math, but got the one she dreaded. She prayed God would help her make the volleyball team, but was cut during the first round of tryouts. And when her grandma caught a life-threatening case of pneumonia,

Kelly had begged God to heal her. And wept at the funeral two months later. So Kelly decided there was no God. Or He didn't care. Either way, there was no point trying to please Him. God had turned His back on her, so she turned her back on Him.

Maybe that was one of the reasons she'd been so thrilled to catch Aaron. Something had finally gone right. And with him by her side, no one could call her a loser again. She'd shown those mean girls. Again, no thanks to God.

The campers bowed their heads as Jill started the closing prayer. Kelly dropped her head as well, trying to not think about what a fraud she was.

"God, please show each of us the empty places in our lives and what we're using to fill them. Help us to look to You instead and allow You to satisfy our hunger and quench our thirst. Amen."

Jill sounded so confident that God was listening. Kelly's stomach twisted with a yearning so intense that it ached.

The girls rushed to clean their assigned sections of the cabin before heading off to the first activity of the day. As Kelly collected the binders, she smiled, trying to look as if everything was normal. But it wasn't. The morning's devotion had been more troubling than the others, and she was angry at herself for letting it get too personal.

When her parents had forced her to come to camp, she'd decided to make a few friends, get a tan, and tune out all the religious stuff. The campfire talks were for the campers, not the counselors. The last thing she wanted to think about was the empty, hungry places in her life.

Jill shouted a final warning and hustled the girls out the door. Kelly finished stacking the devotion books on the shelf. When she reached the door, her hand hovered over the light switch. It would be so easy to leave it on. Lose a point. Knock the cabin out of contention for the ice cream sundaes. Her stomach knotted, and she tried not to think of the eager, hopeful faces of the campers. She concentrated on an image of the sundae, with mounds of rich ice cream, rivers of sweet caramel and generous handfuls of candy toppings. She had no choice. Some form of sabotage had to be done. But not today. The campers knew she'd been the last person in the cabin. The act of treachery would have to wait until she could be sure to escape any blame.

Kelly flicked off the lights and headed toward the maintenance shed. As she approached the brown shack, thoughts of the troubling devotion faded. She may be a spiritual mess, but that wasn't the priority now. Her friends needed supplies. And she still hadn't figured out how to get them.

15 TWO DRAMATIC PERFORMANCES

Kelly hesitated at the door of the maintenance shed, her hand resting on the smooth handle. She'd spent the last five minutes concocting a plan. Not a great one. Not even a good one. But it was all she had. Taking a deep breath, she straightened her back and lifted her chin. Her drama teacher had once said she had a talent for dramatic flair. Time to put that to use.

Kelly turned the knob and strode in just as Tony handed Bob a pair of thick gloves.

"It's dusty in the barn. So wear jeans and a long-sleeve shirt."

The job assignment brought a grin to Kelly's face. Not that she wanted to work in a smelly barn. But at least she'd be close to the vaulting arena, and there might be an opportunity to catch Joel's eye.

Tony turned to Kelly. "I'm sending you back to the craft shack to finish the weeding."

"Seriously?" Kelly groaned. That meant a morning with no hope of seeing Joel. She might as well have been sent into exile.

"Weeding sounds like fun," Bob smirked, his words dripping with sarcasm.

Kelly glared at him. What a chump.

"Careful." Tony leveled his eyes at Bob. "I can find a patch for you, too, if you'd like."

"No, thanks." Bob made a quick exit.

As soon as the door closed, Kelly spun toward Tony. Arms flung wide open, she dropped to her knees. "O Keeper of the Maintenance Shed and Defender of the Weak, I need your help."

Go big or go home. That's what her drama teacher always said.

Tony raised an eyebrow. "Whatever you want, the answer is no."

Clasping her hands together in supplication, Kelly edged closer. "O Keeper of the Maintenance Shed and Defender of the Weak—"

"You've got the wrong shed. Look somewhere else."

Ignoring his gruff tone, Kelly continued in her most pleading voice. "Look upon your loyal servant and show mercy. You alone can help my friends defeat the evil male counselors who would do us harm."

Tony snorted. "I've seen you with a paintbrush—you can defend yourself just fine." His eyes narrowed. "But you mentioned friends. Who else is involved in whatever you're scheming?"

Kelly hesitated. Once she gave names, there'd be no turning back. "Sheila is a damsel in distress."

"And I'm sure her sidekick Marcie is as well."

No sense denying it. "Darren has repeatedly attacked Sheila, though she has done him no wrong. He must be punished. Sheila has a plan..."

"And I want nothing to do with it." Tony moved to step around her.

Kelly threw herself at his feet. "Please, O Keeper of the Maintenance Shed and Defender of the Weak. Without a few critical supplies all will be lost. You're our only hope."

Tony tried to pull his foot out of Kelly's grasp, but she hung on tight.

"I do not want to hear any more." He pronounced each word slowly and deliberately. "Because that would make me an accomplice. The less I know, the better."

Kelly released Tony's foot and looked up. His lips formed a straight line, but there was a gleam in his eye. Like someone who enjoyed being a part of trouble.

Kelly felt a surge of hope. "You'll help us, won't you?"

"If you're caught and tortured, my name is not to be mentioned."

"You have my word." Kelly mimed locking her lips and throwing away the key.

"All right. What do you need?"

Kelly leaped to her feet. As she rattled off the list, Tony moved about the shed, pulling items off shelves and stacking them on one of the work benches.

When he'd finished, Kelly pulled a piece of paper out of her back pocket and bowed low as she presented it to Tony. "Please accept this two-dollar gift certificate for the camp store as a token of our appreciation. May it buy you much chocolate, and may the chocolate bring you happiness and long life."

Tony growled. "That's getting a bit thick." But he took the certificate. After pocketing it, he turned his back and began rearranging paint cans on a shelf. "Now would be a good time for you and all your supplies to disappear."

Kelly snatched the items and was gone in sixty seconds. As she raced back to the cabin, she laughed out loud in triumph. Her lousy plan had worked. She could hardly wait to share the victory with Sheila and Marcie. After hiding the supplies in her locker, she set off for the remaining jungle of weeds by the craft shack.

The morning passed in agony. Her already sore leg muscles cramped every time she changed position. When noon finally rolled around, she kicked the weeds into a pile, surveyed the finished job with a bitter grimace, and struck out for the lodge. She'd barely walked through the doors when someone caught her by the arm. Kelly spun around and looked into the smiling face of a counselor from the adjacent cabin. Hannah, if she remembered correctly, the assistant in the craft shack.

"Everyone's waiting for you at the back table."

Kelly frowned. "Why?"

"We've got it all worked out. And Jill said it was fine with her."

"What are you talking about?"

Hannah motioned for Kelly to follow her. They made their way to the corner of the dining hall, where all the assistant counselors had gathered, chatting and eating lunch. Kelly's eyes fixed on Cindy as she snuggled with Joel at the far end of the table, looking as if she was trying to morph into a Two-Headed Monster. One that Kelly would be happy to rip apart. The Men in Hats sat together on the opposite side. Mike had a pad of paper in front of him and a pen in his hand.

Hannah laughed at Kelly's confused expression. "Jill's been bragging about how you put all the campers to sleep last night with a story. And you did it in record time. The head counselors want each of us to tell the same story to our campers tonight. So we need you to teach it to us."

Everyone at the table gazed expectantly at her. Kelly felt her cheeks grow warm.

"Did you want to grab some lunch first?" Hannah moved around to an open spot on the bench. All the counselors had plates filled with food in front of them.

Kelly shook her head. "I'll get something later." Or not.

Darren leaped up and pulled a chair out for her. So he could be a gentleman–when he wasn't messing up Sheila's hair. Kelly perched on the edge of her seat, feeling awkward at the head of the table.

Taking a deep and shaky breath, Kelly gathered her thoughts. "'Hardships is a bedtime story my dad used to tell me. He was a master at using details to drag out a story, and he always spoke in a low, soothing tone. I was hardly ever able to stay awake till the end."

Mike scribbled frantically as she talked.

Darren peered over Mike's shoulder. "Why are you taking notes?"

"I've never told a bedtime story before. I don't want to mess it up."

Darren tapped on the page. "How are you going to read the notes in the dark?"

"With a flashlight."

Darren hesitated for a moment, then reached for a pencil in the middle of the table. "Can you pass me a few sheets?"

A few other counselors also asked for paper. As Kelly waited for them to get ready, her eyes locked with Joel's. She held his gaze and sent him a bold smile. She had Joel's full attention. And she meant to make the most of it.

Launching into the story, Kelly breathed as much energy and creativity into her performance as possible. When she finished, the counselors burst into applause. Kelly rose and bowed.

"That's the dumbest story I've ever heard."

Kelly glanced up in surprise, unprepared for Cindy's sudden attack.

"If I tell a story with such a lame ending, my campers will think I'm an idiot." Cindy's eyes spat fire.

Kelly clenched her jaw. "If you tell it right, they won't be awake to hear the last line."

"No matter how it's told, it's still stupid."

"No, it's not!" Darren waved his hand in protest. "Puns are an advanced form of humor." He pushed his page to the center of the table and drew a large triangle at the bottom of his notes. "My math teacher is always saying that without geometry, life is *pointless.*"

While everyone at the table groaned, Kelly sent Darren a warm smile, grateful for his defense.

Mike drew an oval on his page. "And a boiled egg is hard to *beat.*"

After a quick high five, Darren nudged Mike. "Did you know that the horses at Timberlake Camp are happy?"

"Why is that?"

Darren grinned. "They all have *stable* environments."

Mike opened his mouth, but Cindy cut him off. "I still think it's a lame ending." Her mouth was set in a thin, tight line.

"Do you know any more stories like that?"

Joel's question caught Kelly off guard. She turned to him, and the look of admiration on his face sent a thrill coursing through her. But she wasn't the only one watching Joel's face. Suddenly, Cindy's anger made sense.

Her heart pounding, Kelly nodded to Joel. "Tonight I'm going to tell the tragic tale of Molly the Moth. It's a love story."

Joel flashed a heart-stopping grin. "I'd like to hear it."

"I'd like to tell it to you." Kelly gave him a playful smile.

Someone else asked a question, but Kelly pretended not to hear. She had more important things to do. Like flirt with Joel, right in front of his pouting girlfriend.

A metallic pounding from the front of the dining hall shattered the moment. Kelly twisted around in her seat as Bill gave a final bang with the serving spoon. "Clean your tables. Afternoon activities start in fifteen minutes."

Kelly's stomach growled, protesting the lack of lunch. And breakfast. And dinner the day before. But she ignored the rumbles, along with the lightheaded and dizzy feelings that hit her as soon as she stood up.

The assistant counselors surrounded Kelly to express their thanks. As they moved off to join their campers, Kelly looked for Joel, hopeful to continue their conversation. But Cindy had maneuvered him off to the side.

"Brilliant job." Mike tipped his hat to Kelly.

Darren tucked his notes under his arm and bowed low. "I loved the ending."

Of course he would, being a master of the pun himself.

Bob hung back until the Men in Hats had moved on. "Couldn't keep your eyes off him, could you?"

Kelly's back stiffened. "I don't know what you're talking about."

"You'll never get him. Cindy's got her claws in too deep."

Kelly cast a quick look at the golden couple, still locked in a private conversation. Kelly felt a flicker of doubt as she watched Cindy place a possessive hand on Joel's arm, pulling him close to whisper in his ear. Maybe she'd only imagined Joel's interest in her after the story. But she didn't imagine the light kiss he planted on Cindy's cheek.

Bob gave her a nasty smile. "You've got no hope against a hot babe like Cindy."

Which is exactly what Kelly feared. She spun around and walked away, with Bob's taunting laughter ringing in her ears.

As she headed out of the lodge, Sheila and Marcie raced to catch her. Marcie rubbed her hands on the front of her apron and kept glancing behind, as if she'd just escaped from the clutches of a predator. Or a tyrant kitchen manager.

"Did you get everything we need?" Sheila's eyebrows rose in an anxious arc.

"You doubt me?" Kelly sniffed, acting insulted. "I got it all. No problem."

Sheila punched the air, her eyes alight with excitement.

Marcie twitched her nose like a curious rabbit. "Why were all the assistant counselors listening to you at lunch?"

Kelly had a sudden vision of Cindy's face, flushed red with raw jealousy. She knew she hadn't imagined that. A feeling of hope surged within her, and she burst out laughing. "I was just stirring up trouble."

Sheila nodded her approval. "Excellent. And we'll stir up even more tonight."

16 A MESSY TUG-OF-WAR

Kelly's fingers curled around a weed, but she paused before yanking it out. She closed her eyes to focus on the thoughts swirling in her mind. Joel liked the story. She was sure of it. And he liked her too. She'd seen the expression on his face as he listened. Focused, intent, and approving. More important, she'd seen the look on Cindy's face. Fuming and jealous, which meant she was scared. And that was a good sign.

"Are you sure you're strong enough to pull out that thistle?"

Kelly's eyes snapped open and she glared at Bob. She didn't mind so much that Tony had sent her to weed around the flowerbeds at the front entrance of the camp. But did he have to assign Bob to the same task? She had better things to do than listen to his taunts. Like daydream about Joel.

Kelly plucked a thorny nettle and threw it into her overflowing garbage bag. Then she moved a few feet over and turned her back on Bob. Partly because that patch of weeds needed a lot of work. But mostly because she knew that being ignored would irritate him.

Something soft hit her on the back of the head.

"Hey!" She pulled a prickly thistle out of her hair.

Bob looked her up and down. "That weed could push you over. You're the skinniest girl at camp."

Kelly beamed. Not that she cared about Bob's opinion. But if he'd noticed how thin she was, maybe others had too. Like Joel.

Bob's brow furrowed, and she almost laughed at his confused expression. He had no way of knowing she'd interpreted his insult as high praise.

"You're so skinny that if you turned sideways, you'd disappear. And Joel wouldn't be able to find you. Even if he was looking."

The weed she hurled hit him full in the face.

Bob wiped the dirt from his eyes. "You're going to pay for that." He reached into his bulging sack, pulled out a handful of thistles, and launched the green mass at Kelly. She ducked and flung a thorny shrub at his head, snickering as the dangling roots showered him with soil. The barrage of weeds continued until their bags were empty. Bob jumped into the middle of the flowerbed and yanked out a fistful of daisies.

"Those aren't weeds!" roared an angry voice.

Kelly turned and saw Tony lumbering toward them. His timing couldn't have been more perfect. Bob dropped the yellow-and-white blooms.

"I sent you to pull weeds, not flowers," Tony thundered. "Now, clean up this mess."

Kelly bent over and raked the ground with her fingers, stuffing the thistles and roots back into her garbage bag. Tony folded his arms and watched as Bob did the same. When the ground had been cleared, Tony pointed at Kelly. "Leave your bag and head down to supper."

Kelly dropped her bag and turned toward the road. Bob heaved his bag beside Kelly's and moved to join her.

Tony held up his hand. "You're not finished yet, Bob."

"Why does Kelly get to go and I don't?"

"I didn't catch her ripping up flowers."

"But that's not fair," Bob protested.

"Take both bags and dump them behind the maintenance shed in the yard waste bin."

Kelly caught Bob's eye. "I win," she mouthed.

Scowling, Bob picked up the bags and shook them menacingly in her direction. Kelly gave an innocent smile. Just to irritate him further.

As Kelly made her way down the road, she overheard snatches of Tony's lecture to Bob on how to be a proper gentleman, all the more funny coming from a gruff and grumpy grizzly. She covered her mouth to stifle the giggles.

When she neared the cabins, Kelly ducked into the bathroom to comb the dirt and leaves out of her hair. Once she was satisfied with her appearance, she hurried to the lodge, hoping to run into Joel. She'd barely stepped foot inside the room when MaryAnn intercepted her.

"I'd like to chat with you for a moment."

Kelly stiffened. Had Tony snitched about the paint fight with Bob? Or ratted on the supplies for the prank? With feet dragging, Kelly followed MaryAnn to a quiet corner.

"When your mother signed you up for camp, she told me about some of the struggles you've been facing."

Kelly clenched her jaw. She should have known her mom would blab all her private business.

"I'm concerned about how little you're eating."

"I'm fine," Kelly murmured through tight lips.

MaryAnn fixed her with a penetrating stare. "I know you skipped lunch yesterday, as well as breakfast this morning and lunch again this afternoon."

Who was the tattletale? Probably Sandy. Maybe Jill. "I didn't make it to lunch yesterday because I was covered in paint and it took forever to wash off. This morning, the campers asked a lot of questions about a story I told last night. During lunch, the assistant counselors asked me to tell them the same story. I just didn't have time to eat."

MaryAnn's steady gaze never left Kelly's face. "Bill tells me he sees you jogging on the road every morning."

That solved the mystery of the figure she'd seen in the distance. "He must really love hiking to get up so early."

"He likes to walk while he's praying for the campers and staff members."

Prayer. What a waste of time.

"Kelly, do you often feel cold? Or tired and weak? Had any fainting spells? Headaches? Trouble sleeping?"

Kelly looked at her hands. She'd experienced each of those issues almost every day for the last year. "I feel the same as always."

"Are you able to concentrate? Think clearly? Do you experience mood swings? Have feelings of failure or depression when you eat?"

Kelly flinched. The symptoms MaryAnn listed were classic signs of anorexia. Having been through this with her mom, doctor, and counselor, she knew it would be wise to admit to one or two symptoms, just to satisfy MaryAnn's suspicions.

"The cabin does get a little cold at night. I was thinking of asking for a blanket. Jill sleeps with an extra one on her bunk."

"I have several thick quilts. I'd be happy to loan you one for the week."

"That'd be great. I'm also having a little trouble sleeping, but that's because the girls in the cabin make a lot of noise. When I told them a long story last night, they fell asleep a lot faster." Kelly hoped her smile was reassuring.

Doubt etched MaryAnn's face. After an awkward pause, she inhaled deeply. "Please let me know if you experience any of the other symptoms."

"I will." Even though that was never going to happen.

A grin lit up MaryAnn's face. "I heard about your story. It sounds fabulous."

"Thanks."

"I've been watching, and you're doing a great job with the campers."

The compliment swirled around Kelly like a warm breeze.

"I noticed you've befriended Amber. I was worried about her because this is her first time at camp and she's extremely shy. I thought she might hide behind a book for the entire week, but you've drawn her out."

Kelly glowed under the praise.

MaryAnn motioned to the food line. "I'll let you join your cabinmates. But please make sure you take a healthy portion for supper. Maintenance work takes a lot of energy. So does fighting with your work partner. Although I heard you got the better of him." MaryAnn winked.

News sure traveled fast at camp. Kelly's lips curved into a wide grin. "He deserved it."

"I'm sure he did."

They shared a chuckle, then Kelly turned to join the serving line.

"By the way..."

Kelly froze. She'd gotten off too easy. MaryAnn would no doubt ask her to drop the morning jogs. Or announce that she'd be monitoring every plateful.

"Don't be surprised if I pop into your cabin one of these nights. I love a good story."

Relief flowed through Kelly's body. She'd escaped any consequences. For now. "I have enough stories to last the whole week. Drop in anytime." Just please not tonight. Or she'd never be able to sneak out to help Sheila and Marcie with the prank. Which might be a good thing.

Kelly glanced at her campers, already seated and eating. Hoping that MaryAnn and Sandy were watching, she hurried to the front counter, grabbed a plate, and loaded it with three slices of pizza, a generous portion of salad, and two massive chocolate-chip cookies. That should satisfy any prying eyes.

As Kelly approached the table, Amber motioned to her, then slid her book to the side to make room. Same steamy novel, but the bookmark hadn't made much forward progress.

Kelly smiled. "How was your afternoon?"

"I had archery." Amber sighed. "I'm hopeless. I shot at least a hundred arrows and not one even came close to the target. How about you?"

"Bob threw weeds at me." Kelly echoed her sigh. "But I threw more back."

Kelly pushed the salad around her plate with a fork and took a few bites. Just in case someone was spying on her. When MaryAnn strolled by at the end of supper, Kelly's plate was clean. But only because she'd slipped the pizza and cookies to the campers who'd wanted seconds.

Kelly felt too tired to participate in the evening games, so she and Amber returned to the cabin to hang out. A few other girls joined them, working on colorful friendship bracelets, the latest project from the Craft Shack. Kelly spent the next hour chatting with the girls as she helped to untangle knotted threads.

When it was time to leave for the evening campfire, Amber approached the door, the ever-present romance novel tucked under her arm.

"Hey, Amber, why don't you leave the book behind this time?" Kelly suggested. She didn't really expect the Amber to listen, but it was worth a try.

The girl's grip on the book tightened and she hesitated, chewing on her bottom lip. Then, without argument or protest, she walked to the back of the cabin and slipped the book into her suitcase. Kelly worked hard to hide her astonishment.

As they made their way to the campfire area, Kelly snuck a few sidelong looks at Amber. She fidgeted with her sleeve, as if she didn't know what to do with her empty hands, most likely the natural result of giving up a security blanket she'd probably carried for a long time.

Kelly felt proud of Amber's choice. Not that she had anything against comforting items. She had her stuffed beagle, after all. But if Bill's talks about love were true, any lessons found in Amber's books were seriously flawed and worth dumping.

As they approached the benches, Kelly saw yellow and orange flames dancing in the fire pit. What a relief. She didn't feel like going on another hike.

Amber poked Kelly and pointed to a large, circular mound on the ground in front of the fire, covered with a large tarp. "Wonder what that is."

Kelly shrugged. "Knowing Bill, it could be anything."

"Maybe it's something to eat, like a giant cherry pie." Amber rubbed her hands together.

"Under a tarp?" Kelly wrinkled her nose. "I bet it's something for tonight's lesson. Girl and Guy should be afraid. Very afraid."

Once everyone arrived, Stan and Amy stepped to the front to lead the singing. When the last note faded, Bill strode forward, carrying a thick coil of rope on his shoulder.

"The tug-of-war is the ultimate test of strength." Bill grabbed a corner of the tarp and whipped it off, revealing a large wading pool full of mud. The campers cheered wildly, and Bill had to shout to be heard over the thunder of clapping hands. "Tonight we're going to have a competition between male and female counselors. Any volunteers?"

Kelly wrapped her fingers around the bench. No way was she going anywhere near that muck. Normally, her competitive spirit would have pushed her to the front. But brute strength wasn't her thing. Neither was a mud bath.

Kelly leaned toward Amber without relaxing her tight grip. "I can't imagine anyone being crazy enough to volunteer."

"Men in Hats rule!"

Darren leaped over, around, and between the campers as he made his way to the front. Mike, Charlie, and Zach followed close behind.

Kelly gave a snort. "Okay, I can't imagine any girl counselors being crazy enough to volunteer."

Amber giggled.

As the four guys assembled at the front, Kelly shook her head. The female team was going swimming in the muck. Guaranteed.

Bill directed the Men in Hats to one side of the mud pit. "We've got our crew of guys. Now we need some ladies to challenge them."

Kelly had already been covered in paint and weeds this week. She didn't need to add mud to the list. Especially not with Joel in the audience.

The campers shouted names, pushing various counselors forward. Kelly resisted the temptation to yell Cindy's name. It would be a pleasure to see her covered in thick sludge. But calling out might draw attention to herself. And thus far, she had escaped notice.

Jill jumped to her feet and strode to the opposite side of the pool, receiving a roar of support from the female campers.

Amber gasped. "She'd better not track any mud into the cabin. She'll be in big trouble if we lose points in the Clean Cabin contest."

Kelly switched her allegiance in an instant. She'd be cheering for the guys to pull the girls to a messy loss, which would save her the effort, and guilt, of sabotaging her cabin.

Campers shoved Amy, Hannah and Cindy forward. Kelly relaxed her grip on the bench. She was safe. Her cabin might lose the sundaes. And Cindy was going to get filthy. This was turning out be a great evening.

"Choose your spots and wait for my signal," Bill instructed.

Darren took the anchor position at the back, wrapping the end of the rope around his waist. The girls huddled for a moment. Then Jill called to the guys, "How about making this fair and giving us an extra team member?"

The campers shouted their approval. It was a wise move on the girls' part, although unlikely to make a difference. It would take more than one player to give them a fighting chance.

Darren held up his hands for silence. "Go ahead. The Men in Hats will still win."

Jill pointed at Kelly and beckoned her forward. Shaking her head, Kelly stayed in her seat. But the nearby campers shoved her to the front.

Not everyone seemed pleased with Jill's selection. Cries of "She won't make a difference' and "You should pick someone bigger" rang out. Kelly's cheeks grew hot. She might not be the biggest member of the tug-of-war team, but she wasn't a wimp.

As the girls took their positions, the Men in Hats flexed and struck classic body-builder poses. Tall and skinny, Mike was the furthest thing from a muscle-bound strongman. He looked ridiculous, but Kelly wasn't in the mood to laugh. Not when she was about to take a bath in a mud pit.

Kelly stepped behind Jill and pinched her arm. "Why did you pick me?"

"You're my assistant."

"I'm asking for a transfer."

Jill laughed as she picked up the rope. Kelly grabbed hold, debating whether she should leap out of the way at the last minute or allow herself to be coated in mud so she could ensure a mess in the cabin. She searched the crowd for Joel's handsome face, and found his eyes focused on her. That settled it. She'd be staying clean. No matter what.

Bill pointed to the guys' heads. "Do you want to remove the hats...just in case?"

Mike ran his hand along the brim. "Impossible. We can't take them off."

Kelly frowned. Why not? Had they glued the dumb things on? That would complicate Sheila's plans for the theft.

"Suit yourselves." Bill raised his arm. "On your mark, get set, go!"

Instantly, the girls were dragged forward. The outnumbered guys had no trouble pulling their squealing opponents toward the deep circle of sludge. But just when it looked as if the girls were going to be hauled in, and Kelly was about to leap to safety, she saw Bill wink. Darren dropped the rope and stepped to the side.

A startled gasp rose from the campers. The male cries of 'foul' were drowned by the frenzied screams of the female campers. The female counsellors felt the shift in power, and pulled with new energy.

With the odds now five against three, the girls managed to drag the guys back over the ground they'd gained. And right into the pool of brown muck.

Chaos erupted. The girls' team jumped up and down in victory. The campers hollered and jeered. And Bill couldn't stop laughing.

Darren approached his teammates as they struggled to climb out of the slippery mud bath. "Sorry, but I had to let go. The Men in Hats are gentlemen. It would have been wrong to pull the girls into that slime." He extended his hand to Mike.

From the shocked expressions on the faces of the other Men in Hats, Kelly guessed they hadn't been in on the plan.

Mike, completely caked in mud, grabbed Darren's hand. "I understand."

The moment of maturity shocked Kelly. Maybe she'd misread Mike.

Then, without warning, Mike pulled Darren into the pool.

Kelly grinned. She'd read him right after all.

Mike and his teammates wrestled with Darren, knocking off his hat, which hadn't been glued after all. Mud splattered everyone standing nearby. Kelly ducked but it was impossible to avoid the flying muck. She was splattered with brown spots.

The campers shouted with laughter. But one voice seemed sharper than the others. Turning, Kelly looked straight into Cindy's eyes, gleaming with delight as she sneered at Kelly's dripping face. The picture-perfect model had kept clean by hiding behind Jill.

Kelly scanned the crowd, her eyes darting back and forth as she searched for Joel's blond hair. She spotted him in the back, his head thrown back in laughter. But at who? The Men in Hats? Or her? Impossible to tell.

Still chuckling, Bill approached the guys. "Come on out, Gentlemen in Hats. Clean up as best you can." He tossed a towel to each of the guys. "You can shower after the campfire. But Tony won't be happy if the drains get plugged, so jump in the lake first."

When a number of campers shouted their intentions to join the late-night swim, Bill held up his hand. "*Only* the Men in Mud will be jumping in the lake. If the rest of you want to get wet, take a shower."

Bill tossed a few towels to the girls, and they wiped the dark clay off their faces and arms. Kelly's mind raced as she watched the Men in Hats shake the mud off their hats. Surely they'd leave their precious headgear on the shore when they jumped in the lake. Maybe they could swipe the hat then and stash it in a nearby bush.

Kelly searched the crowd and made eye contact with Sheila. She raised her eyebrows, inclined her head toward the lake, and pretended to adjust an invisible hat. Sheila's forehead creased in a deep frown, and she mouthed the word *no.*

Kelly held back a groan. It would have been worth a try. Unless Sheila was looking forward to the midnight canoe ride.

As Kelly and the others returned to their seats, the campers parted to give the still-muddy counselors plenty of room.

Bill brought Girl and Guy forward and reconnected the green ties between the cardboard figures. "Many dating relationships are a lot like the tug-of-war we just witnessed. Girl and Guy form opposing teams, in constant conflict over every decision. What movie should they watch? What music should they listen to? Where should they go to eat?"

Bill motioned for Tony to come forward. They each picked up a figure and carried it to the pool of mud, propping Girl on one side and Guy on the other, with the ties stretched taut between them.

"Dating isn't supposed to be competitive, combative, or messy. Every discussion shouldn't turn into a stubborn struggle for victory. In fact, there shouldn't even be winning or losing."

Kelly's mind flashed back to an action flick she and Aaron had gone to see with Annalisa and her then-boyfriend, Gary. There had been more fighting off screen between Annalisa and her guy than in the movie.

"It's not hard to understand why these battles happen. Most of us have strong opinions, and we believe that our opinions are right. Some of the issues that cause disagreements are serious, but others are simply ridiculous."

Bill had that right. Annalisa and Gary had argued about which movie to see and who should pay. Then they'd debated over which snacks to buy. When they finally decided on a medium-sized bag of popcorn, they battled over who should hold the bag. A decision about where to sit in the theatre followed that. And when the movie started, they quarreled about which actors or actresses were better. They didn't stop until Kelly threw popcorn at them and threatened to move to a different row. When they walked out of the theatre, Annalisa called the evening a disaster. Gary didn't argue. It was the only thing they'd agreed on all evening.

Bill gestured to the cardboard couple. "It's impossible for Guy and Girl to have the same opinion on everything. Guy might want his pizza covered in mushrooms while Girl may believe that edible fungal growths belong on the ground."

Mike snorted. "I'm with Guy. No stinking mushrooms for me."

"Too bad." Darren shook his head. "I always thought you were such a *fun-gi*."

Fun guy. A low rumble rose from the benches as the campers groaned.

"No mushrooms for me either." Amber clutched her throat and made gagging noises.

"I'll skip them too," Kelly agreed. And the whole greasy pizza, for that matter.

"There's nothing wrong in disagreeing with the opinion of another person. The real issue is how we disagree." Bill paused to allow his words to sink in. "Girl and Guy don't need to cut their ties just because they can't agree about mushrooms. If our couple can compromise, chances are excellent that their relationship will survive and even thrive."

Bill turned to Tony, who was standing beside Girl. "Tony, what does compromise mean?"

The maintenance director pulled a piece of paper out of his back pocket. "*Compromise* is 'a settlement of differences in which each side agrees to make concessions.' *Standard Heritage Dictionary*, page one hundred eighty-nine."

A book that Tony should use more often. Or at least some form of spell check.

Kelly smiled. Bill had finally picked a topic where she could shine. She didn't argue with Aaron. She just let him make all the decisions. It kept him happy. And as long as Aaron was happy, he'd stay with her. It was a great strategy. Except when he wanted to take the car, and she wanted to say no.

Bill unrolled a clean white tarp. He motioned for Tony to grab the other end, and they pulled it across the mud pool. A large piece of paper with the word compromise had been duct-taped to the top.

"Compromise makes it safe to disagree. And the correct way to disagree is through a mature and respectful discussion. Perhaps Guy will let Girl pick the movie. Or Girl will let Guy choose the radio station. Or Girl will let Guy decide where they eat supper. Or Guy will ask for mushrooms on the side, even though he prefers them baked into the cheese. If they can't reach a decision, they can always flip a coin."

The campers laughed. But Kelly wished Annalisa and Gary had thought of that. A coin toss would have been much better than stretching the popcorn bag between them until it ripped and fluffy white kernels spilled everywhere. Followed by angry words and name-calling.

"Once a decision is made, both people honor it. *Compromise* is critical to a safe and successful relationship. It deserves a place on our list of New Romantic and Sexy Words."

Tony brought the chart to the front and added the word. Kelly wondered how he'd found the term in the dictionary when he clearly couldn't spell it.

"Of course, it's one thing to compromise in areas of preference, like toppings on pizza. But no one should ever sacrifice morals, values, or faith. We'll save that discussion for a later time. When I have a donkey."

Another farm animal? Still, it sounded safer than a pool of mud.

Amber sniffed. "He'd better not hog-tie it, like that poor calf."

"I'd like to see him try." Kelly smiled, but Bill's words rang in her head. Never compromise when it comes to morals, values, or faith? That's what she'd done. And it hadn't turned out so well. She'd lost her guy.

"Tug-of-war relationships rarely succeed. That's because the focus is on winning, not sharing."

Annalisa and Gary never made it to a second movie, and their relationship didn't last much longer than a week.

Bill picked up Guy and walked around the mud pool to place him beside Girl. "Rather than pushing against each other, our couple should be pulling together."

Tony stepped behind the fire pit and returned, pulling a little red wagon with the words "Difficulties and Dreams" painted on the side.

Kelly joined the campers in a chuckle. A big bear of a man like Tony looked ridiculous pulling a toy wagon. But the metal cart probably wasn't his. The printing on the side was far too neat, and there weren't any spelling mistakes.

Tony positioned the wagon behind Girl and Guy. Bill reached into his back pocket and pulled out a short length of rope. He looped it through the wagon handle and attached it to the ties between Guy and Girl.

"Life is not easy."

No argument there. Kelly felt weighed down by homework, grades, college choices, parental pressure, expectations, friends, sports, clubs...not to mention romantic relationships. And she knew her friends felt the same.

Tony reached around the pool and strained to lift a massive canvas bag, which he dropped in the back of the wagon. From the clashing sounds, Kelly guessed it was filled with rocks.

"During challenging situations, Guy and Girl can pull together and share the load. If one grows weak, the other will keep him or her from falling or giving up."

Tony strained to lift another huge sack, which he also dropped in the wagon.

"Pursuing dreams is also a heavy, uphill climb. Guy and Girl can pull together and help each other accomplish their goals."

Kelly closed her eyes and tried to imagine Aaron pulling a heavy wagon with her. She couldn't. She did most of his work in drama, cheered for him at every basketball game, and arranged her plans to suit him. She couldn't think of any times when he'd helped her pull toward any of her goals.

Logan had sure pulled Lucy though. To a place where she didn't want to go. And when things didn't turn out the way he liked, he dumped her and walked away.

But as tempting as it was to shine the brightest spotlight on Logan's faults, Kelly knew that wasn't fair. Aaron said he loved her. But he'd been willing to risk getting her in trouble with her parents and even the law just so he could get what he wanted. That didn't sound like love, and she couldn't keep making excuses for his selfish behavior.

Bill slipped his arm around Guy and Girl. "When two individuals combine their strength and pull as a team, they can climb mountains." He rapped on the side of the heavy-laden wagon. "When we respectfully compromise with preferences, but hold fast to our beliefs, values, and faith, both partners win. And no one is covered in mud."

Bill stared at the Men in Hats. "Speaking of being covered in mud..." He pointed to the lake.

Darren, Mike, Charlie, and Zach let out a whoop and raced one another to the water. The campers jumped to their feet, cheering them on. The Men in Hats ran down the length of the dock and leaped off the end, hats and all. Which left no chance to snatch the ugly headgear from the beach.

Seconds later, the four friends scrambled back on to the wooden planks, shouting about the freezing-cold water. They stood dripping on the dock, wringing water from their soggy hats before jamming them back onto their heads. Kelly hoped Darren's hat liked the lake because it would be visiting it again soon. This time for an extended stay.

With the fun over, Bill dismissed the campers to head back to their cabins. Kelly stretched and yawned. It had been a long evening. And she still had a bedtime story to tell and a prank to pull before she'd be free to go to sleep.

As campers scampered over and around the benches, Sheila brushed against her. "Meet at the maintenance shed at eleven."

Kelly nodded. That should give her enough time to tell the story.

"We're going to squash Darren like a bug." Sheila's eyes glowed in the firelight. Then she disappeared into the crowd.

Kelly let out a long, deep sigh. Sheila had it wrong. This had nothing to do with swatting one annoying pest. They were about to poke a hornet's nest.

17 THE PERFECT PRANK

"Before I start tonight's story, we need to set some ground rules." Kelly stood in her pajamas with one hand on the light switch. "No flashlights. No sitting up or moving around. And no asking questions."

"I'm not going to fall asleep this time." Joyce punched her pillow several times before twisting and flopping backward. "Not that it's worth staying up for. I just want to prove that I can do it."

Of course. Joyce would never admit to enjoying anything at camp.

"I'm staying up too." Emma crawled into her sleeping bag and lay back, folding her arms behind her head.

As the other campers settled into their bunks, they declared their plans to remain awake as well.

"Good luck." Kelly winked at eight determined faces before flicking off the lights.

After picking her way through the darkness to her bunk, Kelly settled in a comfortable position and wrapped herself in the thick quilt she'd found lying on her sleeping bag. She sent a mental thank-you to MaryAnn.

Tonight's tale was one of her favorites, with endless possibilities for adding details. The odds for victory were on her side. "There once was a moth named Molly. She lived in Mothland, which is..."

An hour and fifteen minutes later, Kelly finished the story. The soft hum of steady breathing assured her that not one girl in the cabin was awake. Not even Jill.

Stifling a yawn, Kelly pulled a T-shirt and sweatpants over her pajamas, then slipped into her flip-flops. After removing the bag of gear from her locker, she tucked it under her arm and tiptoed to the door. It creaked as she opened it. Kelly froze and held her breath, but no one stirred. She stepped into the chilly night air and gently closed the door behind her.

As she stood on the veranda, allowing her eyes to adjust to the darkness, Kelly shivered. Behind her was the warm, safe cabin. Ahead was a flaw-filled prank that required breaking several major camp rules and risked severe punishment if caught. Which was likely. Kelly took a deep breath and stepped off the porch. It felt like an act of sheer madness. She hoped she wouldn't regret it.

Kelly slipped past the other cabins, keeping to the shadows. She'd heard rumors that the camp was patrolled at night by Bill and Tony. At any moment, she expected one of them to jump out and grab her. But as she crept along without meeting anyone, she gained confidence and picked up her pace.

A few feet from the maintenance shed, Kelly paused. A dim light above the front door cast a faint glow, but she couldn't see anyone. Had Marcie and Sheila gotten tired of waiting and gone back to bed? Or already been caught?

She snuck around the back. Two familiar figures huddled by the wall. A wave of relief rolled over her.

"Hey," she whispered.

Both girls jumped. Marcie let out a shriek and switched on a flashlight, shooting the beam directly into Kelly's face.

"Don't blind me!" Kelly shielded her eyes with her arm.

"Sorry." Marcie pointed the flashlight to the ground.

"Where have you been?" Sheila hissed. "We've been waiting forever."

"I had to put the entire cabin to sleep," Kelly replied in a hushed voice. "My story did the trick. Not one of them heard the ending!"

"Who cares? You made me spill my Coke." Sheila held up a shiny can. "Did you bring everything we need?"

Kelly raised the bag. Sheila snatched it, then motioned for Marcie to shine the light inside. After she'd rifled through the contents, Sheila let out a long, relieved breath. "Darren is going down!" She punched the air in triumph. "Or at least, his hat is going down...to the bottom of a cold, dark lake!"

Kelly stared at their empty hands. "Where's the hat?"

"We hid it." Sheila pointed to the bushes. "In case we got caught."

Marcie disappeared into the shrubs. A few minutes later, she emerged holding the hat high.

After a quick check to make sure the road was clear, they struck out for the lake. Except for the crunch of footsteps, the girls walked in silence until they'd left the cabins behind. As they neared the lodge, Kelly's curiosity overcame the need for stealth. "How did you get the hat?"

Sheila's steps took on a swagger. "Marcie has a friend whose little brother is in Mike's cabin. He lives on sugar, and he's been going through serious withdrawal at camp." She sighed. "It's sad, really. He should get help for his addiction."

Kelly glanced at the can of soda in Sheila's hand. And Sheila should listen to her own advice.

Marcie sniffed. "By exploiting the poor boy's weakness, we convinced him to sneak into Darren's cabin and grab the hat while the guys were showering."

Sheila waved the hat in the air like prized plunder. "When he delivered it to me, I slipped him a huge bag filled with candy we snitched from the Super Sundae supplies."

Kelly raised an eyebrow. It sounded too easy. "Aren't you afraid this kid will turn traitor?"

Sheila shook her head. "We told him that if he rats us out, the guys might reward him. But then they'll punish him for stealing the hat in the first place."

"We also promised a steady supply of sugary treats for the rest of the week if he keeps his mouth shut."

Kelly laughed. "That's perfect." She felt her confidence growing. The crazy plan just might work.

"It's *hefty.*" Marcie gave a pleased smile.

Kelly tugged on Sheila's sleeve. "Translation, please?"

She rolled her eyes. "It's her latest attempt to create a famous buzzword."

"This one's logical." Marcie sniffed. "Cool became phat. And hefty's another word for fat. Get it?"

Kelly swallowed her laughter. "I don't think it's going to catch on."

Sheila poked Kelly in the arm. "Why were all the assistant counselors gathered around you at lunch today?"

As Kelly told of the success of her bedtime story, she couldn't resist gloating over Joel's interest and Cindy's jealousy. "I've never seen her face so red!"

"What a little snot," Sheila spat out. "Cindy can't stand it if all the attention isn't focused on her. Especially Joel's attention."

"I'm glad you flirted with him." Marcie giggled. "It serves her right!"

"I don't know what he sees in her," Sheila murmured. "I wish he'd dump her. If he ever does, I'll be—"

"We're here." Marcie pointed forward.

Kelly wondered what Sheila had been about to say. But there was no chance to ask. Sheila had already rushed ahead.

No lights illuminated the lakefront, but a bright moon reflected off the water, bathing the dock and buildings in a soft glow. Kelly saw the outline of the canoes, pulled in far from the shore and stacked across several logs.

"I'll get paddles and lifejackets." Sheila yanked open the door to the boathouse and ducked inside.

"Don't they lock things up around here?" Kelly asked.

"There's no need." Sheila's voice sounded hollow from deep within the building. "Who would be crazy enough to take a canoe out in the middle of the night?"

The girls stifled their giggles.

Motioning for Kelly to follow, Marcie grabbed the end of the nearest canoe and rolled it over. Kelly gripped the other end and stumbled under the weight as they carried it to the dock. Sheila set the life jackets and paddles off to the side.

Marcie knelt on the wooden planks and pulled out several large zip-lock bags from her pocket.

"Another *donation* from the kitchen?" Kelly asked.

Marcie shrugged. "You could say that."

"I had no idea Lady Katherine was so generous."

"She's not. We asked Sandy."

Marcie squashed the hat, stuffed it into one of the plastic bags, smoothed out the air, and sealed it. She shoved that bag inside another one. After sealing it too, she grabbed a third and repeated the process.

Kelly raised an eyebrow. "Are you absolutely sure that's going to keep it dry?" The hat was cheap and ugly, but she didn't want it to get ruined.

Marcie adjusted her glasses. "I've run several controlled experiments in the kitchen sink. After a test period of twelve hours, the seals on the bags remained airtight. However, it was impossible to replicate the variables present in a lake and we don't know if—"

Sheila gave an exasperated grunt. "So there's no guarantee it'll work. Guess we'll find out."

Sheila took the brick from Kelly's supplies and tied the rope to one end of it. Her fingers flew as she created an intricate web of knots. Marcie passed her the triple-sealed bags and she stuffed them inside a larger bag with a clasp, which she attached to the middle of the rope. Finally, Sheila fastened the neon-orange floating marker to the free end of the rope and lowered the jumble of bags and ropes into the middle of the canoe. The contraption wouldn't win any awards for appearance. But that wouldn't matter as long as it kept the hat safe. Unfortunately, there was no time for a trial run.

Sheila lifted her can of Coke in a salute. "For luck," she said, and guzzled it down. Then she set it on the dock and slipped into her life jacket. She nudged Kelly with the end of her paddle. "Ever been in a canoe before?"

"No." Kelly struggled to fasten the clips on her bright orange vest.

"We'll put you in the center."

Kelly stepped into the canoe with one foot. She gasped when it pitched beneath her. Arms flailing, she tried to regain her balance as she straddled the ever-widening gap between dock and canoe. She let out a piercing shriek.

"Quiet," Sheila hissed. She grabbed Kelly's arm and pulled her back onto the dock. With an exasperated sigh, she knelt, grabbed the edge of the canoe, and held it steady. "Stay low. Step in the middle."

"And never stand up," Marcie added. She sat on the dock, swung her legs over the side, and lowered herself into the tippy craft.

"I could have used that advice earlier." Kelly followed her example, crouching low and grabbing the sides to steady herself. Normally she loved the water and was an excellent swimmer. But she had no plans to take a dip tonight.

Sheila took her position in the back and used her paddle to push off from the pier. Reluctant to release her grip on the canoe, Kelly ignored her own paddle, which lay along the bottom of the canoe.

While Marcie and Sheila coordinated the rhythm of their strokes, Kelly became lost in the beauty of the night. The moon cast bright beams across the dark waters of the lake, and the prow of the canoe cut smoothly across the glassy surface.

Marcie took a deep breath and let it out slowly. "This evening is so *rotic*!"

"Rotic?" Kelly groaned.

"It's *romantic* without the *man*," Marcie explained. "I think it's my best word yet."

Kelly agreed. But that wasn't saying much.

Once they hit open water, Sheila directed the canoe toward a thick forest of reeds. It stretched at least a mile down the shoreline.

Hiding the hat in that jungle would be easy. The problem would be finding it again.

The canoe plunged into the sparse reeds. The tall stalks brushed against Kelly's arm and face. Marcie and Sheila strained with each stroke, but the reeds grew denser as the boat continued forward, and they made slow progress. Kelly grabbed her oar, which was heavier than she'd expected. She watched Marcie and tried to copy her movements. Several times, she misjudged the timing of her stroke and clonked Marcie's paddle with her own. When she tried to change sides, she swung her dripping paddle too low and smacked her friend on the back of the head. Marcie screeched.

"Sorry." Kelly pulled her paddle in.

"Let's drop the hat before we get stuck." Marcie rubbed her skull. "And before Kelly makes me bleed."

"We haven't gone far enough." Sheila leaned harder on her paddle. The canoe moved mere inches.

"Any farther and we'll never get out." Marcie pulled her paddle in and laid it across the sides.

Sheila gave a sigh of surrender. "All right. This spot will do."

Kelly picked up the cement block and leaned over to drop it into the lake. The shift in weight caused the canoe to dip dangerously close to the surface of the water. Kelly squealed and lurched back to the center of the boat. She crouched low as the canoe rocked back and forth.

"The *hat* is supposed to go in the lake. Not us." Sheila motioned for Kelly to pass her the gear.

Kelly used her foot to push the bag, rope, and block to Sheila. Keeping her weight balanced, Sheila picked up the block and lowered it over the side, using the rope to control its descent. Kelly lost sight of it as it sank in the dark water. The rope continued to slip through Sheila's fingers, pulling the plastic bags and hat under with a gurgling sound. She'd almost reached the end of the rope when the tension relaxed.

"The brick must have hit bottom." Sheila tossed the remaining rope over the side. It sank quickly, leaving only the neon-orange marker floating on top of the water.

Kelly and Marcie exhaled slowly.

"It worked!" Sheila exclaimed.

"We hope," Kelly added. A vision of water seeping into the bags and soaking the hat played through her mind.

"Let's get out of here." Marcie massaged the back of her head. "I need an aspirin. Maybe two."

The girls dug their paddles into the muck, but the canoe didn't budge.

Marcie grunted. "These stupid reeds are too thick."

"We can't go back over the same path." Sheila groaned. "We'd be sure to bend even more reeds and leave a trail as wide as a highway."

After several minutes of straining and heaving, the girls slouched in their seats.

"Now what?" Marcie's voice quivered.

"I'll have to push us out." Sheila swung her legs over the side of the canoe.

"What are you—?"

Before Kelly could finish her question, Sheila slipped into the lake. The light boat rocked precariously. Marcie and Kelly screeched and grabbed the sides. Once the boat settled, Kelly twisted around to stare at Sheila, who had positioned herself at the back of the canoe. Dark water lapped gently over the tops of her shoulders.

"Start rowing," Sheila ordered through chattering teeth. "This water is cold, and my feet are sinking in the mud."

Kelly and Marcie strained hard with their oars as Sheila pushed the canoe through the reeds. They edged forward slowly. Finally, the canoe broke through and floated into open water.

"I can't touch bottom." Sheila gasped. She swam to the left side of the canoe, then gripped the metal edge with both hands. "Lean hard to the right and I'll pull myself in."

"No!" Kelly hissed furiously. "You'll tip us for sure."

"You can swim beside the canoe." Panic raised Marcie's voice to a shrill pitch. "It isn't far."

Kelly considered using her paddle to push Sheila away. Or whack her on the head.

"I can do it."

Kelly recognized the stubborn pride in Sheila's voice. And knew she couldn't be stopped.

The canoe lurched left under Sheila's weight, and Kelly and Marcie threw themselves to the right side. Water sprayed as Sheila kicked hard. For a moment, Kelly thought the crazy plan might work. But Sheila lost her grip and fell back. Kelly and Marcie were unable to adjust their weight quickly enough. The canoe plummeted right, pitching them into the water.

A stabbing shock of cold shot through Kelly's body as she plunged into the lake. She kicked hard for the surface, struggling with the awkward weight of her layered clothes and pajamas. When her head broke the surface, she heard Marcie gasping for air beside her. Kelly pushed wet hair out of her eyes and searched for Sheila. Intending to drown her.

"Grab the paddles before they float away." Sheila's voice came from the other side of the canoe, which had somehow managed to stay upright and afloat.

Kelly sputtered. "You tipped us into the lake and that's all you can say? Get the paddles yourself." She was done helping Sheila.

"I'm sorry." Sheila sounded anything but apologetic. "But we'll be in real trouble if we lose those paddles.

Kelly scanned the water for the oars. She hadn't hit Sheila earlier, which was a mistake. But she could make up for it now.

"We'd better get going. It's a long swim back." That was Marcie, always practical. Even after being dumped into a cold lake in the middle of the night. Kelly was glad to see she'd managed to keep her glasses on her face.

Three loud clunks meant Sheila had found the paddles and tossed them into the canoe. She positioned herself at the back and pushed from behind. Marcie swam alongside, doing a sidestroke, with one hand on the boat to help guide it.

"Why don't we just pull the canoe to shore and get back in?" Kelly couldn't stop the shaking in her limbs.

"No way," Sheila said. "We'd have to go through the reeds, and that would make a huge trail."

"So let's carry it on land."

"We'd leave too many tracks in the sand."

Kelly grit her teeth. Sheila wouldn't care if they caught pneumonia as long as the prank went ahead as planned. She'd only been in the water a few minutes and already her fingers and toes were stiff with cold.

Tense silence reigned as Kelly kicked alongside her friends. She didn't even care about all the calories she was burning. She just wanted to get back to her cabin, out of her sopping clothes, and into a warm sleeping bag.

When they finally reached the dock, Marcie pulled herself up and flopped onto the wooden planks. Kelly crawled out beside her. She looked at her friend, the moonlight shining off her bright-yellow life vest as she lay gulping in air. Kelly couldn't help but giggle.

"What?" Marcie panted.

"You look like an enormous beached guppy."

Sheila hauled herself onto the dock and peeked around Kelly. She snickered.

"It's not funny." Marcie sounded annoyed.

"What did I tell you?" Sheila stood and rung water out of her hair. "That wasn't so bad."

Kelly and Marcie exchanged a quick glance, then together reached out to give Sheila a shove. She flailed wildly before slamming into the lake with a huge splash. Kelly felt a warm glow of satisfaction. Justice had been done. Or at least it was a start.

Sheila dragged herself onto the dock again. "I might have deserved that."

The girls smothered their laughter. Even Sheila chuckled.

When Kelly could breathe again, she sat up and poked Sheila. "So, was it worth it? Just to sink one hat?"

"Absolutely!" Sheila's eyes shone in the dark. "Darren's never going to find that ugly thing."

Kelly glanced back at the long stretch of reeds. Odds were good they wouldn't be able to find it either.

Kelly helped Marcie drag the canoe back to its place while Sheila grabbed the life jackets and paddles.

"If I hide them at the back of the shed, they'll dry before anyone finds them."

Kelly hoped Sheila was right, although the icy trickle of water running down her back was a cold reminder that might not be the case.

After Sheila emerged from the boathouse, they struck out for the road. The only sound was the squish of their sopping clothes and shoes. Which was rather amazing. Between the shrieking, splashing, and laughter, they'd made enough noise to wake the entire camp. Or at least alert Bill and Tony.

"How do you like working on maintenance?" Marcie gave Kelly a curious look.

Kelly shrugged at the out-of-the-blue question. "It's great...if you like mowing lawns, painting fences, and pulling weeds."

Sheila nudged Marcie. "Ask her what you really want to know. What it's like working with Bob?"

Kelly couldn't believe what she was hearing. Marcie actually liked Bob? She had to be blind. And deaf. Especially after his cruel comments and mocking laughter when she'd been soaked by the water pitcher. Kelly searched for something positive to say about her work partner that wouldn't be an outright lie.

"Well, he did move picnic tables for me once." But only because Tony made him. Kelly ran out of compliments.

Sheila snorted. "He's only here to knock off volunteer service credits. I guess it's a requirement at his fancy private school. He said the other option was working in some soup kitchen where the people smelled and the food was bad."

That sounded like Bob.

Marcie sighed. "My dad says that Bob's father owns a really successful international company and Bob will likely take over one day. Being with Bob could open doors to so many opportunities. Whoever dates him will be set for life."

Who cared if Bob ran a hundred companies? He was a jerk. Maybe Marcie wasn't as smart as she seemed. Kelly hurried to change the subject. "What's it like working in the kitchen?"

The question brought instant groans.

"It's awful." Marcie's hand flew to her chest as if in sudden pain. "There are thousands of dishes to wash every day. When we finish with those, we have to scrub the big pots and scrape the baked-on gunk from the pans."

Sheila kicked at a rock. "Then we have to mop the floors. If we're lucky, we get a short break before it's time to set the tables for the next meal. It never ends."

"And Lady Katherine is so picky!" Marcie moaned. "She's always lecturing about surprise inspections from some health-and-safety group. I guess there's at least one every summer."

Sheila gave a bitter laugh. "She has nothing to worry about. You could eat off the floor in her kitchen."

"At least we have Sandy." Marcie's tone brightened. "She's always singing and joking, even with Her Royal Highness."

Sheila nodded. "I've seen her make Lady Katherine smile twice. And that's a miracle."

"Sandy asks about you sometimes." Marcie spoke with hesitation, as if choosing her words carefully.

"What does she want to know?" The question came out harsher than Kelly would have liked.

"Weird things, like how much you eat, how often you exercise. Even whether you go to the bathroom after meals." Sheila's forehead crinkled.

So the spying kitchen worker wanted to know if she purged after eating. Kelly's stomach knotted. She'd been down this path before. It started with an interfering do-gooder asking questions. And it ended with some sort of ugly confrontation to force her to eat more.

Sheila gave a little chuckle. "This morning she asked if we thought you were happy."

The question stung. It was too personal. Too sensitive. And too perceptive. "It's none of her business what I do or how I feel."

Sheila waved off Kelly's anger. "I told her you were fine. Then she said people might look happy on the outside, but on the inside, they feel like someone took a bat and beat them black and blue."

"I can't believe she said that!" Kelly felt as if she'd been punched in the gut. She struggled to breathe. She'd never thought of it in those terms. But that's how she felt in the deepest, darkest parts of her heart. How could Sandy have known?

"She really cares," Marcie assured Kelly. "She's like the camp mom."

Kelly had just escaped from one prying mother. She didn't want another.

"When I came to camp last year, I was a mess." Sheila spoke in a rare serious tone. "Sandy noticed how depressed I looked, and one afternoon she took me on a canoe ride. We rowed out to the middle of the lake, and Sandy unloaded a huge backpack filled with pillows and snacks. We drifted for an hour, talking and dunking cookies in milk." A contented sigh escaped her lips.

"Lots of campers and staff have gone on one of Sandy's famous canoe rides," Marcie said. "But I didn't know she brought refreshments."

Sheila kicked at another stone in the middle of the road, sending it off into the bushes. "I told her about all my troubles back home. My older brother picked at me constantly, my former best friend had started some nasty rumors about me at school, and my parents were talking about getting a divorce. Sandy didn't fix anything, but it felt good to have her listen. When we got back to shore, we prayed, and she told me she'd keep praying for me. After camp was over, I went home to the same old problems. But every month, I got a card in the mail from Sandy. When she saw me this summer, she asked about everything."

Marcie nodded. "I hear that she writes to a lot of campers during the year. And even staff members."

Kelly's throat was too tight to speak. Counseling sessions in a canoe were fine for Sheila and the others, but she didn't need Sandy's help. Or cards. And especially not the milk and cookies.

As the girls approached the cabins, Kelly stopped. "What do I do with my wet clothes? And I'm wearing my pajamas underneath. I don't have another pair."

Sheila drummed her fingers against her chin. "I've got extra pjs. You can change in our room. We'll dry your clothes tomorrow and —"

"What are you girls doing out of bed?"

Sheila and Marcie screamed.

Kelly recognized the gruff voice. She stepped forward and dropped to her knees. "O Keeper of the Maintenance Shed and Defender of the Weak..."

"Not that again!" Tony stepped out of the shadows. "I am also Patroller of the Camp and Punisher of Those Who Break Rules. Now, I expect answers and you'd better tell the truth. Did you meet up with any boys?"

"No, sir," all three girls answered at once.

"Did you break anything?"

"No."

"Did you put the canoe back?"

Kelly froze. No one answered.

"Well?"

Sheila stepped forward. "We did. Thanks for helping with the supplies."

"I don't know what you're talking about. And you forgot this." Tony held up a can of Coke.

Kelly stared at it for a moment, uncomprehending. Then her mind flashed back to the dock, Sheila taking a swig for luck, then leaving the soda can on the edge. And now it was in Tony's hands.

"It's late. Get to bed." Tony growled his displeasure. "And I don't want to see you out again. Is that clear?"

"Yes, sir."

"Nice work, by the way. Except for the tipping. And all the screaming."

Kelly nearly laughed in relief. He was on their side.

The girls hurried to the staff room. Kelly grimaced when Sheila handed her a pair of red-and-white pajamas with Coke-a-Cola written all over them. But they were dry, and she wasn't in a position to be picky. She changed quickly, left her wet clothes with her friends, then crept to her cabin. As she opened the door, it creaked again. Kelly froze and peered inside. No movement. She tiptoed to her bunk and slipped into her sleeping bag.

For a moment, she considered searching for her calendar, but decided not to risk making any noise. She'd find it in the morning. Besides, crossing the days off wasn't as satisfying as it had been.

Kelly snuggled deep into her covers, damp hair clinging to her face. Her fingers and toes were stiff. She ached all over. And there was a strong possibility she'd catch a nasty head cold. Kelly pulled her stuffed beagle close and buried her face in her pillow to stifle a sudden burst of laughter. This was the most fun she'd had in a long time.

18 CAUGHT IN CONVERSATION

Sirens blared in the distance. Police! Tony must have ratted them out. But surely Kelly wouldn't face criminal charges over a stolen hat.

Hands grabbed her. They didn't have to shake so roughly. She wasn't resisting.

"Kelly, wake up!"

She struggled to focus bleary eyes on Jill's frowning face.

"Your alarm's been ringing for the past five minutes."

"Sorry." Kelly reached under her pillow and fumbled for the switch.

With a disapproving snort, Jill crawled back into her bunk and pulled the covers over her head.

Kelly stared out the window at the dim light. How could it be morning already? She could have sworn she'd just come in from the prank. Kelly listened to the deep, contented breathing of the campers with a jealous twinge. She wished she could skip her daily jog and go back to sleep. But that wasn't an option.

Pushing her covers back, Kelly tried to roll out of bed. But her exhausted limbs refused to obey. It wasn't the first time her body had rebelled. She pulled out the strategy she'd developed for moments like this, when she needed to motivate herself.

You're only as good as you look. Kelly chanted the horrible truth over and over in her head. *Fat girls don't deserve cute guys.* Aaron had taught her that. And she knew that if she gained weight, Joel would never look at her. Cindy was pretty and thin. He'd choose her instead.

The combination of fear and shame gave Kelly the strength to sit up. With aching muscles protesting every move, she changed clothes, slipped outside, and stumbled down the path past the cabins.

Once she reached the paved road, Kelly tried to maintain a steady jogging pace, but the lack of food and sleep had taken their toll. Halfway to the turn-around point, her wobbly legs refused to move any faster than a shaky walk.

A figure appeared in the distance, growing larger. Must be Bill on his way back to the ranch. There was no place to turn off and no trees to duck behind. An encounter was unavoidable.

When Bill reached her, they both stopped. "You're off your usual schedule. Late night?"

Kelly nodded, wondering how much he knew.

"I hope you put the canoe back."

She gulped. He knew everything.

"You'll be late for breakfast if you don't cut your jog short. How about we walk back to camp together? I'd like to chat anyway."

He phrased it as a request, but the firm tone left no choice. She turned and walked beside him, hoping the punishment wouldn't be too severe.

"Are you enjoying your week at Timberlake?"

"Camp's not exactly what I expected," she admitted, relieved he'd dropped the subject of the previous night's escapade.

Bill raised an eyebrow. "I hope that's a good thing."

"Yes and no. Working with the campers is challenging, but I'm having fun. I like the campfires. They're crazy, and I never know what to expect. The girls seem to be learning a lot." And so was she, even if she didn't want to admit it out loud.

"Glad to hear it. We've never done anything quite this intense, but I believe it will make a huge impact in the lives of those who are listening."

Kelly ducked her head, wondering if he was referring to her. She searched for a way to shift the conversation back to him. "You should have been a teacher."

"I am. My classroom is just bigger than most." He gestured to the camp in front of them. "Instead of posters on walls, I have horses in fields. Instead of lessons in classrooms, I tell stories at campfires. But I do follow a textbook." He held up the worn, black Bible he'd been carrying. The edges of several loose papers tucked into the book rustled in the breeze. "I couldn't live without it."

"You'll have to survive somehow when it falls apart." Kelly giggled. "Maybe you should buy a new one."

"I suppose." Bill sighed. "But it'll take a while to transfer all my notes. So this one will have to do until summer is over."

Kelly frowned. "Can't you just take all those pieces of paper and put them in the next Bible?"

Bill held the book in front of her and flipped through it. Almost every page had been marked in some way: highlighted text, notes in the column, underlined sentences, circled paragraphs with names and dates written beside them. Kelly had never seen a book so marked up.

"I read a chapter from the Old Testament and one from the New Testament every day. Been doing that for twenty years. And I never read without a pen in my hand."

Kelly's jaw dropped. "You really do read your Bible."

"This is a personal record of my faith in God and His faithfulness to me. I've worn out three Bibles already." He closed the book and ran his hand lightly over the cover. "Each time one falls apart, I buy another and copy all my notes, page by page."

Kelly thought of her Bible, left at home under her bed. Other than being dusty, her book was neat, proper, and in mint condition. But Bill's looked tattered, worn and...treasured.

He pulled out a couple of loose sheets from the front. "I keep a list of people and their needs. As I walk every morning, I pray for each one." Bill turned the papers over. Both sides were filled with small printing. "Sometimes God answers right away. Other times, it takes longer. There are a few requests on these pages that I've been bringing before the Lord for over thirty years."

That was a long time to pray without a response. And it seemed foolish. Kelly knew all about unanswered prayers. She had many of her own. But unlike Bill, she'd been smart enough to stop asking. She couldn't help feeling curious about why Bill hadn't given up as well.

"What do you do when God doesn't answer?" She tried to keep her voice even and steady, as if she didn't care.

"I keep praying. It's not my job to make things happen, just to keep asking. And while I'm grateful for every yes, I'm learning to be just as thankful when He says no or wait."

"What about when God does nothing?" Kelly clenched her fists. It wasn't a question so much as an accusation. And she couldn't hide the anger behind her words.

"Just because I don't see God's hand doesn't mean He isn't working. My sight and comprehension are limited. I don't expect to recognize all His answers during this lifetime. But I know that I'll understand when I see Him face-to-face."

The warmth in Bill's tone wrapped around her like a soft blanket. She felt the fight draining from her.

They walked in silence for a few moments, listening to the crunch of the gravel under their shoes. Bill's faith was real. She could hear it whenever he spoke at the campfires. He knew God. And deep down inside, she felt a twisting stab of envy. She'd tried to know God like that. Why hadn't it worked for her?

They slowed their steps as the cabins loomed before them.

Bill faced her. "Kelly, do you have a relationship with God?"

She dropped her gaze. "I thought I did once. But now I'm not even sure if He exists." No point denying the truth.

"Oh, He's real." Confidence rang in Bill's voice. "I'll be praying for you," he added with a wink.

Kelly shrugged. He could pray all he wanted. No one was listening.

"When you see Sheila and Marcie, tell them to be careful."

Her throat went dry. "Are you going to punish us?"

Bill chuckled. "Let's just say there's more to that hat than any of you realize."

Kelly's brow furrowed. "It can't be all that special. Darren bought it at the dollar store."

"Just tell the girls what I said." Bill strode off toward the lodge.

Kelly hurried to the cabin and found it empty. Which meant she was late for breakfast again. While she would have been happy to skip the morning meal, she didn't need any more questions or lectures.

Kelly rushed to get ready. But by the time she burst into the lodge, her cabinmates were already halfway through the food line. After grabbing a bowl, she slipped in behind Amber and took her usual miniscule helping of cereal.

The aroma rising from the fresh blueberry muffins was irresistible. She chose the smallest one and nibbled on the corner. Her taste buds thrilled to the perfect blend of sweet, juicy berries with a sugary crumble on top, melting slowly in her mouth. Incredibly delicious. Without a second thought, she wolfed it down. Then silently berated herself, but grabbed another.

As soon as she settled at the table, Kelly scarfed down the second muffin. Loathing her lack of self-control, she vowed to skip lunch to make up for the morning's pitiful jog and excess calories.

"Did you hear the news?" Joyce's excited voice carried down the table. "Darren's hat is missing. He's sure it was stolen."

Kelly assumed her best shocked expression. "Does he have any idea who did it?"

"Darren accused one of the kitchen workers." Joyce pointed toward the front counter, where Sheila was removing an empty muffin tray as Marcie replaced it with a full one. Both looked half asleep, and their movements were slow and strained. As if every muscle hurt.

Kelly's lips twitched in wry amusement. She knew exactly how they felt.

An angry roar rose above the usual dining hall noise. Kelly glanced nervously toward the source and saw at least twenty male campers and counselors crowded around Stan and Darren's table. Darren sat in the middle of the group, mouth set in a firm line and unruly hair sticking up where his hat should have been.

"If we raid their cabins and take all their clothes, they'll give it back," shouted a camper, pointing wildly in the direction of the nearest table of females.

Shouts of outrage rang from the girls. "If you touch our stuff, we'll throw everything you own in the lake," one camper hollered.

Mike, sitting to Darren's left, jammed his hat tighter on his head and motioned for the group to lean in. They spoke in hushed tones.

No need to guess the subject. Kelly turned away, fighting a nauseous rolling in the pit of her stomach.

More loud accusations and equally loud denials were tossed from table to table until Bill banged the serving spoon against the front counter.

"A personal item belonging to one of our male counselors is missing. Whoever is responsible has until this evening to correct his or her poor choice." Bill cleared his throat. "Let me be clear. Darren will have a hat back on his head by supper tonight."

Heart pounding, Kelly risked a peek at Sheila and Marcie, now standing beside the kitchen doors. Hands clasped in front of them, they were the picture of innocence. Neither glanced her way.

Bill picked up a pen and wrote the scores for each cabin on the contest chart. Kelly was grateful for the distraction. The campers immediately switched their focus to the chart, cheering or complaining depending on the results.

"We're still winning!" Amber squealed.

"Tied for first place," Kelly corrected. "Stan's cabin has a perfect score too." She avoided mentioning Darren's name for fear it might spark another discussion of the missing hat.

"Campers are free to head to morning devotions once their tables are cleared." Bill disappeared into the kitchen without a glance in Kelly's direction, much to her relief.

After dumping her cereal and placing her bowl in the rack, Kelly exited the lodge with Amber and the rest of the girls. Halfway to the cabin, she tapped Jill on the shoulder. "Could I be a few minutes late to devotions? I need to talk to someone."

Jill raised an eyebrow. "Now?"

Kelly nodded. "It's really important."

Jill fixed her with a penetrating stare. "You must have been really tired this morning to sleep through your alarm. And I could have sworn you were wearing a different pair of pajamas when you went to bed last night."

Kelly froze. "The first pair wasn't comfortable, so I changed." Which was true. No need to mention that the original pair had been uncomfortable because it was sopping wet.

Jill grinned. "Say hi to Sheila and Marcie for me." Then she winked.

Kelly melted with relief. And felt a sudden rush of appreciation for Jill.

Kelly zipped back to the lodge, thankful to find the dining hall empty of campers. Armed with dish rags and a bucket of soapy water, Marcie and Sheila worked at the back of the room, washing down the tables.

Kelly rushed over. "What are we going to do?" she moaned.

"Don't worry." Sheila scrubbed at a crusted bit of something on the table. "Darren will have a hat on his head at supper tonight." She dipped her hand in the pail and flicked suds at Kelly.

Kelly narrowed her eyes at Sheila's nonchalant response. There was no way the redheaded tornado was going to wind down that easily. Not after all they'd been through to pull off the prank.

Sheila plunged her cloth in the bucket and rung it out. "Bill didn't specify that we had to return Darren's hat. As long as Darren has a hat on his head, we've met the terms."

"And just how are you going to make that happen?" It wasn't like there was a large selection of ugly hats in the camp store.

Sheila twirled her rag in the air. "When we go on our break this afternoon, we'll make a paper hat that looks just like Darren's old one."

Kelly's fingers itched to dump the bucket of dirty water on her friend's head. "It's one thing to mess with Darren, but I don't want to cross Bill. He can make the rest of the week miserable for us. And he told me this morning there's more to that hat than we know."

Sheila let out a low growl. "Tony must have snitched."

"Is Bill going to punish us?" Marcie's hands flew to her mouth.

Kelly shook her head. "I think we're safe. He—"

The lodge door swung open and Stan entered, carrying his devotion binder. His entire cabin trooped after him, with Darren bringing up the rear.

The campers ambled along in a loose line until they saw the girls at the back of the hall. Then they surged toward them, surrounding Kelly and her friends.

"We know you did it."

"You'd better give it back."

"If you ruin it, you're going to be in big trouble."

"Ever been tarred and feathered?" squeaked a scrawny camper who resembled a bright-eyed weasel.

Darren remained silent, but his scowl spoke louder than any verbal threat.

"What possible motive could I have for taking a hat?" Sheila toyed with a strand of her straight red hair while staring pointedly at Darren. "I feel just awful that it's gone." The pleased grin on Sheila's face looked anything but sympathetic. "It would be terrible if anything happened to that lovely hat."

The campers snarled in response. The scrawny one lunged for the bucket of dirty water, but Darren held him back.

"We've got devotions to do. Let's move," Stan ordered the boys. He walked to the door connecting the hall to the gym.

The campers hollered more threats as they followed their lead counselor. Darren resumed his position at the back, prodding the stragglers.

Kelly had devotions as well, which Jill had probably started by now. She tried to slip past Darren, but he placed a hand on her shoulder.

His light brown eyes looked straight into hers. "There's still time to save yourself."

Kelly froze. She could feel her heart beating wildly in her chest. Which she considered a reasonable response after being threatened by an angry mob of ruffians.

Darren gave her shoulder a slight squeeze. Then joined his campers.

Kelly's shoulder felt warm where Darren's hand had been. She stared after him and wondered what the warning meant, and why he'd try to protect her. With a shake of her head, she pushed the question aside. She had other things to worry about, like how much it might hurt to be covered in tar and feathers.

19 BEWARE OF THE SCISSORS

Kelly waited until Darren had followed the last of his campers out of the gym before she whirled to face Sheila. "Would they really cover us in tar and feathers?"

Sheila glanced at the gym door, as if sizing up the boys and their threats. "Anything's possible. Although no one really uses tar. They might cover us in maple syrup and feathers. It's sticky, but it washes off in a warm shower...eventually."

Kelly frowned. Joel had already seen her covered in brown paint and splattered with mud. Maple syrup and feathers would surely be even less flattering. And she wasn't about to sacrifice her chance at Joel for a stupid hat.

"This prank thing has been fun. But I'm getting out. I didn't sign up to be attacked by a cabin of vengeful campers." Kelly headed for the door.

Sheila blocked her escape. "But we've got a plan!"

"So does Darren." Kelly tried to duck under Sheila's arm, but Sheila covered her every move. "Why don't you just tell him that if he stops messing up your hair, he can have his hat back?"

Sheila rubbed her hands together. "I want to see him sweat first."

"The only people sweating will be us. As we run for our lives." Kelly dodged left and bumped into Marcie.

"We went to a lot of work to hide the hat." Marcie pressed her hands together in supplication. "Could you just give it one more day?"

Kelly stared into the pleading faces of her friends. She couldn't betray their alliance. At least not yet. "All right. I won't say anything...for now. But that will change if I see a single sticky feather."

With a grateful smile, Sheila stepped aside. Kelly hurried off to devotions. She could only hope that Darren and Sheila would work this out before someone got maimed. Like her.

When Kelly reached the cabin, she found the campers sitting in a circle. Their binders lay closed on the floor in front of them. Had they already finished? Kelly hoped not. She grabbed her book from the shelf, and then nearly dropped it, struck by the sudden realization that she'd actually be disappointed to miss out on the devotion.

"I heard Darren's offering a reward for any information about his hat." Emma leaned forward, as if sharing a piece of tantalizing gossip. "His whole cabin is going to pitch in. A dollar each."

"Ten dollars?" Joyce's lip curled. "That's not much."

"I don't know." Emma looked off into space, as if counting in her head. "I could use it to buy a chocolate bar every day I'm here."

Jill cleared her throat and made a show of opening her binder. "We can talk about the hat after devotions."

So she hadn't missed anything. Kelly quickly took a spot beside Amber.

Joyce shifted to face Kelly. "The boys in Darren's cabin said your two friends took the hat. Did they?"

Without waiting for an answer, Nadia jumped in. "The boys think you helped them. Did you?"

Every camper stared at Kelly.

"Me?" Kelly gave a light laugh. "I was here in the cabin last night, telling the story of Molly the Moth. It took forever for all of you to drop off. How would I have time to be part of a prank?" A weak argument, but she didn't have much else.

"Are you going to give it back?"

"Where did you hide it?"

"If you tell us, we'll share the reward."

The girls hadn't heard a word she'd said. Or at least hadn't believed it.

Jill rapped her devotion book with a pencil. "Enough crime solving." She passed out a set of notes and the campers inserted the sheets into their binders. Grateful to escape the interrogation, Kelly examined the top page. A large pair of scissors filled most of the space. "The Break-up" was printed in bold above the clippers.

"Our couple has a rough morning ahead of them," Jill said. "The pictures tell the story."

Pages rustled as the girls flipped through the drawings. The first sketch showed Guy and Girl as a connected couple. Smiles beamed from both faces. Next, Guy burped the alphabet while Girl watched with a disgusted expression. The following scene showed Girl with a pair of scissors. The drama concluded as Girl snipped through the ties that bound them together. The look on Guy's face was a mixture of shock and misery.

This wasn't going to be a light and happy lesson.

Jill read the caption below the last sketch. "When the connection between two individuals is cut, the relationship ends. The severed ties are like damaged, exposed nerve endings. The pain can be excruciating."

"When my boyfriend broke up with me, I cried for days," Emma said. "My mom told me I was too young to be in love and I should just get over it. But I really liked him."

Jill gave a sympathetic smile. "Ties hurt when they're cut, whether you're thirteen, twenty-three, or fifty-three."

Kelly flinched as she thought of Aaron. It had hurt when he broke up with her. After her parents had driven her home, Kelly had grabbed her cell phone and locked herself in the bathroom. Aaron answered on the first ring but wasn't interested in her tearful apology. He told her she'd humiliated him, and he was done with her. Then he called her a few nasty names and hung up. She'd sent frantic texts. And he sent one back that left her sobbing on the bathroom floor for hours.

Kelly glanced at the young girls around her. She didn't think it would be appropriate to share details of her story. Even if she couldn't forget them herself.

Joyce's sharp voice cut into her thoughts. "I dated a guy for a week. It didn't hurt at all when we broke up."

Kelly was surprised that anyone had lasted that long with Joyce. The guy must have had skin as thick as an elephant to handle her prickly nature and sharp tongue.

Jill circled the ties from the last image of Guy and Girl. "A week is a short time to form a connection, so there were probably fewer ties to cut. That means less heartache."

Several other campers shared details of their romantic splits. By Kelly's account, five of the eight girls had been in a romantic relationship. More than she'd expected.

Jill flipped to the next page in her binder and the girls followed her lead. "The Dump" had been printed in bold letters at the top of the page. This section also began with a picture showing Guy and Girl as a connected couple. In the next scene, Guy yawned as Girl blathered on. The following frame showed Guy throwing the ties at Girl. In the final sketch, Guy walked away as Girl, wearing a hurt expression, clung to the ties, which dragged in the dust on the ground.

"I don't get it," Emma said. "What's the difference between a *dump* and a *break-up*?"

"The relationship is over in both cases. The difference is how that happens." Jill tapped on the picture. "In a break-up, one person simply cuts the ties. But in a dump, the ties are thrown back in the other person's face. It's a deliberate act of disrespect. And it's all about blame."

Kelly could still hear Aaron's mocking words and feel the wave of icy shame that soaked her.

Jill turned to the next page, which was blank except for one sentence in the middle. "You're too _____, and you're not _____ enough."

"What's that supposed to mean?" Terri asked.

Kelly congratulated herself for finally being able to tell the ponytail-wearing twins apart, which had only happened after Jill pointed out a small beauty mark near Terri's right ear.

Jill rose from the floor, grabbed pencils from one of the shelves, and passed them out. "In a dump, the relationship ends because one person blames the other for being too much of something or not enough of something else. Think about people you know, or your own dating experiences, and fill in the blank spaces. Add as many examples as you can."

Kelly wrinkled her nose as she stared at the exercise. This wasn't going to be hard. But it wasn't going to be pretty either. At least not if she was honest.

As she filled in her answers, Kelly glanced around the circle. Pencils scratched at a furious pace.

After several minutes, Jill rapped on the floor. "Let's go around the circle and each share one answer." She tapped Fiona, who was sitting on her right.

"You're too ugly and not pretty enough." Fiona adjusted her thick glasses. "That's what Ryan told his friends when he dumped me."

How cruel. Kelly felt like reaching across the circle and giving Fiona a bear hug. Her boyfriend deserved something else. Like a fat lip.

"You're too stupid and not smart enough." Kelly could hardly hear Tanya's soft voice. She wondered if those words had been said to her or one of her friends.

"You're too boring and not exciting enough." Terri's lips twitched.

"You're too fat and not thin enough." Nadia pulled her jacket closer around her. "The guys don't have to say it. It's the way they look you up and down...and sneer."

Kelly winced. She knew that look. Or at least she used to. But not anymore. And she was going to keep it that way.

Emma swallowed. "You're too clingy and not confident enough."

"You're too clumsy and not athletic enough." Joyce's tone was loud and defiant. Or maybe defensive.

"You're too serious and not funny enough." Michelle's shoulders sagged. "But what did he know?"

Amber hesitated when her turn came. She ducked her head, then said quietly, "You're too geeky and not cool enough."

Kelly's heart ached at the pain in the young girl's voice.

Amber gave a weak shrug. "My mom likes to quote that saying about sticks, stones, and breaking bones. She says words can't harm."

Not true. Amber knew it, and so did the rest of the girls. Words cut as deep as any physical blow. Maybe deeper. And left scars that lasted for years.

Everyone looked at Kelly, the last in the circle to share. She forced a reluctant smile "You're too plain and not sexy enough."

No one looked surprised, which probably meant it wasn't a new message. A heavy silence followed.

Jill put down her pencil and leaned back. "Dumps aren't usually stated this bluntly, but the message is always clear." She gazed around the circle, making eye contact with each girl, including Kelly. "But you don't have to accept the blame. Your worth doesn't depend on what someone says. Your value doesn't change even if some guy says you're not good enough and dumps you."

Fingernails bit into Kelly's palms as her hands clenched into tight fists. Jill had spoken the truth, but it came too late. The campers had already been wounded by the shameful accusations of others. And so had she. How were they supposed to erase the damage of those ugly words?

The girls sat in silence for several moments before Nadia cleared her throat. "Is there any way to split from a guy without the pain?"

Jill shook her head slowly. "It's possible for both individuals to decide the relationship isn't working and lay down their ties at the same time. But it's far more common for one person to snip or drop the connection. And that will always hurt."

"So there's no hope?" Nadia's voice carried a raw edge.

"The amount of pain you experience depends on what you keep in your hands." Jill gave a light chuckle at the quizzical looks from the girls. "Let go of the ties. Release bitterness. But hold on to forgiveness."

Joyce erupted with an outraged gasp. "There's no way I'm forgiving my ex! After we broke up, that idiot spread all sorts of nasty lies about me."

Several of the girls muttered supportive comments. "Loser" and "moron" were two of the kinder adjectives.

Joyce lifted her chin, her eyes glittering with pride. "I gave that jerk double for my trouble. For every insult he said about me, I spread two worse ones about him."

The girls broke into applause and cheers. Kelly thought it best to refrain from joining in. But revenge did sound fair.

Jill raised her hands to signal for silence. "Forgiveness doesn't make what he did right. It doesn't excuse his poor behavior, and it doesn't mean you have to remain in any type of relationship. It just means letting go. And when someone treats us poorly, we still need to treat him or her with respect."

"Why?" Joyce snapped. "He didn't deserve it."

"It's not about your ex-boyfriend. It's about you. You are a person of character and maturity, regardless of who the other person is. That's how you act, regardless of how the other person behaves. My mom had a saying too. She said that keeping bitterness or unforgiveness in your heart is like drinking poison and expecting the other person to die."

Kelly's thoughts drifted back to Aaron. She knew he was saying nasty stuff behind her back. Annalisa had made that clear. And he talked that way about all his past girlfriends. Despite her staunch defense of Aaron, there were secret moments when she had a wild desire to grab a megaphone and shout to everyone what a dirty, lousy, selfish, no-good scoundrel he was. But it wouldn't do any good. The other girls wouldn't care that he was selfish and aggressive. He was too popular to be damaged by insults. And maybe it wasn't her job to accuse him. Just hold her head high and move forward.

Jill flipped to the last page in her devotion book. "When we end a romantic relationship, we should be mature about it. Part of that involves breaking up in person and not through a friend, e-mail, or text. No ripped pictures. No silent treatment. No poor behavior, hoping they'll get the message. We treat the other person the same way we'd like to be treated."

Kelly imagined Jill sharing such a message in the halls of her school. Some students would ignore her. Others would laugh, or even mock. But how many would secretly long to be treated with such respect? Kelly definitely would.

Jill closed her binder. Assuming they'd reached the end of the lesson, Kelly uncrossed her legs and found that her left one had fallen asleep. Everyone stretched and a few campers stood.

Jill held up her hand. "We're not quite done. I have one last story to share."

The girls resumed their places, and Kelly rubbed her aching limb.

"When I was in high school, I had a close friend named Ally. She started seeing this older guy and became completely obsessed with him. They dated for a few months, and during that time, she dropped me, along with all her other friends and activities. Ally put everything into her romantic ties with this guy. All her value, hopes, and dreams."

Surprised by Jill's solemn tone and grim expression, Kelly stopped massaging her leg and leaned forward.

"When this guy dumped her, he said some cruel things. He made it clear they'd never be together again and immediately started going out with another girl. Ally didn't come back to school the next day. Her mom found her body in the basement of their house, hanging from a rope."

The girls let out gasps and moans. Then Kelly heard the muffled sound of crying. She wished Jill would hurry and finish the story. Surely they found that poor girl in time and cut her down. But Jill remained silent, and the truth slammed into Kelly. There wasn't going to be a happy ending. Not for Ally.

Jill put an arm around Tanya, who had buried her head in her hands. "Ally let her relationship with this guy become the most significant connection in her life. When she lost it, she lost everything."

Kelly fought the urge to beg Jill to stop, to tell her it was too much for the campers to handle. Almost too much for her. But hadn't those same thoughts crossed her mind? Feeling powerless about the mess she was in. Wondering if life was worth living without Aaron. Wondering if it would be easier just to end it all.

Kelly hadn't succumbed to the temptation. Maybe because she still hoped Aaron would take her back. Maybe because despite all the fighting with her parents, she knew she still had their love and support. And despite her doubts and anger at God, a tiny seed of faith remained. But she didn't know what the campers had for support, and it would be wrong to shelter them. The girls needed to hear the story, because some day they might be in the same place as Ally, pushed to the edge by shame, loss, and despair. She didn't want them to follow the desperate girl's example.

A somber silence settled on the room. Several girls sniffed and wiped their eyes, and even Joyce sat with shoulders hunched. Kelly wondered what Jill could say to give these girls hope when Ally had found none.

Tears ran down Jill's cheeks. "That's why it's so important to look to God as the source of your value. It will hurt to be dumped by a guy you really like. But if you know God, His love will keep you from being devastated."

The campers leaned closer, as if straining to hear every word. Kelly felt overwhelmed by the importance of the moment. She'd assumed devotions would be like school lessons, taking notes and writing down correct answers. But this was more. These truths could mean the difference between life and death. Kelly was humbled to be a part of it.

Jill gently pried Tanya's hands from her face and lifted her head. "God knows you at your shining best. He knows you at your absolute worst. And He loves you more completely than anyone else ever can or will."

Even though Jill had spoken softly, the words resounded throughout the cabin. And Kelly knew that was the only answer. Cruel words spoken by others couldn't be undone, but they could be replaced. Someone had to speak louder. Someone had to speak a message of grace and love. And who could speak with that much insight and authority? Only God.

Jill flipped back a few pages in her devotion book. She drew a cross over the dump comments she'd written, then motioned for the campers to do the same.

"It doesn't matter what some guy says about you. God, who created the heavens, the earth, and everything in them, is crazy in love with you."

Tears threatened to spill out of Kelly's eyes. Tears for Jill's friend Ally, who hadn't known God's love. Tears for herself, because she couldn't believe God felt that kind of love for her.

Jill glanced at her watch and yelped, "We're late for canoeing!"

The moment was broken. Jill collected the binders from the girls. After a quick scramble to straighten up the cabin, the campers rushed out the door.

Kelly stayed behind, knowing she had a few extra minutes before Tony would expect her. She sank onto the edge of her bunk and reached for her beagle. As she stroked the soft ears, the words Bill had spoken on the first day played back in her mind. *Dating ties aren't all good. They don't always lead to happy endings. We're going to show the campers how to keep love straight in the tangled world of dating.* How tragic that Ally hadn't had a chance to hear that message.

Kelly looked at the empty bunks in the cabin, with the nametag of each girl dangling from the posts. It was too late for Ally. But not for these girls. They had the opportunity to hear the voice of God assuring them how awesome they were in His sight. But she'd already had a chance with God and had walked away. Had she moved beyond His reach?

Kelly forced herself to push aside all thoughts of the devotion and pulled her calendar from its hiding place under her pillow. With slow strokes, she crossed off Tuesday, which she'd missed the night before. Five days to go. She'd reached the halfway point, but didn't feel as excited as she'd thought she would.

An image of Darren's hat, anchored in the reeds of the lake, sprang to mind. It hadn't been a perfect plan. But they had succeeded in hiding the hat. And most important, they'd escaped any punishment—so far.

She chalked that up to a run of good luck. And that worried her. It was about time for something to go wrong.

20 A FAIRY-TALE RIDE

Kelly raced down the path leading to the maintenance shed. She'd lingered too long in the cabin after devotions, thinking about the tragic story of Ally's suicide. And now she was late to report for her morning job assignment.

She was about to rush into the shed when the sounds of a heated conversation inside caused her to pause. Her curiosity roused, she leaned close to the door, which had been left slightly ajar.

"But it'll take us all night if we only get one or two!" Bob's muffled voice rose in frustration. "We need at least four or five."

Something that would take all night? Kelly felt a shot of excitement race through her body. That could only be a retaliatory prank from the guys. And she was in the perfect position to eavesdrop on all the details of their devious little plot.

"They're far too valuable to risk being lost." Tony's words were followed by a metallic grating noise, as if he were lifting some type of lid. Maybe from one of the toolboxes stacked on the back shelves.

"Darren's not going to be happy."

Kelly held back a giggle at the sulking tone in Bob's voice.

"You can tell Darren and his friends that there'd better not be any damage done. Take both of these. And I want them back by tomorrow morning."

Eager to catch a glimpse of the mystery items, Kelly tried to crack the door a few extra inches. It didn't budge. She gave a nudge with her shoulder. A little too hard. The door burst open and she stumbled into the room.

Bob dropped two screwdrivers on the floor, and his fancy cap fell off as he bent over to pick them up.

"Late as usual," Tony barked.

Kelly fixed her attention on Bob. "I believe I'm right on time."

Bob straightened up, hid the tools behind his back, and scowled at her.

"What kind of maintenance job takes place at night?" Kelly raised an eyebrow.

"You'll find out soon enough."

Kelly's throat tightened. She knew it wasn't an empty threat, and Bob was capable of nasty stuff.

Suddenly Darren strode in. He skidded to a stop at the sight of Kelly, then recovered with a broad grin. As if he was glad to see her, and not concerned about what she might discover.

"What a surprise," Tony grunted, looking anything but surprised. "Something I can do for you?"

"Just wanted to see how things were going." Darren held out a hand to Bob. "Did you get what we need?"

As he passed the screwdrivers to Darren, Bob's eyes shifted to Kelly. He smirked.

Darren approached Tony. "Could we get a few more? I can pay for them." He held up two chocolate bars. "You prefer dark chocolate, right? Without nuts."

"Glad to see you did your homework." Tony placed one of the bars on the table. He ripped the wrapper off the other and took a huge bite.

Kelly stared in disbelief. Tony had just accepted a bribe for tools that would likely be used against her and her friends. And he wasn't even trying to hide it. She hoped he choked on his candy.

As Tony rummaged through the toolbox, Kelly couldn't contain her outrage. "I didn't realize Darren was working on the maintenance crew. He must have a big job if he needs so many screwdrivers." Her words dripped with sarcasm.

"Actually, he needs them for a prank." Tony pulled out two more screwdrivers and handed them to Darren.

Kelly glared at Tony. Easy for him to be smug. He wasn't going to be attacked.

Darren pulled a wrinkled piece of paper out of his pocket and passed it to Tony. "I'd like to keep the screwdrivers until noon. This should cover it."

Kelly recognized the two-dollar voucher their team had won during the staff training weekend. The same coupon she'd used to bribe Tony earlier. Which made Darren a copycat.

With a grunt of approval, Tony accepted the payoff. "Pleasure doing business with you."

They shook hands, and Darren headed for the door. Before leaving, he turned and locked eyes with Kelly. "Tell Sheila that if I get my hat back, these screwdrivers won't be necessary. But if not..." Darren shrugged and exited the shed. Bob followed close behind.

"You know, Darren could teach you a thing or two about how to conduct a proper bribe." Tony patted the shirt pocket where he'd stuffed the store coupon. "None of that 'Defender of the Weak,' on-your-knees nonsense. Just a fair exchange of goods."

Kelly folded her arms. "Personally, I thought the presentation was a little bland." Tony only liked it better because he'd been blinded by the dark chocolate. Without nuts.

Tony handed Kelly a sponge, several old towels, and a bucket of soapy water. "You'll be washing the screens and windows in the girls' cabins today. Make sure you vacuum the dead flies and spiders from the sills."

Kelly's nose wrinkled in disgust. She wondered if Tony stayed up late devising the worst possible jobs for her.

She was almost to the door when Tony called out, "I've seen the way all you girls fantasize over Joel."

Kelly spun around to face him, eyes narrowed. She didn't know which was more surprising—that he noticed or that he cared enough to comment.

"Someday one of you is going to wake up and realize that you've overlooked the best choice of all. Darren's twice the man Joel is."

Darren? Was he kidding? "You're giving me advice about guys?" Kelly sputtered. "Those screwdrivers are going to be used in some evil plot to harm me and my friends. And you're saying the guy who's going to carry out the crime is a great catch?"

"Chase Joel all you want, but you'll be disappointed if you snag him."

"I doubt any girl here would agree with you." The entire female population at camp couldn't be wrong.

Tony's eyebrows rose. "None of you really knows Joel. You're only attracted to his image."

Kelly resisted the temptation to roll her eyes. Of course they were attracted to his image. Joel was good-looking, muscular, and athletic. What more was there to know?

"Being seen with Joel is just an ego-boost. That's not love. That's selfishness."

Kelly didn't want to hear any more. She placed a hand on the doorknob.

"Hang on." Tony tossed her a pair of gloves. "These will help with the creepy, crawly things."

"Thanks...for the gloves." Not the advice.

"I'll be working with Bob up at the barn. When you're done, you can report to me there."

Kelly stormed off to the cabins. As she scrubbed the dirty windows, her mind jumped back and forth between trying to solve the mystery of the screwdrivers and coming up with a clever reply to Tony's comments about Joel. By the time she finished, she had a splitting headache, but no ideas about the prank and no witty response for Tony.

It was almost noon when she stepped out of the last cabin and dumped the dirty water into the bushes. She dropped the equipment at the maintenance shed, and for a moment she wished that Tony had said to meet him there rather than making the trek to the barn. But the longer trip would burn off calories and make her late for lunch. She might even miss the noon meal completely if she took her time coming back. And there was always the possibility of running into Joel.

On her way to the barn, Kelly passed campers heading to the lodge for lunch. But instead of walking on the road, they were shuffling through bushes, ducking behind buildings, rifling through storage bins, peering into garbage cans, and climbing trees.

A slow grin stretched across Kelly's face. The whole camp was being turned upside down as the campers all searched for one ugly hat. But there was little chance any of them would think to check in the lake.

Kelly found Tony and Bob near the arena. "The cabin windows are all done."

"That was fast. I didn't expect you to finish until this afternoon." Tony nodded in Bob's direction. "You can both check in with me after lunch. I'll have a new assignment for you, Kelly."

Eager to avoid another lecture on love, Kelly struck out for the lodge.

Bob fell in step beside her. "Everyone knows Sheila took the hat, and you and Marcie helped."

"I don't know what you're talking about." Kelly picked up the pace. So much for her plan to waste time and skip the meal.

"If you don't—"

The sound of thundering hooves drowned out his words. She and Bob jumped to the side of the road as the horse staff galloped past.

Riding to lunch on horseback was a nice perk. No wonder Sheila had been envious. Kelly had yet to find any fringe benefits to working on maintenance.

A rider at the tail end of the group stopped beside them. Kelly looked up to find Joel's mesmerizing blue eyes, flashing smile, and wind-tossed blond hair.

"Hey, Kelly. Want a lift to the lodge?"

Like a fairy tale come true, her prince had come. And he was offering a ride on his noble steed.

"What are you doing, Joel?" Bob snapped, ruining the moment. "She's the enemy. You should drag her behind your horse until she confesses."

Kelly sent Bob a withering look. Now would be a great time for a fairy godmother to appear and turn him into a toad. It couldn't be hard. He was already halfway there.

"There are better ways to get a confession." Joel extended a hand to Kelly. "What do you say?"

"I'd love a ride." She wasn't a big fan of horses, but nothing was going to stop her from getting on this one.

"Can you give her a leg up?" Joel asked Bob.

Reluctantly, her partner cupped his hands. Kelly stepped into them, grabbed Joel's hand, and swung up behind him. The bold scent of cinnamon spice filled her senses, and she barely resisted the temptation to rest her cheek against his back and breathe in deeply.

"What about me?" Bob complained.

Joel shrugged, then urged his horse into a slow lope. Kelly immediately slipped to the side. She grabbed Joel's waist to steady herself. The warmth from his lean muscles radiated through his shirt. She considered pinching herself to make sure it wasn't a dream. But then she'd have to relax her grip on Joel. And there was no way she was doing that.

"So," Joel said over his shoulder, "have you got the hat?"

"Of course." She grinned. "I carry it with me everywhere. It's in my back pocket right now. Would you like me to give it to you?"

Joel burst out laughing. "I didn't expect an admission of guilt that easily."

"And you didn't get one," Kelly replied smoothly.

"When I first saw you, I took you for the shy, quiet type. But I'm beginning to think I was wrong. You can hold your own with a paintbrush. You tell bedtime stories that drop off entire cabins. And you're part of a prank that has the entire camp in an uproar. Not bad for your first week."

"Just trying to keep things interesting." Kelly's cheeks felt as if they had burst into flames. But his mention of this being her "first week" was a reminder that her time at camp was short. If Joel thought she'd be staying longer, he might not make his move until it was too late. "I'm only here for one week, so I have to make the most of it."

"Just one week? That's too bad."

Did he really mean that? Or was he being polite? Kelly wished she could see his face.

Several campers called her name as she rode past. She smiled down at them, ignoring the jealousy written on many of the girls' faces. Tony's words crept into her mind. *Ego boost. Selfish.* With a toss of her head, she banished the thoughts.

Far too quickly, they arrived at the lodge. Kelly could almost hear a clock striking midnight, signaling the end of her fairy-tale ride. The porch was packed with campers making their way into the lodge. Joel pulled up a few feet from the steps.

Kelly sat still for a moment, unsure how to dismount. The ground was a long way down.

Darren stepped off the porch and approached the horse. "Need some help?" His lips were set in a tight, straight line.

Kelly wondered at the disapproving expression. He probably shared Bob's opinion that she should be dragged behind the horse until she confessed. "No thanks."

Darren's frown deepened. His eyes remained focused on her face.

Kelly looked around for something to step on, a stool or raised platform. Nothing. She relaxed her hold on Joel's waist. Leaning to the side, she swung her leg over the back of the horse. But with nothing to grab, she was unable to control her descent. Kelly's feet hit the ground hard. She stumbled, then landed on her backside.

There was an outburst of laughter from the campers. And Cindy was probably somewhere in the group, enjoying her embarrassment. Kelly didn't look up to confirm. She winced from the pain and the humiliation. Tears came to her eyes, and she let out a low hiss. Which was a big mistake. Joel's horse tossed its head in alarm and made a series of short, stiff-legged jumps, as if escaping from a snake, its hooves coming dangerously close to her. The campers on the porch gasped. Kelly cringed and tried to scramble back.

In a blur of motion, someone jumped between her and the large animal, shielding her body from danger with his own. Kelly heard Joel's soothing voice as he dismounted and led the horse to a safe distance. Kelly relaxed and looked up to find Darren's anxious brown eyes. He reached down to help her stand, putting a protective arm around her shoulder as he guided her to the veranda.

"You should be more careful around horses."

An unexpected warmth filled Kelly. She murmured a quiet thank-you.

"You're welcome."

Darren glanced over at Joel, who had passed the reins to a counselor and was rushing toward them. When he turned back to Kelly, the concern in his eyes had hardened. He gave her an intense look, then disappeared into the lodge.

Joel reached her side, leaving Kelly no time to ponder Darren's shifting attitude. "Are you okay?"

Kelly tried to read the expression in Joel's blue eyes. Concern for her safety? Amusement from her awkward dismount? Disappointment at her clumsiness? She couldn't tell.

"I'm fine." Kelly brushed off her pants. "Thanks for the ride. And for rescuing me from Bob."

"No problem."

The corners of his lips curved into a grin. "You still need to tell me about Molly the Moth. My cabin is begging for another story."

Kelly gave a half-hearted smile. "I thought I was the enemy."

"Not to me." He returned to the horse and led it to a post where the other horses had been tethered.

Kelly watched him for a lingering moment. Her handsome prince had come. And she'd nearly blown her chances with him by falling on her butt. But the gallant hero had overlooked her idiotic blunder. There was still hope for a positive outcome. Maybe even a happily ever after.

21 TENSIONS RISE

"We've got to talk." Kelly leaned across the serving counter, her tone hushed but urgent.

Sheila glanced up and gave a withering scowl. Then she plopped a huge spoonful of mashed potatoes in the middle of Kelly's empty plate.

"I didn't ask for potatoes."

Sheila dropped a second heaping portion on top of the first.

Kelly shot Sheila a scathing look and moved down the line to where Marcie stood serving peas.

"What's the matter with Sheila?" Kelly pulled her plate back to avoid getting any more food added to it.

With a hesitant glance at their friend, Marcie whispered, "I'll tell you later."

"We need to talk as soon as possible. I overheard a conversation, and I know the guys are up to something."

Marcie chewed on her lip. "We get a break about an hour after lunch. Could we meet in your cabin?"

Kelly nodded. "The girls will be at archery, so it'll be empty. I'll duck out of whatever job I'm doing on maintenance."

Kelly made her way to her table and joined the campers.

Amber slid to the side, making room. "Why do you have so much mashed potatoes? And nothing else?"

"My friend was playing a joke on me." A mean one.

Kelly stuck her spoon into the mountain of spuds and stirred in aimless circles. It was tempting to indulge in just one or two bites of the creamy richness. In self-defense, she closed her eyes and imagined the potatoes slapped all over her hips, waist, and legs. She'd be fat, and Joel would find her disgusting. When she opened her eyes, she had no problem pushing the plate away.

The other girls shot a barrage of questions at Kelly.

"Why were you riding with Joel?"

"Does he like you?"

"Do you like him?"

"What about his girlfriend?"

"Are you going to kiss him?"

Kelly gave a slight shrug, hoping to strike an air of indifference. "He thinks I have inside information on Darren's hat. He tried to trick me into giving something away."

Jill waved a spoon in Kelly's direction. "Watch out for that guy. He's a player. When he was a camper, he had a reputation for kissing all the girls."

The campers giggled.

Jill cleared her throat. "Let's revisit our strategy for the clean cabin contest."

Kelly was grateful for the obvious redirection. She'd like to kiss Joel. But that wasn't information she wanted blabbed around camp.

She cast a fleeting glance toward her prince. He stood by his table, talking with Cindy. Kelly was too far away to hear their conversation, but there was no mistaking the angry sparks flying from Cindy's eyes. Could Joel's ride with Kelly be the source of the eruption? She hoped so.

Joel tucked a long golden strand of hair behind Cindy's ear. Then he leaned close to whisper something. Cindy's pout softened and she smiled. Pierced by a hot stab of jealousy, Kelly looked away.

Her attention strayed to Stan's table, where the weasel-like camper who'd threatened tar and feathers was jabbing Darren in the arm with a fork. The kid's arms were smudged with dirt, and ketchup stains colored the corners of his mouth. From the look of his greasy hair, Kelly guessed that he'd managed to ditch the mandatory cabin shower night. Or at least skipped the shampoo.

Kelly elbowed Amber and pointed in their direction. "Who's the Mad Stabber?"

"Marvin." Amber's lip curled in disgust. "We have vaulting at the same time as his cabin. No one can stand him."

"Is he always that dirty?"

"Yes. And he's starting to stink."

Darren removed the fork from the camper's grasp. Marvin snatched it back and plunged it into the back of Darren's hand. Darren's face twisted into a grimace.

Amber gasped. "Is that blood?"

"Sure looks like it." Kelly watched with curiosity. Serious injury at the hands of an annoying camper was a topic that hadn't been covered during staff orientation.

Darren wrestled the weapon out of Marvin's hand and placed it on the opposite side of the table, out of Marvin's reach.

"Guess he took control of that situation," Kelly quipped.

Amber rolled her eyes. "You don't know Marvin."

The boy seized a spoon and beat a frantic rhythm on Darren's back. With a quick twist of his wrist, Darren snatched the modified drumstick from Marvin. For a moment, Kelly thought Darren might smack the camper in the head with it. Instead, he breathed on the spoon and rubbed it on his nose. When he released his grip, the spoon remained in place, dangling off his face.

"I could never get that to work for me," Amber said, admiration in her voice.

Kelly didn't find it particularly attractive. But the cheap party trick did the job. Marvin grabbed another spoon and, instead of using it to beat on Darren, struggled to get it to stick on his own nose.

Kelly glanced back toward Joel's table. Cindy was nowhere in sight, but two female campers had taken her place. Grinning broadly, Joel appeared to be enjoying the flirtatious attention. Kelly felt another sharp stab of jealousy, even though she had no claim on him.

A burst of applause drew her attention to Darren's table. Both Marvin and Darren had spoons hanging off their noses. As she compared the two scenes, Kelly felt a flicker of doubt. While she disagreed with Tony's assessment that Darren was twice the man Joel was, he was certainly not a flirt. She watched as Darren exchanged a high-five with the outcast camper.

Amber fixed Kelly with a penetrating look. "I think Darren's really great."

"He's a nice guy," Kelly said matter-of-factly. Except for the fact that he was about to exact revenge on her and her friends.

"He jumped in front of a horse to save you."

True. Which meant he couldn't be too mad at her, despite all his frowns. She turned to consider him again. His tousled hair and warm brown eyes had a certain charm. And she remembered the warmth of his hand on her shoulder. But he wasn't Joel.

Bill strode to the front of the dining hall and tapped his watch. "Time's running out. If a certain item is not returned by tonight, there will be consequences."

Kelly shuddered. With Bill's unpredictable creativity, who knew what kind of punishment he'd devise.

She poured a large glass of water and guzzled it. Another successful meal. She hadn't eaten a thing. And hadn't been caught.

Bill dismissed the campers, and Kelly and Amber carried their plates to the slop bucket at the front of the room. Kelly's mashed potatoes, which she hadn't touched, covered the bottom of the pail.

Kelly made her way to the maintenance shed, hoping the afternoon assignment wouldn't involve dead bugs. A job in some remote place would be perfect. That way no one would notice when she slipped off to meet with Marcie and Sheila.

Tony held out a garbage bag and a pair of gardener's gloves. "The area around the lodge needs to be weeded."

Kelly grimaced. "Maybe you shouldn't plant so many weeds."

"Then what would you do all day?" Tony chuckled. "Bob will be helping me at the barn for about an hour and a half and then he'll join you."

Perfect. She'd be able to start on her task, have her meeting with Sheila and Marcie, and get back before Bob showed up. Kelly hoped her relief wasn't too obvious.

She headed to her assigned spot and worked for forty-five minutes, constantly checking her watch. Then she slipped off to her cabin. Once inside, she paced the room, trying to guess what had put Sheila in such a hostile mood.

Ten minutes later, Sheila swept in like a cool breeze. She shoved Kelly's stuffed beagle out of the way and sat on the bunk, arms crossed.

Marcie perched on a neighboring bed. "So, what's the news?"

Kelly described the screwdriver-and-chocolate-bar exchange that she'd witnessed.

Marcie bit her lower lip. "They're definitely up to something." She turned to Sheila. "Any idea what it could be?"

Sheila shrugged and stared out the window.

"What is your problem?" Kelly had enough of watching Sheila pout.

"Nothing's wrong with me," she snapped back. "And apparently nothing's wrong with you either. You're probably feeling great after your cozy ride with Joel."

Instantly, everything clicked. This hat thing wasn't about getting Darren's attention. It was about getting Joel's.

"You're jealous!"

"Am not!" Sheila looked as if she were going to burst into tears.

Kelly's anger drained out of her. "I had no idea you liked Joel. Honestly. I thought you had a thing for Darren."

Sheila picked up Kelly's beagle and stroked the long ears. She remained silent for a few moments, then let out a loud sigh. "I fell in love with Joel the first time I saw him."

According to Bill and his theory of ties, love at first sight wasn't possible. But this didn't seem a good time to remind Sheila of the campfire message.

"When was that?"

"Two years ago. We were both campers, and he paid a lot of attention to me the whole week. I felt so special." Sheila lowered her head. "We even kissed once."

It was only one kiss, years ago. But it still bothered Kelly to hear about it.

Sheila took a ragged breath. "We both came back to camp the next year, and I thought things would continue. But he found a new girl to take my place. And this year he's got Cindy."

Tony's comments lingered in Kelly's mind. "What do you like about Joel, anyway?"

"He's just so good-looking. Athletic. Confident. Flawless. Everything you could want in a guy."

All external qualities. So Tony was right. Sheila couldn't really be in love with Joel because she didn't know him. And, Kelly admitted, neither did she.

Sheila put the beagle aside. "If you can get Joel, you should go for him. I'd rather he chose you than that stuck-up snit Cindy."

Kelly gave her friend a big hug. "Right now we have more important things to think about, like surviving whatever Darren and Bob have planned for us."

Marcie stood and stretched. "All the Men in Hats are probably in on the scheme. Since Charlie works in the kitchen with us, maybe we can get something out of him."

"He hardly ever says a word." Sheila frowned. "It would take a miracle to get him to spill confidential information."

"Bob and I will be weeding together this afternoon," Kelly said. "I'll work on him."

Marcie gave a wistful sigh. As if pulling thorns with Bob was the most romantic activity in the world.

Sheila glanced at her watch. "Unfortunately, our break is over." She stood. "But at least we have a plan."

The girls left the cabin and walked together to the lodge, where they parted ways.

Kelly returned to her weeding and worked alone for another half hour. When Bob joined her, garbage bag and gloves in hand, his face twisted in a scowl.

"You haven't gotten much done. Having a lazy afternoon and saving all the work for me?"

Bob was such a charmer.

Kelly bit back a sarcastic reply and greeted him with a bright smile "I'm glad you're here. This has to be the worst job in camp. It's so...lonely." Her drama teacher would have groaned at that performance.

"This is a switch." Bob crossed his arms. "You're acting friendly. You wouldn't be fishing for information, would you?"

Kelly grit her teeth. "Of course not."

"Why don't you go ask Romeo for another ride on his mule? Maybe he'll tell you what you want to know."

Kelly wished she could wipe the smirk off Bob's face. With a silent apology to her friends, she abandoned the quest for clues and escaped to the opposite side of the lodge. Plopping herself down near a patch of weeds, she worked in solitude. After considering every possible trick that would require a large number of screwdrivers, she came up blank.

A shadow fell over her. She looked up into Tony's eyes.

"It's quitting time."

Kelly rose slowly, limbs stiff from crouching.

Tony picked up the bag. "Looks like you left some weeds for another day. You're free to go."

Instead of leaving, Kelly dropped to her knees. "O Keeper of the Maintenance Shed and Defender of the Weak, please tell me what the guys are planning. I promise I'll buy you enough chocolate to last the rest of the summer."

"Chocolate bars are for new deals only. They can't be used to purchase information on other deals."

"Are you quoting from some *How to Bribe the Maintenance Manager* handbook?" Desperation brought out her sarcastic side.

"I wrote the book, and I'd be happy to provide you with a copy. In exchange for a chocolate bar, of course."

Kelly resisted the temptation to throw something at him. "I'll pull every weed in this camp. I'll paint every fence post. I'll clean every screen in every cabin."

Tony crossed his arms. "You'll do all that if I tell you to anyway."

It was no use. He wasn't going to turn informant. She spun around and headed to supper.

As Kelly got into the food line with her cabin, dizziness swept over her. The room spun slightly. Her knees gave way. Scared she might pass out, she leaned on the counter for support.

"Are you feeling all right?" Jill touched her arm. "Your face is white."

"I'm fine." Kelly took several deep breaths to steady herself. She'd never felt this sick before, but then again, she'd never eaten so little. Back home, she'd had to deal with her mother's constant vigilance. Wearied by the battles at each meal, Kelly had compromised with low-calorie snacks. But that hadn't been the case at camp. Combine the skipped meals with the lack of sleep and constant activity, and the only surprise was that she hadn't collapsed sooner.

The feeling of nausea passed. Kelly gave Jill a shaky smile and brushed aside her hand. "It's been a long day." She put a small amount of pasta on her plate. No sauce or meatballs, of course.

"You're setting a bad example for the campers," Jill whispered in her ear.

Kelly glanced back and saw that several of the girls had also taken small portions and skipped the sauce. A huge wave of guilt slammed into her.

Sandy walked through the swinging kitchen doors, her gaze sweeping across the half-empty plates. She grabbed a ladle from one of the pots and motioned for the girls to wait. "Two meatballs per person," she announced, then scooped a generous amount of marinara sauce, with the required meatballs, onto each plate, including Kelly's. "It's the Timberlake Law of Spaghetti."

Kelly's hands trembled as she walked back to the table. With so many eyes watching, she had to eat every morsel on her plate. As she struggled to swallow, she determined to take an extra-long jog the next morning to make up for eating so many calories.

At the end of the meal, a stern-looking Bill strode to the front of the room with a hatless Darren by his side. "I was very clear this morning when—"

"Ahem."

All eyes turned to the staff table at the back of the hall.

Tony rose to his feet. "Sorry to interrupt, Bill, but I found this on my workbench." He held up a shoebox. "It had a chocolate bar on it and a message asking me to deliver the box to you at supper time." Tony walked to the front and handed the package to Bill.

Bill raised the top, peered inside, and pulled out a note. As he scanned it, a hint of a smile flickered across his face. But it was quickly replaced with a frown.

He read aloud:

We heard all the words that Director Bill said.
"A hat must be back upon Darren's head."
We've provided a hat for Darren to wear.
Next time choose your words with a little more care.

Darren reached into the box and pulled out a paper hat nearly identical to the original in color, shape, and size. Sheila and Marcie had done a great job. As Darren held the hat high, applause and jeers rose from the campers. With a sweeping bow, he placed it on his head and headed back to his table.

Bill addressed the camp. "It appears that whoever took Darren's hat has returned a hat. Let me be clear this time. *Darren's* hat needs to be back on his head by supper time tomorrow. If not, Bernice has a couple of extra shovels and pitchforks. And things are really piling up in the barn."

Kelly wrinkled her nose. She'd never shoveled manure before and had no desire to start now. Sheila and Marcie had better see reason and return the hat. Or she'd row out on her own to get it.

Tony held up an empty candy wrapper. "And please note that I am not doing any more delivery work if there are nuts in the chocolate bar."

Only Tony would be so blatant. And greedy.

"I'll pretend I didn't hear that." Bill coughed. "Campfire will be indoors tonight. We'll meet in the gym in five minutes."

Kelly exhaled slowly. The paper hat had bought them another twenty-four hours. She might have felt relieved...if not for those four annoying screwdrivers.

22 AN EVENING OF REBOUNDS

Kelly struggled against the current of campers and staff members as everyone swept toward the narrow doorway leading into the gymnasium. This was all Bill's fault. He knew there was only one door from the dining hall into the gym. Did he have to give the entire camp only five minutes to get through it before campfire started?

Bodies slammed against her on all sides. Someone stomped on her foot, and she yelped. But the sound was lost in the raucous tumult of the crowd. Fingers bit into her arm. Kelly twisted her head to find Amber hanging on as if she were a life preserver.

"Why are we meeting inside tonight?" Amber shouted.

"I have no idea." Except that Bill didn't seem to like campfires with actual fire. He had to drag them somewhere else. Like the riding arena. And now the gym.

MaryAnn stood in the center of the room, arms swinging like a policeman directing traffic. "Find your cabinmates and sit together along the walls."

Kelly caught sight of Jill at the far end of the gym. She and Amber made their way over and squeezed in alongside the rest of their group. Kelly wasn't thrilled about sitting on the hard, cold floor. She leaned back against the rough wood paneling and hoped the campfire wouldn't take too long.

Once the campers had settled, Bill jogged through the gym door, wearing a referee's black-and-white-striped shirt and dribbling a basketball. A predominantly male cheer burst from the crowd.

Kelly leaned forward, her discomfort forgotten. Basketball was one of her favorite sports, and she'd played on the junior team in middle school. She lost interest when she got to high school and instead turned her attention to drama. But after she started dating Aaron, captain of the varsity team, she hadn't missed a match.

Amber groaned and slumped against the wall. "That's why we're here? To watch basketball?"

"What's wrong with that?" Kelly clapped along with the other campers. For once, she wouldn't mind being chosen if Bill needed a volunteer.

"I don't like playing sports. Or even watching them."

Kelly didn't doubt that. Judging from Amber's selection of books, the only sport that could hold her interest was the steamy game of love.

Bill stopped at center court and blew a short blast on the silver whistle that hung around his neck. "I've already recruited two teams for tonight's competition. Huddle up!"

So she'd have no chance to show off her athletic skills in front of Joel. Kelly felt a twinge of disappointment.

The four Men in Hats jumped up, raced to the left side of the court, and pulled into a tight circle. Joel, Bob, Stan and a counselor named Brent who taught archery formed a second huddle on the right side of the gym.

No question which side Kelly would support. Team Joel had her cheer. And her heart.

Amber pointed to the far group. "Darren's wearing his paper hat."

"Not for long." Kelly laughed. It would be impossible for that flimsy thing to stay on his head during a fast-moving game.

Bill sounded the whistle again, and the teams lined up at center court. Darren, Mike, Charlie, and Zach pulled thin pieces of string out of their pockets and secured their hats onto their heads. They looked goofy. But the campers showed their approval by cheering wildly. Kelly had to admit that Darren was being a good sport about the prank.

Mike faced Joel for the tip-off. Bill tossed the ball in the air and Joel leaped high. But Mike was taller, and the extra inches gave him the advantage.

Mike knocked the ball to Charlie, who dribbled down the court. The Men in Hats pressed toward the basket. Charlie faked a shot and tossed the ball to Zach. But a flash of blond came out of nowhere and intercepted the pass. Joel tore down the court and performed a flawless layup. Kelly clapped so hard her hands stung. This was turning out to be the best campfire yet.

Bill shouted something, most likely the score, but his words were drowned out by a wave of cheers. Overwhelmingly female. Joel slapped hands with his teammates and jogged back to his zone.

On the far end of the gym, Mike threw the ball in from the side. Charlie caught it and moved down the court. The ball flew from Charlie to Zach. Zach threw a wild pass to Darren, who managed to catch it and send it back Mike. He took a shot, but it rebounded off the rim.

Leaping high, Mike caught the ball. Bob tried to knock it away but ended up smashing Mike on the arm. Bill called a foul and motioned for Mike to step out of bounds. He tossed the ball to him. Mike looked for an open teammate, then passed it to Charlie. A lob to Darren was intercepted by Joel. Again.

The crowd cheered harder as Joel took off down the court. Kelly put her fingers to her lips and gave a piercing whistle. She fixed her eyes on Joel as he moved across the room with the smooth, relaxed stride of a professional athlete. She could have watched him all night. This was his game and he ruled the court. The only person who came close to matching him in skill was Mike.

Unfortunately, Joel's breakaway ended when Zach ran into him. The campers erupted with boos. Bill awarded Joel two free throws. Both shots swished through the hoop. The female campers yelled themselves hoarse. Kelly included.

Amber yawned loudly.

"How can you not enjoy this game?" Kelly shouted above the pandemonium.

"I wish I'd brought my book."

Reading was good. Watching Joel was better.

Kelly's attention turned back to the game just in time to see blood dripping from Charlie's nose. She picked up the words *elbow, cheap shot,* and *Bob.* Kelly knew her maintenance partner too well to be shocked. Her only surprise was that he hadn't fouled out of the game in the first five minutes. She hoped Marcie was watching—and taking notes on her malicious glamour boy.

Bill asked Charlie if he wanted to make a substitution, but he shook his head and wiped his nose on his sleeve. The play resumed.

Bill gave a two-minute countdown. Joel's team had possession of the ball. They passed it back and forth with lightning speed, fighting furiously for the chance to make one last basket. Despite numerous shots, every attempt missed.

As the campers counted down the final ten seconds, Mike intercepted the ball and threw a wild long shot. It bounced off the backboard. To the amazement of all, the ball dropped through the hoop. The campers leaped to their feet, chanting Mike's name.

Bill blew his whistle and waved the guys in to shake hands. The players, chests still heaving from the effort of the game, shook hands, then waved to their adoring fans.

Kelly had eyes for only one athlete. Even with his face flushed and blond hair matted with sweat, Joel was gorgeous. Kelly wished he'd find her in the crowd and smile. Or at least nod. But he didn't even look her way.

The court had barely cleared before Tony and MaryAnn brought out Guy and Girl, placing them under one of the baskets. MaryAnn connected the cardboard hands with ties. Then she and Tony walked off to the side.

Kelly leaned back and crossed her legs. Time for the spiritual stuff. A letdown after the exhilarating game.

Bill, still wearing the referee's uniform and whistle, jogged over to the paper couple. Kelly wondered how he was going to pull something meaningful out of a basketball game. And link it with romantic love. And God. It seemed like a harder move than Mike's long shot across the gym.

Bill motioned for quiet. "Tonight we're going to talk about a strategic move called the rebound. A rebound happens when a shot misses and bounces off the basket rim or backboard. We saw several great examples tonight. Grabbing the rebound is a great play in basketball. But it's a lousy move in dating."

Not in Kelly's playbook. If Cindy messed up her chance with Joel, Kelly would be ready to move in, grab him, and take him away.

Bill pulled a pair of scissors out of his pocket and snipped through the cords connecting the cardboard pair. "Guy took a shot at dating Girl, but she broke up with him. However, don't count him out of the love game yet."

Tony sprinted in from the side, carrying the cut-out figure of a different Girl. He elbowed the original Girl out of the way and placed New Girl next to Guy.

Kelly shook her head in amused disbelief. Only Bill would dream up two cardboard characters. And now there were three.

Bill motioned toward the cutouts. "Our friends are no longer a couple. But in a classic rebound move, Guy grabs the next girl who walks by. He shoves the ties into her hand. That gives him another shot at a relationship."

As Tony connected the cut ties from Guy's hand to New Girl's hand, Kelly's thoughts drifted to Aaron. He was probably hooking up with someone new. Only he wouldn't have to grab anyone. Half the girls in the school would be throwing themselves at his feet. Funny, though, the thought didn't bother her as much as before. Probably because she had her sights set on a rebound of her own with Joel.

Bill blew his whistle. "The rebound worked! Guy has scored. He sure looks happy...for now."

Mike booed. "We want our Girl back!"

The campers followed his lead. Kelly joined in, glad that none of her friends from home could see her getting caught up in the romantic lives of two paper cutouts. Absurd as it was, she felt loyal to the original Girl. She didn't want to see Guy with anyone else.

Bill raised his hands. Once the crowd had quieted, he walked over to Mike. "Why do you think Guy connected with New Girl so fast?"

Mike shrugged. "I guess he doesn't want to be alone."

"Correct. He didn't choose New Girl based on her personality and character. We know that because he didn't even have time to get to know her. Guy picked her because she was available."

Aaron wouldn't be looking for someone based on personality or character either. He'd take any good-looking girl who would do whatever he wanted. Rather than feeling jealous, Kelly realized she felt sorry for whoever that would be. Because Aaron probably wouldn't care for the new girl any more than he'd cared for her, and he'd drop her just as fast if something went wrong. And she wondered why she hadn't seen Aaron in this light before.

Bill walked back to the new cardboard couple. "See any other problems?"

A female camper shouted, "Guy used the old ties to connect with New Girl."

"Two points for you." Bill applauded. "There wasn't time for Guy to let go of the previous cords. As with a substitution in a basketball game, the new person is expected to pick up right where the old one left off."

Kelly's thoughts drifted to her school friend Annalisa. She'd secretly been dubbed Miss Revolving Door because she was never without a boyfriend. The moment one guy left, she snagged another. Perhaps a better nickname would be Miss Rebound.

Bill pointed to Mike. "What does a coach do when the game is at a critical place?"

"He calls a time-out."

"That answer was a slam dunk," Darren called out.

Mike faked a high-five. "What could I do? The ball was in my court."

Bill waited for the camper groans to die down. "The answer was correct. But the puns were foul."

More moans from the crowd. The humor was obvious, and rather simple. But even if Mike and Darren didn't earn points for clever puns, they scored on consistency. Kelly smiled at her own mental wordplay.

Bill walked back to New Girl and Guy, unfastened the ties, and then moved both cardboard girls off to the side. Left by himself with loose ropes hanging from his hand, Guy looked forlorn.

Bill put his arm around the solitary figure. "After a break-up or a dump, Guy needs to wait awhile before dating again. Then he won't be dragging old ties with negative emotions into the new romance. But until that time comes, he's got a problem. Guy's lonely."

Kelly had never thought about why Annalisa always had a guy on her arm. She'd assumed Miss Revolving Door was just a self-centered flirt. But even though Annalisa was a part of the cool group, she didn't have a lot of close friends. Jealous of her constant parade of boyfriends and anxious to protect their own guys, many of the girls had shunned her. If what Bill said was true, Annalisa might just be lonely.

Bill pointed to Guy. "God created each of us with a need to be loved and to give love. If Guy is taking a time-out from dating, how can he meet those needs?"

A loud knock on the gym door caused Kelly to jump.

Bill nodded to Stan, who was sitting to the left of the door. "Would you see who's there?"

Stan stood and swung the door wide. Two cardboard characters stood in the frame. Around their necks were signs labelling them "Guy's Mom" and "Guy's Dad." The paper mother wore an apron and the father had a rolled-up newspaper in his hand. Kelly laughed along with the campers. The cardboard population was expanding rapidly.

MaryAnn carried the figures in and set them beside Guy.

Bill shook the stiff hands of the new arrivals. "Who knows us best and annoys us most? Family. Who has the courage to say what we need to hear? Who has our best interest in mind? Who will always be there for us? Hopefully, it's our family."

Kelly had another question Bill could add to his list. Who forces you to go to camp when you want to stay home? But she didn't feel the biting anger she'd experienced when her parents first announced their decision. She hadn't realized it until that moment, but during the past few days, the bitterness had drained away.

Bill put his arms around Guy's mother and father. "I know this isn't always the case. And no parent is perfect. But in families that function as they should, there's a shared commitment to one another."

A startling thought struck Kelly. If things went well with Joel, she might end up thanking her mom and dad for signing her up for this week. She would never have predicted that.

MaryAnn took several of the ties dangling from Guy's hand and connected them to his parents' hands. Just before she finished, there was another loud knock.

Bill motioned to Stan, and he opened the door again.

Tony strode in, carrying three cutout figures and a large paper sack.

Kelly laughed. Cardboard people were taking over the world. Or at least Timberlake camp.

"Some of Guy's friends have come to hang out with him," Bill explained.

Tony tossed the sack to Bill, then arranged the characters around Guy. Using a handful of ties, he connected Guy to his buddies.

Bill reached into the bag and pulled out four matching baseball caps. "Among good friends, there is trust, support, loyalty, and understanding."

And a lack of good fashion. Although these were definitely an improvement on the ugly fishing headgear worn by Darren and his crew.

As Bill placed the caps on the paper heads of Guy and his friends, the Men in Hats hollered their approval.

A series of raps at the gym door caused Bill to throw his hands up in exaggerated surprise. "Well, who could it be now?"

Stan swung the door wide once more, and Sandy entered. Instead of a cutout person, she carried a large wooden cross and a handful of brown sheets of paper cut in the shape of footprints. She placed the cross beside Guy.

Starting at Guy's feet, Sandy laid out two sets of footprints. A quarter of the way across the gym, she dropped one of the tracks. A single set of prints continued alone. At center court, she scattered the remaining sheets in a haphazard manner. Then she returned to stand beside the cross.

Bill gestured toward the figures surrounding Guy. "When we're feeling lonely, we can meet part of our need for sharing through family and friends. But the most important connection is with God."

Kelly had agreed with everything Bill had said...until now. She'd tried to connect with God. She'd given Him her best. She'd reached up as far as she could. And fell short.

Sandy reached into her back pocket and pulled out a long red tie. Kelly caught the symbolism right away. Red for the blood of Jesus. The kitchen worker attached one end to the beam of the cross and the other to Guy's hand.

Bill followed the trail of brown footsteps. "This path represents our relationship with God. We never walk alone. God is always with us." He pointed to the single set of prints. "During the difficult times in our lives, He carries us."

Kelly recognized the familiar story of "Footprints." She used to have a poster in her room with the poem on it. Her parents had given it to her years ago. As a child, she'd found the message comforting. In all her storms and trials, Jesus would carry her. Last year, she'd taken it down, crumpled it up, and thrown it in the garbage.

Bill reached the mixed-up pattern of steps on the gym floor. The prints crisscrossed, strayed apart, and even faced in opposite directions at times. Kelly frowned. She didn't remember anything like that on the poster.

"Looks like a mess, doesn't it?" A grin stretched across Bill's face. "These are the times when we dance."

Kelly's jaw clenched. When she was younger, her father used to dance with her in his arms. They'd whirl around the house, spinning, dipping, and twirling until she was out of breath. She'd felt so close to her dad in those moments of crazy abandon.

But to dance with God? Out of the question. She'd never felt that close to Him.

With a wave of his arm, Bill directed everyone's attention back to the crowd of cardboard characters. "Guy was lonely when Girl broke up with him. But he doesn't need to rebound into another romantic relationship to avoid the pain. A strong connection with family, friends, and God will provide the support he needs to get through this difficult time."

Kelly wondered what kind of support Annalisa had at home. She didn't have any siblings, and Kelly had never seen her parents at any of the school activities. Perhaps Annalisa hadn't really wanted all those guys. If Kelly and the other girls reached out in true friendship, Annalisa might lose the need to rebound from one boyfriend to the next.

Then she thought about herself. She was lonely now that Aaron was out of the picture. And where was she turning? To another guy, just like Annalisa. But she didn't have a lot of other choices. She'd been fighting with her parents at home, had neglected her church friends, and was being shunned by the cool crowd at school. Joel seemed like her best option.

Bill glanced at his watch. "Tonight's message is over. Head back to the cabins. Lights out in twenty minutes."

Kelly's stomach knotted as she watched Bill pick up the footprints from the floor. She didn't have to ask if he'd danced with God. She'd seen them. On the road every morning. While she stumbled past alone.

Amber nudged Kelly and pointed to the corner of the gym where the Men in Hats had formed a huddle with the campers from Darren's cabin. "Are they starting another basketball game?"

Kelly saw a flash of metallic silver in Darren's hand. "No. They're setting up for something different."

A game called Revenge. With no rules and no referee. And she had no defense against the screwdrivers. This matchup wasn't going to end well.

23 TWO INVITATIONS AND A RESCUE

As Kelly started her morning jog down the road, she tried to keep her attention focused on the route ahead. But she couldn't help glancing over her shoulder to see if anyone was following her—possibly carrying a bucket of tar and feathers. Everything remained clear. No signs of mischief. Nothing appeared out of the ordinary.

A rustle in the bushes made her leap to the opposite side of the road. A rabbit hopped out, and she chuckled at her nervousness.

Kelly wiped a hand across her sweaty forehead and resumed her pace, pushing through the exhaustion. She'd told the girls a bedtime story about a three-legged chicken, then stayed awake half the night, straining to catch the sound of boys wreaking unknown havoc. But she hadn't heard a thing. When she'd finally surrendered to a restless sleep, she'd dreamed of being chased by giant screwdrivers wearing ugly brown hats.

Kelly stopped to shake a stone out of her shoe and took a few deep, steadying breaths. She was being paranoid. Behind her, the camp slumbered in peaceful bliss. Whatever sneaky stunt the boys had planned must have failed.

Forty-five minutes later, Kelly jogged back into camp and she chided herself for being foolish. After all, how much damage could the boys do with a few screwdrivers?

A glance at her watch showed she had just enough time for a quick shower before breakfast. Kelly zipped into the cabin, where a few girls still slumbered, though most of the bunks were empty.

As quietly as possible, Kelly gathered her towel, shampoo, and a clean set of clothes, then slipped out. As she neared the bathroom, she heard a rumble of angry female voices. She quickened her steps, wondering if there'd been a fight over sinks or electrical outlets.

Kelly found it difficult to squeeze her way into the packed bathroom, and the roar of girls arguing all at once made it impossible to ask questions. And then she saw the source of the outrage. And understood why Darren needed so many screwdrivers.

Each of the mirrors had been unscrewed, turned around, and secured back in place. The paper backing reflected nothing, rendering them useless. The shower rods and curtains had been removed, leaving the white tile walls open to view by everyone else in the bathroom. Even worse, all the lavatory stall doors had been removed, exposing the toilets.

A few girls giggled, but most wore furious expressions. Several hopped from one foot to the other, in obvious need of privacy.

Kelly grimaced. *Good one, Darren.*

Jill arrived, carrying an armful of blankets. The sea of girls parted, and Jill draped the quilts over the toilet stall frames. With exclamations of relief and gratitude, several campers dashed behind the make-shift screens.

Amy stuck her head in the bathroom. "I found the doors in the supply closet. I'll go to the maintenance shed and borrow a few screwdrivers from Tony."

A futile plan. Darren had put his five-dollar coupon to good use, and there wouldn't be any screwdrivers until noon. But Kelly didn't bother to share that information. Best not to get involved.

"Thanks a lot, Kelly!" Cindy's angry voice rang from the far end of the bathroom. "This is your fault. You and your friends."

All eyes turned to her.

Kelly took a step back, as if to distance herself from the damage. "Why are you accusing me?"

Cindy pointed to the backward mirror farthest from where Kelly stood. It had a note taped to it, which Cindy seemed only too happy to read aloud.

To all female staff and campers,

This is a warning, loud and clear.
If you were smart, you'd shake with fear.
Wherever you go, you should watch your back.
You never know when we might attack.
You're going to suffer, be sure of that,
Unless you give back Darren's hat.
The Men in Hats and their loyal supporters

PS: Sheila, Marcie, and Kelly, we know you took the hat. We're coming after you first.

PPS: The prank was approved. Complaining will do you no good.

"They're bluffing." Kelly forced a weak smile. "They want us turn on each other."

Cindy gave a triumphant laugh. "I heard you plotting with Sheila about getting supplies, and I told Darren."

So much for the bonds of sisterhood. The guys didn't even need to bribe the smirking snitch.

With a fierce glare, Cindy tossed back her blonde mane and left. Several of the campers walked out with her. Trying to ignore the grumbling aimed in her direction, Kelly focused on draping one of the blankets across a shower stall frame.

The warm water flowing over her washed away the dirt and sweat. But not the images of angry campers' faces. The poem, along with Cindy's accusations, had accomplished its goal. The girls had been stung by the prank, and they had three targets for their frustration. With Sheila and Marcie safe in the kitchen, Kelly was the only one within firing range.

Kelly stepped out of the shower and wrapped her hair in a towel. Amy returned from the maintenance shed—without any screwdrivers, of course. The girls groaned, but Amy produced a handful of butter knives and showed a few girls how to use them as crude tools. With everyone's attention diverted, Kelly snuck back to the cabin. She found the campers huddled around a small handheld mirror.

Joyce waved the mirror in Kelly's direction. "This stinks. I can only see half my head with this thing. And I had to pee so bad this morning I almost left a puddle on the floor."

For once, Joyce had a justifiable complaint.

Emma wrinkled her nose. "I couldn't wait. I used the bushes."

"There's no way I'm going in the trees," Joyce snorted.

"Imagine what they'll do next." Emma waved her arms in the air. "Turn off the hot water so our showers are freezing? Or turn everything off so we have no water at all?"

Even Jill looked irritated. "Kelly, you should give back the hat."

"I don't have it." At least not on her.

Jill frowned. "But I'm guessing you know where it is."

Well, she knew where it was supposed to be. But Kelly couldn't be sure that the line hadn't broken, setting the hat adrift. Or that fish hadn't found the bags and nibbled through to reach the main course within. However, she was certain Jill didn't want to hear about potentially negative complications, so Kelly pressed her lips tightly together.

"You have to talk to Sheila and Marcie. Knock some sense into their heads before the boys do something worse and every girl in camp attacks all three of you."

As if to support Jill's warning, several of the campers shot Kelly dirty looks before returning their attention to the handheld mirror.

Kelly sat on the edge of her bunk and swept her long hair back into a ponytail. She reached under her pillow and pulled out the calendar. With swift strokes, she scratched through the box labeled Wednesday. Only four days left, and camp would be over. With the morning's threats hanging over her head, that sounded like a good thing.

As Kelly pushed the chart back under her pillow, she thought of things she'd miss when she returned home. Not working on maintenance with Bob, that was for sure. But she would miss Sheila and her crazy schemes, Marcie and her quest for academic glory, Joel's mesmerizing blue eyes, and the crazy antics of Darren and Mike.

Kelly frowned. Odd that she'd considered Darren in friendly terms when he'd just turned most of the female campers against her and her friends. And he was such a tease, messing up Sheila's hair and making terrible puns. But he'd played along with the paper hat, and dashed in to save her from the horse's hooves when she fell.

Kelly gave her head a slight shake to dismiss thoughts about Darren. She had bigger things to worry about. Like trying to get Sheila to cough up the hat before more damage was done.

As Kelly walked to the lodge with her girls, she was greeted by taunts from the male campers. Kelly flinched every time she heard her name. But she kept her eyes focused forward.

Once she'd filled her cereal bowl, Kelly sat at her table and stirred the plain oatmeal. She listened half-heartedly as the campers discussed the morning prank. When their voices ceased abruptly, Kelly glanced up, expecting to see Bill at the front with the clean cabin scores. Instead she looked directly into a pair of intense blue eyes.

"Hey, Kelly." Joel's deep voice made her stomach flip. "I'm working on a new vaulting routine this afternoon and I need an extra pair of hands." He swept his blond hair back from his forehead. "If you're interested in helping, meet me at the corral after lunch."

Before Kelly could answer, Jill jumped into the conversation. "You're not planning to put Kelly up on Samson, are you?"

Joel chuckled. "Of course not. Matt usually handles the lunge line, but he's going to spot for me. I need someone to keep Samson moving while I practice a few moves on his back."

Lunge line? Spotting? Joel might as well be speaking a foreign language.

Jill faced Kelly. "Have you ever worked with a vaulting horse?"

"No." But she was a fast learner. And motivation wouldn't be a problem with Joel as her teacher.

Jill spun back to Joel. "Why don't you pick someone who has experience? Cindy knows how to handle a lunge line."

Kelly gave Jill a swift kick under the table. Jill smiled as if nothing was wrong.

Joel addressed Kelly. "You've been around horses before, right?"

"Sure." Although the trip to the petting zoo when she was in kindergarten probably didn't count. There was no need to explain that her first time riding a horse had been yesterday with him. When she'd fallen on her butt and nearly been trampled.

Joel gave Jill a confident smile. "Anything she doesn't know, I can teach her." He leaned close to Kelly. "Are you interested in helping me?"

Kelly felt her face glow. "Absolutely. I'll ask Tony for some time off this afternoon."

"Great." Joel flashed his heart-stopping grin. "See you there."

As Joel walked back to his table, Kelly's campers made smooching noises. The teasing stopped when Bill banged on the side of the serving area with a metal spoon. Shouts and cheers erupted as he filled in the clean cabin scoreboard.

"We're still tied for first place," Jill shouted, her concerns about Joel apparently forgotten—for the moment.

Kelly tried to fake excitement as the girls celebrated with high fives.

"Three more inspections and we'll be feasting on Sandy's Super Sundaes. All we have to do is continue—" Jill's words were drowned out by stamping and yelling from Stan's cabin.

"Victory is ours, and so are the sundaes!" Stan shouted.

An arrogant boast, considering that it was still too early to tell which cabin would win. Though Kelly was privately rooting for the boys.

Bill dismissed the campers, and the girls began clearing the table. As Kelly scraped the majority of her oatmeal into the slop bucket, she felt a tap on her shoulder. She looked up, hoping to see Joel again. Her eagerness vanished when she found herself staring into Sandy's eyes instead.

"It's a great day for a canoe ride. I checked with Tony, and he's released you from morning maintenance duties so you can join me."

Kelly had always thought that working on maintenance was the last place she wanted to be. Until now. She swallowed the lump in her throat. "Canoeing isn't my thing." She'd already been out on the lake once and had no desire to repeat the boating, or swimming, again.

"We won't go far." Sandy's smile was firm. "My plan is to drop anchor in the middle of the lake and relax. There are a few thoughts I'd like to share with you."

Kelly didn't want to go out on a dinky boat with someone bent on sharing, which was clearly a code word for giving a lecture. "I just told Joel I'd help him with vaulting this afternoon. I don't know if Tony will give me that much time off."

"I'm sure Tony can manage without you. Besides, we'll only be out for an hour or so." Sandy glanced at her bare arms and sighed. "Just enough time for me to get a sunburn."

Kelly clenched her teeth. She could refuse. But if Sandy tattled to Tony, that might jeopardize her afternoon with Joel. It would be safest to go and get it over with.

"Meet me in the kitchen when cabin devotions are finished." Sandy walked off, whistling an upbeat tune.

As she headed toward Amber, who stood waiting for her at the exit, Kelly felt nauseated. The thrill of vaulting with Joel had been soured by the dread of canoeing with Sandy.

Just outside the lodge, Kelly noticed several male campers gathered in a tight ring. Marvin, the unwashed boy from Darren's cabin, stood in the center. His face was a splotchy red, and it looked like he was struggling to hold back tears. A growing crowd gathered around the boys.

"You wet your bed last night." A tall camper laughed.

Fists clenched, Marvin took a step toward the boy. "I did not, you liar!"

"Then why is there no sleeping bag on your bunk? It's because the counselors are washing it before it stinks up the whole cabin!"

The other boys snickered and made rude comments.

"We should call you Pee Wee Marvin."

"Do you need a diaper, Pee Wee?"

"I'm glad I'm not on the bunk below him!"

A surge of anger welled up within Kelly. She nudged Amber. "What's the name of that tall kid, the one standing closest to Marvin?"

Amber paused. "I think it's Clint."

Kelly elbowed her way through the spectators and stepped into the inner circle, then glared at Clint. "I'd be careful if I were you."

He looked her up and down. "And why is that?"

"If you keep spreading nasty rumors about Marvin, I'll be forced to reveal some not-so-nice things about you. Just to be fair."

All eyes turned to Clint. Which was exactly what Kelly wanted.

His lip curled. "You don't know anything about me."

"I know what I saw last night at the campfire in the gym." Though Kelly kept her tone soft, there was no mistaking the veiled threat. "I'd hate to spill your secret. But if you keep giving my friend a hard time, you leave me no choice."

Clint curled his lip in a sneer. "There's nothing to tell. I don't wet my bed."

"Really?" Kelly narrowed her eyes and spoke slowly for maximum effect. "Last night, I saw you pick your nose and eat the booger."

Several girls shrieked, and cries of "gross" and "disgusting" rang out. The circle of campers leaped back, distancing themselves from

Clint. Kelly felt a thrill of satisfaction. She couldn't have hoped for a better reaction.

"That's a lie!" Clint shouted, his face flushed purple.

Okay, so it wasn't true. But Kelly felt no remorse for the little fib. He'd asked for trouble, and she was only too happy to provide it. "Don't say mean stuff about other people if you don't want something worse said about you."

The lodge door swung open and Bill stepped out. He frowned as he surveyed the group. "You should all be in your cabins for devotions. Get moving."

The campers split up and hurried off. But Marvin stayed rooted to his spot. Kelly caught a glimpse of Darren, with his paper hat tipped low over his eyes, standing in the doorway of the lodge. She wondered how much he'd heard.

Bill turned his attention to Kelly. "Anything I need to know?"

"Nope. Everything's fine." She winked at Marvin.

Bill gestured up the road. "You'd better head to your cabins or you'll be left behind."

Left behind from what? Kelly was tempted to ask what he meant, but Bill had already turned back into the lodge.

Kelly and Amber had taken only a few steps before Marvin ran over and tugged on Kelly's shirt. "Did you really see Clint pick his nose and eat the booger?"

Kelly shuddered. "No. But if he's going to make up stuff about you, then I felt free to do the same for him."

"Clint didn't make it up." Marvin's voice was so low Kelly barely heard him.

Marvin looked so small and vulnerable, Kelly felt an overwhelming desire to hug him, greasy hair and all.

Darren jogged over and placed a hand on Marvin's shoulder. "I have good news. When you get back to the cabin, you'll find a clean, dry sleeping bag on your bunk."

Marvin stared at the ground. "What if it happens again tonight?"

Darren shrugged. "Then we'll wash it again." He gave Marvin a light punch on the arm. "My first summer as a camper, I wet my sleeping bag four times in one week. I was too embarrassed to tell my counselors, but the smell gave me away."

Amber stifled a giggle, but Darren didn't seem bothered. He was focused on Marvin, who had the beginnings of a smile on his face. "As far as I know, I hold the camp record. Of course, that was a long time ago. And no one knows about it."

"Except us," Kelly teased.

Everyone laughed together.

"I won't try to beat your record," Marvin promised.

Kelly leaned close to Marvin. "If you skip the juice at snack tonight, that will help."

"Thanks." Marvin gave her a broad grin, and Kelly knew she'd found a new friend. One who needed to use a toothbrush.

At the point where the road divided, Kelly and Amber turned off toward the girls' cabins. But Darren stepped ahead to block the path. "Kelly, could I talk to you for a minute?"

She glanced around. No Men in Hats lurking nearby. No buckets of tar or feathers hidden in the bushes. She should be safe. "Amber, could you let Jill know I'll be there in a minute or two?"

"Sure." Amber headed for the cabin.

Darren motioned for Marvin to go on ahead, then waited until the boy had reached the bunkhouse. "Thanks for what you did. I saw what was happening and was on my way to stop it, but you got there first." He lifted his paper hat and ran his fingers through his hair. "It's like the poor kid has a target on his back saying, 'Pick on me.' I try not to leave him alone, but I can't protect him all the time. Thanks for sticking up for him. You were brilliant."

"I'm glad I could help." Kelly enjoyed his look of admiration. "You're really patient with Marvin. He seems to drive everyone else crazy."

"I know what it's like to be the camp loser. Not only did I wet my bed when I was a kid, I also had a stutter."

Kelly was caught off guard by Darren's honesty. And she felt a sudden flicker of shame at the petty prank of stealing his hat.

Darren gave a light-hearted chuckle. "I drove my counselor crazy that summer, but he was patient with me. Too bad he quit being a counselor. But he does make a great maintenance manager."

Kelly's eyes widened. "Tony was your counselor?" She had a hard time imagining him as sensitive or patient.

Darren nodded. "He can balance a spoon on his nose longer than anyone. And he was a terror in pillow fights. You only got one chance to whack him before he flattened you."

Kelly laughed. That sounded more like the Tony she knew.

"I'd better catch up with Marvin. Thanks again for looking out for him."

"His secret's safe with me."

Darren sent her a grateful smile, his eyes lingering on her face. Then he turned down the path, but glanced back after a few steps. "You looked seriously fierce when you were defending Marvin. And really cute." Darren spun around and jogged toward the cabins.

Kelly's cheeks burned. She felt flattered by his compliment. But she hoped it was just a friendly passing comment, not a sign of interest. Darren might be charming in a fun, offbeat way, but he couldn't match the overwhelming attractiveness of Joel.

She waited until Darren was a safe distance away before calling after him, "I told you I'd keep Marvin's secret safe. But I didn't promise not to reveal yours!"

"Tar and feathers!" Darren yelled, but there was laughter in his voice.

Kelly tipped an imaginary hat to him, then ran for the safety of the cabins.

24 HOW TO DRAG A DONKEY

"Ouch!" Kelly rubbed the stinging red mark on her arm where the cabin door had smacked into her moments before. She leaped back to avoid being trampled as the campers swarmed out. Jill was the last to exit.

Kelly raised her hand in protest. "Devotions can't be over already!" She'd only been talking with Darren for a few minutes.

Jill handed her a slip of paper. "This was tacked to the frame of my bunk."

Kelly scanned it.

Meet at the rodeo arena at 9 AM for morning devotions.

That explained Bill's earlier comment about being left behind. He really seemed to enjoy hauling them all over the property for campfires. And now devotions as well. Not that she minded too much. She liked the creativity and variety of the messages. But surely he could have chosen a more direct route. Like sending them straight from breakfast to the arena. But Bill didn't seem to care about simple or easy. Just keeping everyone off balance by doing the unexpected.

Within minutes, the walkway was packed with bodies as the other girls exited their cabins and then joined with the male campers on the road as they all made their way to the barn area.

Kelly nudged Jill. "I need to use the restroom. I'll catch up in a few minutes."

Jill nodded, and Kelly maneuvered through the crush of bodies going in the opposite direction. When she entered the empty bathroom, she was relieved to see the mirrors and doors back in place. The butter knives must have done the trick. Hopefully the memory of the prank would be short-lived and there wouldn't be any new mischief to stir up more resentment. But that wasn't likely if Sheila didn't return the hat. Which she wouldn't do unless Darren groveled and begged forgiveness. And that seemed even less likely. Which left being tar and feathered as a very real possibility.

As Kelly stepped to the sink to wash her hands, she heard someone enter through the opposite door. She glanced up with a cheerful greeting on her lips. The words never left her mouth.

Cindy stood stiffly at the far end of the bathroom. There wasn't a trace of makeup on her pale face. Her eyes were swollen and bloodshot. And her nose had turned an unattractive shade of red.

"You may be Joel's new favorite. But it won't last." Cindy spat the words like a cobra. "Then you'll get dumped too. And he'll come back to me." She grabbed a handful of paper towels, wheeled around, and left.

Kelly stared at the spot where Cindy had stood. There could be only one reason for the nasty message. A wild hope leaped within her as she allowed the thought to take shape. Cindy and Joel must have broken up. And this was her chance to step in and take her rival's place.

Pushing aside any feelings of pity for Cindy, Kelly considered the warning. But only for a moment. Cindy's bitter prediction showed nothing more than jealous spite. And Kelly would be happy to prove her wrong.

Kelly's feet flew as she exited the bathroom and ran to catch up with the others. She fell in step beside Amber, who chattered nonstop the whole way to the arena. Kelly didn't hear half of it. She was too busy scanning the crowd for a handsome face with piercing blue eyes. She caught sight of Joel surrounded by a pack of giggling girls, his head thrown back in laughter as the female campers gazed at him with awestruck expressions.

A sharp squeal from Amber snagged her attention. "He's so cute! Those long ears are adorable."

Kelly guessed Amber wasn't talking about a person. Following her gaze, she saw a small, gray donkey standing alone in the middle of the arena. The peaceful creature watched the gathering crowd through half-closed eyes as it nibbled hay from a bucket. Kelly wondered which rough-and-tumble rodeo event the poor thing would be participating in that morning.

"They'd better not abuse it, like they did that poor calf," Amber said.

"I don't think Bill will repeat himself." But that didn't mean it would be any better for the unfortunate donkey.

Kelly and Amber followed the other campers up the noisy metal stairs and settled beside the rest of their cabinmates.

Bill entered the arena, a long rope and halter slung over his shoulder. As he walked toward the donkey, the docile creature swung its head, observed Bill for a few moments, then resumed munching on the feed.

When Bill reached the gray beast, he gave it a light pat on the neck. "This is Molasses, the only donkey at Timberlake Camp." Bill's voice rang clearly through the arena loudspeakers. "He has a reputation for being stubborn, which you might have guessed considering his species. No one's been able to teach him to follow a lead. But we're going to give it another try this morning."

Amber clapped her hands in delight. "Bill doesn't have a chance."

Kelly agreed. "My bet's on the donkey."

Bill moved the bucket of hay to the side. It must have been close to empty because Molasses didn't seem bothered to see it go. After taking the halter off his shoulder, Bill placed it over the donkey's head and tightened the straps. Molasses barely blinked. A promising beginning.

Bill attached the lead rope and stepped forward, pulling gently. Molasses didn't follow. Bill tugged harder. Molasses extended his neck, but his body didn't move. Using all his might, Bill hauled on the rope. But the donkey remained in place.

Molasses had triumphed, and the campers chanted his name.

Bill raised his arms. “It’s not over.”

Kelly gave her head a small shake. It was hard to tell who was more stubborn, Bill or the donkey.

Bill made a beckoning motion and Tony hopped over the railing and into the arena. Bill passed him the lead rope. An unnecessary move, in Kelly’s opinion. Molasses appeared content to stay exactly where he was.

With no explanation, Bill trotted over to the gate at the far end. He swung it wide open and walked out.

Kelly couldn’t believe he was giving up so soon. Then she heard an engine start, and Bill returned—behind the steering wheel of a huge pickup.

Molasses’s long ears flicked back and forth. But he stood his ground as Bill slowly backed the truck to within a few feet of the gray beast. Bill hopped out of the cab, took the lead rope from Tony, and attached it to the hitch.

It didn’t take much imagination to guess what Bill intended to do. The girls erupted in shouts of protest, drowning out the cheers from the guys. Kelly winced. She wasn’t an animal-rights activist or anything, but this didn’t seem fair.

Bill got back into the truck and inched forward. Molasses was no match for the pickup. The poor donkey was pulled forward, but he didn’t follow willingly. Bracing all four feet, Molasses leaned back on his haunches. His skidding hooves left two rows of tracks in the dirt.

Bill didn’t drive far before he stopped and stepped out of the truck. The boys gave him a raucous standing ovation. Kelly joined the girls as they hissed and booed.

“Relax.” Bill walked over to the donkey. “Molasses wasn’t harmed in any way. We’re still good friends.”

Although the donkey’s eyes remained wide, Molasses allowed Bill to stroke his neck. When Bill pulled a carrot out of his pocket, the donkey relaxed his stance and eagerly chomped on the peace offering.

"Molasses should give Bill a good, swift kick!" Amber looked angry enough to jump over the rails and do the job herself.

Kelly nodded. "And Molasses should kick the truck too." At least a couple of times. And leave a big dent.

Bill rubbed the donkey between the ears. "I think our four-legged friend deserves a larger treat to thank him for being such a good sport."

"A barn full of hay couldn't make up for that stunt," Amber fumed.

Bill retraced his steps to the front of the truck. The moment the driver's door opened, Molasses stiffened all four legs and leaned back, braced for the pull. He may have been a donkey, but he was nobody's fool.

Bill reached into the cab and pulled out a handful of carrots. When he turned and saw the defiant mule, he burst out laughing. "That's a clear message if I ever saw one." He walked back and offered Molasses the orange delicacy, still chuckling. At the sight of the treat, the donkey relaxed again and began chomping.

Bill gave Molasses an affectionate rub. "This donkey is not going to be led anywhere against his will. At least not without a fight. And that's not a bad thing. It's great to be stubborn if you choose to be stubborn about the right thing."

Kelly smiled. Her mother often accused her of acting mulish. She couldn't wait to tell her it was a compliment.

Mike's voice rang out from the stands. "Hey, Darren. That donkey sure is clever."

"I guess that makes him a smart ass."

The male campers roared in laughter at the daring pun. Kelly figured it was bound to happen sooner or later. Darren and Mike had almost been respectful, waiting so long before pulling out the obvious joke.

Bill frowned at the counselors. "Both of you can spend some extra time with Molasses at the barn tomorrow morning, mucking out his stall. Maybe he can teach you about appropriate camp language."

Mike grinned. "Can we p-ass?"

"No. And you just earned yourself an extra morning."

Mike and Darren sat in silence. A wise move considering Bill's stern expression.

Bill motioned for Tony, then untied Molasses and handed the lead rope to the maintenance manager. Then he reached into the back of the pickup and pulled out Girl and Guy.

"They're back together!" Darren led the campers in a round of cheers.

Bill set the couple in place. "Don't get too excited. It's true that Guy's rebound didn't work out, and Girl realized no other cardboard figure compares to Guy. But there's trouble ahead for these two."

Kelly grinned. It would've been disappointing if the message hadn't contained something messy, painful, or dangerous. She'd come to expect it.

Bill dug into the bed of the truck and came up with a halter. He carried the cardboard characters off to the side, then pulled the halter over Guy's head. Once the straps had been tightened, he attached a set of ties to the halter and wrapped the loose ends around Girl's hand. When Bill stepped back, it looked as if Girl was leading a reluctant Guy.

Bill stepped between the couple and held up the ropes. "There are individuals who use the dating ties like a lead rope to pull their partners around. It looks a lot like a 'donkey drag.' One individual leads and the other follows, willingly or not."

Amber poked Kelly. "If Girl could drive a truck, Guy would be in big trouble."

Kelly chuckled. Knowing Bill, she wouldn't be surprised to see that happen.

Bill tilted Guy backward to resist the pull. "It's not necessarily wrong for one person to lead another. Certain people tend to be leaders while others prefer to follow. That's personality. The problem with the donkey-drag relationship is that the one doing the pulling is not giving the other person any choice."

"That's Aaron," Kelly murmured.

"What?" Amber asked.

"Nothing." Kelly hadn't meant to say his name out loud. But his face had come so clearly into focus. Along with a vision of herself, sporting long gray ears.

Bill turned to Tony, who had been holding Molasses's slack lead rope. "We're going to need the list of 'New Romantic and Sexy Words.'"

Tony reached into the back of the truck. He pulled out the familiar easel, which he hung over the donkey's back. Molasses twisted his head to sniff the paper and took a quick nip, tearing a chunk from the bottom corner.

Amber nudged Kelly. "I think Molasses found a way to pay Bill back for the truck."

The campers laughed. Bill chuckled with them. "I guess that makes it our list of 'New Romantic and Tasty Words.'"

Kelly gave a weak smile. But it wasn't funny. At least not to her. Just like Molasses, she'd tried to push back with Aaron. Grumbling when he chose yet another movie that she didn't want to see. Protesting when he told her she couldn't listen to country music anymore. Complaining about always doing what he wanted. All of them subtle kicks to let Aaron know she didn't like his lead. But she still allowed him to drag her around.

Bill tapped the halter on Guy's head. "Tony, are the words *overbearing* and *bully* on our list of romantic words?"

Tony scanned the sheet. "Nope."

"That's because there's nothing loving about being forced to follow someone, especially to places you don't want to go or activities you don't want to participate in. That's why it's important to determine your standards and draw boundary lines *before* you date."

Something both she and Lucy had failed to do. When Aaron and Logan had taken them to a house party where drinks were flowing, Kelly hadn't been pleased. Lucy hadn't looked any happier, especially when Logan told her she needed to loosen up and a can of beer would help. But the girls had stayed. Kelly pretended to laugh and have fun, and even forced down a drink. Poor Lucy drank a lot more, and Kelly didn't like the way Logan was smiling when he took her home.

Bill's voice cut into her thoughts. "If someone tries to drag you where you don't want to go, you need to be like a donkey. Lean back. Dig in your heels. Refuse to move. Even if someone drives up in a truck."

Kelly should have done that. And maybe she would have set an example for Lucy to dig in her heels too.

"In a relationship, you don't want to date a person who pushes or pulls. You want to connect with an individual who will talk with you about the direction you'd both like to take. That type of honor can only come from a humble person."

Tony pulled a pen from his pocket and added *honor* and *humility* to the list. Molasses sniffed at the paper, but Tony blocked him before he could get another mouthful.

Kelly stared at the newly scrawled words. Those terms could never be used to describe Aaron. He was too confident, self-assured, even cocky. Unfortunately, she wasn't sure that words like *honor* and *humble* were a good fit for Joel either.

Bill removed the halter from Guy, detached the ties, and reconnected them to Guy's hand. "When dating, it's important to be stubborn for the right things: your morals, your standards, and your right to be respected. You don't want to be treated like a donkey. But there are times when you might need to act like one."

Bill gave the donkey a final pat and turned to the campers. "You're dismissed to your morning activities."

Kelly's stomach knotted. In just a few minutes, Sandy was going to pull her to a place she didn't want to go. The middle of a lake. But as Kelly imagined paddling around in a tipsy canoe, she realized she was being silly. One hour on a lake was not going to ruin her life. This might even work out for good. She'd escape whatever nasty job Tony had planned for her, burn some extra calories, and maybe even get a bit of a tan.

Kelly sat up a little straighter, her shoulders back. Sandy might want to play therapist. But Kelly could be as stubborn as Molasses when she wanted to be.

25 A MATH LESSON IN A CANOE

Kelly followed the campers as they exited the arena after morning devotions. Then she veered off the main road and ambled down a side path leading to the maintenance shed. Sandy was no doubt waiting for her in the kitchen. But she'd just have to wait a little longer. Kelly needed to secure Tony's permission for her afternoon rendezvous at the vaulting arena first. If the conversation in the canoe didn't go well, Sandy might complain and Tony could block her chance to be with Joel. And there was no way she was going to let that happen.

When she reached the shed, Kelly fixed a bright smile on her face and strode in. Tony stood at the back of the room with Bob.

"Good morning, Tony. I hope you don't mind, but I'd like to ask for a very special favor. I was wondering if I could have some time off this afternoon to help another counselor."

"Hey, that's not fair!" Bob sent Kelly a dark scowl. "She's already skipping out this morning to go floating around the lake."

Ignoring him, Kelly kept her eyes fixed on Tony. She hoped he'd be impressed with her altruistic motives and wouldn't push for details.

Tony folded his arms across his chest. "Who are you helping?"

"Joel." Kelly winced inwardly, knowing Tony wasn't a fan. She kicked herself for not bringing a candy bar. Dark chocolate, no nuts. "He's working on a new vaulting routine. He asked me to handle the lunge line."

Tony raised an eyebrow. "I didn't realize you were an experienced horsewoman."

She wasn't fooling Tony. He knew this had nothing to do with selfless generosity and everything to do with a certain blond hunk. But at least he hadn't said no. Not yet anyway.

"I already told Joel I could help him. He won't have time to find anyone else."

Tony studied her for a few moments. Kelly felt her cheeks grow warm. She hoped she wouldn't have to drop to her knees and beg.

"All right. But be careful around that beast."

Kelly had a feeling he wasn't referring to the horse.

Bob let out a disgusted snort. "She should get double the work tomorrow."

Tony picked up a can of paint and passed it to Bob. "Someone has to do Kelly's work today. I guess you'll be staining the porch outside the boys' and girls' cabins by yourself."

Stifling a laugh, Kelly left quickly. As she walked away, she heard Bob protesting unfair work conditions and favoritism for girls.

Kelly's good humor faded as she slipped through the service door into the kitchen. She leaned against the back wall for a moment, watching the hum of activity. Charlie leaned over a sink in the far corner, scrubbing a large black pot. Marcie pulled a steaming rack of shiny plates out of a massive dishwasher and set it on the counter while Sheila struggled to slide a tray of dirty dishes into the same machine. In the middle of the kitchen, perched high on a stool, Lady Katherine observed the scene with eagle eyes as she whipped a frothy batter in a bowl.

A large door opened to Kelly's right and Sandy stepped out of a walk-in freezer. She noticed Kelly and gave her a quick wave. "I'll be ready in just a minute." Then she grabbed several containers from a shelf and disappeared back behind the thick freezer doors.

Sheila and Marcie rushed up to Kelly.

"Take us with you!" Sheila pleaded.

"We'll do the rowing. You can sit back and relax." Marcie clasped her hands together in supplication.

Lady Katherine glared at them, and they immediately returned to the dishes.

After Sheila started the next cycle on the dishwasher, she moved closer to Kelly and began folding aprons. "We saw the bathroom this morning," she whispered. "The guys did a good job. That was one of the better pranks."

"The campers didn't think so." Kelly glanced at Charlie, hoping he couldn't hear. "There was a note with our names on it attached to one of the mirrors. It said if we don't give Darren his hat back, the guys will strike again. And even if they don't, Bill will do something drastic."

"Don't worry. I've got a plan."

Which did nothing to reassure Kelly. "Does it include another late-night swim?"

"Oh, come on, that was fun."

Kelly snorted.

Sheila continued with supreme confidence. "I'll take care of everything at supper tonight."

Doubtful. But there wasn't time to talk more. Sandy reappeared from the freezer, removed her apron, and grabbed a stuffed backpack from under a table. Kelly felt her muscles stiffen. There had better not be cookies inside that bag because she'd toss the whole thing overboard. And jump ship herself.

Sandy motioned for Kelly to follow, then headed out a side exit. Kelly waved to her friends and left quickly to avoid their miserable expressions.

Sandy hadn't taken more than three or four steps before she began talking. "I was seventeen years old when I signed up to work as a volunteer at Timberlake. A week before camp started, I got a call from the director. Glen was in a panic. He still needed to fill two positions and wanted to know if I was interested in being the canoe instructor or craft leader."

Kelly remained silent, determined to say as little as possible. Sandy didn't seem to notice.

"I'd never held a paddle before, let alone actually been in a canoe on a lake. But I couldn't imagine teaching anything artistic. I draw stick figures. And they're not even good." Sandy shuddered.

Kelly thought of the artwork that her mother had saved over the years. Like the lopsided clay pencil holder sitting on her desk. And the blotchy watercolor painting of horses tacked on the fridge. Art wasn't her thing either.

"I told Glen he was talking to the new canoe instructor. My training consisted of watching a few videos and reading a book. I was woefully unprepared!" Sandy chuckled.

Kelly would have chosen the job of canoe instructor too. And she had experience now. She knew how to fall out of a canoe and drag it to shore.

When they reached the boathouse, Sandy continued her monologue as she sorted through the racks of life jackets. She grabbed one for herself and passed another to Kelly.

"If Bill had been the director, he never would have allowed such an unqualified instructor on the lake. But Glen was more easygoing. He told me I'd figure it out, and I did. It was one of the best summers in my life." Sandy handed Kelly a paddle. "And you should've seen my tan. I was golden."

Kelly glanced at her own arms. Only a hint of brown. Even though the painting and weeding had been outdoor jobs, they hadn't done much for her color.

Sandy searched among the canoes lined up in a row near the shore. "Good old number nine, my favorite." She gave it an affectionate pat, then motioned for Kelly to grab the back end. Together, they carried it to the edge of the lake. "Place your paddle across the gunwales and lean on it to keep your balance. I'll hold the canoe steady while you move to the front."

It was more instruction than she'd gotten from Sheila and Marcie. Kelly followed the directions, and the canoe remained stable as she inched her way forward. Once she was seated, Sandy tossed the backpack in the middle, pushed off, then hopped in. The bow of the canoe sliced smoothly through the still water.

"Perfect conditions." Sandy took a deep breath and exhaled slowly.

Kelly hadn't had a close view of the lake since the night of the prank. Out of the corner of her eye, she glanced down the long length of reeds. To her relief, there were no bent stems or noticeable trail.

Sandy chatted nonstop as they glided across the glistening water. She recounted tales of cramming twelve campers into one canoe and turning it into a water bus. She recalled playing Battleship and ramming other boats, trying to tip them over. She told stories of clueless campers blowing across the lake on windy days, and the hard work it took to pull them back to shore. Kelly couldn't help but smile at the humorous escapades.

Once they reached the middle of the lake, Sandy instructed Kelly to pull in her paddle and stow it at the bottom of the canoe.

"Now, turn around in your seat. Just make sure you're always balanced in the middle. It's a lovely morning for canoeing, but not so nice for swimming."

Agreed. With slow and careful movements, Kelly shifted her position.

Sandy reached into her backpack, pulled out two pillows, and passed one to Kelly. "Make yourself comfortable."

Relieved that Sandy had brought cushions instead of cookies, Kelly leaned back and closed her eyes.

They floated in silence for a while, soaking in the sun while listening to the various sounds from camp that carried clearly across the water. As Kelly relaxed, her thoughts drifted to the work she would have been doing if Sandy hadn't invited her here. She couldn't help but chuckle. "Sheila and Marcie would swim half the lake for the chance to join us. And Bob would swim half the lake to tip us over."

Sandy laughed. "Those poor girls are probably up to their ears in potatoes by now. Their hands are going to be raw before the morning is out."

"I'm sure Bob's up to his elbows in brown stain." Kelly grinned at the mental image. The pity she felt for her friends did not extend to her maintenance partner.

"It's my plan to be a dump truck this morning." At Kelly's confused expression, Sandy leaned forward. "I want to unload everything I've been longing to share since I first saw you."

Kelly tensed at the abrupt change in topic. She'd come close to forgetting why they were out in the canoe. A foolish mistake.

"You don't have to say anything in return."

Kelly gave a slow nod. She would listen, but nothing more.

"When I was fifteen years old, I became anorexic."

The blunt statement caught Kelly off guard. That was the last thing she'd expected to hear. She'd been prepared for a lecture, sermon, even an angry tirade. But not a confession.

Sandy gazed across the water, as if at something far away. "I struggled every day with obsessive thoughts about food. I felt guilty for every bite I took. I lied constantly when questioned about my food intake. Pushed myself to utter exhaustion by exercising for hours at a stretch. I felt driven by the need to lose just one more pound."

Kelly stared at Sandy in shocked wonder, her heart pounding wildly in her chest. She thought she was the only one who felt that way. But Sandy understood. She'd felt it too.

"The struggle lasted for many years. But I finally recovered. Ever since, I've been sharing my story whenever I can. I especially like going into the high schools. I once spoke at a health class, and while the teacher was introducing me, I heard a student whisper to her friend, 'I wish I could be anorexic, just for a week.'"

Foolish girl. Who would wish for such torment, even for a handful of days?

"That student didn't have any idea what I'd been through. How could she? She only saw my ultra-thin body. If she truly understood the hell I'd lived through, she wouldn't want to be anorexic for one day."

Or even one hour. Maybe the girl hadn't understood, but Kelly did. Every word that Sandy said.

Kelly drew in a long, shaky breath. Maybe it was the enchantment of camp. The power of Bill's campfire messages. Or the exhaustion of self-denial. But Sandy's simple and honest revelation pulled an internal admission from Kelly that all the pressure and demands of her parents, doctors, and counselors couldn't—the truth. She was anorexic. It was wrecking her health. Consuming her life. And she was powerless to stop.

Sandy's hand trailed over the edge of the canoe, her fingertips playing in the water. She remained silent, like she was waiting. But for what? In all of Kelly's counseling sessions, there had been a lot of talking, but not from her. Only to her. No one had allowed her to ask any questions. Or share her worries. Or have a discussion. And this was her chance.

Kelly looked into Sandy's eyes. "How did it start?"

Sandy rested her elbows on her knees. "When I was sixteen, two boys at my school began to tease me about my 'curves.' Of course, they weren't that polite."

Kelly gazed at Sandy's trim figure. "Were you...big?"

"Not really. But I developed faster than most of my friends and had gained a few extra pounds. Looking back, I don't know why I cared what some pimply-faced teenage boys were saying about me. But I did."

It was hard not to listen to the taunts of others. And even harder not to care. She'd never forget how crushed she felt when she heard that Aaron thought she was too fat to date. The only girls he was interested in looked like the skinny models in magazines. So that's what she had become. And it was a good thing. Because judging by Cindy, Joel probably felt the same way.

Sandy rubbed a hand across her forehead. "Those boys measured me and said I wasn't good enough. Foolishly, I believed them."

Kelly tried to envision the scene. "The boys held a ruler up to you? Like in a Math class? And the teacher let them do that?"

"No." Sandy chuckled. "I was speaking symbolically" A sigh escaped Sandy's lips, and the moment of humor was gone. "There are so many rulers. Most of us have at least one. Some kids measure their self-worth by their grades. A lot of adults do the same with their salaries or the cars they drive. We might calculate our significance by the clothes we wear, the friends we have, the good deeds we perform, the amount of money in our bank account, our awards and trophies, the popularity of our boyfriends, girlfriends, or spouses."

Kelly thought of the shelves in Marcie's staff room, sagging under the weight of books. Books promoting accomplishment and success. They were rulers. Every one. Kelly felt a twinge of guilt. Was she any different? Her rulers didn't come with pages bound in a cover. She'd been looking to her social group, her boyfriend, and the weight scale to determine her worth.

Kelly frowned. "I thought it was good to set high standards and strive to be the best."

Sandy adjusted the pillows behind her back. "None of those things is a problem unless we use it to calculate our value."

Kelly had felt successful at losing weight, at least in the beginning. Being in control of her food and exercise made her feel powerful, even superior to others who lacked her discipline. She'd loved watching the numbers on the scale go down. But they never seemed low enough. Before long she felt trapped, like a hamster on a spinning exercise wheel. Exhausted, unable to stop, and yet going nowhere.

"Do you know why these rulers don't work? They're all crooked. They can't give accurate results. Because whenever we try to determine inside worth by measuring outside things, we get the wrong answer."

That was exactly what she was doing to herself. Jumping on a scale every morning and letting the numbers determine whether she was a winner or a loser. And even when she won, it wasn't enough. Because every time the sun rose, she had to jump on the scale and prove herself again.

"Our self-esteem only gets worse when we compare ourselves with those around us. We might be happy with our grades, until someone else's grades are higher. Or they drive a nicer car. Or they're thinner. So now we're not just trying to measure up to our own standards. We're trying to measure up to other people and their bent rulers."

The sun's bright rays blazed down on the lake, reflecting off the water. Kelly blinked several times. Her life was a constant competition to eat less, weigh less, and exercise more than anyone around her. She wasn't happy unless she had everyone beat.

Sandy reached into her bag and pulled out a small tube of sunscreen. She carefully applied it to her arms and shoulders, then held the tube towards Kelly. With an impatient toss of her head, Kelly waved away the offer. She didn't care if she burned as red as a lobster. She just wanted Sandy to get back to her story.

"I tried to cope with my fears and insecurities by controlling what I ate. I thought that if I dropped a few pounds, I could earn the approval of others and then I'd feel happy about myself."

Kelly remembered losing those first ten pounds and the compliments that followed. And how Aaron's indifferent gaze had slowly changed into one of admiration and interest.

"I lost five or six pounds and was thrilled. But those feelings faded. So I dropped another five pounds. And I felt great, until that slipped away as well. No matter how much weight I lost, I never felt good enough."

A breeze rocked the canoe slightly, but Kelly barely noticed it. She couldn't argue. Along with the feeling of success came the desire to gain even more approval. She'd managed to get in with the popular crowd, but her parents constantly argued with her about her choice of friends. She tried to study but all her grades–except for Drama–took a nosedive. She became desperate to excel in something. Diet and exercise were two things she felt in control of. And every pound she lost became a symbol of her success in at least one area in her life.

"Everyone thinks that anorexic people are worried about being skinny, but they're not. They're anxious about their self-worth." Sandy gazed into Kelly's eyes. "You are more than your weight. Your value doesn't fluctuate with the size of your waist."

Those words hurt. Because she desperately wanted to believe them.

Kelly focused on the beach and the tall wooden cross standing beside the campfire pit. "Were you a Christian when you were anorexic?"

"Yes. I accepted Jesus as my Savior when I was eight years old."

"So where was God?" Kelly didn't bother trying to keep the resentment out of her voice. "Why did He let you suffer? He could have stopped the boys from teasing you. He could have sent someone to help you." Kelly choked on the bitter words.

"He did send someone. Himself. He was right there in my heart, but I didn't look to Him. When those boys told me I was fat and ugly, I listened to them. I got mad at God for what I perceived as my flaws."

Angry tears stung Kelly's eyes. "God didn't protect you. You had to look after yourself."

"The boys told me that my appearance was the most important thing about myself. But I didn't have to believe that. If I had opened my Bible, I would have learned that God doesn't look at the things people look at. He looks at the heart."

Kelly hid a sneer. Guys like Aaron and Joel would never see what was on the inside if she didn't look good on the outside.

Sandy checked her watch. "Lunch prep will start soon. We need to start heading back." She handed Kelly her paddle, then picked up the second one.

Kelly took the paddle but didn't put it in the water. She wasn't ready for the conversation to end. Not until she had an answer to the most critical question of all. "How did you recover?"

Sandy rested the paddle across her knees. "One Sunday night, when I was feeling completely overwhelmed and lost, I went to church with my family. At the end of the service, I walked up to the altar and asked for prayer. The pastor's wife and I had a long talk. I spilled everything. When I finished, she told me I needed a different way to measure my worth. I had no idea what she meant."

Kelly caught herself holding her breath. Waiting for a simple answer. One that she could grab on to and use to climb out of the pit she'd dug with her own hands.

"The pastor's wife must have seen the confusion in my eyes. She said that God saw every part of me, even the deepest, darkest parts that I tried to hide."

Kelly swallowed hard. She'd always thought of herself as a decent person. But she hadn't been proud of the things she'd said and done over the past few months. Lying to her parents and going out behind their backs. Joining in the school gossip and failing to defend the victims. Going to parties and drinking, when she swore she'd never do anything like that. Being controlled by jealousy, envy and selfishness. She'd been surprised, and shamed, to discover how weak she really was.

Sandy reached into the collar of her shirt and pulled out a thin silver chain. A beautiful shining cross dangled on the end. "The pastor's wife was wearing this necklace that night. She took it off and gave it to me. Then she said that this is God's ruler. He knew that I could never measure up to His perfect standards. But Jesus came to earth and lived the life that I should have, died in my place, and now He measures up for me."

Sandy let the pendant rest outside her shirt.

Disappointment washed over Kelly. She shouldn't be surprised, since this was a church camp. But she'd expected to hear something more than 'Jesus is the answer'. Kelly was tempted to turn around and paddle straight for the shore. But then she noticed the expression of peace illuminating Sandy's face. And it made her wonder. She knew a lot about Jesus. But Sandy seemed to know him like her closest friend.

Sandy's hand strayed back to the necklace, and her fingers stroked the smooth surface. "The pastor's wife told me it didn't matter what others thought of me. It didn't even matter what I thought of me. God's opinion was the only one that counted. And He loved me so much that He sent His Son to die in my place and save me. I just needed to believe it."

Kelly wanted to believe that too. But she didn't know if she could. "You make it sound so easy."

"It wasn't." Sandy gave a wry smile. "I had accepted the lie that my significance came from my appearance. I had to exchange that for the truth of how God sees me. I went to a counselor for close to a year, and she helped me work through all my faulty beliefs. She kept me accountable and helped me establish new habits. Every day now I read my Bible. I pray and listen to worship music. I study with a group of Christian friends. Each of these steps keeps me walking in freedom."

Kelly thought of her habits. Exercising to utter exhaustion. Denying food to the point of starvation. Chasing after popularity no matter the cost. Sandy's approach seemed refreshingly simple.

Sandy glanced at her watch again, and Kelly knew their conversation was drawing to an end. Her mind felt full to bursting with all she'd heard, and she was grateful for Sandy's invitation to go canoeing that morning. She would have missed so much if she hadn't come.

"I'm still tempted to do things to prove my value. When I find myself reaching for some cheap way to measure myself, I stop and remember that I am of great worth simply because Jesus said so. There's nothing more I need to do."

Kelly tried to envision what it would feel like to have that kind of confidence. To be free from the grip of anorexia. To go out with friends and eat a hamburger without any guilt. To sleep in and not worry if she missed her morning jog. To find friends who liked her for who she was, not what she wore or how she looked. And to not care what guys like Aaron said or thought. "Do you still care about how much you weigh?"

"Yes. And I work hard to stay a healthy size. I feel great satisfaction when I step on the scale and discover I'm in my target range. But I'm not devastated if I'm off by a pound or two. I choose to find my significance in God. That has made all the difference." She tucked the cross back into her shirt. "I have a new Ruler now."

Kelly turned around, dipped her paddle in the water, and matched the rhythm of Sandy's long, deliberate strokes. If only she could stay on the lake for the rest of the day. She'd even miss the meeting with Joel if it meant she could keep listening to Sandy. Kelly chucked softly. That would have been unthinkable a few hours before.

Far too quickly, the bottom of the canoe scraped on the gravel of the shore, and Kelly stepped onto the beach.

Sandy took the paddle and life jacket from Kelly and gave her a tender smile. "Thanks for listening."

"Thank you for sharing." Kelly embraced Sandy in a long, tight hug. Then she straightened and stood still for a moment, basking in the golden warmth of the sun's rays. Deep within, she felt the stirrings of a powerful emotion she hadn't experienced in a long time.

Hope.

26 A STRANGE BLACK OBJECT

A wave of frustration rolled over Kelly as she stood at the serving counter in the dining hall, holding an empty plate. Rows of grilled cheese sandwiches lay stacked on long trays. Kelly replayed Sandy's message in her mind. This lunch meal wasn't a measure of her worth. These calories weren't her ruler. She should be able to eat a stupid sandwich without being overwhelmed by guilt and fear.

Someone behind her shouted, "What's the holdup?" Heads craned to see why the line wasn't moving.

"Don't be picky," snapped another irritated voice. "Just grab one."

Kelly remained rooted in place. Before camp, the rules had been simple. Eat as little as possible. Exercise constantly. Be thinner than everyone else.

But the conversation with Sandy had challenged her thinking. She had a choice to make. And it started with those two pieces of toasted bread with cheese oozing out the sides.

She willed her hand to reach out and take a sandwich. But it wouldn't budge. The hope that shone so brightly after her talk with Sandy faded. An ugly reality took its place. She'd never be able to change.

Impatient campers jostled in the line, pushing Kelly forward. She moved to the end of the counter, spooned a small portion of fruit onto her plate, and made her way to the table.

All heads were bent close together, and the girls spoke in hushed tones.

"So he really dumped her?" Emma sounded doubtful.

"Yep." Joyce wore a delighted smile. "The girls in Cindy's cabin said she's been bawling all morning."

Kelly searched the hall for Cindy and spotted the blonde sitting with her campers. Heavy makeup masked the red, puffy eyes that Kelly had observed when she'd run into her in the bathroom. Cindy seemed to be enjoying a lively conversation. But Kelly thought she talked too loud and laughed too long.

Jill slid onto the bench beside her. "Be careful this afternoon. Vaulting is more dangerous than it looks. And be even more careful around Joel."

Kelly stiffened. Jill meant well, but Kelly didn't need a second mother.

Jill looked at Kelly with concern. "Joel's a good guy, but he collects hearts for fun. I don't think he means to break them. But he doesn't handle them with care."

Thoughts of Sheila's jealousy and Cindy's tears flashed through Kelly's mind, but she pushed them aside.

After Bill dismissed the campers for their afternoon activities, Kelly stopped in the bathroom to brush her hair and pull it into a high ponytail. She stared at her reflection in the mirror. Not even close to Cindy's glamourous perfection, but hopefully good enough. Then she headed toward the arena.

When she reached the vaulting ring, she found Joel placing a thick saddle pad on a massive brown-and-white horse. Kelly had seen the animal during the tour at staff training, and when she'd accidentally spooked him the next morning. But he seemed much larger now.

Her confidence faltered. What was she doing here? She had no business being in charge of such a beast, especially while someone performed risky tricks on its back. Kelly was about to turn around and flee when Joel looked over at her with an inviting smile. Desire trumped fear. Kelly climbed through the rails, unwilling to miss her chance at the hottest guy at camp.

Joel's arm encircled her, and he guided her to the animal's side. "This is Samson."

When Samson turned his massive head toward her, Kelly took a quick step back. She hoped the horse couldn't sense her fear.

Joel didn't seem to notice her nervousness. He led the horse to the center of the vaulting circle. Kelly followed close behind.

"Your job is to keep Samson going at an even pace," Joel explained. "You'll control his gait using the whip."

Kelly gasped. "I don't want to hurt him."

Joel burst out laughing. "You don't hit Samson. You hold the whip low for walk, hip height for trot, and vertical for canter."

Kelly ducked her head, angry at herself for sounding like a naïve fool. "You make it sound easy."

"It is." Joel passed her the lunge line and a long leather whip. "Stay in the center of the ring. As Samson moves around the circle, dig in your left heel and pivot."

Kelly hoped Joel couldn't see her hands trembling.

"Don't worry." Joel put an arm around her shoulders. "Samson won't bite."

He was laughing at her, but Kelly didn't care. Not as long as he had his arm around her.

Matt ducked through the rails and entered the ring. He'd been with Joel the day she threw rocks at the shed and gotten him thrown from the horse. Maybe he wouldn't remember.

Joel gave Kelly's shoulder a gentle squeeze before releasing her. "Hi, Matt. You know Kelly, right? She's going to work the lunge line for us."

Matt nodded. "You covered Bob with paint and told that bedtime story."

Kelly gave a quick bow, grateful that Matt's memory had selected only her finer moments. "It's been a busy week for me."

"And you're one of the infamous hat thieves."

"Innocent until proven guilty." Kelly winked.

Joel and Matt laughed.

Joel positioned Samson along a dirt ring that had been worn into the ground. "Give a clucking sound with your tongue, let him walk for a few paces, and then raise the whip to hip height."

Kelly followed the instructions, and to her relief, Samson began to trot. Joel ran alongside, matching his steps. Grasping the handles on the saddle pad, he swung himself up and onto the horse.

Joel knelt on the saddle pad, then extended his left leg and right arm. "This is a basic flag."

Kelly had never watched vaulting before, except for the short glimpse when the campers first arrived at the beginning of the week. She found it fascinating. Or at least she found Joel fascinating.

He lowered himself to a sitting position. "And now for the scissors." He swung his legs several times to gain momentum, then lifted himself from Samson's back, twisting his legs so that he came down sitting backward. Then he swung his legs again and twisted back to face forward.

Kelly let out a low whistle, impressed with the balance, agility, and strength needed to execute gymnastic skills on a moving animal. "What's next? Are you going to do a handstand?" she teased.

"Great idea." Joel leaped up to a crouching position, both feet on the saddle pad. Then he lowered his head to Samson's shoulder, pushing his legs up into a perfect line. He held the move as Samson circled the arena.

Kelly laughed. "I'd clap, but my hands are full."

Joel returned to a seated position. "Save the applause. You haven't seen anything yet." He motioned for Matt. "I'll need you to spot now."

Matt joined him, running alongside and keeping his eyes trained on Joel.

Joel gave Kelly a thumbs-up. "Samson needs to pick up the pace."

Kelly raised the whip higher and the horse moved into a smooth canter.

Joel performed a cartwheel across the back of the horse, then grabbed onto the handles and flipped his body over one side. His feet hit the ground and he pushed off, launching back over the horse, where his feet hit the ground again. He did this several times before he returned to a seated position on the saddle pad. Kelly let out a cheer. This was a show worthy of selling tickets for.

A group of staff and campers paused to watch. Kelly kept her eyes trained on Joel but stole quick peeks at the growing audience. She spotted Cindy at the back of the crowd, hiding behind dark sunglasses, with arms crossed and a sour expression on her face.

Marvin waved wildly at Kelly. She gave him a brief nod and a smile. Darren stood beside him, eyebrows furrowed in a dark frown. Kelly wondered if Marvin had been more annoying than usual.

Matt's voice brought her attention back to the ring. "Shake the whip a bit. Samson's starting to lag."

Kelly did as she'd been directed. Joel explained each move before he executed it, as if she were the only one watching and he performed for her alone. A surge of confidence rose within her. It looked like Joel had made his choice, and it was her.

Joel stood, then flipped backward in a thrilling dismount, landing on his feet with perfect precision. Kelly lowered the whip, and Samson stopped.

The girls on the fence burst into cheers and applause. Joel acknowledged them with a quick bow.

Matt stopped to catch his breath, then jogged over to Joel and clapped him on the back. "Good work." He gave Kelly a quick nod. "I'm looking forward to hearing your next story."

Kelly grinned, then turned back to Joel. He was breathing heavily from exertion and glistening with perspiration. She couldn't take her eyes off him.

Joel took her hand and kissed it lightly. "I knew you could do it."

Surprised and flattered by the unexpected gesture, Kelly gave Samson a pat on his sweaty neck. "I think this big guy should get more credit than me."

Joel took the lunge line and whip from Kelly. "Well, I'm not going to kiss his hoof. But he does deserve a good rub-down and a long drink."

A strand of hair from Kelly's ponytail blew across her face. Joel tucked it behind her ear. Kelly held her breath as his fingers lightly brushed her cheek.

"Jill was right," he said softly. "I probably should have found someone with more experience to help today." He leaned close. "But I'm glad I asked you."

Kelly looked into his mesmerizing blue eyes. For an instant, nothing else existed. Until the girls from her cabin shattered the moment.

"Samson is my favorite horse!"

"Can we pet him?"

A few of the campers stood gawking at Samson. But most stared openly at Joel.

He waved the campers into the ring. The girls surrounded them, patting the horse and peppering Joel with questions about vaulting.

Amber stepped beside Kelly. "We're on our way to the store. You want to come?"

Kelly sent Joel an apologetic look.

"Go on," he said. "I'll catch you later."

Or sooner, if she had anything to say about it. Kelly watched Joel lead Samson toward the barn. The campers tugged on her sleeve. She turned and walked with them toward the lodge.

"Hey, Kelly, your face is all red."

The girls giggled at Joyce's taunt.

"Vaulting is hard work. I'm hot and tired, that's all."

"Hot for Joel." Joyce smirked. "I saw him kiss your hand."

There was no use arguing with Joyce. Especially since it was true.

"And it's obvious he likes you."

Kelly smiled at Joyce. She hoped so.

Nothing could spoil the moment. Except for Bob, walking toward her on the road. He stopped in front of her and adjusted his fancy snapback cap. "I hope you had a good day doing nothing."

Kelly motioned for the girls to go on without her. "As a matter of fact, I had a great day."

"Well, that's about to change."

Kelly didn't care for the smirk on his face. "Why is that?"

Bob pulled a round black object out of his pocket and held it up. It was about the size of a marble but looked like it was made out of a soft, spongy material. A few dark threads hung from it, and it appeared torn or ripped on one side.

Kelly squinted at the strange item. "What's that supposed to be?"

"Revenge." Bob tossed the object in the air a few times. "Darren's not empty-handed anymore. Now he's got something on you."

Bob's threat made no sense. What could Darren have on her, and what did it have to do with that squishy-looking black ball?

Bob shoved the item back in his pocket. "I'm supposed to tell you that Tony doesn't have any work for you. You get the rest of the afternoon off."

That message must have been painful to deliver. But Bob didn't appear bothered. In fact, his good mood was disturbing.

As Kelly watched him go, she noticed two people standing close together outside the vaulting ring. Cindy's teasing laughter carried on the wind as she rested a possessive hand on Darren's arm.

A sour taste filled Kelly's mouth. Surely Darren was too smart to let Cindy dig her claws into him.

A small movement caught her eye, and she realized she wasn't the only one watching the pair. On the far side of the arena, Joel stood beside Samson at the watering trough. But his eyes weren't on the horse. They were on the smiling couple. As he stared at them, his face darkened with unmistakable anger.

A cold chill ran through Kelly. She was so close. She couldn't lose Joel now. Her eyes darted back, and she watched Cindy snake an arm around Darren and steer him down the road. But not before the blonde siren cast a backward glance at Joel.

Joel wasn't the only performer today. Cindy was putting on her own show. Kelly spun around. Time for her to join the action. She hadn't taken more than a few steps toward Joel when she heard Amber calling her name. Kelly hesitated. In that moment, she saw Joel swing up on Samson's back, dig his heels into the horse's side, and gallop off to the barn. The opportunity was lost.

As Kelly hurried to catch up with the campers, she tried to think of a clever way to turn Joel's focus back to herself. But she arrived at the store without a plan.

Jill approached, eyebrows raised and finger shaking, with an amused light in her eyes. "As your head counselor, it's my duty to remind you that physical affection between staff members is forbidden. Even if it is just a quick kiss on the hand."

Kelly bristled at the warning. "How do you know already?"

"Camp news travels fast. News about Joel travels even faster." Jill grinned. "The assistant counselors are all begging to learn another one of your stories. I told them you'd tell them one at supper tonight. I hope you don't mind."

Kelly could have hugged Jill. For being understanding, and for unknowingly giving her an opportunity to shift Joel's attention from Cindy and shine the spotlight on herself.

An hour later, when Kelly entered the lodge for supper, she found the counselors sitting at a back table. She walked directly to Joel and squeezed in beside him on the bench. The warmth of his arm pressed against her and his gentle squeeze just above her knee infused her with courage.

She glanced around the group. "Is everyone ready to hear the tale of Molly the Moth?"

Mike sat across from her, paper and pencil in front of him. He slid a few sheets and a pen to Darren on his left. "What do insects learn in school?"

"I don't know." Darren glanced at Kelly, then looked away. Muscles contracted in his tightly clenched jaw.

Kelly looked at him in surprise. Darren had never failed to come up with a reply in the two-man comedy routine. And he seemed angry. Was he frustrated that he hadn't gotten his hat back yet?

"Insects learn *mothmatics*." Mike chuckled.

The counselors groaned.

"This story ends with a better pun than that." Kelly reached across the table and tapped Mike's paper. "Let's start. Molly the Moth lived in Mothland with her mother, father and..."

Just as she began her story, Cindy slipped in next to Darren and snuggled. Kelly could feel Joel stiffen, and she felt helpless against Cindy's obvious ploy.

A few minutes later, Joel put an arm around Kelly's shoulders and pulled her close. She leaned in and tried to find reassurance in his affectionate touch. But she couldn't shake the uncomfortable feeling that she was being used like a pawn. Especially when she looked at the perfect blonde sitting across from her, looking so annoyingly confident.

As Kelly spun the tale, she spotted MaryAnn walking toward the back table. Recalling Jill's reminder about the rules against public affection between counselors, she sat up straight. Joel dropped his arm just in time. The director's wife passed the table of assistant counselors and continued across the dining hall.

Kelly relaxed. As much as she missed the warmth of Joel's well-muscled embrace, her mind raced with MaryAnn's warnings during staff training about the consequences of counselors breaking the rules. Kelly had no desire to spend the evening shoveling manure from the barn stalls.

Except for the sound of utensils clinking on plates, the assistant counselors were silent as Kelly told of the romantic rise and fall of poor Molly the Moth. Mike and Darren scribbled notes, just as they had with the first story. But Darren kept his eyes focused on the paper, and he seemed uncomfortable. Was he irritated by Cindy's attention toward him? Kelly felt a satisfied swirl of pleasure. She didn't want a nice guy like Darren getting trapped by calculated feminine wiles.

Kelly paused dramatically in preparation for her grand finale. "Molly sighed as she watched Hercamur fly away with another female moth. She'd lost him forever. Molly folded her wings and sobbed. And there's nothing sadder in the world than seeing a *moth bawl*."

A mixture of laughter and groans rose at the final pun.

Matt scrunched his eyebrows together. "I don't get it."

Mike rolled his eyes. "B-a-w-l. B-a-l-l."

Matt's eyes widened in sudden understanding, and he applauded in Kelly's direction.

Joel pulled Kelly into a hug. "Brilliant. As usual."

Kelly's moment of joy didn't last long. Bill ruined it by banging on the side of the serving table.

"I made it clear this morning that Darren's hat was to be returned by supper. Since that hasn't happened, I have no choice but to—"

Someone cleared his throat loudly, and all eyes turned to see Tony striding to the front of the room. "Sorry to interrupt, Bill, but I was asked to deliver this to you."

He waved a flat yellow envelope in the air, and a surge of frustration swept over Kelly. That wasn't a hat. Which meant the prank wasn't over. So much for Sheila and her plans.

"That envelope had better contain instructions for the safe return of Darren's hat," Bill said.

Kelly doubted it.

Tony passed the envelope to Bill. He pulled out a single sheet of paper and skimmed it. "Shelia, Marcie, and Kelly have admitted to taking the hat."

Kelly gasped as a chorus of boos and cheers erupted from the campers. She hadn't agreed to a confession. Was Sheila trying to get her killed?

"So it was you." Joel squeezed her close, admiration in his voice. "Congratulations on an awesome prank."

Kelly's anger at Sheila was instantly forgotten, and she flashed Joel a flirtatious grin.

At the front, Bill banged loudly. The campers quieted.

"The girls have agreed to return the hat if Darren promises to leave Sheila's hair alone and never mess it again. I'll give Darren time to consider that offer. He can respond tomorrow at supper, either accepting or rejecting the terms."

The male campers called for Darren to say no, urging him to mess up all three girls' hair. Maybe even cut it off. As she turned to see his reaction, she was surprised to find Darren's eyes on her. Her lips twitched in a weak smile. She hoped he'd accept the terms before someone got scalped. Like her.

"In the meantime, the girls have requested a protective order, which I will grant to them and all of their belongings, beginning immediately and extending for the next twenty-four hours."

The male campers complained, but Kelly breathed a sigh of relief. At least she was safe from Bob and Darren, and whatever they'd planned to do with that strange black object.

Bill banged again. "I'll see everyone at the campfire in half an hour. It's going to be a cool evening, so bring jackets."

As Bill dismissed the tables, campers swarmed around Kelly. Most claimed they'd known it was her all along. Others begged her to tell where she'd hidden the hat. Still others speculated on what Darren would do.

Kelly wondered too. She couldn't figure Darren out. He was full of contradictions, teasing her about tar and feathers, protecting her from horse's hooves, calling her cute, but now confusing her with angry stares and cold silence. Maybe he'd fallen for Cindy after all.

Joel leaned close. "I'd better get back to my campers. Thanks for the story." He brushed his lips against her cheek.

When she turned to smile at him, she realized Joel's gaze wasn't fixed on her, but on Cindy. As the beautiful blonde rose, she whispered something in Darren's ear, then walked away. Joel leaped up and followed her. Kelly lost sight of them in the crowd.

A nosy camper poked Kelly in the back. "Did you bury the hat? Or hang it in a tree?"

Kelly nodded, only half-listening to the question. Her shoulders still felt warm where Joel's arm had held her. And her cheek tingled with the memory of his lips. But had the kiss been for her benefit? Or for Cindy's?

27 THE FIRST ROMANCE

Kelly should have been happy as she walked with Amber to the outdoor campfire site. After all, Bob and Darren's schemes had been thwarted by Bill's guarantee of protection. But she felt a growing sense of dread when she thought of Cindy's obvious flirtation with Darren, and Joel's jealous reaction. The blond heartthrob seemed to be slipping through her fingers and back into the outstretched talons of that sneaky siren. And Kelly was helpless to stop it.

Amber chuckled.

"What's so funny?" Kelly followed the direction of Amber's pointing finger. She saw the cardboard couple leaning against each other, at a safe distance from the blaze.

"I wonder what terrible tangles are in store for Guy and Girl tonight."

Kelly craned her neck. "They're starting to look bent and creased."

"I hope they survive the week and live happily ever after."

Just like Kelly hoped to do with Joel.

The two girls joined their cabinmates in the middle section of the benches. After several songs and a few skits, Bill walked over to the cardboard duo and put his arms around them.

"Guy and Girl have had it rough lately. So I've decided to give them a break tonight and focus on a different couple. A real one. We're going to examine the very first love story. It comes straight out of the Bible, from the book of Genesis."

Kelly slouched on the bench. She'd heard the story of Adam and Eve countless times, and there wasn't much romance to it. Or anything else exciting.

Bill stepped off to the side and returned a moment later, dragging an old flannel board and a small, foldable table.

Kelly groaned at the sight of green cloth stretched across a square surface. When she was in preschool, she'd had a Sunday school teacher who used a similar board every week to tell the story. The lessons had been as flat and lifeless as the thin felt shapes the teacher placed on the board.

Kelly shook her head. Bill had dreamed up calf roping, a donkey drag, and a tug-of-war over a mud-filled wading pool. How could he possibly believe that the campers would be entertained with a simple flannel board? It was insulting, as if he thought they were still in elementary school.

MaryAnn joined Bill at the front, carrying several clear Ziplock bags full of multi-colored cloth pieces. She opened the bags and spread the contents across the table.

Bill gestured to the blank board. "The first chapter of Genesis tells us that in the beginning, God created the heavens and the earth, and every living creature on the land and in the seas."

As Bill was speaking, MaryAnn selected a handful of pieces. First, she placed a huge cloud with the word God written on it in big, gold capital letters in the middle of the board. Then she stretched a long strip of blue felt across the top of the easel to form a sky, and filled it with white clouds. Next came a narrow piece of brown felt across the lower portion. MaryAnn added green grass and tall trees. A wavy piece of dark blue formed an ocean in the bottom corner.

MaryAnn searched through the pieces and pulled out an assortment of animals. Within minutes, a small rabbit sat in front of a towering giraffe. A black horse stood beside a resting lion. Colorful birds flew through the air while a majestic killer whale leaped high out of the waves.

Kelly stifled a yawn. At least MaryAnn had a better variety of felt pieces than her Sunday school teacher. And the family of fat hippos added a humorous touch. But Kelly almost wished Bill had taken them on a trek to the arena. Not that she wanted to watch the mistreatment of another donkey or calf. But it would be more entertaining than this.

Bill nodded to the flannel scene. "Then God formed Adam."

MaryAnn selected a skin-colored felt man and added him to the garden scene, strategically placing bushes in front to hide his lack of clothes. Then she connected Adam to God using green flannel ties that matched the larger ones Bill used with Guy and Girl. Kelly had never thought of Adam being joined to God in that way. But she supposed it made sense.

"But it wasn't good for Adam to be alone. So He created Eve to be the perfect partner for him."

MaryAnn placed a skin-colored felt woman, also clothed in green bushes, on the board. The campers snickered, and Kelly chuckled with them. Her Sunday school teacher had never used naked characters. Trust Bill to add a twist to flannel people.

MaryAnn connected Eve to God. Then she searched through the pile for more flannel strings and joined Adam and Eve to each other, forming a triangle of connection.

"God placed these clothing-challenged individuals in the garden of Eden to share and work in His perfect creation. And in that garden, God walked with Adam and Eve."

The first love story. Not that Adam and Eve had a lot of other options for partners.

"Most of you know how the story goes," Bill continued. "Adam and Eve disobeyed God and ate the fruit from the one tree that was off limits. But their rebellion was more than breaking a rule. It was a choice to break away. The consequence was separation from God."

MaryAnn reached into her back pocket and pulled out a pair of scissors. She snipped the flannel connection between God and the only two people on earth.

Kelly felt an unexpected rise of resentment within her. That was how she felt—cut off from God. But in her case, she hadn't done anything to deserve it.

Bill's deep voice broke into her thoughts. "This disobedience is what we call sin, and a holy God cannot be connected to anyone stained by it."

MaryAnn covered Adam and Eve with small black felt dots. It made them look dirty, or sick. Which was most likely what Bill intended.

Kelly had heard lots of sermons on the subject of sin. She settled back, waiting for Bill to warn the campers about the evils of drinking, swearing, smoking, doing drugs, and having sex outside of marriage. Actions that always ranked among the top offenses at her church. Kelly had a clean record in all those areas. Well, mostly clean. Just a little drinking, and a few lies to her parents. But she'd committed none of the big bad sins, so the sermons didn't bother her. In fact, she felt quite comfortable whenever a pastor railed against such immoral actions.

But Bill didn't call out any sins by name. Did he think the campers were too young to be participating in these activities? Bill wasn't naïve. Which meant he'd omitted the typical list of wrongdoing on purpose.

Bill tapped on the flannel couple. "This sin against God didn't sever the connection between Adam and Eve. But it introduced tangles that weren't there before."

MaryAnn rolled a handful of ties in her palms and placed the snarled mess between the felt couple.

Bill picked up a few of the sin spots and added them to the couple. As if they didn't already have enough. "A holy God can't connect Himself to sin-stained people. And sin-stained people can't meet the perfect standards of a holy God As descendants of Adam and Eve, we are all born sinners. That means we're disconnected from God right from birth."

With fingers flying, MaryAnn removed the animals from the scene. In their place, she added an assortment of flannel people, of all shapes, sizes, ages, and races. Small black dots covered each of them. Some of the individuals were linked to each other with snarled ties, but none were connected to God. Several stood with arms stretched up. As if trying to reach God, but failing.

Kelly's thoughts wandered back to staff training. MaryAnn had said this might be the first time many of the campers heard what Jesus had done for them. And Bill had chosen to use a flannel board to show it. At the beginning of the evening, she'd laughed at the absurdity of it. Now she was impressed by the simplicity. She'd heard salvation explained in a multitude of ways, most of them long and complicated. But she'd never seen such a clear picture as the one before her.

"Many people think they can earn ties to God by living a good life, going to church, and giving money to charity. Those are all good things, but none of them is good enough. There's absolutely nothing we can do to reconnect with God."

As the sun sank behind the trees, the evening chill descended on the rows of campers. Kelly shivered, though she wasn't sure if it was from the dip in temperature or Bill's despairing picture.

"Looks hopeless, doesn't it?"

Yes, it did. The campers gave quiet agreement as they sat in silence, staring at the bleak scene on the board.

Kelly studied the cloth characters. One stood out to her, a girl with brown hair tied back in a ponytail. As she studied her look-a-like, Kelly felt annoyed. Surely the flannel girl didn't deserve all those dark sin spots. What if the girl had worked hard to be good? What if she had perfect attendance at church, always knew the answers in her Sunday school classes, and others looked up to her? Kelly's fingers twitched, and she was tempted to snatch some of the black circles from the cloth figure.

Bill tossed several logs on the fire and stoked it with a poker, causing a blaze of light to glint off the sequined eyes of the flannel girl. For a crazy moment, she seemed to look straight through Kelly. As if she could see the jealousy, anger, bitterness, and pride hidden deep in her heart. And suddenly Kelly thought she understood why Bill hadn't read off a list of sins. Because he couldn't count them all. And the worst ones weren't the obvious, outward choices that everyone could observe.

Bill strode back to the flannel board, now easier to see as the crackling flames burned with growing strength. "When I mentioned we were going to talk about the first love story, most of you probably assumed I was referring to Adam and Eve. But I was talking about God. The first romance was between God and Adam. Soon after came the romance between God and Eve."

Kelly's lip curled in disbelief. A romance with God? Ridiculous. Maybe even disrespectful. God was love and all that, but going on a date with God? Dinner and a movie? Bill was stretching it too far.

"God loved us too much to let us be eternally lost. On our own, we could not approach Him. So He came near to us. This is the first and greatest love story. God loved the world so much that He sent Jesus to reestablish those original ties with us."

MaryAnn held up a flannel Jesus. She placed the robed figure among the other people on the board. Then she added ties between God and Jesus. He was the only character on the flannel board with such a connection. And the only one without the black spots.

"Because Jesus was born of a virgin and lived a perfect life, sin did not cut His connection with God. But He willingly traded places with us. Through an excruciatingly painful and torturous death on the cross, Jesus took our sin on Himself. He experienced our punishment and paid the price for our disobedience. The price of separation from God."

MaryAnn placed Jesus on a cross, covered him with the dark spots, and put a spiky crown on his head. Then she cut the ties between God and Jesus, creating a wide gap in the connection.

Kelly couldn't turn away from the flannel board. The story of Jesus' crucifixion was as familiar to her as that of Adam and Eve.

She'd heard it from the pulpit every Easter and watched more church plays than she could count. She knew Jesus had given His life. But she never considered that He'd lost His relationship with God at the same time.

MaryAnn laid Jesus in a flannel cave, then placed a large cloth stone in front, sealing him in.

Bill's voice rang out in the stillness. "Once the debt was paid, death and hell could not hold Jesus. Three days after He laid down His life, God raised Him from the dead. The connection between God and Jesus was restored."

MaryAnn took the stone away, revealing Jesus again. But now, instead of a sin-stained man wearing a crown of thorns, He was spotless and clothed in white. Kelly wasn't sure how MaryAnn had made the switch, but the effect was startling.

A cheer rose from the campers. Kelly joined in the applause. These were the stories that Kelly liked best, where it looked as if all was lost but in a sudden turn, good triumphed over evil. She read her favorites over and over. She'd never thought of the Bible as fitting into that category. But then, she'd never heard the story told in this way.

MaryAnn placed the transformed Jesus halfway between the land and sky, then added ties to reconnect Him to God.

"Now Jesus holds out His nail-scarred hands with ties of forgiveness. When we reach out to take hold, we are reconnected to God through Jesus."

Bill searched his pocket and pulled out a handful of ties identical to the ones that MaryAnn had been using. Except the cords in Bill's hands were bright red. Just like the ones that had connected Guy to the cross during the campfire in the gym.

As Bill connected Jesus to several of the flannel people using the red ties, MaryAnn pressed new white outfits over the sin-stained ones. "God's greatest desire is for everyone to be reunited with Him, but that can only be done through His Son. Jesus gave His life in order to save you. This is the greatest love story ever."

Kelly considered the brown-haired flannel girl again. She was among the characters who held red ties connected to Jesus and who'd been newly clothed in white. Looking ready to live the ultimate happily ever after.

Bill tapped on the board. "The story doesn't end here. Salvation is only the beginning–the first tie of many. After we're saved, we can continue to add ties."

MaryAnn cleared most of the flannel board, leaving one individual who had ties connected to God through Jesus. Kelly knew there was more to being a Christian than saying one prayer. Things like living a good life and trying to please God. Although that hadn't helped very much when she'd been faced with pressure from Aaron. Kelly leaned forward, wondering if Bill had something new to say.

Bill stepped away from the flannel board and stood in front of the fire pit. Bright flames crackled behind him. "Some of you have already asked Jesus to forgive you–possibly here at camp. You went home full of excitement, determined to serve God. But within a week or two, life returned to normal and you lost your enthusiasm."

A low murmur rose from the audience. Apparently many campers could relate. Kelly had experienced the same swing of emotions, sometimes feeling close to God and sometimes far away. She'd assumed something was wrong with her faith, but maybe she wasn't the only one.

Bill's face glowed in the firelight. "If we want to serve God, then we deliberately build ties with Him throughout our lives. And as with all ties, that involves sharing. We share with God by developing a daily routine that includes praying and studying the Bible."

Kelly frowned as MaryAnn added a flannel Bible and praying hands to the board. It seemed too simple. Besides, she'd done all that and it hadn't brought her any closer to God.

"It's easy to add ties with God at camp. But after you go home, it requires deliberate effort. Especially if you don't have the support of a Christian family or friends. You'll want to attend church and a youth group or Bible study. Make Christian friends. If you can't find any at home, write to your counselors or other campers."

Kelly dropped her head. She'd hoped for some trick she might have missed. And she'd gotten nothing.

"If you do these simple activities every day, by the time next summer comes around, you will have a tree trunk of ties connecting you with the Lord. And there's nothing more important or life-changing than that."

MaryAnn added a large number of ties between the flannel individual and God.

Bill stood in front of the campers. "If any of you would like to reconnect with God right now, I'd like you to raise your hand."

Kelly's head snapped up, startled by Bill's instruction. At church, her pastor always asked everyone to close their eyes during the altar call to spare them the pressure or embarrassment of a public decision.

To her surprise, hands rose all around her, including several girls from her cabin. Terri, Emma, Fiona, even Amber.

Bill's gaze traveled slowly across the rows, and he gave an affirming nod and smile to each individual.

As Kelly looked at the glowing faces around her, she remembered the hope she'd felt when she first committed her life to God. How old had she been? Somewhere around seven or eight. She'd never forget how excited she'd been, knowing life would be so much better. And it had been great, for a while.

How would these campers feel when everything didn't work out perfectly? When prayers went unanswered? When things fell apart, and God allowed it to happen? Shouldn't Bill warn the campers that being a Christian wouldn't give them a pass on trouble? No one had warned her.

Bill motioned for arms to be lowered. "Now, is there anyone here who already has the tie of salvation but hasn't added many others? If you'd like to make your relationship with God a priority and recommit to adding ties, please raise your hand."

Again, arms lifted all around the campfire. Mike, Charlie and a few other staff members held their hands high. Kelly felt an urge to join in, but not in front of everyone. She didn't want to admit that something was lacking with her faith. She'd made that mistake before.

When she'd first had doubts about God, she confided in a close friend in the youth group. There had been a look of shock on her friend's face, then pity in her eyes. The friend must have told her mom, because news of Kelly's faltering faith hit the church prayer chain that evening, and her friends waged an intense intervention program. Annoyed and embarrassed, Kelly pretended to renew her trust in God. That was the last time she talked about her doubts. She'd been faking her faith ever since.

Bill signaled for hands to be lowered, and he closed his eyes. "God, I thank You for every hand that has been lifted to You tonight. We confess our selfish choices, disobedience, rebellion, and pride. We ask for Your forgiveness, bought with the precious blood of Jesus." Bill's voice choked with emotion, and he paused for a moment. "Jesus, thank You for reconnecting every person with a raised hand to God the Father. Help them to continue to follow and grow in their relationship with You, adding ties for the rest of their lives."

When Bill finished his prayer, there was a moment of silence. Then someone started clapping. Others joined in, and the applause turned into a roar of shouts and cheers. Kelly clapped until her hands stung, caught up with the excitement of the moment.

MaryAnn began a worship song. The campers joined in, and their voices swelled to fill the air around them. Kelly closed her eyes, soaking in the music. She couldn't deny it. There was a God, and these campers needed Him. She needed Him too. But how could she trust that He wouldn't let her down? And that she wouldn't fall away again?

When the song finished, Bill took Guy and Girl and propped them beside the flannel board. "The first romance was the love that

God has for us. He moved heaven and hell, literally, to rescue us. In devotions tomorrow, you'll learn how this first romance will help all other romantic relationships. It's time now to head back to your cabins. But anyone who would like to talk or pray can stay a little longer."

A handful of the campers rose to leave, but many lingered, including Kelly. A few sat alone, heads bowed. Some paired off with a counselor or talked quietly in small groups. A handful of girls huddled in the front row, softly singing worship songs. Jill gathered the girls from the cabin who'd raised their hands into a circle.

But it wasn't only campers who'd been touched by Bill's message. MaryAnn had her arms around a weeping Amy. Sandy and Cindy carried on a tearful conversation in an isolated spot. Tony and Stan stood near the fire, deep in discussion.

Kelly watched in amazement. She'd never expected the other staff members to have any questions or doubts about their faith. As she watched them seek guidance, the sharp spikes of jealousy pricked her. She'd been afraid to raise her hand. But they hadn't. And now they were getting help. She desperately wanted to speak to someone and ask why being a Christian hadn't worked for her. But who could she talk to? Who could she trust who wouldn't judge her for being a failure?

A gust of wind caused several pieces of loose flannel to flutter off the table. Kelly followed their flight to where they landed on the far side of the board at the feet of three figures. With the fire burning low, she hadn't noticed Bill, Darren, and Marvin, who were caught up in an intense conversation as they rearranged the flannel pieces on the board. The teasing light was gone from Darren's eyes, and his eyebrows creased into a serious line. She heard Marvin's voice raised in agitation, but couldn't make out the words.

Bill opened his worn Bible, pointing halfway down a page. Heads bent together as they read, then Marvin's small shoulders shook. Bill and Darren each put an arm around the weeping camper, and they bowed together in prayer.

Kelly felt guilty for intruding on a private moment but was too fascinated to turn away.

When they finished, Marvin lifted a glowing face, streaked with clear spots where tears had washed away the grime. Bill folded Darren and Marvin into a giant bear hug, and they all burst out laughing.

And there was her answer.

If Bill could help a small, lost boy, maybe he'd have something for someone who felt small and lost inside. Someone like her. Kelly settled back on the bench, waiting for her opportunity to approach him.

28 BITTER REVENGE

Kelly shifted on the hard bench as the campfire burned low. She didn't want Bill to rush his conversation with Marvin and Darren. But if he didn't finish soon, it would be too late for her to talk with him. Besides, they seemed to be doing more laughing than talking now. And she had crucial questions that needed answers.

Kelly glanced around, looking for someone else with whom she'd feel comfortable sharing her innermost doubts. Sandy was still busy with Cindy, who'd stopped crying but sat with her head buried in her hands. And MaryAnn had a comforting arm around Amy as they sang quiet worship songs together.

Bill raised an arm and cleared his throat. "It's time for everyone to head back to their cabins for lights out." He cleared the pieces from the flannel board, sweeping them into one of the bags. Then he folded the small table.

Kelly saw her opening. It wasn't ideal, but she could walk with Bill, at least as far as the lodge. That should give her enough time to slip in a question or two. She leaped to her feet and took a few steps in his direction. But before she reached him, the Men in Hats surrounded the camp director. Darren picked up the table, Mike tucked Guy and Girl under his arms, Charlie and Zach scooped up the bags holding the flannel pieces. They joked together as they struck out for the road, a raucous group surrounding the director.

Kelly sighed. What a great time for them to become the Helpers in Hats. Now she'd missed her opportunity. Catching Bill alone was going to be next to impossible. Unless...she could join him on his morning prayer walk on the road. It would mean giving up her jog. But she was surprised to find, she didn't care.

Kelly felt a soft tug on her sleeve and turned to find a radiant Amber at her side. "It's dark out, but somehow everything looks brighter. Is that weird?"

Kelly recognized the glowing expression on Amber's face. The wonder of new faith. She'd felt the same excitement for God once.

She gave the young camper a squeeze. "No, it's not weird at all. It's God." But a pang of worry twisted her insides. She hoped Amber's enthusiasm wouldn't fade, like it had for her.

The girls joined the others headed back toward the cabins. Kelly's heart skipped a beat when she saw Bob coming their way, still tossing in the air the strange black object that he'd threatened her with earlier. She braced for some sort of confrontation, but he passed by without a word. Just a smirk in her direction.

Kelly and Amber entered the cabin with Jill right behind them. She called out a fifteen-minute warning till lights out and the girls scrambled all around the room, pulling pajamas out of suitcases, grabbing soap and towels, and dashing off to the bathroom. Kelly snatched up her toothbrush and toothpaste and rushed to join them.

When she returned to the cabin with the last few stragglers, Jill motioned to her. "I thought I'd give you a break tonight and read the girls a bedtime story myself."

"Thanks." Kelly grinned. She could fall asleep early for once.

Jill pulled a book off the shelf and shouted a two-minute warning. The girls scrambled to get ready. Kelly slipped into her pajamas and crawled into her sleeping bag. As she adjusted her pillow, her arm brushed against a soft lump underneath it. She pulled out a small package wrapped in pink tissue. Someone had left her a present. She started to unwrap it, then stopped. It could be a trick, a nasty surprise from Bob or the Men in Hats. She fingered the package warily, then shook and sniffed it. Seemed harmless enough. And pink tissue was a little much for the guys. A glance around the cabin showed the campers climbing into their bunks. She turned so her body blocked the package, in case anyone was watching. Then she carefully opened the first fold and found a note.

Dear Kelly,

I thought you might like a new ruler. This is the only one that will give you an accurate measure of your worth. I wear mine every day because I need a constant reminder that God's opinion is the only one that counts. Remember, God loves you with unfailing, unending, immeasurable love.

Sandy

Kelly was eager to see what kind of ruler could be small enough to fit inside such a tiny package.

When she carefully removed the tissue, tears filled her eyes. With trembling fingers, she pulled out a thin, black leather cord with a small wooden cross dangling from the end. Kelly recognized it at once, and knew where Sandy had found it. It was one of the religious trinkets from the camp store. Cheap junk that would have been a waste of her store coupon. Or at least that's what she'd thought a few days ago.

At the beginning of the week, she would have been offended and even furious at being given such a gift. She might even have thrown it in the trash. But things had changed. She still had doubts and questions that needed answers. But she no longer felt hostile toward God. If possible, she wanted to reconnect with Him.

Kelly unfastened the clasp, then hesitated. It didn't feel right to wear it yet—not until she had the kind of faith that Sandy and Bill talked about.

She tucked the cross back into the folds of the tissue, refolded the note, and placed both under her pillow. As she did, her fingers touched the calendar.

Jill clapped her hands. "Okay, lights out in ten...nine...eight..."

Kelly grabbed a pencil and crossed off another day. Only three squares remained. Camp was coming to an end so quickly. But she wasn't looking forward to that anymore. And she no longer needed the chart. Kelly pulled out her suitcase, shoved the calendar deep inside, and pushed the luggage under the bunk again.

Jill flicked off the lights, plunging the room into darkness. Then she switched on her flashlight and opened the book. "Once upon a time..."

Kelly snuggled deep in her sleeping bag and reached under the covers for her beagle. It wasn't there. She quietly slipped to the floor and felt underneath the bunk. No stuffed animal there either.

Jill stopped reading and shone the flashlight on her. "What's wrong?"

"I can't find my beagle. Has anyone seen it?"

No one had.

Jill yawned. "It probably got mixed up with someone's clothes or shoved into a locker when we were cleaning up. I'm sure we'll find it in the morning."

Kelly climbed back into bed. Jill resumed reading, but Kelly couldn't concentrate on the story. Ever since her father had given her the beagle, she'd fallen asleep stroking its long ears and playing with its soft black–

A chill coursed through her body. She bolted upright. "It's my dog's nose!"

Jill stopped reading again and let out an exasperated groan. "What?"

"N-nothing," Kelly stammered. "I'm going to run to the bathroom." And once she got there, she'd keep going. All the way to Sheila and Marcy's room.

"But you'll miss the story."

Kelly leaped out of bed. "Don't wait for me." She barreled out the door.

She raced to her friend's room and pounded on the door. It opened a crack, and a disheveled Marcie peered out, pajamas rumpled and hair in a mess.

"Kelly? What's wrong?"

Kelly pushed past Marcie and flipped on the lights.

Sheila squealed and flung an arm over her eyes. "This had better be important," she snapped.

"My beagle is missing, and Bob stole it."

Her friends stared at her with blank expressions.

Kelly let out an exasperated groan. "I had a stuffed beagle on my bunk, and it's gone."

Marcie rubbed her eyes. "You woke us up for a missing toy?" She crawled back into her bed and pulled a pillow over her head.

Sheila yawned. "Maybe it fell off the bunk, or one of the campers hid it as a joke."

Kelly shook her head. "I checked. And the girls don't know where it is."

"That doesn't mean Bob took it."

Ignoring their skepticism, Kelly struggled to put her racing thoughts into coherent words. "He worked alone this morning, painting the walkway outside the girls' cabins. There was no one else around. Jill had us all put name tags on our bunks, so Bob would've known which one was mine. And he's been taunting me all afternoon with a small, round, black thing."

Marcie emerged from under her pillow. "Sorry, but I have no idea what you're talking about."

"Bob cut off my dog's nose!"

Marcie's eyes widened. "He wouldn't dare! There's a camp rule about not taking or destroying other people's property."

Kelly threw her hands in the air. "Yes, I know, because we broke it days ago."

Marcie's cheeks turned pink. "We didn't harm the hat."

Kelly snorted. "We won't know that for sure until we pull it out of the water. It could be covered in thick, green algae. Minnows could be nibbling on it for breakfast!" She paced in the narrow room. "Bob told me Darren wasn't empty-handed anymore, that he had something on me. Don't you see? Bob and Darren took my beagle as ransom for the hat. And they cut off its nose as a warning."

Sheila sat up. "You don't know that for sure. Besides, Bill gave immunity to us and all our property."

"But Bob already had the nose. We've got to get my dog back!"

Sheila bit her lower lip. "Even if you're right, we can't do anything about it until tomorrow. If your beagle doesn't turn up before breakfast, we'll confront the guys."

Kelly took several deep breaths. She hated to admit it, but Sheila was right. Marching down to the guys' cabin in her pajamas and attacking Darren in the middle of the night was not the best idea. No matter how much she wanted to do it. There was nothing she could do but wait for the morning. After a feeble goodbye, Kelly dragged herself back to the cabin. She slipped into her sleeping bag just as Jill finished the story.

Jill tiptoed to Kelly's bunk. "Is everything ok?" she whispered.

"Fine," Kelly lied.

As she tried to sleep, her fingers instinctively stroked the pillow. It was no substitute. That beagle may not have looked like much, just a worn and faded dog with droopy ears. But it was important to her. A sharp stab of guilt shot through her. Bill had said there was more to the hat than they realized. What if Darren's hat was as important to him as her beagle was to her?

The prank didn't seem so harmless now.

29 ANSWERED QUESTIONS

Kelly leaped off the fence the moment she saw Bill emerge from the private drive leading to his house, situated to the left of the camp entrance. He walked with his Bible open and head down. She hurried to join him on the road. "Hey, Bill. Sorry to interrupt, but I really need to talk to you."

To her relief, Bill closed the worn book and tucked it under his arm. "No problem. How can I help you?"

As they started walking, Kelly wished she'd written her thoughts out on paper. She'd rehearsed the questions in her mind all night. But in Bill's imposing presence, everything became foggy. She blurted out the first thing that came to mind. "I liked your talk last night. But what you said doesn't work."

Kelly sucked in her breath. She hadn't planned to be that blunt, but there was no turning back now. "I've already done everything you talked about. Ever since I was little, I've prayed, read my Bible, and gone to church. I've even done extra stuff like working on outreach projects with my youth group and going to the soup kitchen to serve meals. I used to feel close to God. But then things started to go wrong, and He stopped answering my prayers. When I had trouble at school and with my parents, God didn't do anything."

Kelly snuck a side glance at Bill. He was staring off into the distance. There was no discernible expression on his face. No way to know what he was thinking. Or if he'd even heard her.

"I feel like I did my part, but God didn't do His part. I've been questioning if there even is a God. If He does exist, it doesn't seem like He cares about me."

There. She had said it out loud. A sense of relief filled her. She turned expectantly to Bill, eager for his response.

They walked in silence for so long Kelly was tempted to poke Bill, or kick him, just to remind him she was still there. Doubts rose up within her. Had Bill decided not to answer? What if he didn't have anything to say?

They'd nearly reached her turnaround point on the road when Bill turned to look at her. "So you've worked really hard at being a good Christian?"

Kelly grimaced. "It sure feels like I have." But clearly it wasn't enough.

"Why did you do all those things?"

She couldn't hold back a snort. "Aren't Christians supposed to try to please God by living a good life?"

Bill gave a brief nod. "All the things you mentioned do please God. But did you really do them for the Lord?"

"Who else would I do them for?" Kelly found it hard to keep the irritation out of her voice.

"For yourself."

For a moment, Kelly thought she'd heard wrong. Because Bill couldn't have just taken everything good she'd done and smeared it with selfishness.

"It sounds like you expected some kind of payment. As if God owes you."

Kelly opened her mouth to argue, then closed it. She had no answer. At least not one she wanted to admit out loud.

"You're angry with God because you believe that living a good life should earn certain benefits. When God didn't reward you, you dumped Him. You want what He can give, but you don't really want Him."

Kelly chewed on her bottom lip. The way he put it made her sound self-serving and greedy. Like she was mad at God because she was giving way more than she was getting. Which was pretty much how she felt.

Bill checked his watch. "We'd better head back or we'll be late for breakfast." He turned and began walking toward camp. Kelly fell in step beside him, her mind racing. If Bill was right, she'd behaved like a self-centered brat. Blaming God when she didn't get what she wanted. Absolving herself from any fault.

Bill looked directly at her. "Can you imagine dating a guy only for what you can get from him?"

An image of Aaron sprang to mind. He'd used her for what he could get. A good grade in drama class. A boost to his ego. But she'd used him too. She'd wanted the attention and popularity that came with being on his arm. She was ashamed to admit it, but she would never have been interested in Aaron if he'd been ugly or unpopular.

And it was the same with Joel.

Kelly listened to the rhythmic crunch of the gravel under their feet. She'd had it all wrong. Expecting God to guarantee her a perfect life because she'd earned it. "I've blown it. Big time."

"We all have," Bill said. "But Jesus gives second chances. As a matter of fact, He gives as many chances as we need."

"But I still don't understand why God allows bad things to happen," Kelly muttered.

"Neither do I. God created a perfect world. Sin broke that. Someday God will fix this world and make it perfect again. But for now, we experience troubles of all kinds. And God uses those hard times. That's often when we grow the most. I can't explain why God allowed you to go through whatever struggles you've had. But I can tell you from experience that you can expect more difficult times to come."

More trouble? She'd thought Christianity was like a golden ticket that would exempt her from the hard moments. Her mind raced as she tried to figure out a whole new way of understanding how faith worked.

Kelly scrunched her nose. "Sometimes it feels like God isn't listening. Or at least He isn't answering."

"Even when God is silent, that doesn't mean He's not there, watching over us and working in our lives."

It was true. Kelly hadn't heard God's steps or seen His hand, but He hadn't forgotten her. She knew, because He'd brought her to this camp.

When Kelly saw the Timberlake entrance growing closer, she slowed her pace to a crawl. She needed time to ask one more question. Perhaps the biggest of all. "How can I handle the struggles without losing faith...like I did before?"

She needed an answer, and it had to be clear. Because in a few short days, she'd be heading home, and she would have to face the mess she'd left behind.

Bill slowed his steps. "When the hard times come, I hang on tight to what I know. That God is good. He loves me. And He's in control. God doesn't promise that I won't suffer, but He promises to be with me always. That's enough to get me through the day." He turned to her with a grin on his face. "And I sing. That's one of the reasons I walk on this deserted road every morning. So I can sing as loud as I want and no one can hear me." He winked.

Kelly laughed. "What do you sing?"

"It depends on the day. Some songs are uplifting. Others are full of questions and pain. However, I do have a favorite."

"Yes?" Kelly prompted.

"I won't torture you with my off-key voice, but I'll quote the chorus. 'On Christ, the solid Rock, I stand. All other ground is sinking sand.'"

Kelly recognized the old hymn. The congregation sang it regularly at her church. It wasn't one of her favorites, mostly because she didn't care for the slow style of music. But for the first time, she thought about the words. She'd been sinking for a long time. And she wanted to stand firm again.

Bill stopped at the fork in the road, one path leading back to his house and the other into camp. "I need to pick up MaryAnn for breakfast, so I'll let you head to the lodge on your own."

Kelly gave a reluctant nod. She wished they could talk more. She looked into Bill's eyes. "Thank you so much." She hoped he would know how much the conversation meant to her.

Bill opened his worn Bible and pulled out a tattered sheet. His list of prayer requests. "Remember, I'll be praying for you."

She knew he would. But it was time to say a prayer herself.

Kelly followed the road into camp, hurrying past the arena and the cabins. Halfway to the lodge, she found a narrow path that led to the lakefront. The clear water shone like a mirror, reflecting the sun's rays. Tall grass by the side of the shore rustled with the morning breeze. Ducks floated in pairs, and a fish jumped in the middle of the lake.

Kelly closed her eyes and tilted her head so she could feel the heat of the sun. Like heaven bestowing a warm kiss of grace.

Kelly took a deep breath and spoke aloud. "God, I've been serving You for all the wrong reasons, and I got angry because You didn't give me what I thought I deserved." She cupped her hands and held them up, as if making an offering to God. "I don't know if You can use this mess of a life, but I'm giving it to You. I want to know You. And I want to love You. Amen."

She opened her eyes. Nothing had changed around her. But deep down, Kelly felt a stirring of joy that she hadn't experienced in a long time.

Excited voices broke into her solitude. She turned and saw a large group of campers on the road, heading toward the lodge for breakfast. Kelly hurried up the path to join them. She spotted Darren and Marvin trailing behind the crowd. They waved when they saw her, and then Darren leaned down and whispered something to Marvin. Both of them burst out laughing. No doubt gloating about her stolen and maimed beagle.

A surge of anger shot through Kelly. The morning joy forgotten, she stormed up the path to meet them. "You may think you got me back. But I'll cut your ugly hat into pieces if anything happens to my beagle."

Eyes wide, Darren held up his hands. "What are you talking about?"

Kelly swallowed hard, her eyes burning with tears. She'd thought Darren and Marvin were her friends. But they'd cut up her dog, and now they were laughing, like it meant nothing. Like she meant nothing.

Joel shouted a greeting and trotted over. He took one look at Kelly's face, and frowned. "Are you okay?"

Kelly turned back to Darren. "Don't play dumb. You know what I'm talking about. My dad gave me that stuffed animal when I was five. Bob showed me the nose yesterday, and it wasn't attached to my dog!" She stopped, unable to trust herself to say any more without dissolving into an ugly, uncontrolled bawl session.

Darren took a step nearer, looking at her with a steady gaze. "I don't know anything about your dog."

Kelly studied him through blurry eyes. Either Darren was a really good actor, or he really didn't know what had happened to her precious stuffed animal.

She swallowed hard. "I want my beagle back."

Darren reached out a hand, but she jerked away. An image of her poor dog's mutilated face came to mind. Her shoulders shook, hot tears rushed down her face, and she turned into a blubbering, sobbing mess. In front of Marvin. In front of Darren. And worst of all, in front of Joel. She couldn't imagine what they all thought of her getting so broken up over a stuffed toy. Like she was a spoiled toddler.

The joyous peace of the morning was gone. She'd made a complete botch of everything. Kelly stumbled backward, then turned and fled.

30 TWO TESTS

Kelly stumbled into the lodge, gasping for breath. She kept her head down as she raced on wobbly legs straight to the bathroom. Five minutes of splashing cold water on her tear-splotched face did little to cool her flaming cheeks. Darren had to be lying. Bob had all but confessed that they'd taken the dog to use against her.

Kelly wiped her dripping face with a paper towel, then leaned against the wall, not ready to leave the safety of the bathroom yet. Because then she'd have to face the embarrassment of yelling like a fool at Darren. And sniveling like a baby in front of Joel.

When she finally emerged in the dining hall, the serving line was empty and the girls from her cabin were at the table, halfway through breakfast. She grabbed a cereal bowl, barely covered the bottom with flakes, and added a touch of milk.

Kelly made her way to the table and slid in beside Amber. As the sounds of happy chatter floated around her, she stirred her cereal and watched it turn into a soggy mess. Just like her morning. After a few bites, she shoved the bowl away.

Amber nudged her arm. "We searched the cabin this morning, but we didn't find your dog. I asked around, and no one has seen it."

"Thanks." Kelly gave a half smile.

She saw Joel walking toward her and cringed. For a crazy moment, she considered ducking under the table to hide.

"Any sign of your beagle?" Joel placed strong hands on her shoulders and rubbed the tense muscles with firm strokes. She tried to relax under his massage.

"We haven't found him yet. But thanks for asking." And thanks for not mentioning her earlier freak-out.

Jill sent Kelly and Joel a motherly glare. Which they both ignored.

"Well, I hope it turns up soon." Joel gave her shoulders a gentle squeeze, then returned to his table. Kelly paid no attention to the kissing sounds made by the campers at her table, which ended the moment Bill posted scores for the clean cabin contest.

Most of the other cabins had dropped out of contention for the ice cream treats. But Stan and Darren's cabin continued to match the perfect scores for Jill and Kelly's cabin. Until this morning. In a careless moment, one of the guys left a light on in their room. And that gave the girls the lead by a single point. Cries of disbelief were drowned by the roar at Kelly's table as the girls pounded their fists on the table in raucous celebration.

Kelly hadn't cared about winning. But right now, she actually wanted the giant sundae. To dump on Bob and Darren's heads. Since the bowl was so big, there'd be enough ice cream to cover them both. That should pay them back for her dog, or at least make a start

After congratulating the girls, Jill tossed a few gloating remarks toward Stan's table. Insults flew back and forth, but Kelly wasn't in the mood to join in. Instead she focused on scraping her cereal into the slop bucket.

A finger poked her in the back. She glanced behind and found a red-faced Marvin, shifting from one foot to the other.

"This is for you." He shoved a crumpled piece of paper into her hand. "From Darren." Message delivered, he scampered off.

A confession and apology? Instructions on where to find her dog? Or more denials? Tamping down her rising curiosity, Kelly tucked the note in her pocket. She'd read it later, when she could be away from prying eyes.

Kelly slipped out of the lodge and made it back to the cabin without any new humiliations. Quite an accomplishment considering how the morning had been going. Once inside, she joined the other girls on the rug.

"We're going to break from the usual format this morning." Jill passed out the next section of notes, which the girls added to their binders. It seemed normal enough, until they looked at the first page.

"Pop quiz?" Joyce scowled. "This is summer camp. We aren't supposed to have tests."

"Think of it more as a review." Jill picked up a stack of pencils and handed them out. "Bill wants to see if you can take what you've learned this week and apply the concept of the ties to real life."

Kelly gulped. At the beginning of the week, she'd been so angry about being at camp she hadn't paid much attention. And she'd already been through enough failure for one day.

"Oh, and Bill asked me to report our cabin score to him."

"We're being graded too?" Joyce's lip curled in scorn.

Kelly didn't like the idea either. Knowing Bill, he'd post the results somewhere. Like on the wall beside the pictures of love. Kelly didn't want her failure broadcast all over camp. Bob and Darren should love it, though.

"Bill gave me these to pass out when I grade your responses." Jill held up a clear bag filled with a colorful assortment of wrapped hard candy. "One piece for trying. Two for a correct answer."

The girls cheered, and Kelly couldn't resist smiling. Bill understood human nature, and the value of a sweet treat. Too bad it wasn't chocolate, or she could have saved it for a future bribe with Tony. Assuming she earned any.

Jill tapped the notes. "On the left side of the page, there are two new pictures of Guy and Girl along with a brief description. Analyze the scene as if you were at a campfire talk. In the blank lines on the right, identify the problem and then describe how knowing God shows us the right way to form a romantic connection."

Jill set a timer for ten minutes, and pencils scratched at a furious pace. The quiz wasn't as hard as Kelly had thought it would be. Or maybe she'd been listening more closely than she'd realized. When the timer rang, she put down her pencil, feeling confident in her answers.

"Let's go around the circle, and everyone can take a turn making a comment about these pictures." Jill pointed to the first one, titled "The Flirt." It showed Girl waving multiple ropes in the air as several guys leaped high in an attempt to grab them.

Jill dangled the bag of candy in front of the girls. "Who wants to go first?"

With an eye on the treats, Joyce raised her hand high. Kelly grinned at how quickly the brick wall had changed her mind about the test.

"So what's the problem, Joyce?"

"I don't think flirting is a problem. It's just harmless fun. And how else are you supposed to let a guy know that you're interested?"

All eyes turned to Jill and the bag of candies. Joyce had taken a different point of view and made a logical statement. But it clearly wasn't the expected answer.

"That's a great perspective." A broad smile spread across Jill's face. "Bill was actually hoping someone would realize that flirting isn't always wrong. You've just earned two candies."

Jill leaned forward to pass the sack of treats, but Joyce held up her hand. "I'm not done yet."

Kelly sucked in her breath. Would Joyce make another excellent point? Or would she blow up the whole exercise by being negative and argumentative?

Joyce tilted her head and stared at the image on the page. "There's something wrong with this picture. It looks like Girl is dangling ties in front of as many guys as possible but doesn't really want to connect with any of them. It's not right to flirt if Girl is just using these guys to get attention for herself."

Kelly couldn't hold back a grin. Joyce had been listening and absorbing the campfire messages. Perhaps the brick wall was more like a thick sponge. It was a good lesson for Kelly not to prejudge or make assumptions. That would be very helpful with the next group of campers. Or it would have been if she were staying another week. Which she wasn't. The thought left her feeling disappointed.

Jill passed the bag of candy to Joyce. "Perfect answers."

After digging to the bottom, Joyce pulled out two green-and-white-striped candies. She ripped the wrapper off one and popped it in her mouth. A satisfied smile spread across her face as she crunched noisily on the treat. "Peppermint, my favorite."

Kelly licked her lips. She couldn't remember the last time she'd had a peppermint. Or any candy. Everyone in the cabin knew she didn't eat much. It would be easy to pass when her turn came. Or take one and tuck it away, saying she was saving it for later but really intending to chuck it in the garbage. But the candies looked good. And Kelly was tired of the tricks and the lying.

Jill nodded at Amber, sitting next to Joyce. "Any thoughts you'd like to add?"

"I don't think it matters how many guys Girl flirts with or how much attention she gets." Amber bit her lower lip. "It will never be enough"

"Excellent point."

Amber looked pleased with Jill's praise. And the bag of candy worked its way around the circle.

Fiona waved her hand. "Some flirts are never satisfied. They're always looking for someone better."

"Very true." Jill motioned for Amber to toss treats to Fiona. "So what's the solution?"

Nadia's eyebrows drew together. "It's important to have support and admiration from others. But God's approval counts more than the approval of people. We should be looking to Him."

Jill applauded her answer, and a look of relief passed over Nadia's face. The bag of candy flew across the circle and into her hands.

Jill pointed to the second picture, which showed Girl in the middle of a lake, clinging to a life preserver. A storm raged around her, stirring up huge waves. Sharks circled their prey, each gray dorsal fin labeled with a negative emotion like *depression, anxiety* or *fear.* Guy stood on shore, pulling hard on a rope attached to the preserver.

Kelly chuckled, trying to imagine how Bill would re-enact this scene during a campfire. Maybe Girl floating in a wading pool with a fan creating waves as goldfish circled their cardboard meal. Perhaps it was best for Girl that Bill had chosen to demonstrate this example on paper. The cardboard Girl had survived a lot, but being waterlogged while small fish nibbled on her limbs might be too much.

Jill tapped on the picture. "Bill called this Lifeline Dating."

Michelle's arm waved in the air. "I think it looks like Girl is drowning and she's surrounded by a lot of personal problems. Girl is clinging to the hope that Guy can pull her out of her trouble."

Jill gave a thumbs-up, and the bag of treats was passed into the hands of a grinning Michelle.

Jill motioned to Emma. "Anything else?"

Emma didn't even look at what she'd written. "I think it's great that Guy is trying to help Girl. We should try to help anyone who has struggles, especially someone we love."

After Emma finished fishing for her candy reward, Jill nodded to Terri. "What is God's solution?"

"I think that God uses other people to help rescue us sometimes." Terri read her answer from the page. "And people are good, but God is better. Because sometimes the waves and sharks are just too big, and God is the only one who can save us."

Kelly's thoughts drifted back to the comments Marcie had made during the training program, when Bill had first introduced Guy and Girl. Marcie hadn't understood how romance and ties could teach the kids about God's love. Kelly hadn't either. But here was the proof. Bill's eccentric plan had worked. Perfectly.

All eyes turned to Tanya, the last camper left to give an answer. "I don't have anything different to say. But can I still get a candy if I come up with a new picture of ties?"

Jill raised an eyebrow. "Sure. If makes sense."

Tanya chewed on a fingernail. "With the last guy I dated, I felt like I was walking a tightrope. He held the ties way up high and I had to balance on them and do everything exactly the way he wanted. And there was no safety net. If I took one wrong step, he'd drop the ties and let me fall."

Kelly joined in the applause from the other girls. Bill would be thrilled to hear that the girls had not only learned the lessons of the week, but gone beyond.

Kelly imagined Aaron, holding the ties high. Demanding that she walk the way he wanted. And when she wouldn't, he dropped her. But that wasn't going to happen again. Because she was getting off the tightrope. For good.

Kelly sat up straighter. She was walking with God now, and she didn't have to perform to please Aaron. She was only concerned with pleasing God.

"You've definitely earned a treat." Jill tossed the candy bag to Tanya. "I can't wait to tell Bill. He'll probably add that to his list of campfire messages. Although I can't imagine who he'd get to walk a tightrope."

The girls shouted out suggestions of different staff members. Kelly laughed the hardest when Tony's name came up. The mental image of the maintenance manager in a tutu, arms flailing for balance, had her rolling on the floor.

Tanya held the bag but didn't open it. "Instead of candy, do you think Bill would give me some ties from the campfire talks? I'd love to take a few home and pin them up on my bulletin board. Or use them as a bookmark in my Bible."

Joyce's face lit up. "I want some too!"

Kelly's mouth fell open. Joyce, the brick wall who'd had a lousy attitude from the moment she arrived, wanted to take home a keepsake to remind her of the lessons and the week at camp. Kelly felt as if she'd witnessed a miracle.

All the girls clamored for ties.

Jill's face beamed with pleasure, and she laughed out loud. "I'm sure he'd be happy to give a few ties to each of you. I'll ask him this afternoon."

Amber waved to get Jill's attention. "Kelly didn't get a candy."

Kelly shrugged. "I don't need one."

Jill motioned for Nadia to pass the treats to her. "I'm sure you had the right answers, even if you didn't get a chance to share them."

Kelly took the bag and pulled out a pink candy. Strawberry, with a soft center. She hesitated for a moment, then removed the wrapper. She couldn't let Joyce have a miracle without experiencing one of her own.

The candy tasted unbelievably sweet. But even more satisfying was the fact that she'd passed a personal test. Just a small one. And there'd be more to come. But it was a good start.

Jill turned the page in her binder. The girls followed her lead. On the final page was a picture of a three-way relationship between Guy, Girl, and God, all connected by a triangle of ties. Jill motioned for everyone to read the final caption together. "When God occupies the proper place in our lives and hearts, the people we love can occupy their proper places. When we love God first, we love others better."

Kelly glanced over the pictures again. So simple that even a child could understand. Or a cabin full of young girls, eager to love and be loved. Or an insecure, anorexic girl who desperately needed God's forgiveness and another chance.

Kelly thought of the cross necklace under her pillow, and her fingers moved to her neck. It was time to put it on.

31 MYSTERY REVEALED

The morning pop quiz devotion ended earlier than usual, leaving the girls with some free time. They spread around the room, pulling out unfinished friendship bracelets, grabbing the art supplies from Jill's shelves, and flopping on their bunks to relax and chat. Kelly used the extra time to pull her hair back in a loose reverse French braid. Amber sat beside her, watching.

"When you're finished, could you braid my hair?"

"Of course." Kelly grinned. Her smile faltered as the other campers ran over, begging her to do the same for them. Forty minutes later, Kelly could barely move her cramped fingers. But she surveyed every camper and their new hairstyles with pride.

Kelly stretched out on the cabin floor, her legs numb from sitting so long. She glanced at her watch and motioned to Jill. "You're late for the first activity."

Jill leaped to her feet. "Two-minute cabin clean-up! And then we've got to run all the way to the barn."

The campers scrambled about the room, tossing candy wrappers into the wastebasket, straightening sleeping bags on bunks, and tucking clothes inside suitcases.

Jill grabbed a sweater and thrust her arms through the sleeves. She spun around the room until she spotted Kelly. "Could you collect the binders?"

"Sure." Kelly fingered the note in her pocket. She'd been hoping to get a few minutes alone.

As the girls dashed out the door, Kelly gathered the devotion books and stacked them in neat piles on Jill's bookcase. Then she sat on her bunk and retrieved the tissue package from under her pillow. Unfolding the layers, she removed the necklace. It took a few minutes of fumbling with the clasp before she was able to secure it around her neck. As she ran a finger along the smooth lines of the cross, a sense of peace flowed over her.

Voices on the veranda of campers rushing past snapped Kelly back to the present. Tony would be expecting her soon. And he probably had a messy job waiting as payment for the missed chores from the day before. If she was late, he might make it worse.

Kelly quickly pulled the crumpled paper out of her pocket and skimmed the short note.

I didn't take your beegle. But don't worry. I'll get it back for you.
Darren

So he was still denying any part in the theft. And it looked like the fate of her beloved dog was in the hands of a guy who couldn't spell the simple word beagle. She wasn't sure if she should laugh or cry. But she had no choice. She had to trust him.

Kelly rose from her bunk, shoved the note back in her pocket, and headed off to the maintenance shed. When she walked in, Tony scowled in her direction. "You're late." He pointed to a pair of heavy canvas overalls. "Put those on. You're painting the boathouse today."

Kelly wrinkled her nose at the sight of the familiar paint-splattered outfit. She spotted several long brown streaks of stain, reminders of her war with Bob. Then she noticed a second grungy pair lying across a nearby chair. "Is Bob painting too?"

"If he ever gets here." Tony tossed an impatient glance at the door. "I'll leave a note and he can meet us there."

Tony scrawled a message and tacked it on the door. Kelly hoped Bob would be able to decipher it. If not, she'd be stuck painting the boathouse alone. She almost offered to rewrite the note more legibly. But Tony didn't seem to be in a great mood, and he was touchy about his handwriting.

Tony grabbed several paint cans and a set of brushes, and they set off down the road. Once they reached the boathouse, Tony set the pails down. "You'll be painting the walls. That includes the window frames and doors. And I want a neat job."

Kelly glanced up the road. No sign of her partner. "What happens if Bob doesn't show?"

"Just paint two sides, and you're done."

Kelly nodded, relieved.

An hour later, she'd melted into a puddle of sweat inside the heavy canvas overalls. But one wall was finished, and she had a good start on the second. She stopped to massage her aching arm.

At the sound of crunching gravel, she glanced up and saw Bob approaching, snapback cap pulled low over his face and hands shoved in his pockets. At least he wasn't tossing her beagle's nose in the air. She considered attacking him with the paintbrush and demanding the safe return of her dog. But that probably wouldn't help the situation. Darren said he'd get her beagle back. She'd give him until supper. And then...she didn't know. But she'd think of something, and it would be painful.

Kelly clenched her teeth and turned her back, vigorously applying paint on the second wall. The rattling of a paint can handle signaled that Bob had arrived.

"I hope you're happy," he snapped, his voice oddly nasal.

"Well, I am halfway done and you—" Kelly turned to face Bob and stopped mid-sentence.

Bob's left eye was swollen and the area around it had turned a nasty mix of blue, black, and green. His nose also looked swollen, and large drops of dried blood covered the front of his fancy jersey. The stain was not going to wash out easily, if at all.

"What happened to your eye?"

Instead of answering, Bob snatched a paintbrush off the grass, dunked it into the can, and sloshed paint on the wall.

"You should really wear overalls so you don't get paint on..." Her voice trailed off as Bob glared at her.

Kelly shrugged. It didn't matter to her if Bob messed up his expensive clothes. He could sulk all he wanted, as long as he painted his half of the shed.

Tony arrived fifteen minutes later and began his inspection with Bob. "Nice shiner."

Bob scowled.

Tony walked around the building, observing their progress. "Once you're finished, bring the cans and brush back to the shed." As he walked away, he tossed a parting comment over his shoulder. "And don't drip any blood on the wall, Bob."

Kelly bit her lip to hide a smile. Bob pulled his snapback cap down low and remained silent, except for the aggressive swish of his brush against the boathouse door.

Half an hour later, Kelly finished her second wall. Bob had barely begun his second side.

Kelly took a deep breath and let it out slowly. She had no idea how long it would take Darren to return her beagle. Or even if he would. But in the meantime, it wouldn't hurt to keep things as friendly as possible with Bob. In case he was planning to cut off her dog's tail as well as his nose.

She approached her sullen partner. "Do you want me to help you finish?"

"No." Bob's face twisted in a sneer. Which was a mistake. He quickly raised his sleeve to catch the fresh red drops dripping from his left nostril. Kelly hoped it hurt.

"Fine. I'll see you later." There was a story behind the black eye, bloody nose, and bad mood. But she wasn't going to get it from him. And there was no point in trying.

Kelly ripped off the overalls, gathered her materials, and headed back to the maintenance shed. Tony wasn't there, so she carried the supplies to the table. She had just placed them on top when she heard a light knock. Turning, she saw Mike standing in the doorway.

"If you're looking for Tony, he's not around." She shook out the overalls and folded them neatly.

Mike cleared his throat. "I just saw Tony. He told me I could probably find you here."

Kelly straightened. "Why are you looking for me?" A twinge of panic ran through her. She was alone and defenseless. If Mike decided to carry out some vengeful act on behalf of the Men in Hats, she'd be in trouble.

Mike held out a large paper bag. "I have something for you."

Warily, Kelly reached for the sack and looked inside. A soft bundle of black, white, and tan fur met her eyes. Her beagle! With a shriek of joy, she pulled the dog out, inspecting every well-loved inch. To her surprise and joy, the nose was exactly where it should be. Her beagle appeared completely unharmed.

Kelly leaped at Mike and gave him a tight hug. "Thank you!"

Mike's face turned the color of a bad sunburn. He pried off her arms and took a step back. "Don't thank me. I didn't do anything. Darren's the one who got your dog back."

An image of Bob's black eye popped into Kelly's head and she gasped. "Did Darren have a fight with Bob?"

Mike chuckled. "Well, that's the story going around camp. But it didn't happen quite like that. Last night, Bob was bragging about having stolen this stuffed dog from one of the girls. He put a noose around its neck and hung it from the fan in his cabin. I guess the dog swung in circles for most of the evening."

Kelly's eyes narrowed. One black eye wasn't enough. Maybe if she went back to the boathouse, she could shove Bob into a door and blacken the other eye as well. Or at least give him a fat lip.

Mike pulled out a chair, spun it around, and sat down. "When Darren talked with you this morning, he realized Bob must have your dog. After breakfast, he headed to Bob's cabin, with Marvin trailing along. Bob was there. But the dog was gone."

Kelly hugged her beagle tighter. "Where was it?"

"I'm getting there." Mike grinned, clearly enjoying himself. "Darren asked about the dog. Bob started spinning some plan about how they could hold it as ransom to get the hat back. But Darren insisted Bob return it to you. Well, Bob got all mad. He said he wasn't giving it back, and Darren couldn't make him." Mike shook his head in disbelief. "I don't know what Bob was thinking. He knows Darren has a black belt in karate.

So Darren had never been a part of the plan. And he'd refused to go along with Bob's scheme when he was given the chance. Kelly thought of the angry accusations she'd flung at him that morning and winced.

"Darren guessed he was hiding the beagle in his locker and made a move toward it. Bob blocked him."

Jumping up, Mike reenacted the scene. "While Bob was concentrating on Darren, Marvin snuck behind him, pulled the beagle out of the locker, and threw a high pass to Darren. Darren and Bob jumped for it at the same time. Darren got the dog, and Bob got an elbow in the face. On accident...of course." Mike winked.

Kelly whooped with joy. "I wish I could have seen that."

"There wasn't much to see. It was all over in a few minutes. But you know how rumors get started. Now everyone thinks it was some huge brawl. Anyway, Darren said he was going to be stuck at the barn all morning. Since I had a break, he asked me if I would return your dog. He thought you'd want it back right away."

Kelly gave her beagle a kiss on the head and felt a rush of gratitude toward Darren.

Mike raised an eyebrow. "Girls," he muttered.

Kelly didn't care what Mike thought. He had no idea how much the stuffed animal meant to her.

"Marvin was furious when he found out the dog was yours. I don't know what you did to earn that kid's loyalty, but I think he would have taken on Bob by himself."

Kelly chuckled at the image of small, greasy Marvin attacking a big jerk like Bob.

A pounding of feet and the cries of familiar voices outside the shed preceded Sheila and Marcie bursting through the door. "We heard a camper talking. We know who has your—"

Kelly held up her beagle. Squealing in delight, Sheila launched herself at Kelly and pulled her into a crushing embrace. Marcie wrapped her arms around them, and they nearly toppled over.

When Kelly glanced at Mike, he looked eager to escape. He tipped his hat and took several steps toward the door. Then he swung back around, looking like he was trying to make up his mind about something.

"We swore ourselves to secrecy, but I think you need to know." Mike spoke so quickly he tripped all over his words.

The intense look on his face was out of character for Mike, who was more at home cracking jokes and interrupting Bill during campfires. There was an instant hush in the room as all three girls stared at Mike.

"Darren, Zach, and I have been friends with Charlie forever. We've been coming to camp together every year since we were little, and we always stay in the same cabin. We've been looking forward to working on staff. We planned to stay for the whole two months."

Kelly tried to imagine eight weeks on maintenance, pulling weeds, painting fences, and cleaning window sills. With sleepless nights on a hard bunk as hyper kids refused to sleep. Not a great picture. But there'd also be crazy pranks, special campers, spontaneous puns, and unpredictable campfire messages. Suddenly a whole summer of camp didn't sound so bad.

Mike hesitated, then plunged ahead. "Things have never been good at Charlie's home. He got good grades and stayed out of trouble, but he always had bruises somewhere. At Christmas last year, his eye was swollen so badly he couldn't open it. We bugged him till he told us what was going on. Apparently, his parents had gotten into a big argument. His mom slapped his dad, and he shoved her into a wall. He was about to hit her, but Charlie stepped in to protect her and he got punched instead. Then his dad left, yelling that he was never coming back."

Kelly's parents got into heated arguments sometimes. But she couldn't imagine her parents getting physically violent. And to think of a father hitting his own son? And then abandoning him? Her heart ached for Charlie.

"Charlie started skipping school, and his grades went downhill. He barely passed the year. Darren, Zach, and I tried to help, but he stopped hanging out with us. He even said he wasn't going to camp anymore."

Mike glanced behind him, as if worried someone might be listening. "The day before staff training started, Darren called Zach and me and told us to meet him at Charlie's house. I'd pretty much given up on Charlie. But I went anyway. When we showed up, Charlie refused to come to the door. His mom let us in, and we marched right into his room. Darren opened his backpack and dumped out these four ugly, cheap hats. Then he told us we were like the three musketeers, one for all and all for one. But we were even better. We were the Four Men in Hats. He came up with this crazy plan that we would never take our hats off, except to shower and sleep, for the whole summer."

Kelly glanced at her friends. Sheila's face had lost its color, and Marcie's lower lip quivered.

"I thought it was a dumb idea," Mike laughed. "But Charlie picked up one of the hats, looked it over, and put it on. And he smiled. I hadn't seen Charlie smile in months. He hasn't taken the hat off since."

Sheila choked. "I'm so sorry." She repeated the apology over and over.

Waves of guilt crashed over Kelly. "We didn't know," she whispered.

Mike nodded. "Charlie hasn't told many people. His mom talked to Bill and MaryAnn about it. And Tony knows too. But that's it." He locked eyes with Sheila. "We were really mad when you stole Darren's hat. But Darren said it would be a challenge. Like a quest to recapture the hat. He said we could unite the whole camp in the search. But you guys hid it really well."

Sheila's lips twitched at the compliment.

"Darren drew a map and divided the camp into sections. Each of the boys' cabins was assigned to search a different area. We recruited spies to follow you everywhere and offered a huge reward. We even have a secret agent from the female staff."

Kelly raised an eyebrow. "No way! Who?" She'd bet money that Cindy was the traitor.

"Not telling." Mike grinned. "We thought maybe you hid it off camp property, but Tony said you didn't."

Sheila's eyes narrowed. "He didn't tell, did he?"

Mike took a step back. "We offered him enough chocolate bars to last the rest of the year, but he wouldn't give even the slightest hint."

It looked like Tony's fictitious *Handbook for Maintenance Managers* included a section on loyalty and fair play.

The smile slipped from Mike's face. "Please don't tell anybody what I said about Charlie."

The girls promised.

Mike looked into Kelly's eyes. "Darren took good care of your dog. I hope you're doing the same with his hat."

32 A KNIGHT IN SHINING ARMOR

Kelly and her friends watched Mike leave the maintenance shed.

Marcie started for the door. "We have to get the hat."

Sheila caught her arm. "Lady Katherine only gave us a few minutes for a break. We've already been gone too long."

Marcie tried to pull away. "We've got to return the hat. For Charlie."

Sheila held on tight. "We'll get it later. I promise."

Marcie gave a deep sigh, and Sheila released her. "This is so *tragible*."

"Now's not the time for some ridiculous new word." Sheila snapped.

Marcie gave a loud sniff. "This whole thing is *tragic* and *terrible*. It's the perfect word."

Kelly couldn't argue. The word wasn't great, but it fit.

"Sorry." Sheila ran a hand across her forehead. "I shouldn't have said that."

Kelly chewed on her bottom lip as she considered their options. "I'm sure Tony would let me off work this afternoon. But I can't steer the canoe alone. Could you get time off from the kitchen?"

"We can try." Doubt etched Sheila's face. "But if we don't get back right now, we'll be facing the wrath of Her Majesty."

With a quick wave, Sheila and Marcie dashed out the door.

Kelly tucked her dog back into the paper sack and hurried to the cabin, intending to stash her precious beagle somewhere out of sight. But when she reached the room, it was filled with campers changing out of their riding gear. The girls crowded around her the minute she entered.

"Did you get your stuffed animal back from Darren?" Jill asked.

Kelly pulled it out of the bag. The room rang with shouts and cheers.

Kelly peered at Jill. "How did you know Darren had my dog?"

"We heard about the fight." Jill rolled her eyes. "All ten versions."

"I hope Darren doesn't get kicked out of camp. Bob deserved what he got." Joyce slammed her fist into her palm.

Kelly frowned. "Why would Darren be thrown out of camp?"

"For breaking Bob's arm when he smacked him with that suitcase."

Emma grimaced. "And fracturing Bob's leg when he pushed a bunk over on top of him."

"I heard Bob's lung got punctured." Terri's face twisted. "He'll be in intensive care for the rest of the summer."

Kelly burst out laughing. "I just saw Bob an hour ago. All he got was an elbow in the face. His only injuries are a black eye and a bloody nose."

The girls ignored her and continued to trade rumors of the fight and its resulting wounds, each one more gruesome than the last.

Jill put her fingers to her lips and whistled. "Enough talking. Let's change, clean the cabin, and head for lunch."

Ten minutes later, the girls trooped out the door and started down the road.

Amber fell in step beside Kelly. "We had a riding test today. I had to get my horse to stop with its front feet in a hoop. But this old nag they gave me wouldn't..."

Kelly tried to focus on Amber's chatter. But she couldn't stop thinking about Mike's revelation. She'd missed so many subtle clues. During lunch at staff training, MaryAnn commented on Darren wearing a hat at the table. But she hadn't asked him to take it off. When setting the curfew, Bill had said that Darren could stay out, but his hat had to be in the cabin by 10 PM. The director had known full well that Darren and his hat couldn't be parted. And after they'd stolen the hat, Bill asked her to tell Sheila and Marcie to be careful. He said there was more to the hat than they knew. It all made sense now.

Kelly was still lost in her thoughts when someone grabbed her waist from behind. She shrieked and spun around to find Joel's blue eyes.

"I've been looking for you." He lowered his voice. "I heard you got your beagle back. I'm glad."

Kelly smiled. "It probably seems silly to you. It's just a stuffed animal. But it's special to me."

"Hey, Joel." A group of female campers waved to him. "Could you come here for a minute?"

Joel shrugged. "Sorry. Gotta go."

He jogged over and was quickly surrounded by giggling girls. Cindy joined them, worming her way until she reached his side. Kelly's smile faded, and she turned away.

Amber sighed. "That's so romantic."

Kelly nodded, and they resumed their trek to the lodge. "It was sweet of Joel to let me know he cared."

"Joel?" Amber stared at Kelly. "I was talking about Darren saving your dog. Like a knight in shining armor coming to the rescue."

The poor girl must be reading her romance novels again. But the comment did make Kelly wonder. Why had Darren rescued her dog? She'd acted like a crazed lunatic and falsely accused him of the theft. If he'd gone along with Bob's ransom plan, he could have gotten his hat back. Instead he'd forced Bob to return the dog to her. He'd gotten nothing from the deal, other than the pleasure of hitting Bob. It didn't make sense, and Kelly felt a sudden discomfort.

The girls entered the lodge. As she passed through the serving line, Kelly took the smallest portions she could. She tried to ignore the guilt that nagged her. She wanted to be free of this strangling obsession with weight and eat like a normal person. But she wasn't making much progress. The candy she'd eaten after devotions felt like a small first step. And the last.

Kelly glanced in Darren's direction. He and Marvin were attempting to hang multiple utensils off their faces. With a spoon hanging from his nose, another from his chin, and two dangling from his forehead, Darren didn't match her image of a valiant knight. Not even close. For one thing, he used to wet his bed. His spelling needed work. And he stuck spoons all over his face for entertainment. But a glimpse of armor might have shone through when he wouldn't abandon a wounded friend, refusing to rest until he found a way to bring Charlie to camp. And she had to admit, there was something noble about the way he defended a small, smelly boy who everyone else teased or ignored.

A smile played across Kelly's face. Darren might not be a typical hero. And Marvin was a greasier sidekick than most. But they'd rescued her beagle. At the very least, she needed to express her gratitude for their good deed.

After Bill dismissed the camp for afternoon activities, Darren and Marvin struck out on the road leading to the archery range. Kelly raced to catch up to them.

"Hey, guys!"

They stopped and turned.

"Thank you for saving my beagle."

A proud grin stretched across Marvin's face. "It was awesome! You should have seen the fight. Blood was everywhere."

Darren gave Marvin a playful punch in the arm. "Don't exaggerate. Blood wasn't everywhere. Just on Bob's shirt. Maybe some on the floor. And possibly a bit on his shoes." He blocked the punch that Marvin threw at him, then jabbed him in the other arm. "But you're right about one thing. It was awesome!"

Kelly laughed with them. "I'm sorry about going ballistic this morning. Bob was taunting me with a small black ball, and it looked like my beagle's nose. I thought you were a part of it."

Darren dodged another blow from Marvin. "Not even close. Bob found an old teddy bear in the Lost and Found and cut the nose off it. That's what he showed you. He has no respect for stuffed animals. The guy's seriously disturbed." Darren stopped sparring with Marvin and locked eyes with Kelly. "But you should have known I wasn't involved. I wouldn't do that to you." He ducked another of Marvin's jabs.

Caught off guard by Darren's serious tone, Kelly squirmed. "Well, thanks again," she murmured, eager to move on.

Marvin poked her arm. "What about Darren's hat?"

Kelly shifted from one foot to the other. Better not to say too much until she actually had the hat in her hand. "I can't guarantee anything. But the hat should be back in its proper place very soon." Hopefully without any water damage.

Darren grinned. "After this is all over, I want to know where you stashed it. It's got to be the best hiding spot ever."

Kelly shrugged. "We might be persuaded to tell our secret. But first, since it was Sheila's idea, you'll have to admit that she's brilliant."

Darren grimaced. "That might kill me!" He gave Kelly an intense look. "But I will credit her for one thing. She picks her friends well."

Kelly ducked her head, unsure how to respond.

After a moment of awkward silence, Marvin grabbed Darren's arm and pulled. "Come on. We're going to be late for archery."

"Let us know if you have any other stuffed animals that need rescuing. Consider us your local Heroes for Hire." Darren winked, then raced Marvin down the road.

Kelly wandered toward the maintenance shed. She hoped he didn't think she was flirting with him. Darren was a great guy, and she appreciated what he'd done for her. But he wasn't her type. He just wasn't Joel.

When Kelly arrived at the shed, she found the door propped open with a large stone. The moment she entered, the sharp odor of paint fumes assaulted her senses. Pinching her nose, she glanced around for Tony. He stood at the far counter, pouring something thick and white onto a piece of wood. Then he picked up a golden comb.

Kelly cleared her throat and Tony whipped around, dropping the comb. Kelly giggled. Tony moved to block the board from sight, and scowled at her.

"What's that?" She grinned, savoring the moment. It was nice to catch Tony hiding something, rather than the other way around.

He pulled a sheet of paper over the wood. "None of your business."

"Not even for a chocolate bar?"

"No deal." Tony grabbed a rag and wiped the white liquid from his hands. "How much time do you need?"

Kelly squinted at him. "For what?"

"For you and your partners in crime to retrieve Darren's hat."

Looked like she wouldn't have to drop to her knees and beg the Defender of the Weak. "Since you asked, could I have about an hour off?"

Tony pursed his lips. "One hour. Not a minute more." He tapped his watch. "Meet Bob and me at the barn when you're done. Wear pants and a long-sleeved shirt. We'll be working in the hay."

"Thanks." As Kelly walked toward the exit, she watched Tony out of the corner of her eye. He didn't move from whatever he was guarding until she was out the door.

33 THE BRILLIANCE OF A GOOD PLAN

Kelly's breath came in gasps as she raced to the lodge. Tony didn't have to give her any time to go after that hat. But one hour was hardly enough time to find her friends in the kitchen, convince Lady Katherine to give them an unscheduled break, grab a canoe, and hunt for the neon orange marker. Assuming it was still floating. And then they had to retrieve the hat. Hopefully in good condition.

Beyond that, she had no plan. Sheila could figure out what to do with the hat once they had it.

Kelly had almost reached the kitchen when Sheila and Marcie burst out the door.

Sheila swung a backpack over one shoulder. "Let's go! We've got half an hour to find that hat."

Only thirty minutes? Tony had been more generous than she'd thought.

"How did you convince–"

"No time for questions." Sheila grabbed Kelly's arm and the girls dashed toward the lake.

Halfway to the canoeing area, Marcie waved her hand in protest. "I've got a cramp in my side."

They slowed their pace to a brisk walk.

"How did you convince Lady Katherine to give you the time off?" Kelly panted.

Sheila shifted the backpack to her other shoulder. "When we asked for extra free time, Lady Katherine pointed at three huge pails of raw carrots. She said we could have a break after we finished peeling and dicing them. Which would've taken us all afternoon.

But then Sandy jumped in and said she'd do it. Lady Katherine didn't like that, but what could she do? And then Sandy gave Charlie a break as well."

"Sandy is *swawesome*," Marcie said, holding her ribs.

Kelly raised her eyebrows. "Which means ..."

"A combination of swell and awesome."

Kelly caught Sheila's eye, and they grinned at each other. Another of Marcie's attempts at a catchy new word. And another miss.

Marcie let out a long sigh. "Can you believe how horribly wrong this prank went?"

"Wrong?" Sheila's long red hair whipped from side to side as she shook her head. "Things couldn't have worked out better."

"Really?" Kelly began ticking facts off on her fingers. "We got dunked hiding the hat, the boys are out to get us, the girls are mad about the bathroom prank and will hurt us if anything else happens, and my poor stuffed dog swung from a fan for most of the night."

"Sounds like a grand adventure to me," Sheila grinned.

"My beagle would disagree with you."

Sheila and Marcie laughed, but dropped the conversation as a group of campers approached, soaked from head to toe. They must have just finished a canoe lesson. Though it looked as if they'd done more swimming than paddling.

After the troop passed, Kelly noticed three male campers break off from the group and slip into the woods. No doubt planning to spy on the girls. And snatch the hat and the reward.

Nudging Sheila with her elbow, Kelly pointed toward the trees. "Three campers are watching us," she whispered.

"Let them have their fun." Sheila shrugged, apparently unconcerned by the potential threat. She snapped her fingers. "Let's focus, people. Operation Find the Hat has begun."

Kelly pointed to the canoe on the far end of the row. "Number nine is Sandy's favorite. Let's grab that one."

"Seems appropriate," Marcie agreed, "since she's peeling our carrots for us."

The girls grabbed lifejackets and paddles, carried the canoe to the lake and took the same places as before, with Marcie in front, Kelly in the middle, and Sheila in back. This time Kelly used the move Sandy had shown her and leaned on the paddle as she slid it over the gunwales. A much smoother entrance than her first attempt when she'd nearly fallen in.

After Sheila pushed out the canoe, Kelly twisted to face her. "Let's not go swimming this time, okay?"

"Hey, it wasn't my fault we tipped."

"Yes, it was!" Marcie and Kelly shouted in unison.

"Oh, yeah." Sheila giggled as she directed the canoe into the lake. She steered down the lake, past their original entry point. "We'll come in from the far side of the reeds. That should keep us hidden from those spying campers."

"Won't that make it harder to find the spot?" Kelly asked.

"Probably. But that can't be helped."

The girls traveled down the shoreline, rowing toward the far end of the reeds.

Sheila let out a chuckle. "You know, Bill should really thank us. This prank has been a great experience for the whole camp."

Kelly shook her head. "I don't think Bob and his black eye would agree."

"He deserved what he got."

Kelly watched Marcie closely, remembering her friend's earlier interest in her maintenance partner.

Marcie waved her hand in the air. "Oh, I'm over him."

"She's got her eye on Mike now."

Marcie turned with a finger on her lips. Kelly noticed that two pink spots appeared in Marcie's cheeks.

"He's been coming around the kitchen after supper, trying to pick up extra desserts. That's all."

"It's more than that." Sheila splashed water towards the front of the canoe. "He shows up after every meal and sometimes stays to help Marcie wash dishes."

"He wants to learn Spanish, so I'm helping him."

"That's odd, because he's taking French in school." Sheila raised an eyebrow. "I'm betting he developed a sudden interest when he saw you studying your Spanish textbook."

A smile tugged at the corner of Marcie's lips.

"I think Mike is a much better choice than Bob," Kelly said. "I never understood what you saw in him."

"He's got everything. Designer clothes, a private school, famous parents. He's popular, confident, and bold. People listen to him. They want to follow him." Marcie lowered her head. "He's all the things that I'm not."

"You're more than you think." Kelly wished that she could give her friend a hug. But that would have to wait until their feet were firmly planted on shore.

Marcie slowed her paddle strokes. "I used to think that people who are successful could rise above all their problems. But after watching Bob this week, I think being rich and famous might cause more problems than they solve. So what's the point of working so hard?"

Kelly fingered the cross around her neck. "Maybe you should ask Sandy for a canoe ride. She has a way of explaining things."

The girls reached the end of the reeds and Sheila turned so the canoe entered the forest of tall stalks. Rowing became more difficult. Kelly scanned from side to side, searching for the bright marker. She felt an anxious knot growing in the pit of her stomach. What if they couldn't find it? She couldn't face Darren without his hat, not after he'd worked so hard to return her dog to her.

Marcie drew in a sharp breath and pointed to the right. A wave of relief washed over Kelly when she saw the neon orange marker, sitting low in the water.

Sheila reached over the edge. With slow and careful movements, she lifted the line and drew the marker, the ziplock bags, and the cement weight into the canoe. After opening the bags, she pulled out the hat and held it up for inspection. "Perfect condition," she whispered.

Kelly breathed a silent prayer of thanks.

Sheila crammed everything into the backpack, then pointed the canoe out of the reeds.

After several minutes of hard work, the canoe entered open water. Kelly caught a glimpse of three male campers scrambling into the cover of the trees. She swung around to face Sheila so quickly she almost tipped the canoe.

"Hey," the other girls yelped. "Watch out!"

"Those campers are waiting for us," Kelly hissed. "They'll steal the hat for sure!"

"I'm one genius step ahead of you." Sheila chuckled.

Kelly wished she felt as confident.

A few minutes later, the canoe glided onto shore. Once all three girls were standing on the sand, Sheila slipped a small bottle of ketchup out of the backpack and nodded to Marcie. "Action!"

Marcie banged her leg against the canoe. Falling to the ground, she grabbed her calf and rolled about, howling. "Ow! I cut myself!"

Kelly rolled her eyes at the exaggerated performance. Marcie probably hadn't made any time in her rigorous academic schedule for an artistic pursuit like drama. And it showed.

Sheila motioned for Kelly to step in front of Marcie, blocking her from any eyes that might be watching from the woods. Then she dumped a generous amount of ketchup over her friend's leg.

"Careful," Marcie whispered. "It's supposed to be a cut, not an amputation."

Sheila rose and pointed to the shed. "Kelly, get the first aid kit!" She shouted the words as if Kelly were across the camp rather than right beside her.

Another unconvincing acting job. But Kelly played along, dashing into the newly painted shack and returning with the emergency pack.

Sheila rifled through the contents and pulled out a package of gauze. She passed it to Kelly, who wrapped the entire roll around the fake injury. Ketchup seeped out the edges of the huge mound, and Marcie smeared it over part of the bandage.

Sheila admired her work. "That looks realistic enough," she whispered.

Kelly shook her head. It looked as if Marcie had severed a major artery.

Sheila fumbled with the backpack for a few minutes before swinging it over Marcie's shoulders. Then she clipped the first aid kit around her own waist.

Kelly frowned. This was Sheila's great plan to protect the hat? Give it to the supposedly injured person and hope the campers wouldn't attack someone with a fatal wound? It seemed...stupid.

Marcie staggered to her feet, moaning pitifully.

"That cut looks bad," Sheila announced loudly. "We'd better get someone to check it out." Leaning close, she whispered, "If anyone tries to take the backpack, put up a good fight."

Motivated by a reward and the glory of recovering the hat, the campers were sure to attack. And no matter how good the fight, Kelly wasn't sure they'd win. Unfortunately, she couldn't think of a better idea.

Marcie put an arm over the shoulders of Kelly and Sheila and hobbled in the middle, leaning on her friends for support. As she limped toward the lodge, she continued to call out "Oh, my leg!" with loud, dramatic wails.

Kelly felt ridiculous. "Don't you think this is a little much?" she whispered through clenched teeth.

"Not at all." Sheila glanced around, then answered in a hushed tone. "We can't risk losing the hat now. We'd look like fools."

Kelly shook her head. "I think it's too late for that."

Halfway to the kitchen, the three male campers leaped out from behind a group of trees and lunged straight at Marcie. Kelly stepped in to block her friend, but the campers slipped around her. The tallest boy ripped the pack from Marcie's back, knocking her down. Kelly grabbed one of the straps and hung on tight. But two of the campers wrestled it from her grip. Before they got more than a few steps, Sheila tackled one of the boys and fumbled for the pack. The tall camper grabbed her arms from behind while the third camper tore the backpack free. They sprinted down the road, whooping and hollering as they clutched their prize.

"They got the hat!" Kelly felt sick. So much for Sheila's genius plan. She turned to her friends. "What do we do now?"

Sheila and Marcie had collapsed to the ground and rolled back and forth in the grass, red-faced and shrieking with laughter.

Kelly's shock turned to annoyance. "What's so funny?"

When they caught their breath, Sheila motioned Kelly to come close. She unclipped the first aid pack from her waist and unzipped it. Kelly saw a blur of blue, green, and brown. The hat! Sheila must have switched it to the first aid kit when Kelly was busy wrapping the gauze on Marcie's leg.

Kelly pictured the campers rushing triumphantly to Darren and presenting him with the backpack. He would open it to find a wet cement weight, some fishing line, a few ziplock bags, a faded neon orange tag covered in algae, and an empty bottle of ketchup. But no hat.

Kelly burst out laughing and bowed low in front of Sheila. "You are brilliant."

Sheila raised her arms in victory. "What an awesome first week. We sure have started off the summer in style!"

Kelly's smile faded. "How long are you staying?"

"The whole two months." Sheila combed her fingers through her hair. "And my goal is to pull a new prank every week."

Kelly swallowed. First Jill. Then Mike and the rest of the Men in Hats. Now Sheila. All devoting their entire summer vacation to working at camp. She poked Marcie. "What about you?"

"Me too." Marcie jerked a thumb toward Sheila. "Someone has to keep an eye on her."

Kelly forced a smile. "I hope the camp is still standing at the end of the summer."

The girls laughed, but Kelly felt a pang of jealousy. Eight weeks of wild schemes and crazy escapades. It would have been fun to be a part of it all.

"How about you, Kelly?"

"I'm only signed up for the first week."

"You can change your mind." Marcie nodded several times. "The camp is always in need of more volunteers. I'm sure Bill could find a place for you."

Yeah, probably in the kitchen. She'd escaped that assignment once. Of course, he might choose to give her more time on maintenance. That wouldn't be much better.

When the girls reached the lodge, they ducked into the kitchen and found it empty.

"Where's Lady Katherine?" Sheila peered around the room. "We were gone far longer than half an hour. I was sure she'd be waiting to pounce on us and make us scrub the floors with a toothbrush."

Marcie lifted the lid from a large roasting pot sitting on a counter. She gasped, her eyes wide. Kelly looked over her shoulder. The container was filled to the top with carrots, all neatly peeled and chopped.

Marcie peeked into two other pots, equally full. "I can't believe Sandy finished them so fast."

Sheila strode over to the walk-in freezer and opened the door. After flicking on the light, she headed to the back, searching the shelves as she went. Kelly and Marcie followed.

Kelly shivered and rubbed her arms. "What are you looking for?"

"Our next hiding place." Sheila pulled out a half-empty bag of frozen peas. She stuffed the hat inside and shoved it to the back of a bottom rack. "I checked the menu. We won't be having peas again until next week. The hat will be frozen stiff but safe."

Sheila was brilliant. In a devious, criminal sense. But still brilliant.

Marcie scratched her bandaged leg. "I need to get this gunk off. It's starting to itch."

The friends exited the freezer and headed to the bathroom. Marcie propped her leg over the sink and peeled off the gauze. She squirted a generous amount of soap from the wall dispenser on the remaining sticky mess. After several minutes of hard scrubbing, her limb was shiny and clean, although a stain of light orange remained where the bandage had been.

"My hour is over. And then some." Kelly sighed. "I'd better join Tony and Bob at the barn."

She left the lodge and trudged up the road to the cabins. After changing into pants and a long-sleeved shirt, as Tony had instructed, she headed toward the barn. She hadn't gone far before she heard her name being called. Glancing behind, she saw Sheila and Marcie racing to catch up.

"We're free!" Sheila shouted, performing a perfect cartwheel in the middle of the road. "No kitchen duty this afternoon."

"How did that happen?" Kelly didn't even try to hide her envy.

"We found Sandy and Lady Katherine dumping the carrot peels in the recycling." Marcie said. "I guess they finished the carrots together. They must have had fun because Lady Katherine was in the best mood I've ever seen her in. She gave us the whole afternoon off!"

"I wish Tony would do that for me."

"We'll come along and help you beg," Marcie promised.

"There's nothing we can't do if we put our minds to it!" Sheila added.

For once, Kelly agreed with Sheila. It did seem like there wasn't much the three of them couldn't do together.

34 MOVE OVER

Kelly squinted at the large red barn as she walked down the dusty road, Sheila and Marcie at her side. Tony and Bob stood on the second-level loft, tossing forkfuls of yellow hay into a truck bed below. It looked like hot, dusty exhausting work. She scratched at her arms, already feeling itchy.

Sheila's brows furrowed in concentration. "The three of us could surround Tony and plead for your release from work for the afternoon."

"I don't think that will convince him." Kelly chewed on a nail. "And Bob is sure to pitch a fit in protest."

Marcie clapped her hands together. "Then we'll cry. Guys hate it when girls turn on the tears."

That might work. Even a tough grizzly bear like Tony couldn't withstand a bunch of girls blubbering on his shoulder. And she'd seen Sheila and Marcie's exaggerated acting skills. They'd be sure to drown him in a flood of fake waterworks.

"If all else fails, we can bribe him with a chocolate bar," Marcie added. "Dark chocolate, no nuts."

A rush of gratitude welled up inside Kelly. She had little hope that Tony would give her the afternoon off. But she appreciated the support of her friends.

Kelly couldn't help but think about her friends at home. Not many seemed willing to stick by her now that she'd fallen from favor with Aaron. She really couldn't blame them. They'd never had much in common, other than the shared goal of being popular.

None of them really knew her or cared about her as an individual. And the same was true on her part.

A burst of applause diverted Kelly's attention. A growing crowd of mostly female campers stood around the vaulting arena, clapping and cheering wildly. No need to guess the center of attention.

Sheila must have had the same thought, because she veered away from the barn and headed straight toward the show.

"What about talking to Tony?" Kelly raced after Sheila.

"I just want to see what's happening first." Sheila maneuvered her way through the tightly packed campers around the rails and found an open spot on the far side. Kelly and Marcie squeezed in beside her.

Kelly peered into the vaulting ring, and every muscle in her body tensed. Joel was circling the arena, standing on Samson's back. With his arms stretched wide for balance, he looked like a Greek statue shining in the sun. But he wasn't alone.

Cindy knelt in front of Joel, arms raised and glowing with a radiant smile as her blonde hair floated in the breeze. In the center of the ring, Matt gave his whip a slight shake and clucked to Samson.

A bitter taste filled Kelly's mouth. Joel could have asked her to handle the lunge line. But he'd chosen Matt. She'd been replaced. In more ways than one.

Joel grasped Cindy's hands and lifted her to a standing position, earning more cheers from the crowd. They circled the ring on Samson's back, looking like a perfectly matched couple in love.

Eyes stinging, Kelly looked away. She had no right to feel betrayed. There was no way that Joel could have chosen her as his vaulting partner. Even if he'd wanted to. But her throat tightened anyway.

Maybe it didn't mean anything. Just a doubles routine on a horse. But Kelly didn't like the expression on Cindy's face. It looked too triumphant.

Kelly forced herself to focus on the barn, and the two figures pitching hay from the loft. Tony had given her time off to get the hat, not to gawk at Joel. She really shouldn't take advantage of his generosity.

A gasp from the campers jolted Kelly's attention back to the arena. Cindy's body was splayed awkwardly across Samson's back. Joel knelt precariously behind her, one arm around the blonde and the other clutching the saddle pad handle with a white-knuckle grip. He'd barely kept them from plummeting to the ground.

Kelly sucked in her breath. As much as she disliked Cindy, she didn't want anyone to be injured.

Matt lowered the whip and brought Samson to a halt. Joel sat back, a huge frown creasing his face, and helped Cindy regain her seat. "You've got to kick up harder. You're all over the place."

Kelly grinned at the frustration in his voice.

"It's not my fault," Cindy snapped back, flipping her long blonde hair over her shoulder. "You aren't holding me straight."

"I'm doing my job. You're the one making us look bad."

Cindy flinched, and her face turned a splotchy red, like she was about to cry.

A fight between the two lovebirds. Not good for Cindy, but definitely good for Kelly. She nudged Sheila. "What were they trying to do?"

Sheila faced her with a sour expression. "Joel's supposed to stand on Samson's back. And Cindy would to kick up to a handstand, with Joel holding her in place."

Kelly drew in a sharp breath. "Is that possible?"

Sheila snorted. "If Cindy's good enough."

"We'll give it another try," Joel called to the crowd.

Matt set Samson in motion, with the golden couple sitting together on the horse's broad back. Joel scooted to the rear of the saddle pad, leaving a gap between them. With strong, fluid movements, Joel leaped to a stand.

A few moves later, Cindy stood in front of Joel, supported by his strong arms. Bending forward, she placed her hands on the handles of the saddle pad, then started to kick up her feet. But she lost her balance and crumpled, nearly knocking Joel off the horse. He slipped to his knees, and with arm muscles bulging from the effort, again managed to keep Cindy from falling off.

Kelly's hands flew to her face. Around her, the campers cringed, and several gasped.

Matt lowered his whip and Samson stopped. Joel slid to the ground and gave the horse a pat, as if conceding defeat.

"I can do that move," Sheila called out.

Kelly went numb as her friend crawled through the fence and strode straight up to Samson.

Cindy's jaw jutted out, and she glared down at her challenger. A tense silence fell over the onlookers as they watched Sheila and Cindy wage a silent war, each refusing to budge.

Joel contemplated Sheila for a few moments. "We can give it a try."

The campers cheered and applauded. Cindy had no choice but to dismount and move to the edge of the ring. She leaned against the railing, arms crossed. One of her staff buddies whispered something in her ear, and she shrugged her off.

"What does Sheila think she's doing?" Kelly hissed to Marcie. Did everyone have to throw themselves at Joel?

Marcie's eyes remained locked on her friend. "Bill would be furious if he knew they weren't using a spotter."

The words hit Kelly like a sharp blow. If Joel had asked her to handle the lunge line, Matt would be free to spot. But he hadn't asked her. Apparently he didn't need her. Or want her.

Matt raised the whip to hip height and Samson began to trot. Sheila jogged alongside, her hands resting on the saddle pad handles as she matched the horse's steps. With two short hops, she flung her legs over Samson's broad back and easily pulled herself up. Joel talked Sheila through several warm-up moves, which she performed flawlessly. The campers shouted, clapped, and whistled their approval.

Kelly felt a surge of pride in her friend. “She’s really good.”

“She’s had years of gymnastics training,” Marcie shouted above the noise. “And she’s taken vaulting at camp every summer.”

When Samson’s gait changed to a canter, Joel swung up behind Sheila. Kelly felt admiration for her friend as the new pair stood and circled the arena together. A mixture of joy and pride shone from Sheila’s face.

Joel motioned for quiet. Sheila leaned forward, kicking into a handstand. She was almost vertical when she tilted to the side. Unable to right herself, she tumbled off Samson. Before hitting the ground, she curled up and went into a safety roll. Joel, who had remained on the horse’s back, slipped down to a sitting position.

A derisive laugh came from the inside rails. “I knew she couldn’t do that move.” Cindy tossed her comment to the crowd behind her, a smug smile on her face.

Kelly shot Cindy a dirty look.

Sheila jumped up and dusted herself off. “I almost had it. Let’s try one more time.” With her jaw set in determination, she ran alongside the huge horse again, and Joel helped her up in front of him.

They stood once more, and this time Sheila kicked into a perfectly straight handstand. Joel caught her ankles and held her in place. They maintained the move as Samson cantered around the ring. The campers burst into thunderous applause. Kelly clapped so hard her hands stung.

In the midst of the celebration, someone in the crowd gave a piercing, high-pitched whistle. The giant horse tossed his head and stumbled. Joel lost his grip on Sheila’s legs, and his arms swung like windmills. He fell to the right and tucked into an awkward roll. With no one to hold her in place, Sheila plummeted off the horse and smashed into the ground. Samson’s back hoof caught her in the side of her head. Sheila screamed and curled into a protective ball, hands covering her face. Blood oozed through her fingers.

Kelly gasped. Campers shrieked and shouted for help. Marcie yelled Sheila's name and crawled through the railing. Kelly scrambled right behind her.

Joel arrived at Sheila's side at the same time as Kelly and Marcie, his nose bloody and a small cut under his left eye.

Sheila rocked back and forth on the ground, moaning and clutching her head. Kelly glanced at Marcie. She had a thick medical textbook in her cabin room. And she'd taken a pre-med prep course. Surely Marcie would know what to do. But her face had a green tinge, as if she were about to lose her lunch. So much for book learning.

Joel stared at Sheila, also clearly at a loss.

A strange calm descended on Kelly. She didn't have to read Marcie's medical texts to know the bleeding had to be stopped. Grabbing Sheila's arms, she turned to Joel and Marcie. "We have to get a look at the injury."

They struggled to raise Sheila to a sitting position. Campers crowded close. A group of girls were crying, several boys shouted questions or advice, but most of the kids were just trying to get a closer look.

Kelly turned to Joel. "Can you get the campers to back off?"

Joel leaped to his feet, no doubt grateful for an excuse to move away from the traumatic scene. He ushered the kids out of the corral.

Kelly pried Sheila's hands from her forehead, revealing a nasty cut, at least two inches long and split wide open. Blood flowed from the wound. Marcie made a gagging sound and turned away from the sight. She should probably try to get a refund on her medical books.

Kelly placed her thumbs and forefingers on either side of the gash and pressed the skin together, closing the wound. Sheila tried to jerk away, but Kelly kept her hands in place.

"Hold still. We have to keep that cut closed until we can get a bandage."

Sheila moaned and trembled, but the bleeding stopped. Marcie slipped behind her friend and wrapped her arms around her.

Kelly glanced about, searching for someone who could help. She saw Tony leap out of the loft and into the hay-filled bed of the truck. He started in their direction, then ducked into the barn.

"Tony's on his way," Kelly told Sheila. At least she hoped he was.

Sheila whimpered and closed her eyes. A stream of tears ran down her face.

Kelly examined Sheila's face for other injuries. A long, red gash ran across her cheek. It looked deep, but it wasn't gaping.

"What have we got here? Something for me to fix?"

Kelly nearly melted with relief at the sound of Tony's voice.

He knelt beside her, and placed a first aid kit on the ground, which explained why he'd run into the barn. He peered through Kelly's hands to examine the wound. "MaryAnn's on the way with the camp van. We're going to take you to the hospital. But I want to clean and cover those cuts first." He rifled through the kit and pulled out a packet of antiseptic wipes.

Kelly held the edges of the cut together as Tony dabbed the medicated gauze on the wounds. Sheila flinched, and tried to pull back. Marcie held her friend in place as Tony ripped the tags off three large butterfly bandages, then stretched them across the cut on her forehead and the gash on her cheek.

Once the bandages were secured, Kelly lowered her shaking arms, not sure if the tremors were from exhaustion or relief.

Someone took hold of Kelly's shoulders and raised her to her feet. She turned and faced a solemn MaryAnn.

"Thank you, Kelly. You did a great job. I'm taking Sheila and Joel to the emergency clinic. I'm going to bring Marcie as well. It will help Sheila to have a close friend with her."

Kelly opened her mouth to beg to go along, but MaryAnn shook her head. "I need you to help with the campers."

Knowing there was nothing further she could do for Sheila, Kelly stepped back.

MaryAnn addressed the campers standing around the outside of the arena. "Joel and Sheila are going to be fine, but we need to get them checked by a doctor. All afternoon activities at the barn are temporarily suspended. The camp store will open early. Please follow your counselors there and wait there for further instructions." She ignored all questions.

Kelly crawled out of the ring and started guiding the campers down the road. The horse staff and several counselors joined her.

A sobbing camper pulled on Kelly's arm. "Is Sheila going to die?"

"Of course not." Kelly forced a smile. "She'll be back at camp in no time." Her attempt to reassure the camper sounded weak. And the camper continued to cry.

When the bedraggled group reached the store, Kelly collapsed onto one of the steps. As the campers who'd been at other activities arrived, news of the accident spread quickly. Details about the injuries and the amount of blood doubled each time someone told the story. After a few feeble protests, Kelly gave up trying to keep the facts straight.

Amber slid in beside her and gave her a hug. To Kelly's surprise, Joyce joined her on the other side.

"You've got blood on your hands," Amber said.

Kelly looked down and shivered at the red stains. So much blood. Such a bad injury.

"I heard Sheila's head split open and you held it together."

Leave it to Joyce to take something bad and make it worse.

Kelly let out a mirthless laugh. "She just had some really bad cuts." At least she hoped that's all it was.

"My mom sliced her finger to the bone once when she was cutting an apple. I almost fainted at the sight of all the blood. And her finger barely hung on."

This was not what she needed to hear. Kelly opened her mouth to ask Joyce to stop, then closed it again. There was no sarcastic edge in Joyce's voice. Just concern. The pessimistic camper might actually be trying to help.

Kelly gave her a half-hearted smile. "I didn't see Sheila's skull or anything. But it was pretty nasty."

"How did you know what to do?" Amber asked.

Kelly pondered the question. "I don't know. It just made sense to stop the bleeding."

Joyce stuck out her tongue. "Wasn't it gross?"

"Yes. But no one else was doing anything. I had to do something."

Joyce stared at the ground. "Sheila's really lucky to have a friend like you." She coughed, as if embarrassed. "I hope she's not brain damaged. Any more than before, at least."

Kelly smiled at the return of Joyce's abrasive humor. But she wasn't fooled. A caring heart beat behind that stone facade.

The afternoon seemed to drag. Reluctant to go to the next activity, the campers milled around the camp store. The crunch of footsteps on gravel caught her attention. Bill strode down the road and leaped up onto the store veranda. All eyes turned to him, and a hush fell over the group.

"I just got a call from the medi-center. The doctor finished preliminary tests checking for a concussion or possible internal injuries. He's happy to report that Joel and Sheila appear to have no serious injuries. They should return to camp later today."

The campers cheered and whistled. Kelly murmured a quiet prayer of thanks.

Bill motioned for silence. "The store will remain open for the next fifteen minutes. Then we'll continue with the regular afternoon activities, with the exception of vaulting."

"Where do we go instead?" Stan called out.

"Report to the field for outdoor games."

When Bill jumped down from the veranda, Kelly marched up to him, determined to get more details. But he held up his hands before she could bombard him with questions. "Kelly, I want to thank you for your quick thinking with Sheila. If you hadn't kept the cut closed, it would have split further."

Kelly smiled at the compliment but remained focused on her friend. "What's happening with Sheila?"

"Her facial wounds are deep, so she'll need stitches. But if all goes well, she'll be back here before supper."

Kelly felt the tension flow out of her body. Such good news. And knowing Sheila, she'd chug a couple of cans of Coke and bounce back in no time.

"With both Sheila and Marcie gone, Katherine's going to need some help in the kitchen. Tony said that he and Bob will finish off in the barn while you cover for your friends."

The exact assignment that she'd dreaded at the beginning of camp. But she felt happy to have it now. The kitchen was a center of activity, so she'd be among the first to hear any news. Maybe even talk with Sheila and Marcie as soon as they returned.

Bill had already taken several steps when he paused and turned back with a puzzled expression on his face. "Do you have any idea why Bob would cheer when he heard about your kitchen duty?"

Kelly gave a wry grin. "I'm sure he thinks justice has been done."

After listening to Sheila and Marcie's never-ending complaints about the grind of kitchen work, Kelly expected the worst. But much of the preparation for supper had already been done. Sandy told more hilarious stories about her days as a canoe instructor while Kelly chopped cucumbers and cauliflower for several veggie trays, filled pitchers with juice to be placed on individual tables, and mixed a humongous salad. They were tedious jobs, but not hard. Then all Kelly had to do was help Charlie set the tables.

He didn't talk much, except to correct where she placed the cutlery and condiments. Kelly didn't say much either. She felt awkward, now that she knew the real story behind the hat fixed firmly on his head.

Once the dining hall had been prepped, Kelly and Charlie returned to the kitchen. He pulled two aprons out of a drawer and tossed one to Kelly. She unfolded it and wrinkled her nose at the multiple stains. She'd traded filthy overalls for an equally dirty apron. It didn't matter if she was on maintenance or in the kitchen. She was destined to get all the dirty jobs. And lousy uniforms.

Kelly pulled the apron over her head and donned a pair of yellow rubber gloves. With a sigh, she filled the deep sink with soapy water. In the background, the raucous sound of campers filled the hall. She hoped someone remembered to let Jill know she wouldn't be at supper.

A lump formed in Kelly's throat. She was missing the meal, which should have made her happy. But it didn't. The only reason she wasn't sitting at her table with the other campers was because her friend had been hurt. Bill said Sheila's injuries weren't serious, but they could have been.

Kelly grabbed a scouring pad and began to scrub the larger pots that wouldn't fit into the dishwasher. All afternoon, she'd been fighting the overwhelming feeling of fear for her friend. But now a surge of anger rose up to take its place. Why had Sheila been up on the back of that horse? Showing off with a dangerous vaulting move? It was all for a guy.

A trembling began in Kelly's legs, and wouldn't stop. She dropped the pad and leaned against the sink for support. Sheila had risked her life for a handsome face. How stupid. And yet how could she judge her friend when she'd been just as stupid. Chasing after Aaron. Starving herself for his approval. Turning her back on friends and family to gain his acceptance. Sacrificing what she knew was right to please him. Risking her own life and future for a handsome face. And then she'd come to camp and instead of learning from her mistakes, she'd found a new face to pursue.

Enough. The one word echoed through her mind. Enough starving. Enough throwing away her life and future for the approval of others. With the help of God, she was going to change, and it was going to start tonight. When the kitchen staff took a break to have their supper, she was going to eat. A real meal. And that would be the beginning of real change.

A burst of cheers came from outside the dining hall. Which was unusual. The kids had never cheered when a meal was brought out. Kelly wondered if Bill given out the clean cabin scores early. She turned off the water and listened. In the midst of the applause, she heard campers shouting out names. Her heart leaped.

Sheila, Marcie and Joel had returned.

35 ASK THE CHICKEN

The thunder of applause from the campers shook the dining hall. Kelly ripped off her rubber gloves and tossed them beside the kitchen sink. Bill had said that Sheila, Marcie, and Joel would be back by supper, but she hadn't thought it possible. The quick return could mean just one thing. Bill had been right, and Sheila escaped any serious injury from the vaulting accident.

Kelly dashed to the door and peered out. The campers were on their feet, clapping and whistling. Joel stood in front of the serving counter, waving to the enthusiastic crowd with one hand. The other rested casually on Sheila's shoulders. She slumped beside him, her head lowered. Marcie stood close by her friend.

Kelly couldn't understand why Sheila looked so dejected. She'd been kicked in the face by a horse and had managed to walk away with a few bandages...and Joel's arm around her. Sheila should have been doing cartwheels.

Bill motioned for the campers to take their seats. As Joel headed to his table, Kelly got a glimpse of his face. Only Joel could make a black eye and a puffy red cheek look good. She was about to wave to catch his attention when she realized he was heading straight to Cindy's table. He leaned close and whispered in the blonde siren's ear.

Kelly ducked back inside the kitchen, her heart feeling as bruised as Joel's cheek. How many times did she need to see it before she accepted the fact that Cindy was back in favor with Joel and she was out? It hurt. But when Sheila and Marcie walked through the door,

Kelly pushed her pain aside and leaped toward them, grabbing them in an exuberant hug.

"Careful!" Sheila pulled away from Kelly's embrace.

Stepping back, Kelly took a close look at her friend. A thick bandage covered most of her forehead. A square piece of gauze was taped across her left cheek. The skin around both bandages looked swollen and discolored. Their eyes met and Sheila ducked her head.

Marcie stepped forward, as if to shield her friend. "Samson's hoof caught Sheila at an angle. A direct blow would have crushed her cheekbone. Or worse. The doctor said Sheila was fortunate to walk away with only stitches and a bad headache."

The kitchen door swung open and Charlie carried an empty serving tray to the sink. He glanced at the three friends before grabbing a pair of rubber gloves. With his back to them, he began to scrub the pots.

Sheila swayed slightly, as if dizzy, and Kelly pulled up a stool for her. "How long do the stitches stay in?"

"They'll dissolve after two or three weeks." Sheila's voice came out high-pitched and strained. She blinked several times as her eyes filled with tears.

"That's not too bad." Kelly put a reassuring hand on Sheila's shoulder, but the redhead jerked back.

"Not so bad? I'm going to have scars for life. On my face!" She spat out the words. "My bangs will cover the one on my forehead. But I can't hide a gouge that runs across half my cheek! Who's going to date a scarface? Who's going to take me to the prom and have their senior picture taken with me? Why would Joel ever—" She stopped abruptly, taking several ragged breaths.

Kelly imagined the types of comments the kids at her school would make if she showed up with a scar on her face. None were nice.

"Sheila, Marcie, and Kelly," Bill called from the other side of the door, "your presence is required in the dining hall. We have a contract negotiation to settle."

Bill's timing couldn't have been worse.

Sheila ran her fingers through her long red hair, pulling it forward as if to hide the bandages, and the three friends walked out. Darren stood waiting beside Bill at the front of the room, the paper hat set at an angle on his head.

At last the prank was about to come to a safe end. Unless Darren did something crazy, like refuse to leave Sheila's hair alone. Then his hat would stay hidden in the bag of frozen peas, the prank would continue, and Bill's order of protection would expire. And that would be terrible.

Bill motioned for the girls to come forward, then had Sheila and Darren face each other. "Darren, you've had twenty-four hours to consider Sheila's proposal. Do you accept or reject it?"

"I accept." Darren raised his hand. "I solemnly swear that if Sheila returns my hat, I will never touch her hair again."

The campers cheered. And relief flooded over Kelly. Now they all could live happily and safely ever after. And that included her beagle and Darren's hat.

Darren and Sheila shook hands, like two opponents congratulating each other after a good match. Then he reached under the counter and took out a large bag. "I offer this token as a sign of my good will."

Sheila opened the bag and pulled out the plank of wood Kelly had seen Tony working on. A large golden comb was attached to the top, and a short message ran down the middle. At the bottom, Darren had scrawled his signature.

As Sheila displayed the homemade peace offering, Darren read the message. "Roses are red, my promise is true. If my hat is safe, then your hair is too."

Rather corny. But also really sweet. And he'd spelled everything correctly.

Sheila gave a short laugh, passed the plaque to Marcie, and slipped into the kitchen. Minutes later, she returned with Darren's hat. With a deep bow, she presented it to her former tormentor. After a careful inspection, he took the paper hat off his head, secured the real one in its place, and raised his arms in victory.

Mike jumped to his feet, chanting, "Men in Hats!" The male campers joined in, hooting, hollering, and stamping their feet. The dining hall vibrated with the noise.

Laughter bubbled up within Kelly. They'd actually pulled off the prank. The hat was back in its rightful spot. Kelly and her friends hadn't been tarred and feathered. And despite a few panic-filled moments when her stuffed dog had been kidnapped, it had been a blast. Even the late-night swim in the lake had been a crazy part of the grand adventure, though she'd never admit that to Sheila.

Bill motioned for quiet. "It's starting to rain, so we'll hold campfire inside today."

As Bill gave instructions, Darren tapped Sheila on the arm. His eyebrows creased in a frown. "My hat is freezing."

Sheila smirked and then winced. Her hand moved quickly to her injured cheek, and she dashed into the kitchen.

Marcie and Kelly followed. Sheila stood close to Sandy, who was transferring the leftovers from supper into storage containers.

"I'm starving." Marcie groaned. "We missed supper when we were at the medi-center. Can we grab a bite before we start the clean-up?"

Sandy nodded. "If Kelly stays to help, you'll finish in no time."

Charlie and the other girls piled food onto their plates. Kelly took a slice of chicken, a spoonful of mashed potatoes, peas, and some salad. It was the most she'd eaten at one meal in a long time.

Each bite brought on a wrestling match between guilt and her will. Every now and then, she ran a finger over the wooden cross around her neck. But she finished the meal. As she looked at her empty plate, she felt full. A little bloated. And very proud.

While Sheila picked at her food, Marcie kept up a constant stream of chatter. Charlie remained silent, but he cast a few furtive looks at Sheila. Kelly hoped he wasn't planning some sort of revenge.

After they finished eating, Bill came in to check on Sheila, and told her to take a break from kitchen work for the rest of the evening. She sat on a stool as Marcie, Kelly, and Charlie washed and dried the remaining dishes. She watched in silence, looking like she might burst into tears at any moment.

The sound of singing from the front of the lodge signaled that the campfire had begun. Kelly hurried to dry the last few pots, then tugged her apron over her head and tossed it into a laundry bin. Halfway to the door, she realized Sheila and Marcie hadn't moved. "Aren't you coming?"

Sheila gave a noncommittal shrug.

Marcie glanced at Sheila. "We'll catch up with you later."

Judging from the miserable look on the redhead's face, that wasn't likely. Kelly couldn't do anything at the moment, but she'd have to think of something that might get the tornado spinning again. Maybe plans for another prank.

With a wave to her friends, Kelly hurried out and spied Amber and the other campers sitting near the back of the risers. She slipped in beside them and scanned the front of the room, looking for clues to the campfire theme. Guy and Girl had been propped several feet apart, and the usual connecting set of green ties was missing. Instead, standing between the cardboard pair was a long clothesline, with an upper and lower rope stretched between two poles. Blank sheets of blue paper were attached with wooden clothes pins to the top rope, and a similar set of red sheets hung on the line below.

Kelly settled back in her seat, wearing a pleased smile. It was exactly what she'd come to expect from Bill's campfires. Something unique and unusual. She could try to guess the purpose for the laundry line decorated with colored paper. And she might come close. But most likely not. And to be honest, she liked it that way.

Bill strode through a side door, carrying a small wooden crate. White feathers poked through the slats, and clucking sounds came from within. Kelly's nose wrinkled. What did a chicken have to do with a clothesline? This definitely raised the evening's props to a new level. Slightly bizarre. And a little disappointing. If she had to make a list of the most boring barnyard animals, a chicken would be at the top.

"What does Bill have against helpless animals?" Amber sat up stiffly. "You know he's going to torture whatever poor creature is in that crate."

Kelly shrugged. She didn't feel much sympathy toward the bird. She preferred animals that she could cuddle and pet. And the live props did keep the messages entertaining. For the campers, anyway.

Bill set the wooden container on the floor. "Tonight we're going to consider an important question. Should Guy and Girl continue dating each other?"

Mike waved his hand in the air. "It's not like there are a lot of other cardboard choices."

"It's true, Guy and Girl don't have a lot of options for romantic partners. But the rest of you do."

Not Kelly. It was highly unlikely that anyone at school would give her a second glance. Aaron would see to that. And at camp? She'd come close to snagging Joel, only to have Cindy snatch him away. Who else did she have? Bob was good-looking, but a complete jerk. Darren was a nice guy, but he didn't have that wow factor. Charlie? Zach? Matt? None of them had shown any romantic interest in her. And the lack of attraction was mutual.

"How do you know if you should start a romantic relationship, or continue adding ties to a relationship you're already in?" Bill scanned the crowd. "No ideas? Not even Mike? Well, let's ask the chicken."

Bill pulled on a set of heavy work gloves, raised the lid on the crate a few inches, and pulled out a squawking chicken. Feathers flew everywhere as the bird flapped its wings, trying to escape Bill's firm grip on its legs. Several girls shrieked and the campers in the front row scrambled back. Bill cradled the hen tightly in his arms. After a minute or two, it settled down. And so did the campers.

"I want you to take a good look at this chicken."

Why? The hen wasn't cute like the calf, or adorable like the donkey. Kelly wished Bill had picked a more appealing animal, like a kitten or a lamb. Even a pig would be more interesting.

"Note the sharp beak, long legs, and beady eyes." Bill displayed the bird as if it was something special. "Now, raise your hand if you think this chicken lays a lot of eggs."

About a quarter of the campers put their hands in the air.

"Raise your hand if you think this chicken *doesn't* lay many eggs."

Another quarter lifted their hands.

Knowing Bill, it was probably a trick question. So Kelly didn't raise her hand at all. And judging from the number of campers who kept their arms at their sides, many felt the same.

Bill paced the room. "How can I know for sure if I'm going to have an egg for breakfast tomorrow?"

All eyes turned to Mike, including Bill's.

"Why's everyone looking at me?" He raised his eyebrows, assuming an air of indignation.

Bill snorted. "That's what happens when you always have something to say."

Mike grinned. "Since you asked...I think you should make the hen lay an egg. Then you'd know."

Kelly almost laughed at the ridiculous answer. Then half-choked at Bill's nod of approval.

"You're on the right track. It's pretty hard to force a chicken to produce, but if I want to know if this little gal is a good egg layer, I'll watch her for a while. A few days. Weeks. Months. The chicken's actions, or lack thereof, will tell me whether I'll be eating eggs in the morning or settling for toast and jelly."

That was the plan for the campfire? Sit around and wait for a chicken to lay an egg? Kelly stifled a yawn.

Bill put the chicken back into the crate and pulled the lid over the top. "This hen happens to be an excellent producer. She lays an egg every other day." He carried the box to Tony, who waited off to the side. "We'll send her back to the henhouse so she can do her job."

Amber gave a sigh of relief as Tony carried the clucking bird out of the lodge. It had certainly fared better than the calf or the donkey, having escaped without being chased, hogtied, or hauled around by a truck.

Bill took the gloves off his hands. "Now, how can you know whether you should start or continue dating an individual? The chicken gave us the answer. You watch that person for a few days, weeks, and months."

"But girls don't lay eggs."

Mike again...of course. Kelly rolled her eyes, but the campers showed their appreciation with hoots of laughter.

Bill shook his head. "You're not looking for eggs. You're checking for clues to see if she is a person of integrity and moral character."

"*Eggsactly*," Darren called out. "I apologize for Mike. He's being a bit of a bird brain."

"What's the matter?" Mike grunted. "You don't like my *yolks*?"

Darren frowned. "They're not all they're *cracked up* to be."

A mixture of groans, boos, and cheers rose from the campers. But Kelly was glad to see Darren back on form. Whatever reasons had prevented him from responding to Mike's puns the night she'd told the story of Molly the Moth must have been resolved.

"You'd better knock it off or you'll both end up scrambled." Bill tossed the comment over his shoulder as he walked over to Guy and Girl.

Mike and Darren tipped their hats to each other, then faked a high-five.

Bill stood beside the clotheslines of colored sheets hanging between the cardboard couple. "Determining someone's moral character isn't as easy as checking a nest for eggs. But if you watch a person's actions over time, you'll get your proof. What people *do* is far more important than what they *say*."

Kelly could have shouted her agreement. Aaron had said a lot of things to her. Like how he loved her and would never hurt her. But that changed real fast when she did something he didn't like. Joel had said sweet things to her as well. But then he acted like a flirt and a heartbreaker.

Bill gestured toward the blank sheets of blue paper. "I'm going to give the girls six specific tests that will determine if their guy is a creep or a keep."

Kelly leaned forward. This campfire might be more interesting than she'd thought. Now that the chicken was gone. And she'd be happy to play along with Bill's quiz.

Bill unhooked the first sheet, flipped it around, and held it up. He read the words printed in thick black letters. "How does he treat his mother and other women?"

Kelly's forehead wrinkled. What kind of a question was that to ask when sizing up a cute guy?

Bill clipped the sheet back in place. "Watch how the boy you're interested in acts toward his mom and sisters. Does he speak to them in a rude way? Act like they're inferior? Expect them to serve him? These are significant women in his life. If you connect with him, you'll become a significant woman in his life. That means he'll treat you the same way. Maybe not at first. But it will happen."

Kelly's thoughts flashed back to an after-school basketball game. She'd been chatting with Aaron while he waited for his mother to pick him up. When mom drove up, he'd snapped at her for taking so long, and then asked if she was too stupid to check her watch. His friends had snickered. Kelly felt sorry for the small woman in the driver's seat, but she hadn't reacted at all to the nasty comment. Perhaps it was nothing new.

Joel wouldn't get points for this question either. He treated girls well, but Kelly had a feeling it was mostly for his own amusement and ego-boost. He'd gotten snappy with Cindy when they couldn't get the vaulting move right. Kelly had been happy to see them quarreling. But she realized now how quickly he'd put all the blame on his partner.

Bill turned over the second sheet and read the bold print. "Does he treat you differently in front of his friends than when you're alone? When you're around his friends, does he make jokes at your expense, call you names, allow others to talk disrespectfully to or about you?"

Several girls murmured. Kelly recalled chatting with Lucy at her locker one day when Logan, Aaron, and a bunch of other guys from the basketball team walked over. Aaron had punched Logan in the arm and asked if he ever played connect-the-dots with the freckles on Lucy's face. Logan laughed, then said he'd tried but her big nose kept getting in the way. Lucy turned away, but not in time to hide her flaming cheeks. Or the hurt in her eyes. Kelly had expected some snarky remark in return. But Lucy said nothing. And neither did Kelly.

After the guys left, she told Lucy that she didn't think Logan's comments were very funny. Lucy had ducked her head and said it was just guys being guys. She said he was really sweet to her when his friends weren't around. But when Lucy wanted to quit the party scene and clean up her life, he dumped her. So much for whatever sweet things he'd told her in private.

Bill turned the third paper around. "How well does he lose?"

A rumble of protests rose from the male campers and counselors. The girls broke into spontaneous applause and Kelly joined in. Even her mild-mannered father became a complete grouch if he lost a game, whether it was cards or mini-golf.

Bill motioned for quiet. "Here's a test that will provide immediate results. Get some friends together for a volleyball game, but set up unequal teams. Make sure your guy is on the weak side.

Then serve the ball and watch. Your guy will likely get frustrated and angry. Males are competitive, and they hate to lose. That's just the way we're wired."

Bill's comments earned him moderate grunts of approval from the males. Kelly wondered if he had set the bar too high, considering this was part of the male design.

"The objective of this test isn't to see if he *likes* failure. No one does. It's about how he *handles* failure. It's okay if he gets grumpy. But not if he gets mean."

Aaron hadn't directed his temper solely at his mom. She'd seen him take out his frustration on his teammates as well, chewing them out during practices and games.

Her dad might pout after being defeated on the checkerboard, but he never said anything harsh. And Darren had handled the theft of his hat quite well. He hadn't lost his temper or attacked the girls. Just the prank in the bathroom, and that was kind of funny. Now that it was over.

Kelly gave her head a quick shake. She wasn't supposed to be evaluating Darren. Although, if she was honest, he'd probably earn a higher score than either Aaron or Joel.

"Life is tough. You and whoever you date will be a team. You want someone who celebrates when you win. Even more important, you want someone who won't take it out on you when your team suffers a loss."

The guys squirmed in their seats.

Bill flipped the fourth paper. "How does he treat animals, children, and handicapped people?"

"Does that include cats?" Mike shouted. "Because they don't deserve any kindness. I've been clawed by those nasty fur balls too many times, and I've got the scars to prove it."

The campers laughed, but Kelly stiffened at Mike's choice of words. She snuck a glance at Sheila, who sat in the last row of campers with her head down and hair falling around her face. Had she heard the comment about scars? Was she trying to hide her own?

Bill snorted. "Those cats were probably just trying to get you to be quiet."

The campers giggled, and Kelly grinned. She didn't blame the cats.

Bill tapped the sheet. "People who are cruel to animals are likely to be cruel to people as well. Your boyfriend doesn't have to *like* cats." Bill stared at Mike. "But he shouldn't be mean to them. He can ignore the cat. The cat will most likely ignore him, too."

Darren half-rose from his seat. "Maybe Mike should *paws* in his war on cats."

Mike folded his arms. "Sounds *purrfect* to me."

"How can I *purr-suade* you to *paw-lease* let that be the last of your puns." Bill waited for the laughter to stop. "Now, back to our lesson. You want to watch how a guy treats children too. It reveals the type of father he'll be. At the moment, becoming a parent may be the furthest thing from your mind. But it's important to connect romantically only with men who are husband/father material."

Kelly wondered how Aaron and Joel would have reacted if they'd been stuck in a cabin with an annoying camper like Marvin. Would they have been patient with him? Defended him when he wet his bed, like Darren? Or mocked him, like the other campers?

Bill flipped the fifth blue sheet. But instead of clipping it back in place beside the others, he held it out.

MaryAnn stepped forward to take it from him. "This question was my idea, so I'm going to ask it. Does your guy pass the Spider Test?"

The girls squealed. Kelly glanced at Bill, checking to make sure he didn't whip out any eight-legged creatures as an object lesson. Thankfully, he kept his hands in his pockets.

"Spiders freak me out." MaryAnn's body shuddered. "If I spot one in the house, I'll grab the vacuum cleaner and suck it up."

A shiver ran through Kelly's limbs as well. She had no love for anything with eight spindly legs. But she preferred to use a shoe.

"I once had a boyfriend who'd heard about my arachnophobia. One day he chased me around a park with a big, ugly spider. I was almost hysterical with panic. I nearly dumped him right then. But after he stopped laughing, he apologized. So I explained that I really was terrified of spiders and I gave him one more chance. A few days later, he did it again. And that was the end of our relationship."

The male campers snickered. But the girls broke into applause.

"That may seem extreme, but I saw his actions as a sign of immaturity. His behavior told me I couldn't trust him with my vulnerabilities. You can learn a lot by watching what a person finds funny."

Kelly's eyes turned to the hat-wearing comics. Mike and Darren were always cracking jokes and making puns. But none of them had been at anyone else's expense. The jokes may have been groaners, but they weren't mean-spirited. Which earned both Men in Hats a point.

Bill took MaryAnn's sheet and clipped it in place. Then he flipped the final blue page. "This is our last test. What's your guy's definition of a 'real man'"?

Mike sprang up and flexed his muscles. The campers burst out laughing. With his long, skinny limbs, he was a far cry from a body builder. Bill cracked a smile as he motioned for Mike to take a seat.

"As Mike attempted to demonstrate, manliness is often pictured in terms of being rough and tough. But in the book of Proverbs, God defines the ideal man as one who fears the Lord and finds delight in His commands. Real men may come with or without biceps. But they always have respect for themselves, for others, and for God." Bill walked to the center of the room and stood facing the campers. "Don't pass up a guy just because he's not what you'd consider attractive on the outside."

Kelly thought of Marcie's recent switch in the object of her affection. On the outside, Bob had Mike beat in every way. But

Marcie must have looked deeper and seen Mike's fun-loving, loyal, and honest heart. And she'd chosen the *truly* handsome guy. While Kelly had been a complete fool and fallen for the most handsome face. Twice.

Bill swept his arm toward the second clothesline, which held five blank red sheets. "Now it's time for tests that guys can use to determine if they should begin or continue a romantic relationship with a particular girl."

Bill's announcement brought thunderous applause from the males. No doubt in relief that the spotlight was going to be turned off them. Kelly braced herself. If she was going to put Joel and Aaron to the test, it seemed only fair to take it herself and see how she fared.

Bill flipped over the first red sheet. "Is she into you or into your wallet?"

More cheering from the guys. Even some foot stomping. Kelly smiled. She'd pass this test, thanks to her mother's good example. When her mother had met Kelly's father, he was a poor college student, struggling to finish his last year in school while holding down two part-time jobs. Kelly's mom said her friends had teased her for going out with a guy who drove a clunker of a car and couldn't afford to take her to eat at a nice restaurant. But she'd looked past the lack of money and saw a hard-working guy with ambitious goals and a caring, sincere heart. She always ended her story by saying she got gold in the end.

"Be wary of a girlfriend who expects you to take her to fancy places and purchase expensive gifts for her. Make certain you're *forming* ties, not buying them."

Kelly loved her parents' story and tried to follow their example. Some of her friends made demands of their boyfriends, but she'd never asked Aaron to buy her things. She awarded herself a point. A good start.

Bill flipped the second sheet. "Can she say no?"

"Every girl I ask out tells me no," Mike shouted. "I'm looking for a girl who can say yes."

The campers roared in laughter. Bill struggled to keep a straight face. "Mike, your girl troubles would take a separate campfire to cover. Maybe even a whole week."

Mike shrugged.

Still chuckling, Bill returned his focus to the question on the red sheet. "Girls who struggle with insecurity will change themselves to match your interests. This is flattering in the beginning, but becomes boring and burdensome as the relationship progresses. If a girl can say no to you, that shows she is strong enough to have her own opinions and has the self-confidence to express them. And that strength is an attractive quality."

Kelly flinched. She'd said no when Aaron had pressured her to let him drive the car. But then she'd given in. She'd panicked when he was about the leave the party and drive drunk. She'd taken the keys and called her parents. So she passed that test. Barely. And mostly because her parents had come in time to save her. What if he had pressured her again? Would she have had the strength to say no another time?

Bill walked back to the clothesline and flipped the third sheet. "Is she possessive?"

From the murmur among the male campers, Kelly guessed this one hit a nerve.

"Constant phone calls, e-mails, and text messages filled with questions, insinuations, and accusations are signs of a possessive girlfriend."

Another personal fail. She'd been a mess while dating Aaron, following his every move. She knew every girl he talked to, was always by his side, called him every evening, and hung on tight. She knew how easy it would be to lose him, and how many girls were waiting to pounce.

Bill clipped the page back onto the clothesline. "Possessiveness can be flattering. It makes you feel like you're such a hot item your girlfriend is afraid of losing you. But it's not about you. It's about her—her insecurity, fear, and jealousy. Those emotions will eventually strangle the relationship."

Kelly studied the floor. When it came to Aaron, she'd done everything out of fear.

Bill flipped the fourth sheet. "Does she pass the Chicken Test?"

Mike raised his hand, "Is that like the Spider Test? Because I'm not afraid of chickens, and it wouldn't bother me if a girl chased me with one."

Darren bobbed up from his seat. "That sounds like *fowl play*. But at least you wouldn't be cooped up."

Kelly laughed along with the rest of the campers. Mike and Darren were really pulling out all the puns tonight.

Bill shook his head, but he couldn't keep a grin off his face. "I wish I could say your jokes were *im-peck-able*, but they're not. And this test is about how she treats people who aren't popular. On a farm, chickens have a pecking order. The top chickens eat first, take the best nests, and harass the lower-ranking hens. Humans also have pecking orders. Especially girls."

Bill's comment sparked a flurry of grumbling among the female campers and staff. Kelly suspected that every girl in the room had been pecked at once or twice, if not more. Herself included.

"Many girls ignore those who have no influence and play up to those who do. Popular girls often step on anyone they consider to be beneath them. That's how they boost their own status and ego."

When Kelly joined the ranks of the coolest kids at school, she already knew that most of them got there by stepping on others. And stayed there by cutting down anyone who threatened their position. Protected by her connection with Aaron, Kelly had managed to stay out of the social bloodbath. But she sat by silently when she should have defended the poor girls who were being targeted. Unfortunately, she'd been too afraid of being cut down herself.

Bill waited for the room to quiet. "You may be a 'top chicken' in your girlfriend's eyes. But if you don't maintain that cool image, you'll be in trouble. Your girlfriend should like you for who you are, not for your reputation or status."

Several girls squirmed. Kelly shifted along with them. She'd just added another huge failure to her score.

Bill flipped the fifth and final sheet. "How does she look when she's camping?"

The girls hissed and booed. Kelly crossed her arms and glared at Bill. Did it always have to come back to what a girl looked like? She couldn't believe Bill was encouraging that attitude.

He made calming motions with his hands. "This isn't a shallow question. It reveals more than you think."

Kelly hoped, for Bill's sake, that he had a good explanation.

"A few years back, I took a group of teens on a week-long wilderness survival camp. We had only what we carried with us, and there was no running water or bathrooms. One camper wore a lot of eye make-up. I wondered how she'd fare."

Bill chuckled. "Cold mountain stream water doesn't remove mascara very well. The other females gave up wearing cosmetics after the first day. But this camper didn't want to be seen without her makeup. So she kept putting it on. By the end of the week, she looked like a raccoon."

The glares directed at Bill hadn't softened.

"This question isn't about beauty products. It's about where a girl finds her security and confidence."

The girls remained silent.

"Outward appearance is a particular struggle for women. They know good looks are part of a guy's initial attraction. But beauty only goes so far. A strong romance can't be built on the perfect nose, fabulous hair, or a great body."

Kelly's stomach wrenched. This was the biggest fail for her yet. She based everything on physical appearance—her own and that of the guys she liked. She felt as if Bill had held up a mirror to her heart, and she didn't like what she saw.

Kelly recalled the morning her parents had announced they were sending her to camp. She'd snapped back, *"You think some lame religious camp is going to fix me. I'm not broken, and I don't need help."* Kelly swallowed hard. She'd been wrong. About camp, and about herself.

"In Proverbs 31:30, the Bible tells us that charm is deceptive and beauty is temporary, but a woman who trusts in God is worthy of praise. When a girl finds her worth in the Lord, it brings a beauty to her that cannot be taken away."

Kelly straightened. She'd only been at Timberlake for eight days. Not long enough for a complete change. But she'd made a start when she'd prayed by the lake and asked God for help. And when she'd eaten a real meal just hours earlier. A smile played across her face, and her fingers strayed to the wooden cross necklace, hidden under her shirt.

Bill gestured toward the two rows of paper stretched between Guy and Girl. "These questions are designed to uncover an individual's true character, which is revealed by what he or she repeatedly does. This is what you should look for in others. And what you should use to attract others to you. *Character* is so important that it deserves a place on our New Romantic and Sexy Words List."

Tony emerged from the back of the group, carrying the easel. He set it down at the front and added the eleventh word.

Aaron had failed miserably at every test. Joel hadn't done much better. And she'd flunked as well. She should feel depressed. But she didn't. Instead, she felt hopeful. There would be other tests. Even bigger ones. And she was determined to do better the next time round.

Bill adjusted the blank pieces of paper, sliding them over to make room at the end of each row. "When you're wondering whether to start a romantic relationship or continue adding ties to the one you're in, ask these questions. If the individual's character is lacking, find the courage and strength to walk away."

That's exactly what she would do when she got home. She'd move on from Aaron and the popular crowd. And with that thought, it was as if a heavy weight had just rolled off her shoulders.

MaryAnn stepped forward and clipped several blank sheets behind the pages with questions. "This list is not complete. There's plenty of room for other questions. Let me toss out a few that apply to both genders. Is this person honest? Generous? Selfish? How does he or she handle money? Who are their friends? Can they say, 'I was wrong' and 'I'm sorry'?"

Kelly considered the new questions. She'd get a chance to practice admitting she was wrong when her mom came to pick her up at the end of the week, only two days away. And she'd add something to those words of apology. A great big hug.

MaryAnn moved to the other side of Guy and Girl and added a sheet with the outline of a cross at the front of each of the lists.

"Here's the most important question of all. Does the person who is the object of your affection know Jesus? If that individual hasn't made a commitment to the Lord, you shouldn't even move on to the other questions. Don't connect yourself to him or her. You might think you can help this person find God. But it's more likely he or she will pull you away."

Kelly shifted on the bench. That's what had happened with Aaron. He'd had far more influence on her choices and actions, while she'd had little impact on his.

Bill walked over to the list of New Romantic and Sexy Words. He drew a star beside the word *time* and underlined it. "Time reveals a person's character and personality. Eventually, the truth will come out."

Exactly. Kelly had fallen for Joel the moment she saw him. But once she'd had a chance to see more, he didn't look quite as good. There wasn't much time left at camp, and she didn't want to waste it chasing Joel.

Bill turned to Mike. "Since you answered the first question tonight about how to tell if our chicken was a good egg producer, I'll ask you the last one. What's the best way to watch another person's actions?"

Mike rubbed his chin for a moment. "I guess you just have to hang around them a lot."

"Good answer. The best way to begin any romantic relationship is by being friends. Through friendship we discover similar likes, interests, and passions."

So she'd been doing things backwards. Falling in love with a guy before figuring out if they had anything in common. Another area to work on.

Kelly's lips curved in a wry smile. Her parents might not recognize her by the end of the week. And neither would her friends at school.

Bill motioned for MaryAnn to come forward. Together, they removed the clotheslines from the poles and attached the lines to the hands of the cardboard couple, so the questions hung between them. "These tests won't help you find the perfect person or the perfect match. There's no such thing. Start by looking for an individual with character who will be a good friend. As your connection grows, he or she might become your best friend."

Bill gestured to the blue and red question sheets. "Here's my challenge to you. Become the type of person that you would like to date."

Kelly glanced over the sheets and smiled. Her score had been miserable. She had a lot to learn. But she'd passed the most important question of all by reconnecting with Jesus.

And as for the others? Well, if there was one thing she'd learned this week, it was that she could make changes. If she really wanted to. And she did.

36 FIVE KISSES

Kelly followed the mass of campers out of the lodge and stood for a few moments in the crisp night air, allowing her eyes to adjust to the darkness. Somewhere in the shadows, she heard the faint clucking of the chicken Bill had used during his campfire talk. But it was squawking voices that drew her attention to a circle of campers several feet away, with Sheila trapped in the middle.

"How big is the scar?"

"Does it hurt?"

"Did you really almost die?"

"Can we see the stitches?"

Sheila ducked her head and tried to move forward, but the tight ring of curious kids didn't budge. If anything, they pushed even closer. The campers didn't mean to be rude, but they could've shown a little more sensitivity.

"Sheila is supposed to get lots of rest." Marcie took her friend's arm and elbowed a path through the crowd.

Kelly rushed to take a spot on her friend's other side. Amber stuck close to Kelly, and they formed a protective shield around Sheila.

"I wish everyone would stop staring at my face," Sheila mumbled.

"Don't worry," Marcie said. "In a couple of days, no one will care."

"I will," Sheila snapped. "Forever."

Kelly winced at the pain behind those bitter words. But she didn't know how to console her friend. "Would you like me to get you something? How about a Coke?" Perhaps a good dose of liquid sugar would cheer her up.

Sheila shook her head, looking even more miserable. If that was possible.

As the foursome made their way up the road, Kelly noticed a large crowd of campers hanging around outside the cabins, chatting loudly.

She grabbed Sheila's arm. "Let's take the shortcut behind the camp store." She steered her friends onto a dimly lit path.

They'd only gone halfway down the trail when five dark figures stepped out from the trees. The outline of hats gave away their identity.

"Bad idea," Amber whispered.

Kelly swallowed hard.

Mike, Charlie, Darren, and Zach surrounded the girls, accompanied by Marvin, looking proud as could be with Darren's paper hat perched on his head.

Darren held up his hand to halt the girls. "We've got some unfinished business with you."

Images of tar and feathers sprang to Kelly's mind. Surely Darren wouldn't go back on his deal. But now that she thought about it, she realized a glaring omission. In their negotiations, they'd only bargained to keep Sheila's hair safe. Anybody else's was fair game.

Kelly glanced about wildly, hoping to make a break for it. But Sheila wasn't in any condition to take a mad dash through the woods, and she wasn't about to leave her friend behind.

For a moment, no one moved. Then Sheila took a bold step toward Darren and lowered her head. "Go ahead. Mess it up. I deserve it."

Darren burst out laughing. "This isn't about your hair."

The tension drained from Kelly. Perhaps the guys only wanted to talk. A quick check showed the boys weren't carrying any supplies that could be used as instruments of torture.

"You want an apology?" Sheila raised her hands, palms up. "I'm sorry. When we took your hat, we didn't know about Charlie's dad—" Her voice broke off as she realized her mistake.

Mike threw his arms in the air. "Remind me not to tell you anything private ever again."

"It's okay," Charlie said.

"You've got it all wrong." Darren motioned the other guys forward. "This isn't about my hat or your hair."

"What do you want then?" Sheila's voice carried a hard edge of suspicion.

Darren took her arms and held them at her side. "I want you to stand very still and stop talking for one minute. I know that's going to be difficult, but try really hard, okay?"

Leaning forward, Darren lightly kissed the bandage covering the scar on Sheila's cheek. Then he stepped to the side. One by one, each of the Men in Hats softly kissed Sheila's bandaged cheek. When Marvin's turn came, he tugged on her sleeve until Sheila bent down. Even then, he had to stand on tiptoes to reach.

Minutes passed, and no one moved. Then Sheila buried her face in her hands and sobbed, her whole body shaking.

As she watched Sheila break down, Kelly realized she'd underestimated the depth of her friend's pain.

Darren gently pulled Sheila's hands from her face. She took several choking breaths.

Darren looked into Sheila's eyes, his face solemn and determined. "For the rest of your life, every person you meet will see the scar on your face. Those who care about the scar, they don't matter. And those who do matter, they won't care."

Charlie gave a low whistle. "That was really good."

"I had help," Darren admitted. "I told Bill what I wanted to say, and he helped me say it better."

Kelly stared at Darren, as if she'd never really seen him before. She'd viewed him as a silly prankster. Fun-loving but immature. Yet he'd just presented Sheila with the most amazing gift. He'd shown her that not everyone would judge her. At least not guys like Darren and the Men in Hats.

Darren swept his hat from his head and bowed low. "From this day forth, the Men in Hats are your sworn protectors. If anyone ever makes fun of you, just let us know and we'll take care of them."

Mike nodded. "And if you ever need an escort to the prom or anywhere else, you can call one of us."

Kelly remembered Sheila's bitter words in the kitchen and her fears that no one would want to date a scarface. Charlie must have told his friends about the conversation he'd overheard.

Darren gave Sheila a lopsided grin. "Not that you're ever going to have a problem getting a date."

Marvin tugged on Sheila's shirt again. "Yah. You're really pretty." A dark blush spread over his face and he kicked at the ground. "Not that I want to be your boyfriend or anything like that."

Marvin's obvious embarrassment broke the solemn tone, and everyone laughed. Even Sheila—a little.

Darren gave Marvin a playful punch in the arm, then turned back to Sheila. "Trust me. No one is even going to notice that tiny scar. And if anybody does, you can tell them you got it during a very memorable week at summer camp, where you pulled off an historically epic prank!"

Sheila' face brightened into a full-on grin.

"But I have to warn you." Darren's voice took on a teasing tone. "If I take you to the prom, I'm wearing my hat."

Sheila smiled even more broadly. "Maybe I'll wear a hat too. What do you think of that?"

Everyone chuckled, then shifted into an awkward silence. No one seemed sure how to end the moment.

"Well, we'd better get going," Mike said. "We're missing out on an awesome pillow fight."

Whooping and hollering, the guys took off running.

As the girls walked up the path, Kelly replayed the scene in her mind. The guys kissing Sheila's cheek. Darren's words of reassurance. All of the Men in Hats pledging to defend her. It was the most amazing thing she'd ever seen.

When they reached the cabins, Kelly gave Sheila a tight hug. "See you in the morning."

Sheila nodded, her face tear-streaked but glowing. "Tomorrow's a new day, and camp's not over yet."

Kelly saw that familiar glint of mischief in her eyes. Those five kisses had worked a miraculous change in her friend.

When Kelly and Amber neared their cabin, the laughter of the girls inside floated through the open window. Kelly paused outside the door, reluctant to enter and lose the wonder of the evening.

"That was so romantic." Amber sighed. "Darren must really like Sheila."

A sudden sharpness pierced Kelly's chest. But she had no time to ponder the disturbing revelation. The cabin door flew open and several girls dashed toward the bathroom.

"There you are," Jill said. "I just gave the three-minute warning for lights-out."

Amber darted into the cabin.

"How's Sheila doing?" Jill whispered.

"She's upset, but I think she'll be fine." Thanks to Darren.

With a roll of her eyes, Jill launched into a mini-tirade. "Joel should have known better than to let Sheila try a difficult move like that handstand. Especially without a spotter. And Sheila shouldn't have been trying so hard to impress Joel. He's not worth it. Did you know he's back with Cindy?"

Kelly nodded. But the news didn't hurt as much as she'd expected.

"Word around camp is that Cindy started flirting with some other guy and Joel didn't like it."

Cindy sure knew what she was doing. But so did Joel.

"I'd better get moving." Kelly didn't feel like discussing the restored golden couple any further.

Once all the campers were in their beds, Kelly began the bedtime story of The Three-Legged Pig. Another long tale filled with details and a ridiculous ending. Kelly smiled as she heard the girls shifting in their bunks, trying to stay awake. But a week of exercise, fresh air, good food, and late nights had taken their toll. Kelly hadn't even reached the halfway point when the sound of deep breathing filled the cabin.

As snuggled into the sleeping bag with her beloved beagle, Kelly's mind drifted back to Amber's comments. Was Darren really interested in dating Sheila? And why did the thought bother her so much?

Kelly rolled over and tried to lose herself in the blissful forgetfulness of slumber. But she kept seeing Darren's soft kiss on Sheila's bandaged cheek. It must be wonderful to be loved like that.

37 AN UNCOMFORTABLE CAMPFIRE

Kelly woke to dreary skies, with dark clouds threatening to unleash a downpour. Seemed appropriate. This was the last full day of camp. She'd be going home tomorrow. And there wasn't much to look forward to. A messy jog through the mud matched her mood perfectly.

As Kelly sloshed through the puddles, she was grateful to have the road to herself. At the start of the week, she'd thought the end would never come. But now she felt like it had come too soon.

Kelly hit the turn-around point and pounded back down the gravel road to camp and a much-needed shower. As the warm water washed over her, she considered her options. Tomorrow didn't have to be the end. She could talk to Bill. If there was an open spot for her, she could stay another week. Maybe more.

As Kelly hopped out of the shower and rushed to get ready, the plan continued to grow. Her parents would be more than happy to have her stay. But there were so many unknowns. What if she got stuck with another lousy partner in a difficult job assignment? What if she was assigned to a new cabin with an unwelcoming head counselor? And that didn't even take into account the new set of campers and their potential challenges. She'd bonded with Amber this week, but what if the next group of girls was harder to deal with. Then again, if the next few weeks were half as fun as the first, it would be worth it.

At breakfast, Kelly forced herself to eat three small pancakes. Maybe next week, if she stayed, she'd add butter and syrup.

Amber gave a dramatic sigh and poked Kelly in the side. "They're such a perfect couple."

Kelly followed the camper's starry gaze to the front of the dining hall, where Sheila and Darren stood close together. Laughing as Sheila balanced Darren's hat on her head.

Finding it hard to swallow, Kelly stabbed at her pancake. Sheila and Darren liked each other. Why should that bother her? She should be glad that her friend was laughing again. Not feeling...jealous.

Kelly dropped her fork and covered her face with her hands as a flood of guilt washed over her. What kind of pathetic friend was she?

A new sort of pain twisted inside her as she recognized the truth. She liked Darren. Not because he was cool, popular or gorgeous. But because he was fun, kind, and thoughtful. And every other quality listed on Bill's list of New Romantic and Sexy Words. But she couldn't allow herself to like him because Sheila was her friend, and she needed Darren. Which meant Kelly needed to look elsewhere.

The dining hall fell silent, and Kelly glanced up. Bill made his way to the front counter, a felt marker in his hand. "Time for the final scores in the Clean Cabin Contest."

Jill motioned for the girls to hold hands. The campers had been extra careful to keep the cabin spotless and in perfect order. But there was no guarantee they still had the lead.

"Our contest has been a huge success." Bill grinned as he dragged out the moment. "Timberlake Camp has never had such clean rooms. I only hope that next week's campers can live up to the standards you've set."

Kelly tightened her grip on Amber and Tanya's hands. The girls had worked so hard. They just had to win.

With dramatic flourish, Bill added the final numbers. Heads craned to see the results.

Jill leapt off the bench with a shriek of joy. "We won!"

Kelly joined the other girls at the table as they jumped to their feet, shouting and punching the air.

"I don't know how I'm going to finish such a big bowl of ice cream," Amber shouted above the noise. "It's enough for two people. But I'm going to give it my best shot!"

Kelly stopped mid-cheer. Amber's words had given her an idea. "Enough for two. And maybe more," she murmured. Maybe even enough for three.

Bill congratulated Jill and Kelly's cabin, reminded the other disappointed campers that they could try again next year, then dismissed the group. After cleaning their dishes from the tables, everyone left the dining hall and raced through the pouring rain toward their cabins. Kelly shivered and pulled her jacket tighter. At least they'd be snug in their room for devotions.

As Kelly neared the veranda, she saw dripping campers standing around the cabin door, staring at a small piece of yellow paper in Jill's hand. At other cabins, groups stood outside and huddled in a similar fashion.

Terri groaned. "The note is from Bill, right?"

Jill nodded. "It says we have to go back to the lodge immediately for devotions."

"We were just there." Joyce crossed her arms like she had no intention of going anywhere except inside the dry cabin. A few other girls also crossed their arms, and Kelly worried there might be a full-scale rebellion. Which she was tempted to join.

Jill pointed at the paper. "It says to bring pillows if we want to be more comfortable."

Joyce waved her arms, flinging droplets everywhere. "If Bill really cared about our comfort, he could have told us to stay at the lodge. Then we wouldn't have gotten soaked!"

Jill shrugged. "The note says we won't be disappointed."

Too late, Kelly thought, as she started to wring out her hair, then stopped because it was only going to get more wet.

Still grumbling, the girls grabbed pillows and stuffed them under raincoats. Then they became part of the mob of campers slipping and sliding their way back to the lodge, complaining all the way. Kelly bit her lip to keep from adding to the grumbling. She usually enjoyed Bill's unpredictable style, but not this time.

As the campers burst through the front doors of the lodge, the griping stopped immediately. And was replaced with shocked silence.

In the short time they'd been gone, the campfire area had been transformed. The room glowed, despite the lack of sun, thanks to multiple tall lamps placed strategically in the corners. A roaring fire cracked in the fireplace. Tables lined the walls, each set with steaming cups of hot chocolate, huge bowls of marshmallows, and large trays piled high with gigantic chocolate chip cookies. A warm, sweet aroma wafted through the room, and Kelly's mouth started to water.

Bill stepped into the middle of the room. "We're going to have a morning campfire instead of the regular cabin devotions. I sent you back to your cabins so we'd have time to set up this surprise." He opened his arms in a sweeping gesture toward the treats. "I hadn't planned on the rain. Hopefully, this will make up for it. Help yourselves."

The dripping campers needed no further encouragement. They dropped their pillows and surged toward the refreshments. Kelly guessed from the squeals of delight that Bill had been forgiven.

Kelly held back for a moment, her eyes searching for clues that might reveal the morning topic. No barnyard animals. No messy substances. Nothing to indicate the direction of his message. Yet Bill had gone out of his way to make sure the campers would be comfortable and relaxed. There had to be a reason.

Kelly wrinkled her nose. If there was some explanation, she'd find out soon enough. Besides, no one else seemed to care. The campers were too busy grabbing cups of hot cocoa. Kelly forced herself to pour a half cup, then deliberately added a few miniature marshmallows. Because a rational, healthy person could enjoy a few of the sweet white squares. And that's what she was striving to be. Besides, she deserved the extra indulgence after being soaked twice in one morning.

Bill strode to the front of the risers, bringing Girl and Guy with him. Campers scrambled to find their places. Kelly still couldn't spot any gimmicks or props. Which seemed odd. She'd expected Bill to become even more grandiose than ever in the final campfire talks.

Bill considered the cardboard pair for a moment. "Up until this point, all of our connections have started the same way. Guy sees Girl. Girl sees Guy. They build ties between them. We've had several dating disasters. But through it all there has been one very important factor: choice. The relationship began with a choice from both Guy and Girl, and it continued or ended through choice."

As Bill spoke, he paced, rubbing his hands in a distracted manner. His nervous behavior made Kelly tense. She wished he'd taken his own advice and grabbed a relaxing cup of hot chocolate. Or several cups.

Bill stopped beside Girl and let his gaze wander over the crowd. "Unfortunately, not all relationships are formed by choice. Sometimes ties are thrust into our hands through force or manipulation. That's called abuse."

Kelly drew in her breath sharply as the shock of Bill's words rolled over her. She'd come to expect unusual campfire topics. But she'd never expected him to discuss something as terrible as abuse.

Suddenly Kelly understood the reason for the bright room, comfortable pillows, and sweet treats. Bill was trying to make a difficult message easier to hear. But nothing could save this campfire from being anything but ugly, painful, and harsh.

Bill ran a hand across his forehead. "This isn't an easy topic to discuss. It will be especially hard for those of you who have been victims of abuse."

Kelly winced. All around her, campers spoke in low murmurs as they shifted in their seats. Had Bill forgotten how young these kids were?

"Abuse can be verbal, emotional, physical, or sexual. It may happen once or repeatedly. But in all cases, one person is taking advantage of another in a way that is wrong."

Kelly snuck a peek at Charlie. His head was lowered, and he stared at the ground. Based on what Mike said, he'd witnessed years of angry fighting between his parents. And taken many blows as well. The physical bruises may have faded but Charlie was still hurting inside. How many campers were hiding wounds like his?

Maybe Bill was right to bring up this topic.

Bill left the room, and returned with a large, black cardboard cutout of a capital A. He placed it between Girl and Guy. "We're going to imagine that someone we know has been the victim of abuse."

The cardboard Girl stared with unmoving eyes at the campers, her lips curved in a permanent smile. It was the same grin she'd maintained after being roped like a calf, participating in a donkey drag, and coming close to a muddy pool during a tug-of-war. Kelly hadn't really cared about her expression. Until now. The happy Girl standing next to the dark, threating capital A shouldn't be smiling.

"Excuse me." Lady Katherine marched around campers as she made her way to the front. She stood beside Girl, with her back ramrod straight and her graying hair pulled into a familiar tight bun. All that was missing was her stark-white apron.

The formidable cook gave Bill a curt nod, and he picked up Girl and carried her off to the side.

Lady Katherine stepped into the spot where the cardboard figure had been. She cleared her throat, clasped her hands behind her back, and settled her gaze on a spot over the heads of the campers. "On a Friday night many years ago, a young teenage girl snuck out of her house, met up with some friends, and went to a party across town. She drank a lot. Around midnight, a cute guy that she'd had a crush on for years offered to take her home. She was thrilled to go with him. But he didn't drive toward her neighborhood. He took her to an isolated spot and turned off the car. She tried to get out. But he wouldn't let her. She tried to fight him. But he was stronger. He sexually assaulted her. Afterward, he warned her that if she told anyone, he'd say that she wanted to have sex with him. The girl was ashamed, embarrassed, and humiliated. She didn't tell anyone for years."

As Kelly studied Lady Katherine's expression, she realized the regal cook wasn't just telling an imaginary story. She was sharing her own story.

A wave of shocked gasps swept through the room as the campers reached the same conclusion.

Kelly wiped her sweaty palms on her pants. Minutes before, she'd been thinking the paper Girl and her frozen smile didn't belong. But now she wanted her back. Girl might have been comical, but at least she was safe. An imagery cutout with a made-up story. But Lady Katherine was a real, live person. Kelly imagined the forbidding cook as a young, vulnerable teenager desperately trying to escape from a lustful boy in a car.

Tony lumbered to the front. Bill removed Guy, and Tony stood in the place where the cardboard figure had been.

No. Not him too.

"A young boy made friends with an older gentleman who lived in the neighborhood. The older man was friendly and caring. And this kid needed someone like that in his life because his own father had run out on the family when he was just a baby. The older gentleman taught the boy how to throw a baseball, took him to some baseball games, bought him gifts, and occasionally watched him when his mother had to work late. One weekend, he invited the boy to stay overnight. And that's when the abuse began. It didn't end for five long years."

A painful silence descended upon the room.

Bill carried a large bag to the center of the room. He dropped it on the floor, and it landed with a thud. He reached inside, and the sharp clang of metal rang through the room as he pulled out a long chain.

"Shared experiences create a connection, even if the experience is harmful or unwanted. But acts of abuse can't build ties of love, because true love seeks the highest good of the other person. Love doesn't try to fulfill its own pleasure while causing harm to another. The bond created by abuse is a heavy chain."

Bill ran the links through the middle of the dark A and then around Lady Katherine and Tony. The cook flinched as the metal passed over her shoulders, and Tony appeared to sag under the weight. The chain seemed endless. Even with the links wound multiple times around Lady Katherine and Tony, the slack reached to the floor. Kelly wondered how many campers were seeing their own connections to abuse.

"Tony and Katherine are telling true stories. Their own stories." Bill stepped back and gave everyone a few moments to absorb the new picture. "Overwhelmed with shame and fear, they told no one about their abuse. Years passed, and both moved away from any interaction with their abusers."

Bill pulled the black A as far back as the chains allowed, leaving a distance of several feet. But the black metal links remained wrapped around the victims. "Even after the abuse ended, it continued to affect almost every area of their lives."

Lady Katherine clasped her hands in front of her. "Ever since that horrible evening in the car, I have struggled with depression. I earned poor grades, fell into the wrong crowd, and gave in to any guy who wanted to sleep with me."

Tony tugged at the chains on his shoulders. "I started using alcohol and drugs and quickly became addicted. I joined a gang and was sucked into a life of violence and petty crime."

Kelly had judged Lady Katherine only as a cold, harsh, aloof cook. She'd viewed Tony as a gruff, grumpy boss. And she'd never bothered to wonder if there was a reason.

Bill moved to the middle, where the A once stood. "Why is it so hard to move forward after abuse?"

Out of the corner of her eye, Kelly caught the movement of a hat. For a moment she worried that Mike or Darren might crack one of their groan-inspiring puns, which would be horribly insensitive. But it was Charlie who answered Bill's question.

"They can't move on because they've still got the chains."

Kelly flinched. From what Mike said, Charlie couldn't get free of his chains. He wouldn't even be here if it hadn't been for Darren's tenacious friendship and his crazy scheme with the hats.

"That's right. Tony and Katherine are still connected to the abuse, and it will continue to have a toxic influence as long as they remain shackled to it."

Which looked hopeless. Tony and Lady Katherine had broken away from their abusers. But how could anyone be free of the memories of such a horrible experience?

"Those who have been abused need to disconnect from the chains and their poisonous effects." Bill paused, and the only sound in the room was the rain falling like tears on the roof.

"It's not that easy. It's not like you can just walk away."

Charlie's quiet words brought whispers of agreement from the campers.

"That's true." Bill locked eyes with Charlie. "An abused individual will never forget what happened. And abuse should never be denied, ignored, excused, or minimized."

Kelly felt her nails digging into her palm. So what were Tony and Lady Katherine supposed to do with those heavy chains?

What was she supposed to do?

She was through with Aaron, but couldn't free herself from the feelings of guilt and shame that wrapped around her. So many mistakes. So many people she'd disappointed and hurt. Kelly had never thought of those emotions as chains. Not until tonight. But that's exactly how they felt.

Bill's gaze swept the room. "Dealing with the chains is never easy. It takes time and courage. And one more thing."

The whole room froze in place, every camper holding his or her breath.

"You must share what has happened with someone you trust."

Kelly's shoulders slumped. How could Bill give such a simple answer?

"Bill's right." Lady Katherine rattled the chains that wound around her. "My abuser counted on my silence. But that protected him, not me. I was scared, so I told no one. I carried the weight alone. Looking back now, I realize that was a huge mistake."

A scuffling at the side door drew Kelly's attention. Sandy stepped in, carrying three new cardboard characters, all painted in bright white. Signs hanging around their necks identified the figures as a parent, a counselor, and a policeman. Sandy set the cutouts between Lady Katherine and Tony, and Bill arranged the chains to cross over the shoulders of each of the cardboard figures. Lady Katherine and Tony seemed to stand a little straighter as the recently added cardboard characters bore some of the weight of the dark metal links.

"If you have been the victim of abuse, it is important that you talk to someone who is trustworthy. It might be a family member, teacher, counselor, coach, pastor, or friend. If you don't feel comfortable with someone you know, then search the Internet for a list of local crisis centers, teen help lines, and abuse hotlines with professionally trained staff. Find someone who can walk with you and guide you through the necessary steps to healing which are different for each person. If you are currently experiencing abuse, do this right away. You will need guidance from someone who can help you remain safe until you are able to escape."

Kelly considered the parent figure. Would it have helped if she'd talked to her parents about what really happened the disastrous night when she'd allowed Aaron to drive the car to the party? Where he got drunk. And almost drove home. There was no way she could have told them anything that first night. They'd been so angry...and disappointed. But what if she'd tried the next day? Or what if she'd talked to her youth pastor? Maybe he could have helped her work through what she was feeling. And identified Aaron's actions for what she now realized they were: selfish bullying.

Bill gestured toward the white characters. "As wonderful as these people are, none of them can completely handle such a heavy burden. But there is someone who can."

Kelly's hand reached for the cross hidden under her shirt, and she knew what Bill was going to say. Every campfire talk, every morning devotion, and every early-morning walk down the dirt road always came back to Jesus. That had made her crazy at the beginning of the week. But not anymore. She got it now. The cross was the best place to be.

Sandy reappeared with the wooden cross Bill had used at previous campfires. She placed it in the center, directly in front of the black A. Then Sandy lifted some of the chains from Lady Katherine and Tony, looping them around the wooden frame.

Bill placed a hand on the solid beam. "The most important conversation needs to take place with Jesus. Pass the chains through the hands of God. Only He is big enough to bear them all."

Tony looked down for a moment. When he raised his head, his eyes were glassy. "My poor choices led to a stint in a juvenile detention center. I thought it was the worst thing that could have happened to me, but it turned out to be the best. Because one night, when I was depressed and feeling hopeless, I decided to hear a guest speaker at the jail. He said that God loved me, that He could forgive everything I'd done and make all things new. I talked to Jesus for the first time that night, and I asked Him to come into my heart. I haven't stopped talking to Him since."

While Tony was speaking, Bill reached into the bag that had held the chains and pulled out a long piece of silky red cloth.

Starting at the cross and working outward, he wove the bright material around the chains.

Lady Katherine's head remained high as the material transformed the dark links around her shoulders. But Kelly saw a tear run down her cheek.

"After high school, I tried to bury my depression in work. I became a distinguished chef, and I owned several successful restaurants. But it wasn't enough. After a failed suicide attempt, I started to see a counselor who was a Christian. We've met every month for the last three years, and I've been learning to trust God with my past, present and future. I'm so grateful to Sandy for introducing me to God and bringing me to this camp."

Kelly's hand flew to her mouth. Sandy was a professional counselor? Now that she thought about it, it made sense. Sandy was known for finding troubled campers and taking them out for canoe rides on the lake. Which was a pretty cool place for a counseling session. Maybe working in the kitchen as an assistant cook was the best way to spot those who were hurting. After all, that's how she'd found Kelly.

When Bill finished covering the full length of chain with the red silk, he stood beside the cross. "The abuse can't be removed. But if you release everything and everyone into God's hands, the abuse can be transformed. The Bible says that Jesus came to set the captives free. He can help you heal and reach a place of forgiveness."

"But that's not fair," Joyce spewed out.

When Kelly saw Joyce's flushed face and clenched jaw, she suddenly realized there might be a reason for every angry, negative and hostile brick in the wall Joyce had built around herself.

"No abuser should be forgiven."

Kelly agreed. Charlie's dad shouldn't just walk away. Neither should whoever had hurt Joyce. And Aaron shouldn't have the chance to force any other girl to go beyond her limits.

"You're right." Bill held Joyce's glare. "The abuser should have to undo the damage. But that's impossible. And many abusers walk free, without any consequences. But forgiveness doesn't mean giving someone a free pass. It means you let go. And you release everything into the hands of God who said in Deuteronomy 32:35 that it is His job to avenge, and He will repay. Justice may not happen on this earth. But there will come a time when God will settle every score with perfect justice."

Kelly fingered the wooden cross hanging around her neck. There had been moments when she wished she could expose Aaron as an arrogant and dangerous jerk. She'd rejected the idea. Mostly because he was too popular for it to work.

But maybe there was a better reason not to make him pay. It wasn't her responsibility. It would be better to place Aaron in God's hands. And tell the truth when it might help another innocent girl. That sounded like true freedom.

Bill walked close to the policeman. "The act of forgiveness doesn't mean we shouldn't take steps to pursue justice. Legal action may be necessary in some cases. We have an obligation to make sure this abuse doesn't happen again—to us or anyone else. That may involve making the crime public, bringing legal charges, and pursuing justice through the courts. A good counselor can help you sort through which course of action is just and responsible."

Bill motioned to Tony and Lady Katherine, and the three knelt before the cross and bowed their heads. "Let's take the first step to the cross together. Lord, we come before You, bringing the abuse that we have suffered."

Kelly heard a rustling sound and looked up to see Charlie moving down the risers, almost tripping in his haste. Apparently he'd taken Bill's offer to come to the cross literally.

Charlie stopped beside the director, then reached into his back pocket and pulled out a crumpled photograph. Kelly was too far back to see the image, but the paper looked lined and worn with creases, as if Charlie carried it with him everywhere he went. He laid the picture at the foot of the cross and knelt beside it.

Bill put a hand on Charlie's shoulder and addressed the group. "Feel free to come forward if you'd like prayer for yourself or someone you know."

Kelly's vision blurred as a few campers joined Charlie at the front. Then more came. Kelly stared at the grieving faces, knowing there was story behind each one.

She stood and moved forward to pray for Lucy. And herself.

Bill closed his eyes. "Lord, we refuse to be silenced by shame or fear. We will talk, first to You and then to other people who can help us. We bring our abuse and our abusers before You. We place them all in Your hands. Heal our wounds. We pray that You will transform our pain and set us free. Amen."

Charlie embraced Bill as if he'd never let go. Bill smiled down at him like a father proud of his son.

Tears poured down Kelly's face. She really needed a few tissues. Or a whole box. From the sniffling around the room, it sounded as if half the camp was in the same situation.

38 FUNNY HOW THINGS CHANGE

Campers crushed all around Kelly as she knelt at the foot of the cross. Now that she was closer, she could see the crumped photo that Charlie had leaned against the dark wooden beams. His father. She didn't have a picture to lay there. Neither did any of the other campers who had come forward for prayer. But they'd brought other things. Secrets. Memories. Shame. Anger. Fear. The campers laid it all before God. And so did Kelly.

"The campfire is over," Bill said softly. "We'll move on to our regular schedule now. But any campers who need to talk or pray are encouraged to remain behind."

A warm hand settled on Kelly's shoulder. She turned to see Jill behind her.

"I have a favor to ask." Jill pointed to where Emma and Terri were huddled off to the side, their arms wrapped around a weeping Joyce. "I need to talk with a few of the girls. Could you take my place as group leader and go with the others to their morning activities?"

Kelly held back a whoop of joy. She couldn't have asked for a better way to spend the last morning at camp. "But what about my maintenance job?"

"I already asked Tony. He said you'll never make up all the hours of work that you've missed this week, so you might as well take some more."

Kelly chuckled. Sounded like Tony. She should thank him for his generosity. With a bar of dark chocolate, no nuts.

"I'll find you when I'm done, and then you can go to maintenance."

"No rush." Kelly grinned.

Bob would be furious that she'd gotten out of her job again. And without even trying. Or maybe he'd gotten used to it by now.

Kelly searched the room and saw Tony talking to Bob near the back. Probably delivering the news that he'd be working alone. Bob turned and stared straight at her, his eyes narrowed and dark. She didn't know how anyone could sit through these campfires and get nothing out of them. But it appeared Bob had found a way.

She shrugged. Let him be angry. She had her beagle back and the prank was over. He couldn't do anything to her. It was his problem if he wanted to sulk.

Kelly gathered the remaining girls and led them toward the archery range. The rain had stopped, and the sun was beginning to pierce the gray clouds. In the distance, she saw a group of boys already at the hay bales, and recognized Mike's lanky frame standing off to the side.

When the girls arrived, they picked up the bows and arrows, then lined up to take turns shooting at a variety of colorful balloons attached to wooden targets. Brent, the archery instructor, motioned for Kelly and Mike to take a seat on a bench.

"The kids are testing today, so there won't be much for you to do. My assistants will help with keeping the kids in order and recording scores."

Fine by her.

Kelly plopped down beside Mike. He looked at her sideways and pulled his hat down low, as if to secure it on his head.

"Don't worry." Kelly laughed. "Your hat is safe from me."

"I'm just making sure."

"That's probably a good idea. I can't guarantee what Sheila has planned for next week. Knowing her, I suggest nailing your hat to your head."

Mike raised an eyebrow. "Aren't you staying?"

Kelly shook her head.

"You could change your mind. There's always room on maintenance and kitchen." He winked.

No surprise there. Being stuck in the kitchen would knock her out of the best parts of camp, like working with the kids in a cabin. Though Sheila still managed to get in a fair amount of trouble during her week. And Kelly could only imagine what terrible new jobs Tony would dream up if she was assigned to a second week on maintenance. Yet even as she considered the possibilities, Kelly realized it didn't change her desire to stay. In fact, the longing seemed to be growing even stronger. There was nothing to prevent her from staying. Except for one thing.

Kelly closed her eyes. Staying another week would mean watching the budding romance between Sheila and Darren. And that would be painful. But she'd never interfere or betray a friend. An image of Cindy sprang to mind, and she felt a twinge of guilt. As much as she disliked the haughty blonde, she shouldn't have tried to break-up her relationship with Joel. It was rude, hurtful and wrong. She knew she'd caused Cindy pain. Mostly because of how she'd felt when Cindy had done it back to her. She'd acted no better than any of the self-centered girls in the popular group at school. That's not who she wanted to be. And she felt ashamed.

Mike cleared his throat. "Is Marcie going to stick around for the next week?" He looked away quickly.

Kelly raised an eyebrow, suddenly suspicious. "You should ask her yourself."

"I might do that."

Mike jumped off the bale and congratulated one of his campers on a good shot. Which seemed a convenient way to hide his red face.

So despite Marcie's denials, she had caught Mike's eye. Kelly felt a thrill of joy for her friend. Marcie needed someone to make her laugh. Just like Sheila needed someone to remind her that a scar didn't matter. Things were working out well for her friends. And she was determined to be happy for them.

For the remainder of the archery lesson, Kelly cheered on the campers. Then Mike and the boys headed down to the dock for canoeing, while Kelly and the girls made their way up the road toward the vaulting arena.

Kelly climbed to the top rail of the corral and watched as each of the girls, under Joel's expert guidance, took their turn on Samson's broad back. Images of Sheila's accident replayed in her mind, and she flinched every time one of the campers wobbled while performing the basic moves.

Her mind wandered back to the picture of love that she'd drawn at the beginning of camp. Joel was her image in the flesh. But the sketch faded, and was replaced with new images. Darren shouting out crazy puns. Darren and Marvin balancing spoons on their noses. Darren wearing that ridiculous paper hat in the basketball game. Darren leaping to get between her and Samson's hooves. Darren fighting Bob for her beagle. And Darren kissing Sheila on her scarred cheek. If Bill were to ask them to do the assignment again, her picture would look very different.

Raucous noise interrupted Kelly's musing as the boys from Darren's cabin raced up to the vaulting arena. She spotted his hat among the stragglers at the back of the group, with Sheila walking close beside him.

Kelly took a deep breath as the two approached. She needed to get used to seeing them together. She made sure to give them her warmest smile as they joined her on the rails. "How did you manage to escape from the kitchen, Sheila?"

"We got the breakfast dishes done really fast today so Lady Katherine gave Marcie and me the rest of the morning off. Her Highness has really loosened up these past few days."

Kelly glanced down the road. "Where's Marcie?"

"Studying irregular Spanish verb conjugations." Sheila shrugged. "Which will be followed by working through challenging problems in Advanced Algebra. And then she'll probably practice her violin...again."

Kelly couldn't help but roll her eyes. "I got a peek at her practice book. It was filled with insults and threats. That's some strict instructor."

"Didn't you know? Her dad's her music teacher."

Kelly cringed. She'd assumed Marcie's all-consuming quest for fame and fortune came from a personal desire to be a world-famous genius. And maybe it did. Or maybe she wasn't allowed to be anything less.

Sheila gave her head a slow shake. "Her parents don't believe in having fun. They're all about hard work and reaching one's full potential. Marcie's dad didn't want her to come to camp. He said it was a waste of time unless she could earn a medal for something. He only relented because his boss told him that working at a camp looks good on a resume. And Marcie had to promise to keep up with her studies and practice violin for at least an hour a day. She's been getting up at five AM and playing in the kitchen so she won't wake me."

Kelly thought of her parents. Her mom and dad had pushed her *toward* camp, not away. They wanted Kelly to do her best, but not for success or fame. For her health and happiness. She had a lot of apologizing to do when her parents showed up.

Sheila gave Darren a playful punch. "With Marcie practicing, I couldn't stay in the room and I didn't have anything to do so Darren said I could hang out with his guys."

Sheila was bubbling over with joy. And it was wonderful to see.

"Watch me!" Marvin shouted as he climbed up onto Samson.

The small boy looked less greasy than usual. Must have finally taken a shower. But Kelly noticed something else. "Darren, can you take your hat off?"

He raised an eyebrow. But complied.

"Marvin's combing his hair just like yours."

Sheila glanced from Marvin to Darren, then laughed so hard she nearly toppled over. "You look like twins!"

Darren jammed his hat back on his head. "He started doing that this morning. He stood beside me when I was getting ready, copying every move I made."

Kelly smiled. "I think that's cool that he wants to be like you."

"He couldn't have picked a better guy to imitate!" The comment earned Darren an elbow in the ribs from Sheila. "But it gives the guys in the cabin one more reason to tease him."

Darren paused to cheer as Marvin prepared to dismount.

"The other campers have learned to tolerate Marvin's quirks, though, and he's doing a better job of fitting in. I'm going to miss him. But next week will bring a new set of kids, and there's sure to be at least one challenge in the group."

"I'll be out of the kitchen and in a cabin." Sheila raised her arms in triumph. "Bill promised I wouldn't have kitchen duty for the rest of the summer. Unless I break the rules." She gave a sly grin. "So I'll just have to be careful not to get caught."

"The Men in Hats will be on guard against whatever you're planning." Darren laughed. "You might want to be careful yourself. It's going to be hard work to top your prank, but we have a few ideas."

At the mention of possible mischief, Sheila pounced on Darren and spent the rest of the vaulting class trying to pull details out of him. Kelly listened, but didn't join in.

Darren reached around Sheila and tapped Kelly on the arm. "You should really think about staying. It's going to be a fun summer. Besides, with what we've got planned for Sheila and Marcie, they're going to need all the help they can get to survive."

Kelly's stomach turned over as she imagined all the fun she'd be missing.

Several times during the class, Joel waved at Kelly, and flashed his irresistible smile. She turned away in annoyance. He'd already dropped her once, and she wasn't going to give him a chance to do it again.

When the class finished, the girls gathered around Joel while Darren and the boys raced off down the road. Sheila hung back and helped Kelly pry the campers away from the handsome instructor and herd them toward the lodge for lunch. The campers skipped ahead while Kelly and Sheila followed at a more leisurely pace.

Sheila checked her watch. "We should stop by the room and pick up Marcie."

"Sure that's not just a good excuse to grab a Coke?" Kelly teased.

"No, I'm giving up soda."

Kelly snorted in disbelief. Then realized she hadn't seen a can in the redhead's hand since the accident. Maybe it didn't mix well with the medication.

A pickup pulled alongside them, with the horse staff piled in the back.

Joel leaned over the side. "Care for a ride?"

"No, thanks," Kelly and Sheila said in unison.

After the truck passed, Sheila sighed. "If Joel had offered me a lift a few days ago, I would have been in that truck in half a second."

And Kelly would have been right beside her. Or at least beside Joel. "Are you mad at him for the accident?"

Sheila ran her fingers lightly over the bandages on her forehead and cheek. "It wasn't his fault. I was showing off. I tried so hard to get Joel's attention, and instead I got two scars. I was such a fool."

Well, she wasn't alone. Kelly had been just as foolish when she agreed to work the lunge line. But she would have done anything to be close to Joel then, even if it wasn't the safest choice.

When they reached the staff room, Sheila frowned. "I don't hear Marcie." She pushed the door open and found the room empty. "She must have already gone to the kitchen."

Sheila turned to leave, but Kelly grabbed her arm and pointed to the garbage can in the corner, overflowing with empty Coke cans. "You drank all that in one week?"

"Nope. I poured it down the drain last night." Sheila picked up a shiny tin and sighed. "Last summer, when I was a camper, Joel bought us each a Coke at the store. He said it was his favorite drink and the perfect thing to share with someone special. We sat on the veranda for half an hour, sipping them slowly and talking about everything. And then he kissed me on the cheek when we were done. I thought that was the start of something wonderful. But the next day I saw him sharing a Coke with a different girl."

Collecting hearts for fun. That's what Jill had said. And she'd been right.

Sheila shook her head as she stared at the can. "Camp ended, and I went home. I obsessed about Joel all year, and I drank a lot of Coke. I guess I was just trying to hang on to the feelings from that special moment together."

Sheila lifted her chin and dropped the can back into the garbage. "Yesterday I decided to give up two unhealthy addictions. Drinking Coke and chasing Joel."

"Good for you." Kelly gave her friend a quick hug.

Sheila led the way out of the room. "After that night when Darren and the other Men in Hats kissed my cheek, Joel doesn't seem to matter as much."

Kelly understood. Completely. Because she felt the same.

"And then Darren said he'd fight any guy who teased me, and offered to take me to the prom. He's like my special hero, making sure I won't be hurt or alone. No one's ever said or done anything like that for me before."

Amber had once called Darren a knight in shining armor. Kelly had disagreed at the time, thinking that Amber had been reading too many romance books. Which was true. But the camper had been right. So why had it taken Kelly so long to realize his worth? Even Tony had tried to tell her. But she'd been so wrapped up chasing a blue-eyed fantasy that she'd missed the greatest catch of all.

When the girls arrived at the lodge, Sheila made her way to the kitchen while Kelly joined her campers at the table.

Jill motioned for Kelly to sit beside her. "Sorry I didn't catch up with you, but I spent the morning with Joyce. We had to make some phone calls."

Kelly glanced toward the former brick wall. Puffy red eyes hinted at a bout of heavy tears. But she seemed relaxed, and there was a softness in her smile that hadn't been there at the beginning of the week.

Kelly turned to Jill. "No problem. I had a great time at the activities."

"I'm back for the afternoon."

Which meant Kelly was back to maintenance.

After lunch, Kelly headed to the shed. And walked right into the middle of a heated argument.

"She's stronger than she looks, you know," Bob protested.

"You're mowing around the picnic tables, and that's final," Tony growled. "I have other jobs for Kelly."

"Did someone mention my name?" she asked.

Bob scowled. "If Kelly can't handle the mowing on her own, maybe her lover-boy Darren will come to her rescue and do it for her."

Bob's comments stung. Mostly because it was so far from the truth.

Tony raised his eyebrows. "Something I should know?"

Kelly glared at Bob. "You want your other eye black and blue too?"

Tony raised his hands. "That's enough, you two. Bob, mow the grass. Kelly, clean the girls' bathrooms."

They both groaned, then headed their separate ways.

Kelly spent the afternoon scrubbing sinks and showers. And replaying Bob's comment about Darren. He was clearly connected to Sheila. But even if he did like her, she couldn't pursue him without hurting her friend.

Turning her thoughts from Darren, she focused on Amber's comment about the huge size of Sandy's Super Special Sundaes and the idea that had popped into her head. She'd need Sandy's help to pull it off. Hopefully, she'd be easier to bribe than Tony.

After wiping the mirrors with renewed energy, she ran off to the lodge to find her.

That evening, as Kelly entered the dining hall for supper, she noticed that every table except hers had a tray of sugar cookies on it. They didn't need them. As winners of the Clean Cabin Contest, Kelly's cabin would be served massive bowls of ice cream after dinner.

When the campers had finished eating their meal, Bill rang a brass bell attached to a wall behind the serving counter. No more banging a spoon on the counter. Bill had finally gotten his wish.

"It's time for the contest winners to get their just desserts!" Everyone groaned at the pun.

Sandy marched out of the kitchen, carrying a tray loaded with bowls of marshmallows, gummy bears, peanuts, chocolate chips, Oreo cookies, gumdrops, and M&Ms. As she passed tables, campers nearly fell off the benches as they reached toward her, begging for a bite. Sandy dodged the outstretched arms and placed the tray in the middle of Jill and Kelly's table.

Sheila, Marcie, and Charlie, decked out in their French waiter outfits, came out of the kitchen, each balancing a large tray with several dishes of ice cream. When they reached the table, Sandy handed a bowl to each girl except Kelly. With a wink, she placed three smaller bowls in front of Kelly. Kelly gave her a grateful nod.

Sandy clapped her hands several times. "The contest rules state that the winning cabin receives one sundae per person. However, I was approached earlier today with a special request. There are two individuals at camp who performed an act of great kindness and rescued something very important to one of our counselors. This counselor asked if her bowl of ice cream could be divided into three dishes so she could present the sundaes as a token of her appreciation and gratitude. Her wish has been granted."

Sandy held the two extra bowls high in the air. "Darren! Marvin! Come make your sundaes!"

Marvin's forehead furrowed in confusion. Darren whispered in his ear, and a look of realization lit up his face. The little camper's chest puffed out. Waving his arms to the jealous campers all around him, he strutted across the room like a young rooster and grabbed one of the bowls.

"This is awesome!" Marvin elbowed his way between Joyce and Jill and scooped heaping spoonfuls of every topping onto his ice cream.

Kelly grimaced at Marvin's towering mountain of sweet treats. If he managed to eat the whole thing, he'd be sure to collapse in a sugar coma.

Darren came up behind Marvin and placed a hand on the small camper's shoulders. "Make sure you leave some toppings for everyone else."

Marvin sputtered an apology, then grinned as Darren ruffled his hair. He swaggered back to his table, shoving huge bites into his mouth and grinning with candy-crusted teeth at the campers watching him with envious eyes.

Darren gestured to his bowl. "This is really great, Kelly, but you already thanked us."

"Not enough. You rescued my beagle, and that means a lot to me."

"I know. That's why we did it."

Kelly looked into his golden brown eyes, and couldn't speak. She simply nodded.

After Marvin and Darren returned to their table, Amber grinned at Kelly. "Your face is red."

She placed her hands over her warm cheeks. "Oh, that always happens when I eat ice cream."

Amber rolled her eyes. "You haven't taken a bite yet."

Kelly pinched Amber on the arm, then turned to the ice cream. She'd solved two problems at once–paying off Marvin and Darren while reducing the size of her serving to a more manageable portion. And if she couldn't have Darren as a boyfriend, she was glad to have him as a friend.

Kelly took a spoon, dug it into the round scoop of strawberry ice cream, and took a bite. It tasted even better than she'd imagined.

39 STOP SIGN

A lump formed in Kelly's throat as she settled in beside Amber on the risers for the last evening campfire. Kelly spotted the worn and creased figures of Girl and Guy in their usual spot, leaning against the side of the fireplace. She hoped this was going to be a gentle campfire. A rough message just might finish off the cardboard couple.

Amy and Stan led the singing, and campers shouted requests for their favorite silly songs. Kelly joined the girls from her cabin as they tried to keep up with the rapid hand motions to one of the faster tunes. Amber's frantic flailing had Kelly laughing so hard she could hardly breathe. She'd miss these wonderful girls, especially Amber.

As the sky grew dark and the songs turned worshipful, Kelly listened to the praise coming from the lips of the kids around her. She wasn't naïve enough to think that every camper had turned to God or had a life-changing experience this week. But they'd heard truth. Been challenged. And had a lot of fun. And despite her reluctance at the beginning of the week, so had she.

As the last song ended, Bill carried Guy and Girl to the front of the fireplace and connected ties between them.

He put an arm around the familiar pair. "This is a special night for our cardboard couple. Guy has invited Girl to watch a movie at his house. His parents are gone for the evening. When she arrives, the lights are turned down low. Soft music is playing. Our couple cuddles on the couch. Guy puts his arm around Girl, pulls her close, and they share their first..."

"Kiss!" The campers' shouts were followed by a thunder of hoots and hollers.

Bill leaned the figures toward each other and mashed their flat faces together.

Everyone roared in laughter at the ridiculous smooch. Kelly chuckled. If someone had told her a week ago that she'd be applauding a cardboard kiss, she would never have believed it.

She remembered her first kiss with Aaron, and the many that followed. She'd felt so close to him.

Bill pulled the paper pair apart, reached into his back pocket, and pulled out two white bandanas. He fastened them over the eyes of Guy and Girl, then turned to the campers. "Any idea why these two are wearing blindfolds after their kiss?"

Mike raised his arm. "They're going to play a game of 'Pin the Tail on the Donkey'!"

Kelly joined the campers as they applauded. Mike was never one to miss an opportunity, and this would be one of the last. At least for this week. She wondered if he'd pull the same jokes out next week, or come up with new ones. There was one way to find out. A simple conversation with Bill or MaryAnn was all it would take to sign up. Which she could do after the campfire. And she just might.

Bill gave Mike a thumbs-up. "Good try, but wrong answer. Girl and Guy aren't going to play any games that require cloth tied around their heads. Any other guesses?"

Bill was met with blank stares and silence. "When couples kiss, they usually close their eyes."

Mike waved his hand wildly in the air. "I know an animal that doesn't close its eyes when it kisses."

"Must be a *Peking* duck." Darren flapped his elbows like wings.

Kelly laughed along with everyone else. It wouldn't feel right to have a final campfire without at least a couple of comic routines from Mike and Darren.

The camp director shook his head in mock disapproval. "I'm limiting you guys to one joke tonight. And that was it."

The campers booed Bill's announcement while the two friends rose, swept their hats from their heads, and waved to their appreciative fans.

Bill's limit might stop the puns, but Kelly doubted Mike could stay quiet unless someone taped his mouth shut. And even that might not work.

Bill motioned for the boys to take their seats. "Once our couple shares a kiss, it's as if they put on a blindfold. They don't see each other's personalities clearly because they are blinded by physical passion. That's a problem, because our couple needs to be learning as much as possible about each other."

Bill put his fingers to his lips and let out a piercing whistle. Tony, Sandy, and MaryAnn rushed to the front, arms loaded with an assortment of props. MaryAnn unrolled a long gray carpet with a dotted yellow dividing line down the middle. When she stretched it across the length of the room, it looked like she'd just built a highway in the lodge. Tony and Sandy set up six metal signs, each covered with a dark plastic bag, spaced about a foot apart along the length of the new street.

If Kelly had to guess, she'd say that Guy and Girl were about to go on a trip. Destination unknown.

Bill placed the cardboard cutouts at the beginning of the highway. "Our couple has taken the first step on the path of physical pleasure. Let's take a look at where they're headed."

Leaving the couple behind, Bill walked to the opposite end of the road. With a dramatic yank, he ripped the bag off the last sign, revealing a single word, written in dark, bold lettering. Sex.

Stunned silence was followed by nervous laughter and uncomfortable squirming. Kelly felt an overwhelming desire to run from the room. And take Girl with her.

"It was only a little kiss," Mike complained.

"Yes, it was just a kiss," Bill said. "But you can't stop with just one. Not for long."

It was true. The moment Kelly and Aaron had shared their first kiss, he'd started pushing for the second. And then far more.

Bill returned to stand beside Girl and Guy, propped by the first street sign. He removed the bag from the traffic marker and asked the campers to read along with him. "Holding hands." A few steps brought him to the next sign. "Hugging." A few more paces to the third. "Kissing and making out." Bill revealed the fourth sign. "Touching private areas under clothes". Then "Taking off clothes."

Kelly heard some nervous giggling, but Bill's straightforward approach left little room for laughter. Most of the campers stared straight ahead, not making eye contact with anyone. A few studied the ground. No one shouted out any comments. Not even Mike.

Bill pointed to the line of signs. "If you've watched television, movies, or music videos, you've seen this path traveled many times. Very quickly."

Kelly knew that Aaron had been down most of that path. Of course, it was a well-worn route for him. That was part of what made him so attractive—his edgy reputation for being cool, experienced and smooth. But now she saw him for what he was: a selfish player who manipulated girls to get what he wanted.

Bill tapped on the metal sign. "A lot of young people think that as long as they use some form of protection against pregnancy or sexually transmitted diseases, they can enjoy all the sex they want."

There was a lot of talk amongst the girls of the popular group. Lots of bragging, to be more accurate. But no one ever talked about protection. And when the occasional girl did get pregnant, no one asked if they'd taken any precaution. Or pointed out that whatever they'd used had failed.

Bill motioned to the back of the room. MaryAnn came forward, carrying a red stop sign, which she handed to her husband. "God created every sensual part of our bodies, and He intended for sex to be enjoyed. But He draws a clear boundary line for when this should happen."

At school the only warning Kelly heard was about a condom or birth control pills. Her church's pastor had placed a far different boundary: no sex until you're married. But he'd been unclear about what was allowed along the road up to that point. With the lack of guidance and no fixed limits of her own, it had been easy for Aaron to push Kelly farther than she felt comfortable.

Bill carried the stop sign to the end of the road and placed it in front of the final metal marker that read "Sex." "The Bible tells us that sex is to be saved for marriage. God didn't make that rule to stop us from having fun. He did it because the best decision is to wait."

If Kelly's friends at school heard that, they'd laugh. Even some of the ones who went to church. It was old-fashioned to wait for marriage before sleeping together. Sex was expected. Assumed.

Bill scanned the crowd. "I can tell most of you aren't convinced. So let's talk about the dangers of sex before marriage."

Tony strode forward, set up a chart on an easel, and pulled out his pen.

"What should we put on the list?" Bill asked.

One of the campers shouted out, "You could get an STD."

Bill nodded. "Most of you have learned about sexually transmitted diseases in school. They can have unpleasant and even debilitating physical symptoms. Many are incurable and some are deadly. And if you have one, every future partner will be exposed and put at risk of catching it as well."

At least Bill didn't pull out any pictures. The ones Kelly had seen in health class at school had been stomach-turning, for her and the other groaning students. Although that effect seemed lost once students left the class.

A female camper waved her hand. "Even if a couple uses birth control, the girl can still get pregnant."

"That's right. And if that happens, she'll face three options. She can end the baby's life through abortion, keep the baby and raise it herself, or give up the baby for adoption. Each choice has its own consequences, although we don't have time right now to expound on each of these options. However, I do want to make one point. I strongly believe that every child, no matter how they were conceived, is a gift of God. If the mother is unable to care for that child, it is her responsibility to find others who can. The possibility of a pregnancy is a matter to consider very seriously. No matter what decision is made, creating life will change your life."

For the girl, anyway. As far as Kelly could tell, the guys got to live a normal life. She'd heard of a few young dads who took their children on the weekend. Or helped with some expenses. So maybe they hadn't gotten off completely free. But it still seemed unfair.

Bill considered the list. "The physical risks of sex before marriage are typically the only consequences mentioned. But there are emotional factors that are often neglected. Having sex doesn't mean the other person loves you or respects you. And there's no protection from guilt, fear, and shame."

Kelly had thought Aaron cared about her. Maybe even loved her. But he'd only said romantic things to get what he wanted. He sweet-talked her into doing his schoolwork. Giving up all her activities so she could attend his. And giving him the keys to the new car so they could take it on a joyride. She felt stupid for believing him.

Bill pulled a thin golden ribbon out of his pocket and held it up. "Sharing love in a physical manner creates a tie. But it's not a strong tie. It's more like a fragile thread. Physical intimacy isn't meant to be the first tie, and it certainly isn't strong enough to be the only tie in a romantic relationship. It's insulting when someone wants the tie of sex without any others. Our couple needs the safety and protection of a commitment before having sex. Not living together, but an exclusive, permanent commitment. That can only come through marriage."

Bill considered the shimmering cord for a few moments before folding it back into his pocket. "Our couple isn't ready for marriage yet. So they're not ready for sex. And that means this isn't a good place for our stop sign." Bill picked up the red hexagon. "If Guy and Girl enjoy all the physical activities that lead up to sex and then try to slam on the brakes, odds are good they won't stop. If they don't want to go too far, they need to set the boundaries a lot earlier."

Bill carried the stop sign to the front of the road and placed it before the marker labeled "Holding Hands."

Mike groaned. "Are you saying we can't make out at all?"

Bill tapped on the sign. "At the beginning of their dating relationship, a couple shouldn't do anything physical. Not even hand holding."

A rumble of protests rose from the campers. Kelly's friends back home would have scoffed at such a strict set of rules. Well, maybe not all of them.

"After several months of dating, our couple will probably move on to hand holding, cuddling, and light kissing. In my opinion, that's where the physical contact needs to stop. I know that seems limited. But it will keep them from walking too far down that path."

Bill held up a devotional binder. "When your counselors give you the notes from this campfire for your devotion Wallets, they will be including a list of fun ideas that you and your date can do. Activities other than kissing."

"I'd rather kiss," Mike shouted.

"Your girl might prefer to have a gingerbread house competition or a baking contest. She may want to play a board game with stakes on the outcome–maybe the loser has to wash the dog. She might choose bowling, with the rule that you can't throw the ball with your dominant hand. Or she may decide on eating at a Chinese restaurant–with only chopsticks. Or do something that neither of you does well."

Kelly wished she'd had a list like that when she was dating Aaron. It got boring only going to movies and parties. And the only other thing Aaron wanted to do was make out.

Tony strode forward, carrying a large wooden ramp. He slipped it under the carpet about midway down the road, creating a sharp slope.

Bill gestured to the incline. "Certain activities are like steep hills. They'll cause our couple to gain speed and lose control. If our Guy and Girl don't want to travel too far down the road of physical intimacy, they need to avoid things like dirty jokes, crude conversations, and wearing revealing clothing. Most teen girls choose sexy clothes because they believe looking hot helps attract boyfriends or keep the ones they have. Yet they're surprised when they end up with guys who are more interested in their bodies than their personalities."

Kelly bit her lip. Her wardrobe had changed since dating Aaron. Skirts got higher and necklines got lower. Aaron's long and low wolf whistles expressed his approval of the skimpy, revealing clothing. And she'd wanted him to be attracted to her. But she'd meant all of her, not just her figure.

Bill added a street sign showing a slippery slope. "The only thing more dangerous than a sharp decline is an icy one. That's what happens when you go to sexually-themed movies, listen to explicit music lyrics, or take alcohol or drugs. Each of these activities will cause our couple to travel faster and farther than they intend."

Aaron had offered Kelly alcohol multiple times, but she didn't like the stuff. Or the way Aaron had pushed her to drink it.

Bill's gaze swept the room. "I'd like all of the males in the room to rise."

The boys slowly stood to their feet.

"I want to speak to the guys about a danger that particularly affects males. Pornography."

The guys squirmed. So did many of the girls. Kelly thought of Amber's steamy romance novels. They were a popular choice among her friends at school and seemed like innocent fun. But the plots revolved around sex and the bedroom scenes, though illustrated with words, were just as graphic as any nude photo. None of her friends would ever consider those books as pornographic. But it certainly seemed like similar material wrapped in a different package.

"I can't warn you strongly enough to avoid all forms of pornography: pictures, magazines, videos. Porn is highly destructive and addictive. It will warp how you see women and view sex, and that will damage every romantic relationship you have. There is no way to count the number of individuals, and their marriages and families, that have been destroyed because of pornography."

More uncomfortable shifting among the standing males. Out of embarrassment? Guilt? Maybe both.

"Understand that guys are visual and hormonal desires are powerful. It's the way that we're wired. Many guys stumble into viewing pornographic images accidentally. Their curiosity is piqued, and there is a natural pleasure in seeing the pictures. The desires aren't wrong. However, choosing to satisfy those normal passions through the fantasy world of pornography will turn them into deformed desires. Make no mistake. Pornography is a self-centered thief that portrays women as objects to be used, stealing the joy of authentic love and intimacy."

Looking at pornography was normal in school. Just typical, expected behavior. Kids even pulled it up on cell phones in class. Aaron had showed her some of the pictures on his phone once, and she had been shocked at how raunchy they'd been. He promised to delete the images. And then joked that it was time for new ones anyway.

Bill continued. "Even though it may begin with a purely physical motive, viewing pornography can become a coping mechanism to deal with stress, loneliness, boredom, insecurity, anxiety and fear of failure. What started with innocent curiosity becomes a distraction, then a mechanism to escape from negative feelings, and ends up as an addiction. But the momentary enjoyment is outweighed by the guilt, shame and damage that follow."

Kelly leaned forward slightly. This was something new. She'd always thought that pornography was strictly about dirty pictures. Not a way to minimize difficult emotions.

Bill let his gaze wander slowly across the room, making eye contact with each of the boys. Not in an accusing manner. But sympathetic and reassuring. "In order to break the addiction, it will be critical to identify activities or situations that are your weak points. The best way to break a dangerous habit is to replace it with a good one. Come up with alternative ways to deal with the triggers in your life. If you have to block certain phone number or apps, or put your computer in a public place, make the necessary changes. Find a mentor, counsellor or a trusted person who will provide support and encouragement. You can escape from the trap of pornography by changing your habits, rewiring your brain, and finding a support group. This will protect your future relationships so that you can love the whole person, and not lust after an impossible fantasy."

Kelly lifted her chin. She didn't want to be reduced to just a body. But hadn't she already done that to herself, striving so hard to attain the perfect physical image? But not anymore. She wanted to be loved for who she was as a whole person, her strengths as well as her flaws.

Bill motioned for the boys to take a seat. Then he turned his focus back to the whole group.

"In the next set of Wallet notes, I'm going to give everyone an assignment. Think about the boundaries you want to set. Write them down. Pray over them. Think about how you'll handle tempting situations and what you'll do if you slip past your own boundaries. Part of the assignment will be to ask a parent, mentor, leader, coach or pastor to help keep you accountable to the standards you've set."

Her parents would be thunderstruck if she asked them to keep tabs on her! However, considering the huge mess she'd created, she could have used their guidance. And the same was true for Lucy. If her friend had someone to talk to about her relationship with Logan, she might have made different choices. Avoided the parties, the drugs, and stayed in school.

Bill's expression softened. "Some of you have already passed this stop sign. The Bible has a story for you. It's about a woman who was caught with a man who wasn't her husband. Her accusers took her to Jesus and demanded the death penalty. Jesus said that whoever had no sin could throw the first stone. Then he wrote something in the sand. Whatever he wrote caused the woman's accusers to leave. When they were alone, Jesus told the woman that he didn't condemn her, and she should go forward and leave her life of sin."

Kelly had heard the story before, but never really thought about it. Never really thought what it might mean for the campers. Or even for herself.

"If you've already gone too far in intimacy, I want to pass along the same message to you. Jesus has forgiven you. Completely. Now, go and live differently."

That's what Kelly planned to do. Live differently. She was going to pick friends because she liked them, not to be popular. She was going to stop obsessing about her outward looks and worry about her inward heart. And she was going to pick her next boyfriend based on *character*, not on looks.

But that wasn't enough. At the start of camp, she'd had a desire to make a difference in the lives of the campers. And now that same desire filled her as she thought of her friends back home. To tell Lucy that she could live differently. And Annalisa. And any others who might listen.

Bill removed the blindfolds from Girl and Guy. "We haven't added a word to our list of New Romantic and Sexy Words for a while. I'd like to add two now. These are traits that are critical when you set boundaries for physical intimacy. You're going to need a *strategy* and *self-control*."

Tony flipped through the chart until he came to the list of words. He added the new terms, *strategy* and *self-control*, underlining both several times.

"That completes our campfire," Bill said. "You may stand and stretch. But don't go anywhere yet. We have a special event planned for our final evening."

The campers burst into cheers, but Kelly remained silent. She wasn't going to applaud yet. Not until she found out whether Bill's surprise activity was messy, embarrassing, or dangerous. Or all of the above.

40 EVERYONE KNOWS

If Bill hoped to whip the campers into a frenzy, his announcement of a special event for the final evening worked perfectly.

Campers shouted questions, and Bill had to raise his hand for several minutes before the kids finally quieted down.

"Tonight we're going to hold a staff hunt."

The campers roared even louder. Kelly didn't know what that meant, but it didn't sound good. At least not for the staff.

"Counselors will have twenty minutes to run outside and hide. The boundaries for the hunt will be the front of the lodge, the back of the cabins, the fence on the left, and the lake on the right. Hiding inside buildings or vehicles is off limits."

That didn't give the staff much room to take cover. Not with close to a hundred campers swarming over every inch of the facility.

Bill tapped his watch. "Campers will have forty-five minutes to nab as many staff members as they can. Once a camper spots a counselor, he or she will shout out the name and hiding spot. If a correct call is made, the counselor will return with the camper to the deck of the lodge. If the information is wrong, the counselor can escape and try to hide again. I'll be awarding a five-dollar store coupon for each arrest. Any staff members who evade capture will receive a five-dollar coupon once the hunt is over."

Amber tugged on Kelly's sleeve. "If you let me catch you, I'll split the reward."

"Forget it!" Kelly laughed. She preferred the glory of evading capture. If she could.

"Can we use flashlights?" asked a camper.

"No. We'll turn on all exterior lights on buildings. With the moonlight, there should be enough visibility."

"Can the counselors change clothes or use props?" Mike shouted.

"Sure." Bill pointed to the door. "But the clock starts ticking...now."

In a mad scramble, the staff leaped to their feet and rushed out of the building through every exit. Having no idea where to go, Kelly followed a group of counselors who were rushing into the sparse woods bordering the lake.

As the group thundered along the path like frenzied elephants, Kelly realized that staying with the herd would be a liability. She slowed and let the others get ahead of her. If she was going to avoid capture, she needed to think. Sometimes the simplest hiding spot was the best one.

Leaving the trail, Kelly plunged into the bush, ignoring the branches that whipped her face. There wasn't much cover, but she crouched behind the largest clump of bushes she could find and tried to quiet her heavy breathing.

Seconds later, she heard tromping along the path. It couldn't be the campers already. It had to be another staff member. And a clumsy one at that.

Kelly crouched deeper in the undergrowth, biting her lip as the intruder crawled through the brush straight toward her. As if he or she was expecting to hide in her spot!

"Go somewhere else!" she hissed. "This spot is taken."

A thunderous sound came from the direction of the lodge. It wasn't hard to guess what had just happened. The campers had been released. Which left her fellow fugitive with little chance to find a new spot.

Her unwanted companion kept crawling until he or she was nearly beside her. Kelly squinted, trying to identify who it was. But the only feature she could clearly discern was an oddly-shaped hood pulled over the head of the mystery staff member.

"Is that you, Kelly?"

She didn't recognize the muffled voice. And it was foolish to talk.

Campers erupted in shouting, probably celebrating their first capture. Since they still seemed to be concentrated near the lodge, Kelly took a risk and answered. "Yes, it's Kelly. Who are you?"

"Darren."

Kelly's heart pounded so loud she was sure they'd be captured next. She peered closely at her companion. Of course. The hood appeared bulky because of the hat underneath.

"I followed you because I have to tell you something before camp is over, and I don't know if I'll get another chance." He spoke so quietly she barely caught the words.

Kelly felt a thrill run through her whole body. Darren wanted to be alone with her. To tell her something important. Something just for her.

"You're a hot babe, and I've got feelings for you."

Time seemed to stop. Everything but that moment faded away. One shining thought remained. He liked her. Beyond hope, beyond expectation. The words raced around in her mind, leaving her dizzy with joy. Darren liked her!

Kelly's heart thundered in her chest, though she had a nagging moment of doubt. She'd never heard him call anyone a "hot babe". But she clung to the sweet words that came after. Darren had feelings for her!

A mob of campers came rushing down the path near their hiding spot. They stomped through the brush, randomly calling staff names, trying to flush out any counselors foolish enough to fall for their bluff. The campers plunged past without spotting Kelly or Darren.

She had to say something. This might be her only chance to let Darren know how she felt. Kelly took a deep breath, grateful for the darkness that hid her burning face. "I think you're amazing. I can't stop thinking about you. I like you more than anyone I've ever known."

Kelly heard something that sounded like choking. Was he crying?

A lone camper came running down the path and stopped near them. Kelly crouched low. But Darren's muffled hacking sound gave away their location. The camper moved closer and cried out, "Kelly and Bob in the bushes!"

She'd been caught. And the private moment ruined. But at least the camper called the wrong name for Darren. He had a chance to hide again.

Kelly stood, arms raised in surrender. She stepped to the side so Darren could escape. Instead he struggled to his feet, turned to face her, and burst into hysterical laughter.

The camper had been right. It was Bob.

Kelly's breath came in short, painful gasps. What a jerk. She wanted to scream at him. Attack him. Give him another black eye. But she couldn't do any of that, not with a camper standing there.

Bob pulled the hood from his head, revealing his fancy snapback cap. "I was following you to make sure you got caught. And you did. But I never thought I'd get such juicy information."

Even in the dim light, Kelly could see his lip curl in a sneer.

"I'm sure Darren will be happy to hear the good news about your little crush on him."

There was nothing she could say. But there was something she could do. Kelly gave Bob a huge shove that sent him sprawling backward. He lay on the ground, rolling over with laughter.

Kelly started to bolt, but the camper grabbed her arm.

"You have to come with me."

Bob snickered the whole way back to the lodge. Kelly dragged her feet, wishing the ground would open up and swallow her. Or at least consume Bob.

When they reached the lodge, the camper turned them in, collected his coupons, and went out to hunt again. From the crowd on the deck of the lodge, it looked like at least half of the staff members had been caught. Kelly joined them, trying to put as much distance as possible between herself and Bob. But she couldn't escape the dread of what would happen next. How could she have been so stupid? She'd just lost everything. She'd botched any chance of a friendship with Darren. And Sheila would be sure to hate her. Rightly so.

Bob strolled around the deck, smirking every time he caught her eye. But he didn't say anything. That gave Kelly no comfort. She knew his silence was only temporary. Her mind raced, trying to find some way to avoid what was about to happen. Maybe if she acted casual and relaxed, Bob might think she wasn't really bothered by what she'd said. Except she'd shoved him into the bushes. And shot dirty looks at him all the way to the lodge. He'd never buy it. Her mind continued to race. When Bob finally blabbed, she could deny what she'd said. But would anyone–including Sheila–believe her?

Kelly shivered, and tried to distract herself with a nearby conversation. Mike was telling the captured staff members how he'd jumped into an empty black trash bag and hidden among several similar bags stacked beside the lodge. "If I hadn't sneezed, the campers never would have found me," he bragged.

Jill and another counselor confessed to being the first to be captured. They'd been lying flat on top of the lodge veranda, but gave themselves away when Jill accidently kicked down a few acorns.

Kelly stood in the shadows, arms wrapped around herself, listening to the counselors tell their stories. Waiting for Bob to tell his. And ruin her life.

Bill blew a whistle and called everyone still hunting or hiding to come to the deck. Five staff members had escaped detection. Darren and Charlie, dressed in green and black camouflage, were among the last to arrive. They boasted how they'd climbed a tall tree and relaxed as they watched the action below.

Bill counted the staff. "Where's Tony?"

A sudden pounding under their feet caused everyone to jump. With dirt and dust clinging to every inch of him, Tony rolled out from under the lodge steps. He'd been hiding directly beneath them the entire time. Obvious and brilliant. He received the applause that was his due. And a coupon.

Bob turned to Kelly and gave a malicious wink.

"Please," she whispered, holding his gaze. "Don't do this."

He faltered for a moment. Then shook his head. "Hey, Darren, there's something you should know! Kelly has a little confession to make."

There was nothing Kelly could do to stop him. So she fled to the cabin, threw herself onto her bunkbed, and started punching her pillow.

Amber appeared a few minutes later. "Don't worry. It will all be forgotten by morning."

Kelly snorted. Good thing she hadn't asked Bill if she could sign up for another week. That would have given Bob unlimited opportunities to torment her. There was no way she was going to volunteer for that humiliation now.

Reaching under her bunk, Kelly pulled out her suitcase and snatched the calendar. She hadn't crossed off any days since Thursday. She slashed dark lines through all the days she'd missed. The end couldn't come fast enough. The girls began to trickle through the door, and the room filled with the usual late-night banter as the campers prepared for bed. No one said anything to Kelly about the incident, although she did catch a few furtive glances in her direction.

Before turning off the lights, Jill walked over to Kelly and gave her a big hug. "Bob's a total creep," she whispered. "Darren told him to shut up or he'd give him another back eye."

Kelly gave a weak smile. She'd like to see Bob with a second shiner. But if Darren waited one more day, she'd be on her way home and would miss it.

41 KNOTS AND RIBBONS

Kelly reached under her pillow to turn off her alarm clock. The memories of the previous night rushed upon her, and she pulled the covers over her head. She couldn't bear the thought of seeing Darren. Or Bob. Or anyone else. Now that Bob had told everyone how he'd tricked her into confessing her interest in Darren, she'd be the laughingstock of the camp. And she'd probably lost Sheila's friendship. Which felt even worse than all the other humiliations.

Kelly tossed and turned for several minutes, unable to fall back to sleep. With a muffled sigh, she sat up. Might as well get up and go for a run. Bill should've already finished his prayer walk by now, and that would leave the road clear for her.

A fast-paced jog might help clear her head. And all she had to do was tough it out for the next few hours, then she'd be on her way home. Leaving the awkward mess behind.

Kelly dressed quietly, then slipped out of the cabin into the cool air. She stood for a moment, basking in the stillness and the soft glow of the waking world.

After a few stretches, she headed down the well-worn dirt path to the paved road. She jogged to the turnaround point and was on her way back when she saw Bill coming up the road. Apparently he'd had an even later morning than she did.

A knot of anxiety grew in the pit of her stomach. Bill had been on the porch last night when Bob started blabbing. Which meant he'd heard everything. The last thing she wanted was to talk about it.

Kelly didn't slow down as she jogged toward Bill, hoping he'd just let her pass by. Instead, he held up his hand.

Kelly was tempted to blow right past him. But that would be rude. Childish. And cowardly. She had to face the situation. Might as well start now.

Bill turned and started back toward camp, motioning for Kelly to join him. She held back a groan. And wished that she'd stayed in her bunk.

"I asked Jill how you did this week. She said you were the best assistant counselor she's ever had."

A safe topic. Kelly relaxed at the compliment. "Jill's a great counselor. And we had an awesome group of girls."

"She asked if you could stay together. I told her that you only signed up for one week. If you're willing to stay, we could sure use your help."

Kelly took a deep breath. "I've been thinking about that, actually. But now...I don't know."

Bill grinned. "I hope you're not going to let Bob's little trick last night influence your decision."

"He's such a—" Kelly sputtered. She bit her lip to prevent an inappropriate word from escaping her mouth.

"I know." Bill chuckled. "But don't let your wounded pride affect your choice of whether or not to stay."

Pride? It wasn't—

Kelly hated it when Bill was right.

"So, how are you and God getting along these days?"

"Not too bad." Kelly smiled. "I said a prayer the other morning, and I haven't done that in a long time."

Bill stooped to pick up a few rocks, then slung them at the fence posts. "Starting next week, I'm going to hold early-morning prayer walks down this road for any counselors who are interested in building the habit of prayer. I'd love to have you join us—if you choose to stay."

Kelly imagined walking beside Bill, learning from him how to talk to God. She'd have to give up her morning jog. But maybe it was time she concentrated on building some spiritual muscle instead.

"I'd have to check with my mom. But I'm pretty sure she'd be thrilled."

"If it's all right with her, I really think you should stay." Bill winked. "After all, Tony says you owe him a few days on maintenance."

Kelly spun her head to see if Bill was serious. The laugh lines around his eyes told her otherwise.

Bill's joke reminded her of something she'd been meaning to ask since the beginning of the week. "On the first day of camp, you let me out of kitchen duty. Why?"

"I saw the panic in your eyes. I was afraid you'd run down the road and straight out of camp."

She'd considered it.

"I decided that having you stay with a heart that was open to listen was more important than having you in the kitchen."

The camp entrance loomed in front of them. "Let me know when you decide." With a wave, Bill trotted off toward his house.

Kelly drifted toward the cabin, feeling as if her mind was engaged in a fierce tug-of-war. The advantages to staying had a lot of weight behind them. She'd already decided to walk away from Aaron and most of the popular group, but wouldn't mind putting that off for another week. And as eager as she now was to get back in touch with her neglected church friends and work on a more authentic friendship with Annalisa and Lucy, that could also wait. Most important of all, another week would help her grow in her faith. And she'd need that to stay strong when she got home.

The choice to stay seemed to have won...until she imagined the faces pulling on the other side. Volunteering for another week meant putting up with Bob's mockery. It also meant facing Darren. And a necessary but humbling attempt to explain things to Sheila—which was the scariest of all.

For now, she hoped everyone else at camp would be so focused on this being the final day they wouldn't even remember what happened last night. And next week, there would be a new set of campers who wouldn't know the story. Until Bob told them.

Kelly joined the girls from her cabin as they walked down to breakfast. Jill gave her an overly cheerful greeting. The campers looked at her shoes, her shorts, her T-shirt, everywhere except her eyes. Jill probably warned them not to say anything.

As they neared the dining hall, Kelly ignored the fingers that pointed her way and the accompanying snickers. She kept her gaze focused forward, even when she heard several versions of the childish chant "Kelly and Darren sitting in a tree."

At the lodge, Kelly kept her head down as much as possible, even though that meant bumping into a few counters and campers. She dreaded the serving line, certain she'd run in to Sheila there. Would she be furious that Kelly had tried to steal her guy? Or would she be silent and cold, ready to drop their friendship?

Sheila wasn't out front serving food. Kelly caught a glimpse of her through the swinging kitchen doors, washing dishes at the back counter. So she was spared the confrontation, at least for now.

At the table, Kelly stared at her bowl of cereal. Untouched–not by choice but because her stomach felt like it was tied in a huge knot. She scanned the room for Darren and Bob, ready to plot the easiest way to avoid them. She spotted Darren at his table, his back to her. Bob was lounging at a staff table. He caught her glance and winked at her before she could look away. Moron.

Breakfast seemed to last forever. When Bill dismissed the campers for morning devotions, she was the first to rush out the door.

Back at the cabin, the girls took their places in the circle. Kelly relaxed a little. So far, so good. Just a few more hours and she'd be on her way home. She didn't want to go. But she couldn't go through a whole week trying to dodge Bob and Darren, and feeling guilty every time she saw Sheila. She'd be a complete wreck. No matter how Kelly tried to work it out, she just couldn't see how she could stay.

Jill passed out the binders and a typed set of notes. "This is the list of creative date activities that Bill mentioned last night."

Kelly forced herself to focus on the devotion. As she added the pages, she marveled at the thickness of her binder. Bill had covered as much work in a week at camp as she did in a month for some of her classes at school.

"And this is the new set for this morning." Jill passed out more paper.

Kelly stared at the top page. Blank except for the title, which simply read, "The Knot."

"Why isn't there a picture?" asked Joyce.

"Turn to the next page and you'll find out."

A flurry of flipped pages was followed by excited squeals. The sketch that encompassed the entire page showed Guy on his knees, holding out a small box with a ring in it. Tears flowed down Girl's smiling face.

"I don't get it," complained Emma.

"He's proposing!" Joyce shouted at her. But in a nice way. At least for Joyce.

"That's right," Jill said. "And in case you're wondering, she said yes."

The girls cheered. A few hummed the Wedding March. Kelly grinned as she imagined how differently the boys were probably reacting.

The next page showed the familiar picture of Guy and Girl, connected by ties. But this time the ties were fastened around their wrists with a great big knot.

Jill read from the notes. "Through marriage, our couple has bound their lives together for as long as they both shall live. They're knotted to each other for better or for worse, for richer or poorer, in sickness and in health. This commitment is their first priority and it supersedes all others."

Joyce stared at the floor. "My mom and dad never got married. They were living together when they had me. My dad left before my first birthday."

So much pain in a young girl's life. No wonder she'd built a brick wall around herself.

"It's not going to last," Terri muttered. "Girl should sell the ring and at least get some money. That's what my mom did."

The stories kept coming. Painful marriages. Failed marriages. Second and third marriages.

Of all of Kelly's school friends, only a handful had parents who were still together. Most had stepmoms or stepdads. Kelly was lucky that her parents had a solid marriage. They weren't perfect, that was for sure. And they had their fair share of bickering and fighting. But her mom and dad worked through it.

Jill let the girls pour out their hurt and bitterness for a few minutes. Then she guided them back to the devotion. "The next page has some statistics that show that fewer couples are getting married, and many of those who do marry will end up divorced."

Aaron's dad left his mom for a younger woman. But not before running through a number of other lovers first. Aaron's disrespect for his mom made sense. He was following in his father's ugly footsteps.

Jill looked at the girls. "Let's take a vote. Raise your hand if you think Guy and Girl should get married."

Every hand rose into the air.

"Keep your hand raised up if you plan on getting married someday."

A few arms wavered, but they all remained up. Despite the statistics and their personal experiences, the girls continued to believe in marriage.

Jill motioned for the girls to lower their arms, then turned back to the notes and read Bill's next statement. "A wedding is important, but not just because of the rings, the flowers, and the beautiful dress. Marriage vows represent the highest form of commitment two people can make to each other. That's what love does–it commits. This pledge is different from all others, because it is permanent and exclusive. At least it should be"

Even though these girls hadn't seen a lot of examples of marriages staying together, they still believed it was possible. Maybe they wouldn't follow in their parents' footsteps.

"Marriage is God's plan. The Bible says that a man should leave his parents and be united with his wife, and they become one. That's from Genesis 2:24. Marriage is a God-ordained knot, and He plays a part in tying it."

"Then why are there so many divorces?" Terri's voice carried an edge.

Jill pointed to the notes. "Unfortunately, many married couples make one of two mistakes. The first is assuming they can stop adding ties after the wedding. But the secret of winning someone's love is the same as the secret to keeping it. True love never stops adding ties."

Kelly often rolled her eyes at her parents' silly antics. Ridiculous pet names. Dancing in the kitchen. Kisses on the neck. But they made time for each other and even went out on dates. And their relationship kept getting stronger. She'd never thought of those things as adding ties. But it seemed obvious now.

Jill pointed farther down the page. "The second mistake many married couples make is putting more time and energy into building ties to other interests, such as jobs, co-workers, friends, accomplishments, hobbies, sports, children, and other family members. These pursuits aren't bad or wrong. Unless they compete with the spouse."

Kelly's father had turned down a promotion because it would have meant more travel. He said he'd heard too many coworkers complaining that all the time away put a strain on their marriages. That was six years ago. Kelly asked him about it once, and her dad said he'd never regretted his choice.

Jill pulled a mini paper version of Guy and Girl from the back of her binder. "In a dating relationship, the ties can be cut or dropped. That's hurtful. But a married couple is bonded together. They've become one."

Jill used several lengths of green yarn to connect the paper couple, knotting the thick strands around the wrist of each one. She displayed the newly connected characters to the campers. "A divorce rips them apart. They both lose a piece of themselves."

Jill yanked the couple apart. The sound of tearing paper seemed to echo in the silent cabin. Girl's arm came off completely, and Guy's tore so badly that it was barely hanging on.

Kelly winced.

"The kids get ripped up too."

Everyone stared at the sound of Amber's voice. The shy girl never volunteered answers at devotions, but only spoke when Jill called on her.

"When parents go through a divorce, the kids think it's their fault." Amber brushed her sleeve across her eyes. "They think if they just do the right thing, they can keep Mom and Dad together. But it doesn't work."

Kelly wondered about Amber's obsession with romance novels and her desire to write stories about heroes and heroines who stayed together forever. Maybe it was her way of rewriting her own story.

Jill gave a thoughtful nod. "I'll tell Bill what you said about divorce ripping the whole family apart. Maybe he'll add that to the devotional for next week."

Amber's eyes widened slightly, and then she smiled.

Jill turned to the final page "Tough times will come to every couple. But the marriage will stay strong if the two people strengthen the knot between them by continuing to add ties, and hanging on tightly through whatever challenges arise."

Although Kelly's parents always teased each other about how they were stuck with each other, she knew the strength of their ties had been tested many times. When her father lost his job, he went through months of depression. When her mother was diagnosed with cancer, she needed months of chemotherapy. But they'd been there for each other.

A loud snap startled Kelly, and she looked up to find that Jill had closed her binder. If the devotion was done, it was the shortest one ever. Maybe Bill wanted to allow more time on the last day for packing and cleaning. Though that hardly seemed like a good reason to cut short a lesson on God.

Jill held up a stack of papers and fanned through them. They were blank, except for the name of a girl from the cabin written at the top of each sheet "I'll pass these around, and we can all write special messages to each person in the cabin. Let's think about things that we like or admire about each other, maybe mention a special memory, record a funny moment, pass on a word of encouragement. This will become the final page in your Wallet."

The girls spent the next half hour writing on one another's pages while Jill took down the name tags from the bunk posts.

"Please sign the back of everyone else's tag. That way we'll always remember the people who shared this cabin and this week."

After the tags had been signed, Jill passed each girl the page with her name on top. Kelly sat on her bunk, holding her sheet, almost afraid to look. What would the girls say about her? She'd wanted to make a difference in their lives. Had she done that?

Kelly only made it halfway down the page before she had to stop and blink away the tears. *Best assistant counselor ever. So much fun! A great friend. I'll never forget your stories. Camp wouldn't have been the same without you.*

The sniffling campers emptied the tissue box within minutes, and Jill pulled out another. And then another.

As Kelly continued through the messages, she felt overwhelmed. What had she done to earn such compliments? Her mind ran through the past week, searching for some big moment or brilliant thought she'd shared with the girls. There hadn't been any.

The girls thanked her for braiding their hair and helping to untangle friendship bracelets. They wrote how much they'd miss her bedtime stories. They thanked her for listening to them and hanging out during free time.

She'd just been their friend. But apparently that was exactly what they needed. And as simple as that seemed, maybe it was a big part of serving God.

And in that moment, Kelly made her decision. She was staying for the next week. No matter how much Bob teased her. Or how embarrassed she'd feel around Darren. She'd find a way to explain to Sheila that she hadn't tried to backstab and steal her boyfriend. If Sheila was still mad, she'd ask for her help with a prank to get back at Bob. Something really messy. The redheaded tornado wouldn't be able to resist that.

Kelly sat up straight. It was time to dig in her heels and be stubborn for the right thing. And that meant staying exactly where she was.

42 A STRANGELY COLORED GIFT

With the decision to stay made, Kelly felt as if a weight had rolled off her shoulders. And while she felt sad that these campers would be leaving, she could hardly wait for the new group to arrive.

Jill pulled a piece of paper out of her back pocket. "I have a list of things that have to be checked off before we can head to the lodge for the final message. Personal belongings need to be packed, the room has to be vacuumed, bunk mattresses wiped down, and the garbage emptied."

The room had been spotless the entire week. But after they won the sundaes, the girls had let everything stay wherever it dropped. It was amazing how much mess they could make in one day.

Jill tapped Kelly's shoulder. "When you're done packing, could you get the vacuum cleaner from the storage closet? It's across from the bathroom."

"Actually, I don't need to pack. I've decided to work another week. Bill said we could stay together, if that's all right with you."

Jill shrieked and grabbed Kelly in a tight hug. "I'm so glad!" She folded the list and tucked it into her pocket. "There's a lot to do to get ready for the next set of campers. I'll wipe the mattresses if you vacuum."

Kelly grinned. Not at the list of chores, but at the way Jill had given it to her. Not as a commander, but as a coworker. They'd tackle the jobs together.

Kelly went to the closet to get the ancient, bulky vacuum cleaner. Obviously a close relative of the lawnmower she'd fought with at the beginning of the week. She hauled the beast of a machine to the back of the room and had barely begun when Jill tapped her on the back again. Kelly shut off the noisy motor.

"Someone's at the door for you."

Kelly frowned, wondering who it could be. It was way too early to be her mom.

She wove around the campers, open suitcases, and hills of clothes scattered across the room. When she stuck her head out the door, she looked straight into Darren's warm brown eyes. Her face instantly burst into flames.

"Can we talk?"

Her first instinct was to run back into the cabin and hide under the piles of clothing. But that would only be a temporary solution. And a spineless one. She had to face him some time. Might as well get it over with.

Kelly stepped out onto the deck, closing the cabin door behind her. Which was pointless. Every girl in the room had her face plastered to the open screen window, straining to hear the conversation.

Darren glanced at the giggling spectators. "I think we'd better go for a walk."

Kelly nodded, too embarrassed to speak. What was she going to say? Claim she knew all along it was Bob? Tell him she'd changed her mind? She was too uncomfortable to look at Darren as they made their way down the road, heading in the direction of the lake.

Once they reached a safe distance from the cabins, Darren turned toward her. "Bob's a loser."

She couldn't agree more. "Believe me, I know. I worked with him all week. I just didn't realize how big of a cretin he is."

"I don't want any weirdness between us."

"Neither do I." Relief washed over Kelly. The conversation was going much better than she'd expected.

"Did you mean what you said to Bob? About liking me?"

Kelly hadn't expected him to be so blunt. It had been hard enough to tell how she felt in the dark, surrounded by the protective cover of bushes. And now he was looking at her, in broad daylight, waiting for an answer.

She resisted the urge to cover her face with her hands. For a brief moment, she considered denying her feelings. But that would be cowardly. And she wasn't going to let Bob force her into lying. Kelly straightened her back and looked straight at Darren. "Yes, I meant it."

Darren let out a long breath, and a huge smile stretched across his face. "I was hoping you'd say that."

"I shouldn't have said anything." Kelly stumbled over her words. "I don't want to come between you and Sheila."

"Sheila and me?" Darren raised an eyebrow. "We're not interested in each other, not in that way."

Kelly nearly missed a step. That was a surprise. But even if Darren wasn't attracted to Sheila, she was fairly certain her redheaded friend felt differently.

"Talk to Sheila. She'll tell you it's true. We've been friends forever. She's like a sister to me."

Could it be? Did she actually have a chance to be the girlfriend of a truly awesome guy?

"What about Cindy? You got pretty cozy with her this week."

"I was hoping you'd notice." Darren looked pleased with himself. "I figured that if she could use me to make Joel jealous, I could try the same with you."

So Darren had seen right through Cindy's selfish ruse, and hadn't fallen for it. Excellent.

As they reached the lake, a sweet breeze blew across the smooth surface to greet them. Darren led the way to the dock and took a seat on the edge, his feet dangling inches above the water. Kelly relaxed beside him.

"You know, I thanked Bob last night."

"Why?" Kelly had been hoping Darren would punch him, not thank him.

"I didn't think I had a chance with you. I was sure you and Joel were hooking up. When Bob said you liked me, I thought he was trying to get back at me for the black eye I gave him. But when he kept telling the story over and over, I realized he wasn't making it up."

Kelly groaned. She could just see Bob using their private conversation as a bedtime story for the entire camp.

"If he hadn't said anything, I might have let you leave camp without telling you that I'm crazy about you."

Kelly didn't think her face could get any hotter. But with Darren's last words, she wouldn't be surprised to have third-degree burns on her cheeks.

Reaching into his back pocket, Darren pulled out a braided length of string. "I made this for you."

Kelly recognized the gift at once. The campers had been braiding and trading similar friendship bracelets all week. Turning it in her hands, she examined it closely.

The bracelet was a tangled mess. The weave randomly changed from loose to tight, and knots appeared throughout the braid. It was the ugliest one she'd seen. But also the most beautiful.

"I'm not great at art stuff." Darren grimaced. "This is my third try. I had to throw away the others. Marvin tried to help, but he's even worse than I am."

"I think it looks wonderful," Kelly choked out.

They burst out laughing at the blatant lie.

"I thought it could be our first tie."

Kelly slipped it onto her wrist, and it felt as if hundreds of fireworks had just exploded in her heart. "I'd like that."

"What do you think of the colors?"

Kelly considered the mix of black, white and tan, and chose a polite response. "Interesting combination."

Darren gave her a light rap on the arm. "They're the colors of your beagle!"

Kelly turned the bracelet around on her arm and imagined what the cool crowd at school would say when they got a glimpse of the knotted and oddly colored bracelet. They'd mock it for sure. But she didn't care. She'd never received a more thoughtful, endearing, or romantic gift.

Kelly turned to Darren and flashed him a huge smile. "It's perfect. Thank you."

He checked his watch. "We'd better go. I told the campers I'd be back in time to say goodbye. And Marvin's waiting to hear how you like our bracelet."

As they left the private peace of the lake and started back up the road, Kelly chuckled. "I can't believe this is happening."

Darren snorted. "Me, either. I wasn't planning on looking at any girls this summer. I wanted to focus on Charlie. But you just seemed to be everywhere. Grabbing Sheila's clip out of my hand on the first day. Knocking that juice pitcher all over Bob after he made fun of Marcie. Telling mesmerizing bedtime stories. And taking on Clint to defend Marvin. But I think the first time you really got my attention was when you cheated in the relay race during staff training."

"I didn't break any rules! It was good strategy to wrap those dumb socks together."

Darren gave her a playful pinch on the arm.

"Okay, it might have been cheating." She pinched him back. "But Bill said you're supposed to look for character in a potential boyfriend or girlfriend. How is cheating showing character?"

"It wasn't the cheating. It was the courage. When MaryAnn described the race, you looked like a scared rabbit. I thought for sure you were going to turn tail and hop home. But you didn't. And then the relay started and you kicked butt. That's when I knew there was more to you than I'd thought."

Kelly laughed. "Do you know when I first noticed you?"

Darren adjusted his hat. "I assume you were immediately swept off your feet by my charm and good looks."

"Not even close! Although you do look great with a spoon on your nose."

Darren's brow furrowed. "That's not a sign of character, either."

"It was when you were working with a camper no one else wanted to be around."

"I taught Marvin that trick." Darren's chest puffed out. "He can keep a spoon on his nose longer than anyone else in the cabin. Besides me, of course."

Kelly laughed. "When Bob finds out he did us a favor by blabbing what you said, that'll make him really mad."

"Which makes me even happier." Darren said. "I can't believe I wasted so much time by not talking to you sooner. But if you give me your cell phone number, maybe we can get together after I'm done with camp?"

"Actually, I've changed my plans. I'm going to stay for another week. Maybe the whole summer."

"Really?" Darren took his hat off his head and placed it on hers. "That would be great."

Kelly tipped it forward at an angle. The last thing she'd wanted at the beginning of camp was to be wearing this ugly thing, and now she felt honored.

"Since you're my girlfriend now, can you tell me where you hid my hat?"

"No way." A thrill ran through Kelly when he called her his girlfriend. But she wasn't about to let him take advantage of that status. "We may need that hiding place again next week." Kelly tossed his hat back to him. "And is that the only reason you asked me to be your girlfriend? So you could find out about our hiding place?"

"Not at all. I'm willing to pay for the information. How about another friendship bracelet? In the colors of my hat."

Kelly burst out laughing, and Darren pretended to look hurt.

When they reached the path leading to the girls' cabins, Darren said, "See you later?"

Kelly nodded, then ran to the cabin. She barely made it through the door before the campers mobbed her. The girls had had enough of romance between cardboard figures and were eager to hear about a real one.

43 THE FINAL STORY

Kelly hung up the phone and gave a thumbs-up to MaryAnn. An unnecessary gesture. Even sitting on the other side of the camp office, MaryAnn had surely heard her mother's shout for joy when Kelly asked if she could stay. After her mother stopped cheering and then crying, Kelly thanked her for sending her to camp. Then she asked for her Bible and a quilt from home, promising to tell her mother all about the week when she brought the extra items.

MaryAnn had been just as happy about Kelly's choice, though not as loud.

Kelly watched as MaryAnn added her name to the list of staff members staying for the next week, and nearly burst out laughing. There had to be a term for what she was feeling. But she didn't know how to combine "ridiculously happy" into one word. Marcie could probably do it. If she and Sheila were still willing to talk to her. Even if they weren't, Kelly was determined to do whatever it would take for them to consider her a fried again.

After a quick hug from MaryAnn, Kelly left the camp office and hurried to the lodge for the final message from Bill. She'd barely squeezed her way onto the risers with the rest of the campers when she felt a pinch on her arm. She turned and stared into Sheila's snapping eyes.

"You should have told us," the angry redhead spit out the words.

Marcie frowned in disappointment. "I thought we were better friends than that."

They were right. She should have been honest with her friends about her feelings about Darren.

"I'm so sorry. It was a lousy thing to do." Kelly felt the sting of tears in her eyes. "I just lost my head and I didn't know what I was saying. I should have told you—"

Sheila flew into a full tornado spin, arms flailing in the air. "We went looking for you at your cabin this morning. Jill said you're staying next week. We wasted half the morning making a farewell card for you. That's precious time we could have spent working on the next prank. Wait till you hear what I have planned for our next adventure."

"Our next adventure?" Kelly had a hard time believing what she'd just heard. They weren't mad at her after all. Although that might change when she told them about her new status with Darren.

"Of course. You're going to be so glad you stayed. Our next prank is going to be epic. So much bigger than stealing a stupid hat." Sheila's eyes glowed with mischief. "We're going to take that fancy bell that Bill just hung by the kitchen. Nobody ever pranks Bill. At least nobody gets away with it. We're going to need all the help we can get to pull this off, so I was thinking about inviting those hat-wearing geeks to join us."

Marcie grabbed Kelly's arm. "You have to talk some sense into her. Bill will eat us for breakfast if we take his new treasure."

Kelly recognized the stubborn look on Sheila's face. It didn't matter that this plan had even more things that could go wrong than the last one. A certain camp director was about to lose his new bell. Sheila would charge forward, dragging Kelly and Marcie along with her. And Kelly could hardly wait.

"I've got the perfect plan." Sheila rubbed her hands. "We'll steal the bell, put a paper look-a-like in its place, and hold the real one for ransom. We just have to find a place to hide it..." Sheila stopped and pointed at Kelly's wrist. "Where'd you get that?"

Kelly braced herself, uncertain how Sheila would handle the news. "Darren gave it to me."

"Well, it's about time." Sheila gave Kelly a congratulatory smack on the back. "Jill told us you were out talking to Darren. Way to go, girl!"

Kelly flinched as she pictured the campers giggling and making kissing noises.

Marcie leaned over to look. "The bracelet turned out better than I thought. You should have seen the ones he threw away."

"So Darren and Sheila aren't...but I thought..." Kelly couldn't form a coherent thought. She felt as if she'd just stepped off a crazy carnival ride, and the whole world was still spinning. Just that morning, everything in her life had been hopelessly wrong. And in just a few hours, it had all fallen into place. She had her friends. She had a great guy. Her faith in God was growing. And she had another week of camp ahead, with plans for a new prank that was certain to be even more insane than the last. She didn't usually care for thrill rides. But they'd have to drag her off this one.

A hush fell over the room as Bill strode to the front, Guy and Girl tucked under his arms. When he passed Kelly and her friends, he sent them a warning glance, as if he already knew about their plans. And knowing Bill, he probably did.

As Bill propped the cardboard couple at the front of the room, Kelly caught a flash of gold. A closer look revealed paper wedding rings on their fingers and a thin, gold ribbon woven throughout a thick band of green ties.

"Welcome to our final time together." He gestured to the well-worn cardboard pair. "It's been a crazy week for Guy and Girl. They met, dated, broke up, got back together, got married, and just got back from a whirlwind honeymoon. Their future won't be without tangles. But as long as our couple continues to add ties with each other, they will live happily ever after."

Mike jumped to his feet, whistling and clapping. Kelly joined the campers as they followed his lead. Bill waited a few moments before motioning for the group to take their seats.

"I have one last story to share with you."

The campers shifted around, making themselves comfortable. Kelly leaned back, wondering if this final story would be light and funny or inspirational and heartwarming. Bill didn't appear to have any props, animals, or messy substances. And he didn't have much time left. She guessed he'd keep it simple.

"There once was a businessman whose work required him to travel frequently. When he came home from one of his trips, he found his wife crying. She confessed she'd had an affair while he was away."

Kelly stiffened. This was the story Bill chose to end the week with? Betrayal and unfaithfulness? She couldn't believe he'd missed the mark. By a mile.

"The man felt shocked, angry, and deeply hurt. When he asked his wife how she could have done such a terrible thing, she tried to defend herself. 'Don't tell me you haven't had a few flings on all those business trips,' she said. 'I know the kind of women who hang out in hotels and the bars. I can't believe you didn't give in to all that temptation.' The husband assured his wife that he'd never been unfaithful. She didn't believe him. So he handed her his wallet. She opened it and found that it was full of pictures. Photos of their wedding day. Pictures of their honeymoon. Snapshots of their children, family vacations and holidays."

Bill reached into his back pocket and pulled out a black leather wallet. He walked back and forth in front of the campers, flipping through pictures. Almost all of MaryAnn.

Kelly didn't know if her dad had photos in his wallet, but she'd seen his desk at work. And her mother's as well. Both workstations were covered in school pictures, starting with her missing-tooth grin in kindergarten, which she hated. More photos covering all the awkward and gangly years. And then last year's stylish pose in high school, which she loved. She'd always assumed everyone posted family pictures on their desks. Never thought it might be significant.

Bill tucked away his wallet. "The businessman told his wife, 'It's true that I've been tempted to do things that would betray our marriage. But every time, I looked at these pictures. They remind me of what is too precious to throw away on something cheap that sparkles for a moment. After looking at the photos, the temptation never looked quite as good.'"

Bill strode to the fireplace and picked up a devotion binder. Just like the one that every camper had packed in his or her suitcase. Filled with pictures of Girl and Guy. Notes from the campfire messages. The cabin devotionals. The list of New Romantic and Sexy Words. Personal messages from their cabin mates. And blazoned in bold letters across the front were the words "My Wallet".

"Both husband and wife faced temptations. But only one of them had a wallet. That is what made the difference in their choices."

In a flash of understanding, Kelly realized why Bill had labored until his fingers cramped to stencil the title onto each binder, and why he'd chosen this story for the last talk. She should have trusted him to wrap it up perfectly.

Bill flipped through the pages. "Each of you will be going home with a wallet full of pictures. I want these binders to be a permanent reminder of your commitment to God and His commitment to you. When you face temptations, pull it out. Let it remind you of what matters most in life. Nothing is more important than your relationship with God."

Kelly felt a rush of gratitude. Even though she wasn't going home yet, the summer would end. And she'd have to go back to school and face Aaron and the cool crowd.

Thinking of her former boyfriend didn't stir any feelings. She had no desire to reconnect with Aaron or impress the popular girls. But there was going to be a lot of finger-pointing, rumors, and gossip. And she'd likely have some lonely times until she reconnected with her friends from church and found a new group at school. She'd need a wallet then.

And she wasn't the only one. She was looking forward to meeting with Lucy when she got home. And she wouldn't show up empty-handed. Because Lucy needed a wallet too.

Bill closed with a brief prayer. And then, like Santa Claus in western boots and a cowboy hat, he pulled out a sack from beside the fireplace. "It's been brought to my attention that some campers would like to have a tie to take home as a souvenir. Anyone who's interested may grab one on their way out."

Bill must not have realized the impact of the campfire messages, because he seemed surprised when he was surrounded by campers reaching for the thin green ropes. MaryAnn rushed in to help distribute the mementos.

Once all the campers had received their ties, they returned to the cabins to wait for their parents. For the next hour, Kelly greeted the mothers and fathers of her campers, helped carry luggage to the cars, and shared tearful good-byes.

In the midst of the chaos, Kelly noticed one mother standing in the doorway, anxiously searching the cabin. Amber rushed to her and leaped into her arms. "This was the best week of my life!"

Kelly felt a surge of pride, knowing she'd played a part in that experience. She helped Amber carry her belongings outside, listening as the normally reserved camper chattered nonstop to her mom.

Just before she got in the car, Amber wrapped Kelly in a fierce hug. "Promise me you'll write."

"I will." She might even start the first letter that night. Because even though the next week was sure to bring another interesting set of girls, Kelly had a feeling that Amber would always hold a special place in her heart.

When the last camper had left, Kelly wandered down to the nearly deserted lodge, hoping to find Sheila and Marcie. When she entered, she glanced toward the far wall, still covered in the pictures of love drawn during staff training. Kelly located her artwork and chuckled. Blue eyes. Cute smile. Blond hair. Broad shoulders.

Tanned muscles. Cool clothes. She read all the traits she'd scrawled along the border of the page. Funny. Athletic. Smart. Popular.

Kelly reached out to pull the picture from the wall, then hesitated. Perhaps she'd draw a new picture and tack it up right beside the old one. To show that things had changed. That she'd changed.

With a sudden shriek, Sheila and Marcie burst out of the kitchen.

"We're free at last!" Sheila punched the air in triumph.

The girls raced toward Kelly and pulled her into a wild dance of joy. They finally collapsed on the floor in an exhausted heap.

Kelly's gaze wandered to the cardboard couple in the corner, creased and wrinkled after a demanding week.

"What are you looking at?" Marcie asked.

Kelly pointed at the worn pair. "This week has been such a tangle of ties for them." And for herself as well.

Marcie tilted her head as she observed the familiar props. "Yes, but they worked through them."

True. And so had she.

"You know what I see? A girl, a guy, and a summer of ties."

Kelly stared at her for a moment, then started to laugh. "That's it."

"What?"

"You've been trying to come up with some brilliant word. But you just summed up the whole week in one phrase. It may not become a world-famous slogan, but that's how I'll always remember our time at Timberlake Camp."

And not just for a cardboard couple. But for the campers, her friends, and herself. Girls, guys, and a summer of ties.

And tonight, she might just carve that phrase on her bunk, to whisper to those who would sleep there in summers to come.

Sheila grabbed both friends by the arm. "The summer's not over yet. We've got a lot more ties to add."

There was a sudden pounding of feet, and the four Men in Hats burst into the lodge.

Mike headed straight for the girls. "What's this we hear about some kind of truce?"

"We've got a challenging prank," Sheila explained. "We could do it on our own. But we stand a better chance if we all work together. Then we'll all share in the honor—or the punishment."

"Danger, excitement, and glory?" Darren put an arm around Kelly's shoulders. "The Men in Hats are at your service. Where do we sign up?"

"Tell the truth." Mike said. "You just want one of these cool hats so you can be like us."

Mike placed his hat onto Marcie's head. Her cheeks turned a deep shade of red as she reached up to grab the rim. Kelly thought she might pull it off in order to protect her image as a future leader of the modern world. But her genius friend simply adjusted it. And sent Mike a huge smile.

Perhaps Marcie could set a new style for the brilliant and ambitious. Sort of chic geek. Or something like that.

Sheila's arms flew up and she took a huge step back. "If one of those ugly things touches my head, I'm calling off this whole thing and we can go back to being mortal enemies!"

Everyone laughed. Kelly couldn't remember the last time her heart had felt so overflowing with joy. Life wasn't suddenly going to be perfect or easy. And the mess waiting at home wasn't going to disappear. But she was walking with God now, and He could handle everything that came their way.

She whispered a joyful prayer of thanks. For friends. For camp. And for a summer of ties.

NEW ROMANTIC AND SEXY WORDS

1. Balance
2. Respect
3. Time
4. Effort
5. Perseverance
6. Trust
7. Choice
8. Compromise
9. Honor
10. Humility
11. Character
12. Strategy
13. Self-control

ABOUT THE AUTHOR

Working with teenagers has been a passion for Galynne Matichuk, and she has over three decades of experience with young people in a variety of settings.

Galynne has nineteen years of middle and high school teaching experience in public schools in Canada and a private Christian school in the United States. She spent twelve summers working at summer camps, during which time she was a counselor, canoeing instructor, and camp speaker. For two years, Galynne worked with Teen Time, an inner-city teen ministry.

Galynne has enjoyed speaking at several camps, churches, and had the privilege of leading two seminars at the California conference for the Association of Christian Schools International (ACSI) in California.

Galynne recently began working with the T. R. A. C. program (Teen Reach Adventure Camp, specifically designed for youth ages 12-15 in foster care) as a counsellor and camp speaker.

Galynne has one previous self-published book entitled: *How to Bond with Your Child Through Books: One Family's Plan to Read 100 Books Together.*

Galynne can be contacted through the link: fb.me/strongtiestogether.

Made in the USA
Lexington, KY
24 November 2019

57598407R00297